ACTUS

MY BEST FRIEND IS AN

ELDRITCH HORROR

BOOK ONE: BLACKMIST

aethonbooks.com

ALSO BY ACTUS

In a stroke of originality that has never been seen before, I'd like to dedicate this novel to my wonderful readers & supporters. There are too many of you to mention, but an extra thank you to Lord SHAXX, Leander, Winfin, and Ritwik. All the feedback you guys gave me was invaluable.

CHAPTER
ONE

On the day a young Damien Vale nearly brought about the end of the world, his mother made pancakes. This was, of course, something of a problem. You see, Damien wasn't hungry. However, if he left any food on the table, his mother would have known something was wrong.

Normally, Damien wouldn't have found that an issue. There were a great number of things that could cause a young boy to lose his appetite. Rune drawing practice, bullying, contemplating the insignificance of one's mere mortal existence, and girls.

None of these things had even crossed Damien's mind on this day. Well, he might have thought about one particular mortal with short blonde hair and sparkling brown eyes once or twice, but that was it.

Damien's homework had been completed the night before and stuffed under his bed where his mother wouldn't find it, and he counted himself lucky to have no issues with bullies. In fact, he was proud of his ability to blend into the background, watching life pass him by.

Until today. Today was a fateful day, and Damien was

taking no chances. If his mother suspected the slightest thing was wrong, she might have watched him a little closer. She could have noticed how his untrained gaze kept flicking to the giant wooden cabinet covered with runes.

She may have even realized Damien had memorized the password when she'd hastily whispered it that morning in order to get the gold to pay the tax collector. Unfortunately, she saw none of this.

"Mom, when do I get to summon my companion?" Damien asked, tugging on her sleeve as he stuffed the last piece of pancake into his mouth. It tasted as delicious as ever, light and fluffy, with a rich sugary syrup that coated the inside of his mouth. Damien had to keep himself from throwing up.

"In four years, Damien," Hilla Vale said, sighing. "It's no different than the last time you asked me. You're too young to have a summon, and I won't have you romping around Ashfall Academy this early! Just because other kids have done it doesn't mean it's safe! You could die!"

"I could still die when I'm seventeen!"

"Then you'll die more mature. And don't you even THINK of bringing up your father. He was a special case and was lucky to survive. Not to mention, look where it got him! He hasn't been home in months because the queen has him traipsing around the Warfront and hunting monsters," Hilla said, her brow furrowing with anger.

Damien wisely chose this moment to nod mutely. This wasn't the first time he'd had this argument—they occurred on a daily basis. In fact, on this particular day, Damien wanted to do nothing more than pretend summoning didn't exist. That wasn't an option. His mother would have noticed if their morning argument had passed, and he couldn't have that.

The two of them finished their meal at the wooden table meant for three. Damien helped his mother move the dishes to the sink. She sighed and shook her head, ruffling her son's hair with a wry smile.

"Trust me, you'll get your companion soon enough. It feels like a long time, but four years is nothing. With a powerful summon, you might not even have to worry about aging. Just enjoy your childhood while you can. You can make carefree and stupid decisions without ending your life. If you become an adventurer, that privilege is gone. I won't deny it can be exciting, but it can also be deadly," Hilla said.

It was the most she'd spoken on the subject in a long time. Damien jerked his head toward her, wondering if he'd been discovered. Luckily, or perhaps unluckily, for him, she'd turned her attention to washing the dishes. She didn't seem any wiser to his plans.

"I've got a meeting I have to attend with Mayor Leo in a few minutes. I'll be gone for a few hours, and I expect your homework to be done by the time I get back," Hilla said sternly.

"I'll start it right away," Damien lied. No matter what his plans were for the rest of the day, he couldn't leave homework unfinished. After all, it was his favorite subject: Rune drawing.

Hilla rolled her eyes and dried her hands off on a towel.

"I'm sure you will. You're welcome to go play with Jacob when you finish. I've left some sausage and cheese in the ice box, and there's bread in the pantry. You two can grab some food if you get hungry."

Damien nodded, his nerves too tense to allow him to say anything more. Hilla tossed her apron onto a hook and gave Damien a quick kiss on the forehead before she swept out of the house and gently locked the door behind her.

The young boy didn't budge for several minutes. His breathing sped up, and cold sweat trickled down the back of his neck. Slowly, he walked to the door and peered out the small window.

Hilla was nowhere to be seen. She wasn't one to be late for anything, so there was little chance of her turning back now. That didn't help Damien's nerves much.

With a pit forming at the bottom of his stomach, Damien dashed over to the large wooden cabinet. It was bigger than he was, with half a dozen runes he recognized and about ten more he didn't.

"*Lixxar, villo, antov,*" Damien said, his words just barely louder than a whisper.

The cabinet didn't budge. He swallowed and said the words again, this time with more conviction.

The doors of the cabinet popped open with a *click* that nearly made Damien's heart jump out of his mouth. He could nearly hear his pulse now. The young boy pulled the cabinet open.

For the most highly defended object within the Vale household, the inside was rather plain. A large bag of money Damien cared nothing about had been set on the middle shelf. The real prize was at the top.

He reached up, standing on his tiptoes, and felt his fingers brush against hardened leather. A static shock traveled down his arm as he nudged the book over the edge and grabbed it before it could fall. Damien cradled the book like a baby as he absentmindedly shut the cabinet.

"The *Summoner's Almanac*," Damien whispered.

His very short life's greatest desire, the key to my freedom, and the beginning of what should have been the end of mankind.

Damien scurried to his room, clutching the book to his

chest. He grabbed the pouch of chalk from his desk and returned to the dining room, slipping through the back door, and making a beeline for the old shed in the back.

He darted inside and closed the door behind him as carefully as possible. The warm sunlight streaming in through the windows at the top of the barn was just barely enough to see the stone floor.

It had been years since the barn had been used for anything of worth. It smelled like mildew and stale water. The barn was completely empty, aside from some crates of old memorabilia and a wooden sword Damien had made for a school project.

Damien knelt on the floor. He pulled his rough shirt over his nose and brushed as much of the dust away as he could with the back of his hand. He immediately started sneezing as it got all over his clothes and slipped through the small holes in the weaving of his shirt.

His sneezing fit lasted for several minutes before the dust finally decided he'd had enough and let him off the hook. The determined young man wiped his nose on his sleeve. Then he picked up his bag of chalk.

He laid the *Summoner's Almanac* out on the ground before him. Despite the thick binding, the book wasn't particularly large. Damien opened it and flipped through the pages.

It didn't take long to find what he was looking for. It came right after about five pages of warnings and regulations, all of which Damien ignored. The page in question had a single circle drawn out on it.

The circle was made up of hundreds of runes. Two hundred and fifty-six, to be precise. Damien recognized about ten of them. Luckily, recognition wasn't a requirement for casting the summoning ritual.

Damien scanned the book, his eyes flicking over the runes

like two grasshoppers. He only had a few hours to do this before his mother came home. There was no room for mistakes.

He sat there for just over an hour, inscribing the runes into his memory. None of them were particularly complex, so he didn't have any doubts over his ability to draw them. That was all he'd done for the past few years anyway. How much harder could these ones be?

Damien reached inside his bag of chalk with a trembling hand. When it emerged, his fear was gone. All that remained was confidence. The type of confidence that could only come when one knew they only had one shot at something, and failure wasn't an option.

He drew. He started at the bottom of the circle, sketching out each rune with a practiced hand. If he'd wanted to, he could have gone faster. He didn't. Each line, every curve, and every dot were drawn with utter perfectionism in mind.

The young man fell into something of a trance. His hand made the slow trip in a circle around him. He didn't change his pace once. Even when his fingers ached and his wrist burned, Damien continued.

It took him nearly an hour to draw the circle. Damien knew his time counted down, but he pushed the thought to the back of his mind. He rose and examined his work. The circle was large enough for him to lie in. As far as he could tell, it appeared correct. Despite that, a slight frown crossed his face.

Damien glanced from the book to his drawing. It looked the same, but the doubt still nipped at the back of his mind. He grimaced and picked the chalk back up. He moved to the edge of the circle and started drawing again.

This time, it only took him just over ten minutes to finish with his work. He was familiar with the new circle he'd drawn around the summoning one, so he didn't have to try quite as hard.

Damien stepped inside the two circles. He swallowed and picked up the book. His mother could be home at any moment. He narrowed his eyes and forced himself to concentrate on the task at hand. At the bottom of the page was the *Summoner's Almanac*'s final instruction to him: *Earnestly Reach out with your heart and mind. Your call will echo throughout the planes of existence, and your companion shall respond.*

Damien drew in a deep breath, closed the book, and concentrated. Every fiber of his being craved for a companion. More than anything in the world, Damien wanted to be able to cast magic. There was only one way to do that, and it was to summon a companion.

And that was exactly what Damien did. His desires funneled through his body, coursed through the invisible Ether that permeated the universe, and channeled into the first ring of runes around him.

The air hummed and crackled. Damien's hair stood on end, but he didn't relent. If anything, the young boy tried harder. His hands clenched at his sides as his very soul cried out.

That pure, longing note of innocent desire entered the summoning circle. The runes flared with energy and Damien's voice was cast into the universe.

It hurtled through the Ether, tearing free of the Mortal Plane. It traveled through the Plane of Stars, ducked under the Plane of Immortals, and careened straight between the Planes of Fury and Light.

It reached the Plane of Darkness. Then it kept going. It slowed as it passed through the Plane of the Dead, which resided at the farthest reaches of the living universe, but it did not stop.

Damien's plea went where no living mortal's thought had ever been before. Then it kept going. It passed all semblance of what mortals could rationalize. It fell through the cracks in the universe. Then it slipped into the Void.

The Void answered.

A cold breeze kicked up at Damien's feet. The runes glowed brighter as the summoning spell called out to his companion. All the light in the room not from the runes dimmed as if the sun had set.

Damien took a nervous step backward. There wasn't a lot of area in his circle, but the summoning ritual only established the connection between the caster and their summon. It didn't actually pull them into the Mortal Plane.

The air grew colder. What might have been described as an inconsistency formed in the air in front of Damien. The young boy peered closer at it with a mixture of excitement and trepidation.

It wasn't that there was something actually there. In fact, it was more like there was *nothing* at all. It wasn't black. It just didn't exist. A hole in reality. It expanded, drawing a thin line of nothingness before Damien. The line stretched, turning into a large rectangle. Damien's head pounded as the worst headache he'd ever had gripped his skull. He tore his eyes from whatever he'd summoned. Then something stepped out of the rectangle. Despite himself, Damien glanced at it.

A psychic scream tore through his mind. Damien's mouth dropped open, and blood burst from his nose. What he saw could not be described. It was the beauty of the afterlife. It was the hideous face of death itself. It was wonderous. It was terrible. And it tore Damien apart like a house in a hurricane. Damien's soul was torn asunder. His body collapsed to its knees, eyes staring lifelessly into the air.

The shredded pieces of his soul started to dissipate into the Ether around them. Then they froze. Slowly, almost reluctantly, they slithered back into his body. Damien drew a ragged gasp.

The pain was gone. The memory was already fading. It wasn't something a human mind could comprehend, so it was locked away in the deepest depths of his psyche.

Damien couldn't comprehend what had just happened, but the fading memory and his thundering headache informed him it would be wise to keep his eyes firmly on the ground. He didn't know what he'd summoned, but he knew it was something far more horrible than he could even begin to imagine.

"Oops," a voice said. As with the creature's appearance, its voice was impossible to describe. It was like a thousand people of different ages, genders, and languages speaking at the same time. It was gibberish, yet Damien understood it perfectly.

"W-what are you?" Damien asked, not moving his eyes from the ground. His voice was nasally from the blood, and it shook so much it was practically incomprehensible.

"I am It Who Heralds the End of All Light," the creature spoke. Each word thrummed through the air, threatening to rip it apart. "You may call me Henry."

"Why are you here?" Damien forced out. Every word he spoke felt like a punch to the gut. "I did a summoning ritual. You aren't a possible companion."

"How do you know?" The creature genuinely sounded curious. Despite its words, there was no question posed. It was a command.

"The ritual summons a creature from another plane. You aren't in any of the books."

"I could be a demon," Henry said.

It took Damien several seconds to gather the strength to respond. He weakly shook his head.

"You aren't," he said.

"I'm not," Henry agreed. They sat there for several moments, neither of them saying a word. Damien gathered his courage. He tried to swallow, but his throat was dry, and there wasn't a speck of saliva in his mouth.

"C-could you leave? I made a mistake. I didn't mean to summon you. It was supposed to be my companion."

"No, I don't think I will," Henry said in a thoughtful tone. "Mortals got one thing wrong about time, you see. Just because I'm immortal doesn't mean a thousand years pass in a flash. I get bored. Very, very bored. It's been millennia since I last escaped the Void, and I have no desire to return. Besides, why waste an opportunity?"

"An opportunity?" Damien asked.

"Indeed. You asked for a companion, and here I am."

Damien blinked. Bond with this...abomination? The very idea disgusted him. Despite his incredibly rude thoughts, the offer didn't hold up logically. The more powerful a being was, the harder it was to get it to agree to a summon. Many people went through dozens of summons before they located something that would make a pact with them.

To make a deal with a creature that had literally killed Damien with a single glance, well, even Damien wasn't that stupid. However, the fact that Damien was still alive emboldened him. Henry wanted something from him, and that meant he had a chance to live.

"Bonding with a companion you don't know is foolish," Damien said.

"So is summoning me," Henry observed. "Yet, here you are. The offer still stands, foolish one."

A thought struck Damien. He had to force himself to keep

the sigh of relief from escaping his lips. This wasn't the first time a summoning had gone wrong, and the circle had countermeasures built in.

"I refuse," Damien said, shaking his head firmly. "It's time for you to leave."

He shifted his foot and rubbed out one of the runes on the circle beside him. The energy in the runes instantly vanished as the power was cut and the circle broke. Without the contract binding the companion to the Mortal Plane, it would be sent harmlessly back to whence it had come.

"I'd rather not," Henry said.

TWO

Damien's eyes bulged. He nearly glanced up in surprise but stopped himself at the last moment.

"How are you still here?" he stammered, the cold sweat on his back soaking into his shirt.

"Same reason you summoned me. Runes are quite a strict form of magic, aren't they?" Henry asked. "Even the tiniest change can have great consequences. Did you know the rune for 'banish' is only a small line away from the rune for 'offer to exit?'"

Damien swallowed. If the creature noticed, it didn't show it.

"On top of that, you've slightly misdrawn the rune for 'Planes.' Normally, that wouldn't have made much of a difference," Henry said. "However, tonight happens to be the Winter Solstice. The stars are aligned just right for a measly little mortal to call out to the Void. That's amusing. They haven't done that in a few hundred years. It's almost as if you meant to summon me."

Damien looked at the *Summoner's Almanac*. The pages

flipped of their own accord, opening to the summoning circle. The image floated off the page, a single rune lighting up on it.

A single glance was all it took for Damien to confirm Henry's words. The rune he'd drawn on the floor was missing a miniscule line near the top. The pit in Damien's stomach grew heavier. Henry didn't have to show him his other mistake. At this point, there was no need to.

"What do you want with me?" he asked.

"I already told you. You called out for a summon. Here I am. As loath as I am to admit it, you only made two mistakes in your runes. I've been summoned, but it isn't my whole power. It's not even my whole being. The majority of my body is still floating in the Void. I want to explore the Mortal Plane, but I'm too weak to travel far from you. You're my only link to this world, and I'll simply fade away if I leave."

Damien clenched his hands. He hadn't heard of any rules like that in his studies, but he had to admit that much of the summoning ritual was left to those who specialized in it. There was only so much he'd been able to discover himself from the school's libraries.

"What if we make a deal?" Henry offered. "I promise to never harm you if we make the contract. You will be safe from me in every way. We can both walk away happy, Damien. However, if you refuse, we can just say I'm not the forgiving type. Either we both get what we want, or neither of us do."

"I've got another question," Damien said, dodging the eldritch creature's offer. "Why do you talk like...well, a kid? You don't sound like an ancient being."

"This is all to make things easier on you," Henry said in a soothing tone. "I have studied humans for millennia. You are speaking to a façade, a persona, if you will. If you attempted to speak to my true form, well, you know what happened when you saw me. The results of speaking to me would be even worse."

The young man swallowed. It struck him, somehow for the first time, that he'd made a big mistake. It was a big day for wise thoughts such as those, and all things come in groups. As such, Damien was blessed with a second, much more sobering, revelation.

His mother would be home soon. If she went looking for him and looked into the shed... Damien swallowed.

"I'll enter your body. Nobody will get their soul torn apart just by looking at me," Henry said. Damien wasn't sure how he could tell, but something told him Henry would have been smiling if the creature even had a mouth.

Damien's young mind churned as he desperately searched for a way out of his predicament. Unfortunately, he'd exceeded his revelation quota for the day. No ways of escape arose. There was only a single option left open.

"Deal," Damien said, his voice barely a whisper.

Henry didn't respond. A wall of force slammed into Damien. His skin burned, and his muscles screamed in protest as something forced itself into his body. The headache that had been present ever since he'd summoned Henry quadrupled in strength. What felt like an electric shock traveled through Damien's body, setting every single nerve alight with pain.

Then it was done. The pain vanished. Damien's eyes opened, and he drew in a deep breath.

"Well, that was something," Damien's mouth said. It was his voice, too, but it wasn't Damien speaking.

He tried to speak, but his mouth didn't respond. Panic set in when he realized his limbs no longer responded either.

"Don't you worry, Damien," Henry said with Damien's voice. "You're nice and safe. *You* won't be harmed."

It didn't take a genius to understand what Henry meant. Damien screamed within his own mind, desperately trying to move, to blink. To do anything.

Nothing happened. He was a prisoner behind the bars of his own eyes, forced to sit by and watch as Henry forced Damien's body to stand. Henry-Damien stumbled, nearly falling over. Henry slowly wiggled each of his new limbs, getting accustomed to them.

After several minutes passed, he took a weak step out of the summoning circle. Then he took another. And another.

"The time has come," Henry proclaimed, a savage grin crawling across Damien's face. "I am free!"

He took another step forward and promptly walked face first into an invisible wall. A flicker of pain shot through Damien's head as something in his nose crunched, and more blood poured from it.

Henry, unused to piloting Damien's body, lost his balance and fell backward onto the hard ground. The wind was knocked out of his lungs as several more bruises were added to his growing collection.

"What was that?" Henry asked, his voice garbled by the blood in his nostrils. He made Damien rise to his feet and reach out. His hand stopped above the second circle of runes Damien had drawn.

Damien—the real one, not Henry—suddenly found himself in control of his mouth again. Unfortunately, the rest of his body was completely unresponsive.

"I drew an extra ring of runes around the summoning circle," Damien said, a note of pride leaking into his voice despite the situation he was in. "A companion's power is only equal to that of their partner. I made that ring myself. I can't break it from the inside so, now that you're bonded with me, neither can you."

"Clever," Henry said, taking over Damien's mouth once again. "But it gets you nowhere. With your amount of power, this circle won't hold more than a week. A good try, boy. Good, but pointless."

He handed back control of Damien's mouth to its original owner. For a moment, the boy wondered how he must have looked, talking to himself in different voices while covered in blood and trapped within his own ring of runes. He counted himself lucky nobody else was there to see him.

"You're right," Damien said. "But there's no food or water in this circle. I'll be dead before the week is up, and you'll be sent back to wherever you came from."

There was a pause. For the first time in millennia, Henry had escaped the Void. And, after a few short days of captivity in a musty old barn, he was about to be on a trip straight back to it.

"Shit," Henry said. Within his mind, Damien agreed with him.

"You're bluffing," Henry said. "I've watched this world from the Void for thousands of years. I know someone else is aware of your presence. They'll look for you when you go missing, and then I shall be freed."

"My mom will come," Damien agreed, "but she's going to be suspicious when she finds us locked inside my own runes. You won't be able to answer her questions, so she'll know I'm gone, one way or another."

"I can just read your mind," Henry said.

"No, you can't."

"What makes you think that?"

"You didn't know about the barrier I made. I was thinking about it while you were controlling my body."

Henry didn't say anything for a few moments. Then he rubbed his forehead in a remarkably human motion.

"You could survive, you know. If you told your mother everything was fine when she came, she'd let us out. I'd even spare her life, too. Two humans living is nothing in the grand scheme of things. Do you really want to die a slow, agonizing death from dehydration?"

It was Damien's turn to fall silent. As the blood trickled down his nose and dripped onto the floor, thoughts of what his life had been and what it could be flickered through his mind. He didn't want to die, which was a feature shared by the vast majority of mortals.

"I'd even let you have your body back every once and a while," Henry offered. "We could share."

As if to prove his point, Henry released control of Damien. He sank to his knees, his hands trembling. His mouth was parched, and his lips were dry. His nose ached terribly, and the blood made it difficult to breath. His eyes narrowed as he set his decision in stone.

"No. I-I won't let you make others pay for my mistake. I don't want to die, but neither does everyone else," Damien said. He sat and crossed his arms, forcing himself to ignore the terrified screaming that desperately longed to escape his lips. "You can have my body back. When my mom comes and realizes it's not me in this circle, she'll never trust anything I say. It'll be too late. Enjoy your time in the Mortal Plane. My mom is going to be back any minute."

Henry didn't take back over Damien's body, nor did he say anything.

"If my mom gets here and you aren't in control, I'm going to tell her what happened," Damien said, wiping some of the blood away from his lips.

"You stubborn little mortal," Henry spat, saying the last word like it was a curse. "Are you really this suicidal?"

Damien didn't respond.

"Damn it, boy. I'll arrive in the Mortal Plane, with or without you. You're just stalling me until the next fool. You don't get a second chance, you know. Mortals don't come back. You've done no great deeds, so you'll be sent to the Plane of the Dead. There's no coming back from that. If I'm in control, you'll live forever."

Damien said nothing. Several more minutes passed. If anything, the injuries that had accumulated on Damien's body grew more painful as the adrenaline faded into acceptance.

Henry yanked control of Damien's body and shuffled over to the *Summoner's Almanac*. He lifted it and tore through the pages, hunting for any method of release.

"There has to be a way to break the circle." Henry snarled. "I will not go back to the Void. I refuse!"

In his anger, his control over Damien's body slipped.

"That book only has summoning methods and contracts in it," Damien said with a weak laugh.

It was Henry's turn to ignore Damien. His eyes studied the pages at an impossible speed as he scanned the book desperately, searching for any possible way to avoid getting sent back to the Void once again.

Henry forced Damien's body to flip past several pages. Then he paused. Slowly, with a pained grimace, he went back a page.

"This," Henry said, having Damien tap a page with a sore finger.

He was looking at the page, so Damien was able to see it as well. The page was near the back of the book. The word 'obsolete' had been written across the top of page in large, thick handwriting.

The pages contents were quite simple, even for Damien. It described a binding method that involved binding the summoner and their companion together completely. They shared their lifeforce, thoughts, and possibly more, depending on the strength of the bond. In addition, anyone involved with the bond would trade a large portion of their soul with each other.

More than half the page was covered with warnings noting the numerous ways that the bond negatively affected the casters. When one of the two died, the other one would suffer severe backlash or, in the worst scenario, die as well. They were also unable to keep secrets from each other, as each had free access to the other's mind.

However, there were several benefits. The first was that the summoner would be able to better learn the magic their companion could use. Since the souls of the summoner and their companion would be partially fused, they would also be unable to intentionally harm each other or go completely against one another's wishes.

"Half of this page is covered with warnings about how bad of an idea it is to do this kind of bond," Damien said. "This might actually be worse than dying. I don't want to become you."

"I promise it's not worse than a millennium of boredom," Henry said. "And trust me. I have absolutely no desire to become a worthless mortal. We won't become each other. I'm strong enough to keep that from happening. But, look! If we do this, we can both win. You get to live, and I get to experience the mortal world, even if I don't get to destroy it."

Whatever Henry's true intention was, the Void creature had succeeded in planting the seed of hope in Damien's heart. He picked the book up and scanned the page, searching for the loophole Henry was trying to take advantage of.

"Don't take too long!" Henry urged. "If your mother shows up, it's game over."

"I'm not going to make another deal with you until I've read what I'm getting into," Damien snapped. "We both know what happened the first time I trusted you."

"The circumstances are different!"

"Then you'll be happy to take my terms," Damien said. The information in the book was sparse, but he couldn't find anything obviously wrong. That meant Henry was going to try to get him on the terms of the deal.

If Henry could have read Damien's mind, the incomprehensible monster would have winced. Unfortunately, Henry had no such power. There were limits, even to his strength.

Damien scanned through the paper one more time. Then he nodded and picked up a piece of chalk with a blood-stained hand. He drew, moving as confidently and quickly as he dared without sacrificing accuracy.

"You missed a line," Henry said, taking over Damien's hand to draw a small tip on one of the runes.

He glanced at the page. Henry was right. Damien grunted and continued to draw. Between the two of them, they finished the rune circle within just a few minutes. It was simple enough, which was concerning.

"There aren't many runes," Damien said, trying not to concentrate on the pain radiating from his nose. "That means this spell is strong. The less runes it uses, the less energy is wasted controlling the effect."

"Cute," Henry said.

"I learned it in my homework a few days ago," Damien replied, scanning the circle one more time before stepping inside it. "You should be glad I did. It's the only reason I trust this to work."

"Whatever lets you sleep at night," Henry said. "Let's just do the contract."

"Not yet. We aren't just going to do the normal contract,"

Damien said, putting his finger on the page under a small block of text. "It says over here we can set custom terms, and that's what we're going to do. And if you refuse, well, I hope you enjoy the Void."

"You've gotten awful cocky," Henry said with Damien's voice. "Don't forget who you're dealing with, boy."

"I'm doing this exactly because I know what I'm dealing with," Damien said. "And no matter how much I want to live, I think you want to get out of the Void more. You're welcome to kill me if I'm wrong, though."

A low growl escaped Damien's throat. It was distinctly not human.

"What are your terms, mortal?"

"You will not harm any humans, intentionally or not, unless I say you can. By harm, I mean a mortal's definition, not yours. You will also do your best to be a good companion for me, and I will do my best to meet any of your requests I believe are reasonable. I also have the right to end this contract."

"That's hardly a fair contract," Henry scoffed. "More like slavery. You can just end the contract the moment you step outside. Then I get nothing."

"Fine. We have to agree to end the contract. Everything else is the same," Damien said. He cocked his head slightly. "I think I hear my mom coming."

"Damn you." Henry snarled. Damien's body convulsed. He felt like he was splitting in half. For a moment, he thought Henry had gone through with his threat to kill him.

Then a shadowy figure ripped itself free of him. It was vaguely humanoid, but all the features were wrong. Dozens of eyes watched him from all over the figure's body. They faded in and out, appearing in different locations faster than Damien could track them.

Teeth and gaping maws dispersed throughout Henry's body gnashed and growled, dripping purple saliva that sizzled against the ground.

"Very well, mortal," Henry spat. His voice had returned to cacophony of gibberish he'd first spoken in. "Start the spell. I will do my half."

CHAPTER
THREE

Damien swallowed, but his throat was still completely dry. He stood as straight as he could and sent his feeble amount of magic into the runes at their feet. A dark tendril emerged from Henry's side and touched the runes. They flared with a mixture of pulsating white and black light.

"You will not harm any humans, intentionally or not, unless I say you can. By harm, I mean a mortal's definition, not yours. You will also do your best to be a good companion for me, and I will do my best to meet any of your requests I believe are reasonable. We may both agree to end the contract at any time," Damien said, his voice trembling with exhaustion.

Dozens of eyes glared at him with every word he spoke. Once he had finished, Henry repeated the words.

A hammer of energy slammed into Damien's battered head. The runes flared so brightly the barn lit up like a miniature sun.

For the briefest instant, Damien *knew* Henry. He saw the true nature of the creature he'd entered a contract with. It was utterly alien. He immediately understood the persona he'd come to know as Henry was nothing more than a front so Damien could communicate with it. There was no Henry, there was only It Who Heralds the End of All Light. There wasn't a single human thought or emotion to be found within the eldritch creature. Damien saw the inevitable end of the universe, and he knew without a doubt Henry would be there.

At the same time, It Who Heralds the End of All Light knew Damien. For the first time, it truly knew the thoughts of a mortal. Damien's emotions, his determination and fear, mixed with his longing to live. For the first time in a millennia, the creature saw something it didn't understand.

As quickly as it had come, the feeling vanished. Damien was struck with the incredible feeling something was missing. At the same time, he felt...different. He couldn't put his finger on it, but he could instinctively tell that something had changed. Damien's head felt fuzzy. The pain was still there, but it was muted.

"What did you do?" he asked.

"I've acted according to our contract," Henry said. "If you had truly witnessed my entire form, you would have been torn apart so thoroughly I could never put you back together. Even so, you had seen too much for your fragile mortal mind. I locked away the exact details of what you saw to preserve your sanity. I have no desire to be tied to a madman."

Damien searched through his thoughts, but Henry was telling the truth. He remembered dying, but he couldn't recall what he had seen when the eldritch creature had first been summoned.

He couldn't quite bring himself to thank the monster. Damien just sat and closed the *Summoner's Almanac*. The blood had started to dry on his face, but his nose still hurt badly. The bruises on his body pulsated, reminding him of their presence.

Henry transformed into a streamer of dark energy that twirled through the air and entered Damien's body. Unlike the last time, there was no pain. Damien felt *something* shift in his mind, but it wasn't uncomfortable, and he was too tired to care.

Damien watched the doors on the barn, half-looking forward to and half-dreading the moment when his mother came looking for him.

Just under a half an hour after he'd sat, Hilla Vale kicked the doors of the barn open. Emotions washed over her face without restraint. Her expression cycled from relief to worry.

She stormed to the circle Damien had drawn, a bright white light forming in her hand. The barrier shattered like flimsy glass under the mere presence of the energy as she rushed over and wrapped the boy up in a hug, tears streaming down her cheeks. They held each other tightly, sobbing. Neither of them had any words to speak.

"You sly little mortal," Henry said from within Damien's mind. "She never would have killed you."

Damien didn't respond. He didn't need to. Henry sat back within the boy's mind, watching the scene play out with all the curiosity of a cat observing a drowning mouse. Damien was clever, but the contract was far from foolproof.

As rushed and desperate as it was, Henry had already prepared to take a much worse deal. Giving half a soul away was problematic to a mortal but, for a creature as old as Henry was, he wasn't particularly concerned.

For all his plans, though, Henry missed one vital detail. He'd prepared to give many things in order to gain a foothold on the Mortal Plane, but he'd never even considered what he'd be gifted in return.

The half of Damien's soul—no larger than a single speck of dust in comparison with the ocean that was Henry—sank into the ancient creature's very being. Unable to harm it as per the terms of their agreement, Henry could do nothing but watch as the insignificant little speck of mortality set roots into him.

Hilla helped Damien to his feet, still too worried about Damien to be angry, and took him back to the house. They left the *Summoner's Almanac* discarded and covered with blood on the ground in the barn behind them.

"What happened?" Hilla asked, dabbing some of the blood from Henry's face with a wet towel.

Damien' eyes watered again. He opened his mouth to search for the proper words to explain what he'd done, but nothing came out. He just broke down crying again. His mother rubbed the back of his head, waiting patiently until he could bring himself to speak.

"I already know you tried to perform a summoning," Hilla said. "You didn't close the cabinet right. I thought we'd been robbed and you were injured, but no thief would have left the gold while taking the *Summoner's Almanac*. We can discuss that later. I just want to know what happened after you tried to perform the ritual."

"I messed up a line in one of the runes," Damien finally said nasally. His voice quavered.

"And? Did the summoning work?"

It had, and Damien told her as much. He was largely honest, but he kept the details of exactly *what* he'd summoned a secret. *Smart boy. There are beings in the Void mortals don't want to know about. Eldritch horrors they'd prefer to believe never existed. Creatures like me.*

"So...you've got a companion?" Hilla asked slowly. Damien hadn't told her everything. Unfortunately for her, she was smart enough to recognize that. However, she didn't press him further. "What did you make a contract with?"

"A creature from the Plane of Darkness," Damien said. It wasn't a bad choice of a lie, all things considered. As one of the planes farthest the Mortal Realm, humans knew little about it. Many of the creatures that roamed it had yet to be discovered by the inhabitants of this world.

Companions from the Plane of Darkness were few and far in between. Hilla fought to keep the shock from her face. Of all the things she wanted to do, encouraging Damien after an act this foolish was at the bottom of the list.

"Is it intelligent? Did you speak with it?" Hilla asked, running a hand gently along Damien's nose to check if it was broken.

"It is, and I did," Damien said, wincing at her touch. "It... tested me. Wanted to make sure I was strong enough."

"You won a fight against a creature from the Plane of Darkness?" Hilla asked, cocking an eyebrow. She leaned back and let out a weary sigh. His nose wasn't broken, just very badly bruised.

"It wasn't a real fight," Damien said. "But I got disoriented and walked into my barrier."

"Which was the smartest thing you did today," Hilla said, shaking her head. The adrenaline was wearing off, leaving only the worry and stress behind. "You're lucky whatever you summoned didn't just kill you. It could have done immeasurable damage to not just us, but the entire town if you'd made a bad contract! Who knows how long it would have taken other mages to get here and contain it."

"I'm sorry," Damien said, hanging his head.

"We'll deal with it tomorrow," Hilla said. "Mistakes happen in life, but this was a big one. This wasn't a spur of the moment decision, Damien. You planned this out."

He nodded. There was no denying it.

"Don't summon your companion, okay? Contracts have more workarounds than you think, and you've bound something with considerable strength. We need to be very careful."

She had absolutely no idea. Damien nodded once more.

"Good. Go get some rest. You'll be very sore, but you'll be fine. Don't waste too much time regretting your decisions. Instead, think on how to be better in the future."

She gave Damien another quick hug before Damien staggered off to his room and closed the door behind him.

"Fascinating," Henry said. "You were a single ring of weak runes away from ending civilization as humans know it, but your mother told you not to feel too bad about yourself."

"Are you going to talk all night? I'm exhausted," Damien muttered, his voice as low as possible. "And I didn't tell her what you are. We won't be telling *anyone* what you are."

"Very well. In that case, I, too, shall sleep. The journey from the Void was arduous. Do not wake me unless your life is in danger."

"I think I'll live through the night," Damien said. Then he paused. "Wait, how long are you going to sleep?"

There was no response.

CHAPTER

FOUR

Damien and Henry had slightly different ideas on what sleep was. It was one thing to rest for a few hours. Damien could even understand sleeping through the entire day, he'd done it once or twice.

Four years passed before Damien spoke with Henry again. Damien got a girlfriend for all of three days before they broke up. He studied. He trained. He got another girlfriend. That one lasted a whole month before they broke off. He studied. He trained. And thus, life went on.

It wasn't that Damien didn't try to awaken Henry. He lasted all of two weeks before he first reached out and mentally prodded the Eldritch creature, to absolutely no response. The next day, he tried harder.

A whip of mental energy scored across his mind, giving him the worst headache he'd ever had. It lasted for just over an hour before fading away. In some way, Damien was almost glad. Despite his desire to learn magic, the fear he'd slip up and let Henry free on the world never quite left his mind. It ingrained itself deeply within him, and he only tried to contact the creature one hundred and fifteen times after that.

He got closer to waking Henry with each attempt, but the creature stubbornly refused to budge. Whenever Damien pressed hard enough to bring Henry close to consciousness, a powerful sense of impending doom came over him. He got the feeling that waking the ancient entity within himself for a trivial matter would have gone over very badly. However, Damien managed to build an impressive pain tolerance.

On the day Damien turned seventeen, he found himself deep in thought. This was a rare thing for him, as he spent most of his time deep in *other* people's thoughts. He, like many others, subscribed to the ludicrous notion the only way to learn is through copying, so they often had little time to develop their own, original ideas.

Nonetheless, Damien was having one of those days where inspiration struck. He found himself desperately wishing he'd never summoned Henry when he was thirteen years old. He would have taken just about any other companion. Well, not an air sprit, they were notoriously tricksy and generally weak. But any other one would have been fine.

Unfortunately, he'd already summoned Henry. A mage could only have a single companion, and the contract he'd agreed to required him and Henry to agree to the cancelation.

To make matters worse, Damien's seventeenth birthday held more significance than just getting one year closer to death. Seventeen was the youngest age allowed to join a mage college.

Damien found himself in a bit of a haze as he sat at the kitchen table, his mother seated across from him. She'd made pancakes, which only served to strengthen the sense of déjà vu assaulting the young man. Granted, Hilla Vale made pancakes every day, which lessened the feeling a bit.

"Are you going to eat your pancakes?" Hilla asked

Damien. She'd barely aged in the last four years, a benefit of being a mage with a companion.

Damien half-heartedly took another bite. They were delicious, of course. He sighed and set his fork down next to his plate, taking a sip of water to clear the sweet taste out of his mouth.

"I'm worried, Mom. Will the summoning assistants even let me go to the school if I can't summon a companion?"

"What they don't know won't hurt them," Hilla replied. "You'd just better hope your mysterious friend wakes up before the testing or summoning occurs."

"You aren't making this any better," Damien said. He grimaced and shook his head. "I wish I hadn't been such an idiot when I was thirteen."

"You're still an idiot," Hilla said. "You're just older and better able to conceal it."

"Thanks, Mom."

"No problem," his mother said, laughing. "Now, if you're just going to push your food around, you might as well go wait for the mages to arrive. I can already tell you want to go."

Damien rocketed up from the table. Hilla rolled her eyes and rose as well.

"Hold your horses. I've got something for you."

She reached under the kitchen counter and pulled out a large bundle wrapped in paper. Damien took it from her. It wasn't too heavy, but there was some weight to it. The package was a little squishy. He tore it open, revealing a blue coat, along with a huge white scarf.

"It's mage armor," Hilla explained when she saw Damien's confused expression. "You generally get it once you go out into the field, but I figured now was as good a time as ever. Once you get access to your magic, you can channel it into this robe, and it'll turn as hard as steel upon impact."

Damien took the coat and put it on. The scarf was huge, making a large ring around his head and covering the bottom half of his face. If Damien pulled it up, he could have easily covered his head and had scarf to spare.

"You look great. Now, come here. You're not too old to hug your mother, are you?"

Damien rolled his eyes and gave his mother a tight hug. The scarf squished against her face. The two of them laughed as they let go. Hilla gave her son a curt nod and made a shooing motion.

"Now, get out. I've got parties to throw now that I'll have the house to myself," Hilla said.

Damien swallowed. He grabbed the travel bag leaning against his chair and nodded. Despite his mother's words, there was sadness in her eyes. Even so, excitement and fear churned in his chest.

"Git!" Hilla ordered, grabbing the young man and pushing him out the door. "And don't even think about doing bad in school."

"I won't," Damien promised. His mother gave him a nod. Then she blinked and rubbed her eyes.

"Bye, Damien," his mother said.

"Bye, Mom. I'll see you soon," he replied.

Hilla nodded as Damien turned and started down the road toward the center of town. His mother watched him for several more seconds before closing the door and locking it with a final *click*.

There was already a small crowd forming near the glistening fountain at the town square. Damien spotted the mayor, several other kids his age, and a few older than him, and dozens of parents.

A small caravan consisting of three wagons sat by the fountain on the cobbled road. Three men dressed in red robes and all around forty years of age stood beside the cart, talking to the mayor.

"Only eight this year, Mayor Shindal?" the tallest man asked, rubbing his short beard and casting a critical eye over the teenagers.

"Nine," the mayor said as he spotted Damien making his way through the crowd. "Damien will also be going."

The red robed mage glanced at Damien. His eyebrow rose slightly at the young man's coat, but he just shrugged and gave a curt nod.

"The wagons seat eight, so one of you will be in a different wagon from the rest of your friends," the mage said.

"I'm fine with that," Damien said, volunteering himself. He didn't have much in the way of feelings toward his classmates. He'd drawn apart with most of his friends after the incident, and he didn't have any particular desire to rekindle the relationship.

"Very well," the same mage said. "In that case, it's time for us to get moving. We've got a tight schedule to keep. You may simply refer to me as Mage Red. My companions aren't fans of speaking so, please refrain from bothering them if they're in your wagon. We won't be together long, so don't worry yourselves about introductions."

Mage Red pointed at Damien, and then jerked his head in the direction of the back wagon.

"You're in the back. Everyone else, please, get into the second wagon."

Damien nodded and followed the mage's instructions, ducking under the tarp and stepping into the wagon at the back of the line. Four other people around Damien's age already sat on the wooden benches that lined its interior.

Three of them—two boys and one girl—sat on the bench on the left. The girl and one of the boys were dressed in fine clothes and jewelry. The other boy had a rather wicked-looking sword across his lap.

Another girl sat at the far end of the wagon, pointedly not looking in the direction of the other three. Damien glanced between them before carefully sitting in the middle of the bench opposite to the three others, approximately in the middle of the two groups.

"That's a surprise," the wealthy boy said. He had light blond hair and sharp features that gave him a harsh appearance. "I didn't think we'd get another one."

"There is talent everywhere," the boy with the sword said. His clothes were rugged, with bits of metal and leather sewn into them in a form of primitive armor. He had gray hair but looked no older than Damian. "Even in a small town such as this. You should know that well enough, Nolan."

"We're being rude. I apologize. I'm Reena Gray. What's your name?" the girl sitting next to Nolan asked. Her features were so similar to Nolan's that Damian had no doubt they were related.

"Damian Vale," he replied. He glanced in the direction of the girl in the corner of the wagon, but she showed no interest in joining their conversation.

"Mark has already robbed me of the privilege of stating my own name, so I suppose I'll do the same to him," Nolan said, nodding in the direction of the sword wielding boy.

Damian glanced at Mark, and then raised an eyebrow. "Mark has gray hair and your last name is Gray."

"Astute," Nolan said. "It's an amusing coincidence. Say, what's your companion?"

"Nolan!" Reena chided. "Don't be rude."

"It's just a question," Nolan defended. "Right, Mark?"

"I don't care," Mark said. "But you already know my companion. It's an earth elemental."

"From the Immortal Plane?" Damian asked.

"Correct," Mark said, inclining his head slightly.

"Do you know a lot about companions?" Reena asked, cocking an eyebrow.

"A little," Damien admitted, scratching the back of his head with an awkward smile. "I've wanted to become a mage for years, and I didn't have an outlet other than studying."

"That sounds horrendously boring," Nolan said. "I can't imagine wasting so much time learning such an uninteresting skill."

Damien's smile faltered slightly.

"Nolan!" Reena chided. "Stop acting like a child. Damien, my companion is a Wind Wight. Do you know where it's from?"

Her words were kind, but Damien spotted the challenge hidden within them.

"The Plane of Stars," Damien said. "It's a rare form of wind elemental."

"Hey, that's two of us who have told you our summon," Nolan said, leaning forward. "Are you going to tell us yours?"

"Ah, it's from the Plane of Darkness," Damien lied. "I don't exactly know what it's called. I think it's something undiscovered."

The girl in the corner lifted her head for the first time. Her cold black eyes locked onto Damien's back, but he didn't notice.

"Oh?" Nolan asked. "A companion from the Plane of Darkness is a real treat. They're quite rare! I've never seen one myself. Bring it out!"

"I can't," Damien said, grimacing. "It's being a little stubborn right now. I can't actually get it to manifest."

Nolan's interest disappeared. He rolled his eyes and scoffed.

"Right. That's a likely story. Why did they let you into this wagon?"

"The other one was full," Damien replied. "What's that supposed to mean? We all have to get to the mage's college. Why does it matter what wagon we ride in?"

"Look at that. He's just riding along," Nolan said, his face twisting into a sneer. "You aren't one of us at all."

"I have absolutely no idea what you're talking about, but you sound like a stuck-up prick," Damien said, his eyes narrowing.

A shimmer of gray energy danced across Nolan's hands. The well-dressed boy paused for long enough to make sure Damien saw it before allowing it to fade.

"Everyone in this wagon was specifically picked up because of their extraordinary talent or powerful companion," Reena said. The kindness had vanished from her voice. "It's disgusting to pretend to be something you aren't. Lying about your companion is just pathetic. Do you even have one?"

"I'm not lying," Damien protested. Well, he was. Just not for the reasons they thought.

Nolan and Reena averted their gazes, as if being in Damien's presence was some sort of affront to them. Mark shrugged indifferently. He didn't seem particularly bothered, but Damien got the feeling that Mark didn't care about much of anything.

FIVE

On that cheerful note, the wagon jerked into motion. It rumbled down the cobbled paths of Hilltop Vale, taking Damien away from everything he'd known for the past seventeen years of his life.

Two of his companions hated him, one of them was more interested in his sword than anything else, and the last hadn't spoken a single word. On top of that, his companion was still fast asleep. The trip certainly wasn't going anywhere near how Damien had hoped it would.

What followed was an incredibly uncomfortable six-hour trip. Damien did his best to avoid looking at Reena and Nolan. He was embarrassed, even though he knew there was no reason to be.

Their disgusted gazes boring into him whenever he wasn't watching them. He slowly scooted along the bench until he found himself only a few feet from the silent girl. Damien tried not to pay her much attention either. There was no point making another enemy. That being said, he sneaked a glance when he didn't think she was watching.

Her long black hair tied back into a bun. The clothes she

wore were dark as well, and she had two daggers in a sheath at her side. Her skin was tanned from the sun, and her eyes were closed, although something told him she wasn't asleep. Damien quickly looked away before she opened them. Adding 'creep' to his list of titles wasn't something he was eager to do.

The wagon remained silent for the rest of the trip. Damien was vividly aware of each rough bump and pothole they ran over. His backside was just starting to get sore when the road suddenly evened out. The wheels clattered at a steady rhythm.

"We're in Waypoint City," Nolan announced. "What a relief. I don't know if I could have handled more of this."

Damien ignored the insult. He mentally reached out to Henry. His companion didn't respond. He sighed and shook his head. There had been countless times where he'd thought about trying to shake the creature out of its sleep, but he was more tempted to do it now than ever.

The only thing that had stopped him was the fear that Henry would find a loophole in their hastily crafted deal. Damien swallowed. That wasn't an option he could afford to spend time worrying about. If he did, he'd have a mental breakdown before the week was up.

Their trip continued on for several more minutes before the wagon rumbled to a stop. There were several moments of silence before Mage Red pulled the back tarp of the wagon open. He gestured for them to get out.

"We're here. Remain with your wagon group. It makes it easier for us to ensure nobody has gotten lost. Watch your step on the way out. We won't be making any side trips to an apothecary."

Nolan and Reena pushed past Mark, practically jumping out of the wagon. Mark shot Damien an apologetic glance before following after them. Damien rolled his eyes and got to his feet.

He strode to the end of the wagon and hopped to the ground beside Mark. The unnamed girl followed after him silently. Damien looked around the large town square they'd arrived in.

Hundreds of other students mulled about in small groups. Dots of red moving through the crowd marked the mages as they worked to get everyone organized. There were several dozen other wagons, many of which were already pulling out of the square.

The square was large enough that, even with all the people in it, it still almost felt empty. Large stone archways lined the edges of the square, sparkling blue disks of energy shining inside each of them. Large runes covered the stones, both on the ground and on the arches.

There was so much energy in the air that Damien's hair stood on end. His movements seemed slightly slower than normal. Even breathing felt a little more difficult.

A tall gangly mage strode toward them. He carried a large leatherbound book in one hand and a quill in the other. His face was plain and clean-shaven. The mage stopped before the group, scanning them with bored eyes.

"I'll be leading you through the summoning and testing process today," he said. "You may call me Mage Dross. Have any of you already summoned your companion?"

All five hands rose into the air. Reena sneered at Damien, and Nolan let out a laugh.

"This is your only chance to summon a companion, you idiot. Drop the lies, you pathetic fool. They aren't getting you anything but contempt," Nolan said.

"What's that, now?" Dross asked, looking from Nolan to Damien.

"He's lying about having a companion," Reena said, turning her nose up. "He claimed to have one from the Plane of Darkness, but he couldn't even summon it."

"Couldn't or wouldn't?" Dross asked.

"It's hibernating right now," Damien said, feeling the flush creep into his cheeks as he said it. Nobody had ever heard of a hibernating companion.

Dross's lip curled upward, but it was hard to tell if the man smirked or laughed. The mage just shrugged and opened his book, scratching something in it before snapping it shut.

"I don't care what you think. Nor do I care what he thinks. If he has a companion, he will draw upon its powers for the test. If he refuses, he will not attend any of the mage academies. If he does not have one, he will summon one. Nothing else matters."

Reena looked like she wanted to say more, but a cold glare from Dross cut her off before she could start.

"Wise choice, Gray," Dross said. "I don't appreciate backtalk. Your noble title will get you nothing during the testing process. Unlike the colleges, we are entirely impartial. I have absolutely no problem removing anyone who does not comply with my instructions. Is that understood?"

Everyone nodded.

"Good," Dross said. "Come along."

He spun on his heel and strode toward one of the flickering portals lining the square. His long legs forced the five students to break into a light jog to keep up with him.

The mage reached the portal and only paused for an instant to check if the students were behind him before stepping into it. There was a crackle as his body disappeared into the blue light and he vanished, leaving only the faint smell of ozone.

Mark and the Grays followed without an ounce of hesitation. The girl was right behind them. Damien, who had been slightly distracted by the huge runes, scurried after them.

Damien wasn't sure what he'd expected to feel after stepping into the portal, but he wasn't expecting to instantly appear in a large courtyard. It was as if he'd just stepped into it normally—the portal could have been an illusion.

Then his stomach twisted into a knot. The pancakes he'd had that morning decided it was their time to reemerge into the world. Damien staggered and put a hand over his mouth. Luckily, the feeling passed as quickly as it had come.

The other students didn't find the teleportation much easier than Damien did. Reena dry heaved, and Nolan looked like he'd just been punched in the gut. The nameless girl's lips were pressed together, and her face was pale. The only one who hadn't been affected was Dross.

Aside from a single orange brazier upon a pillar in the center of the room, the courtyard was completely empty. The brazier was almost as tall as Damien and made of a strange black and gold stone he'd never seen before.

Cracks spiderwebbed through the floor, originating at the brazier. Some of them were as wide as a foot, but the majority were almost invisible.

"You've all claimed to have a companion, so we won't be attending any summoning rituals. However, I need to know who the mage that officiated your summon was for school records. Do we have any volunteers to go first?"

"I'll go," Mark offered with a shrug. Damien noted the boy's hand still rested on the pommel of his sword, which he had sheathed at his side. "I was helped by Magister Dredd."

"Interesting," Dross said, his eyebrow twitching upward. "I was unaware he assisted in summoning companions for students."

"He made an exception for me," Mark said unapologetically. "What do I have to do?"

"Straight to the point. Good. Go to the brazier and place your hands upon the bowl. Then channel energy into it as if you were powering a rune. I don't care if you already know magic from your companion. You will not use it. The brazier can detect the powers of your companion. If you fail to follow my instructions, you will be removed."

Mark shrugged. He strode up to the brazier and placed his hands on the sides of the bowl. He closed his eyes, and his grip tightened on the bowl. A moment later, a wisp of smoke rose from the brazier.

It was followed by a brown-hued flame. Mark flinched back but didn't let go of the bowl as the fire grew, quickly expanding past his height and continuing into the air until there was a pillar nearly twice his height.

The flames remained within the edges of the brazier, not reaching out for an instant. They were nearly a perfect pillar. It flickered and hissed but didn't move farther.

"That is sufficient," Dross said. "Release the brazier."

Mark let go and strode back to the group.

"How did I do?"

"You did," Dross said. "Who's next?"

It was about at that point Damien realized a little panic was probably appropriate. Nolan volunteered to go next, casting a smug glance in Damien's direction before striding over to the brazier.

Damien paid him no attention. Time was up, and he had no plans of failing the tests before he even got to a mage college.

He crushed the fear and worry building up in his heart. Then he closed his eyes and sent out the tendril of his thoughts. He felt Henry's presence.

It was impossible to miss the creature. Damien could barely use his mental energy without running into the intrusive presence of his companion. Henry was like a huge bear in the middle of his mental space. For lack of a better term, Damien had crept around the monster, trying to make as little magical noise as possible to avoid waking it up.

This time was different. He sent a tiny push of energy in Henry's direction, the equivalent of flicking his companion on the forehead. There was no response. Damien was vaguely aware of the pillar of gray flames that erupted from the brazier in front of Nolan. It was significantly taller than Marks'.

Damien ignored it, squeezing his eyes shut and steadying his breathing. He prodded Henry again, harder this time. Then he slapped his companion with a blast of energy. Henry's mental eye snapped open.

A wave of energy tore through Damien's body. He drew in a choking gasp and staggered. Something steadied him before he could fall, but the young man didn't have time to wonder what it had been.

"You dare awaken me? I told you to let me sleep!" Henry thundered. The eldritch creature's thousand voices carried no magic, but they felt like glistening blades.

"You can't sleep anymore!" Damien hissed as quietly as he could. "It's been four years! I'm about to take the test to get into a mage college. I'll fail it if my summon isn't there!"

The voice echoing throughout his head vanished, and the pain went with it.

"Ah," Henry said. "I suppose that would be problematic. You need to get into that school to get stronger so we can destroy the world, after all."

Damien didn't bother gracing that with a response.

"Stop worrying," Henry said. "I can hear your thoughts

now, you know. It was part of the deal when we swapped souls. And Eight Planes, boy. How can you think like this? Your mind is a disgusting mess of worthless information and fear."

Damien didn't respond again. The less he spoke to himself, the less likely it would be that someone thought he'd gone insane. Besides, if Henry could hear his thoughts...

"More like I have a general estimate of what you're thinking," Henry corrected. "Not super exact. Just...relax, would you? I've spent the last four years improving my form so it will be less likely to make all your little mortal friends shred their souls to bits when they see me."

This is an incredibly important event for me, and you're being flippant about it. Do you understand how vital it is that we do well?

"We'll be fine. I promise," Henry said. "Do you really think something like this is going to be difficult? I could shatter that little bowl with a glance if I wanted to. However, I suggest you release the girl that stopped you from falling over. I think she's starting to get uncomfortable."

Damien snapped back to the real world. He was leaning on the dark-haired girl's shoulder and breathing heavily. Damien yanked his hand back as his cheeks flushed bright red.

"I'm so sorry," he stammered.

"It's okay," she replied with an inkling of a bemused grin. "I thought you'd fainted from the stress of watching the Gray boy do so well on the test."

The pillar of gray fire was nearly three times Nolan's height. Damien grunted and turned away from him.

"He's a dick, but I don't care how well he does. I don't know what his problem is."

"Nolan is part of a powerful noble house," the girl said.

"He isn't dangerous...yet, but you shouldn't have made an enemy of him."

"He did all the enemy making," Damien replied, crossing his arms. "It's not my fault they thought I was lying."

Henry shifted within Damien's mind and let out a laugh.

"You were."

Damien ignored his companion. The gray fire in the brazier reached its peak, flickering steadily at a short bit over three times Nolan's height. The boy stepped back, releasing the bowl, and sending a smug grin at Dross. The fire receded, vanishing into the depths of the brazier. Reena clapped her hands.

"Good job, Nolan!" she cheered.

"It sounds like you'd like to go next," Dross said dryly, gesturing for Reena to step forward. He jotted something else in his notebook and snapped it shut.

Reena followed his instructions, giving Nolan another smile before reaching the brazier. Damien mentally reached out to Henry, well-aware he was still being observed by the nameless girl standing beside him.

She already thought he was weird. There was no point wasting precious time he could spend making sure the test went according to plan.

Henry, is there anything we need to do to prepare for the test?

"Boy, I could burn a hole through the roof if I wanted to," Henry replied, scoffing. "There are two problems with that, though. First, you don't have the ability to handle that amount of my power. You'd probably explode. While that would be incredibly amusing, I'd find myself back at square one. Second, even if you could handle that much of my energy, would it really be wise for you to display such power? We don't need to go looking for attention."

Loathe as he was to admit it, Damien had to agree with

Henry's words. His companion was making a lot of sense, and that worried him. When you start agreeing with the extra-planar eldritch horror you summoned when you were a power-hungry thirteen-year-old, it might be a sign something's wrong.

As Damien conversed with Henry, Reena managed to get the pillar of fire to just a little under where Mark's had been. Her flames were the same gray color as Nolan's, but they flickered and hissed more aggressively despite not reaching as high.

The blonde's teeth gritted as she strained, trying to force the flames even an inch higher. They flickered, reaching up for an instant, then collapsed back into the brazier. Dross wrote in his notebook once again. Then he waved at Reena with it.

"Next," he ordered.

"Can't I try again? I was nervous —"

"No."

"Right, sorry," Reena said, sighing. She sat beside Nolan, who patted her on the shoulder. He still beamed from his apparent success but did his best to repress it for the sake of his sister.

"Don't fret too much, Reena," Nolan said. "There's nothing wrong with your score. The average person can't even get the flames to rise their own height, and this is only a measurement of latent power. Such things can be defeated through skill, or even politics."

"Next!" Dross yelled, staring at Damien and the unnamed girl. "I do not like to be kept waiting. If you don't choose, I'll do it for you."

"I'll go," the girl said. "I was helped by a field operative. He said he would send word and has requested to remain anonymous."

Dross's eyebrow twitched, but he said nothing. He gave her a small nod.

The girl calmly walked over to the brazier and laid her hands on it. She didn't hesitate for a moment, and the flames matched her. The moment her hands were on the stone, a pillar of inky black flame launched upward, stopping nearly exactly at her height.

Calling them flames might have been a mistake. It was more like a single flame, a pillar of dark fire that didn't show a single flicker or fluctuation. Dross's eyebrow twitched slightly. Before he could say anything, the girl released the stone and strode back to the group.

"Interesting," Dross said, jotting something into his notebook. "Impressive control, Sylph."

The other four students goggled at his words. Compared to the other students, Sylph's performance had been pitiful. Yet, of all of them, Dross had complimented her. Damien didn't have long to consider it. The annoyed gaze of the mage fell on him.

He strode toward the brazier, wiping the cold sweat on his palms away on his pants. He stumbled over a crack and had to jog a few steps to regain his balance. Damien heard Nolan and Reena chuckle behind him.

"We're going to have to work on that pitiful persona," Henry growled. "It's honestly sickening. Get some self-confidence, boy. You've got a goddamn Void creature as your companion, but you walk around like a whipped dog."

"Shut up," Damien replied as they reached the bowl.

"Better," Henry replied. "Now, let's get you some bragging rights. I'll not have my partner look pathetic next to these worthless mortals. This world needs to be destroyed with style, and you're out of season."

Damien did his best to ignore the ominous warning

behind his partner's joyous words. It was disconcerting to hear a being a millennium older than him talking about fashion, but now wasn't the time to deal with it.

"I summoned on my own. I didn't receive help," Damien said.

He drew a slow breath and grabbed the stone bowl before Dross could say anything. It was cold and rough like stone generally was. Damien was almost disappointed. His hands tingled, and lines of heat traveled up through the veins in his arms. They reached his chest and expanded outward.

It wasn't exactly uncomfortable, but it was certainly strange. His body felt warm and vibrant, like he'd just woken up after a good night's rest with the sun beating gently down upon him.

A gout of sickly black fire erupted from the brazier. It roared past Damien's face, threatening to spill over the edges of the bowl. The flames were raw and untamed, crackling and popping as they struggled to escape the confines of the brazier.

The pillar of fire rocketed until it was just barely taller than Nolan's pillar had been. Then it inched downward by a foot, remaining steadily at that level.

"That's all you're getting," Henry said. "I could have pushed the fire higher with no problem, but you might have gotten a big head. And don't make the mistake of thinking my power translates to yours. Any one of these four could wipe the floor with your face."

Thanks for that.

"No problem," Henry replied cheerily. "And, before you ask, yes. I intentionally made the pillar of fire taller than Nolan's before dropping it back down. And to the second question you haven't asked yet: also yes. I *am* that petty."

Damien didn't have much of a response for that. A grin

flickered across his face before abruptly fading. The way Henry acted—like he was an old friend his own age rather than a timeless entity seeking the destruction of the world— unsettled him. He knew Henry was simply a way to communicate with his companion, and the familiar tone the monster took on was simply a manipulative tactic. The concerning thing was that it was working.

CHAPTER
SIX

"Get moving," Henry said. "They're watching you."

Four stares burned into Damien's face as he made his way back to the group of students. Dross, however, seemed largely unimpressed. He finished writing and snapped his notebook shut.

"You're lucky to have successfully completed a summon on your own," Dross said. "It wouldn't be the first time it's happened, but it's stupid and dangerous. We're done here. There will be further tests, but not today. You have all displayed sufficient talent to be accepted into a mage college."

"That was a given," Nolan said, recovering from the shock of seeing Damien nearly perform as well as he had. "Did we get into Kingsfront?"

Dross turned a cold eye to Nolan.

"First years are sent to a college at random. These testing results are for your own information not mine. The data will be sent to you so you can get an accurate reading of your abilities. If you wish to apply to a more prestigious mage college, you may do so at the end of your first year. Be aware there are strict requirements for entry, and not a single one of you is anywhere near meeting them at the moment."

Nolan's eyes bugged out.

"Not even close?" he protested. "How is that possible?"

"Welcome to college, Gray," Dross replied. "You aren't the big fish in the pond anymore. You aren't even a guppy. Now, don't look too sad. If you all keep your wits about you and work as hard as you can, you might even pass your first year."

With that comforting piece of advice, Dross returned the book to a holster at his side and gestured for them to follow as he headed back toward the portal.

As he walked, a rectangle of white fire traced itself into the air before him. With a crackle, the air peeled away, and Dross reached into the white box, pulling out a slip of parchment.

"And would you look at that. Right on time," Dross said. "Your college has been assigned. The five of you will all be attending Blackmist for your first year. You will receive a bracelet when you arrive. It will contain information about your current abilities and will update live based on your progress...or regression."

"Wait, the five of us?" Nolan asked, glancing at Damien. "I thought you said it was random?"

"It is. We sort by wagons to make things easier. Generally, students within the wagons already know each other as they're from the same area. You five just happen to be an abnormality. If I cared, I would apologize. Now, get in the portal."

The blue light swirling in the stone arch behind them shimmered, turning a grayish black. Damien felt a slight suction force coming out of it, drawing him in slowly.

Mark was the first to hop through it. Nolan and Reena followed after him, with Damien and Sylph.

This time, Damien was ready for the teleportation. His foot landed on what looked to be obsidian brick seamlessly. He braced himself. Then doubled over and threw up. Turns out, being ready for something doesn't mean you can deal with it.

Damien groaned, wiping his mouth. Before he could even avert his eyes from the vomit on the ground, it vanished. The young man looked up into the cold eyes of a mage in black leather and chain armor. He had a clean-shaven face and short hair.

"It's a long-distance teleport," the mage said. "You aren't the first person to throw up, and you won't be the last."

"Thanks," Damien said, straightening. He took no small degree of pleasure in noting Nolan and Reena looked just as disoriented as he did. Mark and Sylph looked better, but their faces were still pale.

They stood in a large obsidian-tiled courtyard. A massive mountain range surrounded the yard, rising high into the sky on every side and casting them all in shade. The world looked like it was drawn in hues of gray.

"Tread carefully," Henry said, his words cold and lacking the sarcastic tone Damien had gotten used to. "This college is covered in wards. Since we've both got a vested interested in you not dying, you must not reveal my true nature. Mortals will not hesitate to kill you if they discover the truth of who I am."

With that cheery piece of information, Damien felt Henry withdraw into the depths of his mind. All around them, other students popped into existence. Damien couldn't tell exactly how many other groups appeared, as the courtyard was quite large and could have held several hundred people without difficulty, but he guessed there were probably fifteen to twenty other parties of students.

"You five were tested by Dross, right?" the mage asked.

"We were," Nolan said. "I'm Nolan Gray, and this—"

"I know who you are," the mage interrupted. "And, frankly, I'd drop your last name. Nobody cares who you are. Blackmist is at the edge of the continent and just barely under the mage queen's reign. If you want to learn politics, you'd best hope to transfer Goldsilk or Kingsfront. Just survive your first year, and you'll be fine."

The mage traced a circle in the air. He reached inside and pulled out a bundle of metal rings. He checked before handing one out to them in turn.

"Put these on and take a glance at your information," the mage instructed. "That should keep you occupied until everyone arrives and the campus tour begins. I've got to go hand more bracelets out and disappear vomit so, best of luck."

With that, a shadow passed over the man's face. It enveloped his body, turning him darker until he was practically pitch black. Then he sank into the ground and disappeared.

———

Henry shifted, stirring from his idle observation of Damien and his surroundings. A moment later, he faded like smoke from a dying candle.

He reappeared, floating within a black abyss. Miniscule stars in the far distance moved to and fro in a mesmerizing pattern, slowly forming into an enormous face. It looked down at Henry with an expressionless gaze.

There were no words spoken. Henry looked at his chest, where a small mote of light shimmered. Unlike the stars, this light shimmered with a warm glow. A cold wind blew past Henry's face, carrying the distinct air of distaste.

"He appears to be impressionable," Henry said. "The boy has not stopped to wonder why we seek the destruction of the Mortal Plane if it is the only thing that gives us entertainment. With a little more work, he will do as I say without question."

The air around Henry grew cold. He had no skin, but the outer edges of his body grew impossibly cold as his very soul was chilled to the core. The face contorted, its brow lowering ever so slightly in anger.

"We are one and the same. There's no reason to react like that," Henry said, unperturbed by the cold. "We designed me to be like this. You can't complain about our own handiwork. If I was to act normally, the boy would never trust me."

The growing chill relented, but the face looked no less pleased. A moment later, even though it seemed as though they hadn't spoken, Henry flickered.

"The others didn't completely make it? How is that possible? Either they're on the Mortal Plane or they aren't," Henry said. "I'll investigate. I just need to wait for the boy to give me permission to leave. It shouldn't be too hard to get once he's tired."

After a final, miniscule inclination, the head exploded back into stars that flew across the sky, vanishing into the darkness and casting the world into shadows. Henry vanished, reappearing within Damien's mind once more, a pensive frown on his many mouths.

———

"That wasn't dramatic at all," Mark said, rolling his eyes at where the man had melted into the ground. He slipped the band over his wrist without hesitation. His eyes zoned out as he focused on something in the air before him.

Damien inspected the band. It was covered with miniscule runes. They were so small he could barely make them out. He recognized a few of them, but it was borderline impossible to tell what they were doing. With a shrug, Damien put it on. The metal was cold against his wrist. Nothing happened. He reached out with a tendril of mental energy.

The moment his mind touched the metal, light flashed across his vision. Numbers and words etched themselves into the air at the bottom left edge of Damien's vision. He had to keep himself from glancing to check if anyone else could see what was happening.

"It's all in your mind," Henry confirmed. "And, for the record, it's quite invasive. This little thing knows just about everything about you. I've kept myself hidden from it, so you can keep up our little lie about me being from the Plane of Darkness."

Good.

Damien glanced at the numbers at the corner of his vision. The moment his attention was on them, they rose in front of him and enlarged until they were the size of a large sheet of paper.

Damien Vale
Blackmist College
Year One
Major: Undecided
Minor: Undecided
Companion: [Null]
Magical Strength: 3.4
Magical Control: .5

Magical Energy: 8
Physical Strength: .2
Endurance: .3

"How can they just stick a number on my abilities? All they have to go off is what Dross said," Damien said, forgetting to think silently within his own head.

"They don't," Mark said. "It's more of an estimate, but I've heard the mages administering tests are incredibly accurate."

"This is just the basic version, if I'm not mistaken," Reena said. "You can get better versions that have some powerful enchantments on them. Teleportation within campus walls is a common one."

Damien blinked furiously, trying to dismiss the floating paper from his vision. It didn't budge. He frowned and swiped at the air, trying to wave it away. To his surprise, the page vanished, returning to a tiny dot at the corner of his sight.

"That's some really advanced rune work," Damien said. "This must be really expensive."

Nolan scoffed at that, but Damien ignored him. Mark just shrugged in response.

"Probably," he said. "I don't really get how money works. I haven't had much of a chance to use it."

Before Damien could ask what the boy meant, a powerful gale swept through the square. Gentle purple light washed over the crowd as a woman appeared on a translucent platform above them. She wore a cloak made of a motley mix of purple and black that somehow looked garish and fashionable at the same time. For some reason, the woman had two large metal gauntlets on her hands.

"Greetings, new students of Blackmist!" the woman called. Her voice was rich and powerful, with an unmistakable edge of authority. "I'm the acting dean for this year. The previous one is currently off in the Wastes looking for a new weapon after he broke his last one over the head of a devourer beast."

That elicited excited chattering that the woman silenced with a single sharp glance.

"If you don't know what that is, well, there's a reason we've got a general library. You'll be spending a lot of time there, so you might as well get started early. Now, you may refer to me as Dean or Dean Whisp. I've been informed I'm to lead a tour of our main facilities so, please, brace yourselves."

Damien didn't get a chance to wonder what she meant. Henry snarled, and Damien felt the companion's presence condense into a miniscule dot within his mind. Moments later, the world twisted around him, and the young man launched upward. He flew into the air against his will, and his vision seemed to shimmer.

A cold gaze passed over him, threatening to bare the contents of his soul. The feeling remained for a few moments before vanishing. With a start, Damien realized he was looking down on a crowd of students staring blankly into the air.

"For many of you, this is the first taste of real magic," Dean Whisp said. "I won't be telling you what my companion is, but it's from the Plane of Stars and gives me access to Astral Magic. You're currently experiencing something called induced astral projection. Fear not, your bodies will be perfectly safe. Better yet, you'll find yourselves all unable to speak, so we can get this over with nice and quickly. Come along."

Dean Whisp floated into the air, her cloak rippling around her. Damien's vision went along with her as they left the crowd of bodies in the courtyard.

As the dean flew higher, Damien saw the buildings surrounding the courtyard. They were all of different shapes and sizes, but most of his attention was on the enormous mountains surrounding them.

They were much bigger than he had originally thought. They dwarfed the school and surrounded it on every side. There seemed to be thousands of small dots carved into the walls, but it was difficult to make out many details.

"We'll start with the mountains surrounding us," Dean Whisp said. "These are where the majority of students live. The mountains are rich with Ether, which will increase the speed of your magical growth. I'm sure your teachers will go more into that."

The dean shot at the ground. Damien wished he could feel the air rushing past him, but the only sense the dean had brought along with her was sight. Even so, the reminder that he was such a small part of the world was a humbling thought.

Within his mind, Henry scoffed. The boy's realization couldn't have been farther from the Eldritch creature's thoughts, which were almost the exact opposite.

The dean arrived before an enormous gray building within only a few seconds. Great pillars of marble held up tall, beautifully carved roof. In fact, the entire building was one giant tapestry of stone art.

Two massive stone doors at the front of the building towered over them. They must have been nearly two stories high. They sat open, revealing an equally massive library behind them.

"This is the general library," Dean Whisp said. "It's got all sorts of things that will help you in your classes. You'll be paying it a visit later today, after your rooms have been assigned."

She launched into the air once more, forcing Damien to tear his eyes away from the huge building. He tried to turn and get a better look at it, but it was impossible. The woman had complete control of him.

"Absolutely not," Henry said. "I know everything there is to know. I highly doubt some measly little library would hold any information I can't already teach you. I do not want to spend another year of boredom inside the musty walls of some stupid building."

Damien didn't reply. He was already envisioning the countless runes stored within the great library, just waiting for him to learn them.

"Don't you want to cast real magic?" Henry asked. "I can give you access to powers your compatriots can only dream of, but you want to study...writing?"

Why can't I have both?

There was a pause. Then Henry's laugh echoed through Damien's mind.

"That's the attitude, boy. The world is at your fingertips. Never accept compromise. We'll make a conqueror of you yet."

Damien would have winced if he were still in his body. Anything the Void creature approved of was probably not something he should be doing. He mentally shoved Henry away as the dean arrived before the next building. It was long and rectangular, with an obsidian-plated roof that curled upward at the edges.

"This is the mess hall," the dean said. "If you need to eat for free, this is where you'll go. Of course, you may also cook in your rooms. That's actually advisable, especially if you want to become a combat mage. Again, I'm sure your teachers will go into it, and I can't be bothered to explain."

She flew off again, this time coming to a stop only a few

blocks away from the mess hall. The building below them was not much more than a large house. It was made of wood and stone, with a small, quaint-looking door and a single window at the front.

"Student service building," Dean Whisp explained. "In case you've got problems with the college. It's empty, by the way. I'm just contractually obligated to show it to you."

She brought them to the other side of campus, coming to a stop before a large stone building that resembled the library. The carvings were just as intricate and impressive but had more carvings of human mages and their companions. It was slightly smaller than the library and had several men patrolling it. They glanced up when the dean arrived but returned to their duties shortly after.

"This is the Treasure Pavilion," the dean said, gesturing to it. "The school will periodically assign quests for you to complete. Many of them offer rewards that can be claimed from the Pavilion. When I was a student, it was my favorite building on campus."

A smile tugged at her lips, and she flew a short distance away, stopping at a large arch with a glowing black portal swirling inside it.

"This is the portal to the Central Courtyard, in which you are all currently sitting. The courtyard has portals to just about every other area on campus, including the mountains, a large forest outside the college, and several other fun locations I'm sure you'll come to learn of. However, none of them paid enough to get put into my contract, so I'm not giving them any of my time."

The dean took to the sky once again. She rocketed back over to the Central Courtyard. Once she hovered above their bodies, Damien's mind lurched. His vision twisted as he was practically hurled back into his fleshy form.

His stomach twisted and he heaved. Luckily, he'd already thrown up, so nothing came out. Damien groaned and looked into the sky, where the dean was already receding into the distance.

"Nice lady," he muttered.

Nolan grunted in agreement. Then he realized he was supposed to dislike Damien and crossed his arms, turning his nose up and looking away.

CHAPTER
SEVEN

"That was a little close," Henry said with a sigh, the words only audible to Damien. "Stay far away from that woman. If I'd been a moment slower in pulling my presence back, she would have detected me and realized I wasn't from the Plane of Darkness."

Damien gave a jerky nod, too sick to give the eldritch creature a proper response. As people slowly got back to their feet, dark portals swirled into being all around the courtyard. About a dozen people stepped out from within them. Unlike the other mages Damien had seen today, these ones were all quite young.

If anything, they were only a few years older than he was. Their clothing didn't have any sort of apparent pattern to it, although many of them wore dark hues reminiscent of the ones the dean wore.

A woman in casual attire stopped before Damien's group and swiped something away from her face before casting an eye over them.

"Welcome to Blackmist College," she said. Her voice sounded tired. "I've been...elected as your upper-level buddy for your first year here. My name is Beth. You can come to me with any questions about how things work. I'm sure you've got a ton already, but I'd ask you hold them until after we get you all to your rooms."

"We don't have to room together?" Reena asked, breathing out a sigh of relief. The woman pierced her with an annoyed glance and Reena immediately blushed.

"Not all of you," Beth said, staring toward one of the portals and waving for them to follow. "There was a time when Blackmist College was small enough to give each student their own room, but we've grown in the past few years after the destruction of Starfall College. And no, I won't be telling you what happened to it. I don't know myself."

Beth pushed past a crowd of students following another mage through a different portal. She paused in front of the portal a few moments, letting another group pass through, before stepping in herself. The five followed her. They popped out at a small, old-looking arch at the foot of a huge rock slope.

"Anyway, a few of you will have to share your rooms," Beth continued, not perturbed by the teleportation whatsoever.

To Damien's pleasant surprise, he found he wasn't as sick as he had been the last few teleportations. His stomach only twisted uncomfortably before settling. Damien peered up, but he couldn't tell where the mountain ended. There was a winding path that traveled up it, disappearing into the clouds in the distance.

"How many of us?" Nolan asked.

"I'd get to that in due time if you lot would stop asking questions!" Beth snapped. "The five of you have been assigned three rooms. That means two of you will be sharing, while the other one will be alone. And, before you ask, the person who decides who stays in each room is me."

Nolan didn't even have the grace to look sheepish. Beth shook her head and sighed as she started up the sloping path, leading the new students along behind her.

"I'm going to go ahead and stick the two people who can't listen to instructions in the same room. I get the feeling that's what you wanted, anyway," Beth said. Her tone made it very apparent she did not want a response, and Nolan was wise enough to recognize that. He just gave her an appreciative nod.

"Now, do any of you really desire to be in the single room? I'm inclined to give it to Sylph if not. While the school allows coed rooming, we've found people tend to dislike it."

Mark cleared his throat and reached into his jacket, shuffling around for a few moments before pulling out a slip of paper. Beth noticed the motion and stopped walking to take it from him. She scanned it and her eyebrows rose slightly.

"Ah. That's as good a reason as any I've heard. The solo room goes to you, then," Beth said, clearing her throat. She gestured for them to start walking again. "Then the remaining two of you will room together as well."

Her tone booked no room for argument. Damien refrained from glancing in Sylph's direction to see her reaction. He'd already dealt with enough annoyed glances today.

"Now, your rooms will be near the lower end of the mountain," Beth said. "The runes on this pathway can provide a very limited form of teleportation by essentially compressing space in a small area. They're able to recognize who you are, so you can direct them to any room you'd like. If you aren't thinking of one in particular, you'll show up at your own."

Beth came to a stop at a fork in the road. One led further

up the mountain, while the other trailed inwards along a flat area in the mountain. It stopped before three decently sized cave openings lined up within the rock. Damien glanced over the edge of the mountain and instantly regretted it.

It wasn't that he was scared of heights but looking down the sloping edge of an enormous mountain to the clouds below wasn't an experience one should take unprepared. He looked up, but the top of the mountain was so high in the sky he still couldn't make it out.

"Are we meant to make this journey every time?" Reena asked. "What if we fall off?"

"We've yet to have anyone fall," Beth said, leading them along the flat area and up to the caves. "Don't become the first. The runes on the path are enchanted to keep you on them. If you slip off, it'll be on purpose."

Beth stopped before the cave entrances. She reached into a pocket and pulled out three pieces of metal. They shimmered and launched into the air, each one slapping into the stone above the cave entrances. The stone curled around it, sealing them within its grasp. Each piece of metal had a set of names—or a single name, where Mark's was concerned—imprinted on it.

"This is how you'll find your rooms again in the future," Beth said. "Now, you're welcome to do anything you like in your rooms. Anything. They'll be reformed when you leave or graduate, so don't worry about it. I'm going to leave you lot alone for a few hours to get used to your new lodging and figure out what questions you want to bother me with."

She paused, then turned to Damien and Sylph.

"I've got a few more words to say to you two."

She stepped inside Damien and Sylph's cave without waiting for them to respond. Sylph followed emotionlessly after her with Damien close behind.

To Damien's dismay, the cave was small. In fact, miniscule might have been more appropriate. There was barely enough room for the two beds that had been set on either side of the room. There were only a few feet of space between them. There was a small hole behind Beth that led into another room, but it was too dark for Damien to see into it.

Beth strode to the end of the room and gestured for Damien and Sylph to sit on the two beds. Sylph chose the one on the left, so Damien plopped onto the one on the right, doing his best to avoid making eye contact with the dark-haired girl.

"Blackmist takes the safety of its students very seriously while they're on campus," Beth said. "I'm going to be blunt. If either of you overstep your lines, personal or otherwise, there will be *very* serious consequences."

Beth made eye contact with Damien, then turned and did the same with Sylph.

"And I do mean either of you. Blackmist doesn't care who you were. All that matters is that you're now a student. We will do our best to provide a learning environment for you. Any disruptions to that will be dealt with in the most efficient manner possible."

"Understood," Sylph said seriously.

"Same here," Damien said.

"Good," Beth said. Her face relaxed slightly for a moment. "Please, don't take this as me implying either of you would act inappropriately. It's just something we tell everyone sharing a room with someone they don't know."

She stood up, gave them another nod, and strode out of the room. Damien looked around, doing everything but making eye contact with Sylph.

The only light in the room came from the sun outside, and it had already started its downward path. Damien sighed. He grabbed his travel bag and set it on his bed, dumping out its contents just to have something to do. He felt Henry stir within his mind.

"Are you going to let me come out and say hi to your new friend?" Henry asked. "She doesn't have a keen eye like that dean woman so no risk of her figuring anything out. It would be fun to move around on the mortal plane."

Absolutely not.

"Come on, now. You're just being rude, to me and to her. She's been pretty nice to you so far. Just introduce yourself, you wuss. You're going to need pawns if we're going to conquer the world."

"Shut up," Damien muttered under his breath.

"I'm sorry?" Sylph asked.

Henry's laugher faded into the background as Damien forced his companion away from the front of his mind, cringing the entire time.

"I'm so sorry, I was —"

"Talking to your companion?" Sylph guessed.

Damien blinked. That wasn't the reaction he'd expected.

"Yes, actually," he said. "I didn't realize many people did that."

"They don't," Sylph said. "But you had the same spacey look you had before you took the test earlier today, and you were talking to someone then as well. Your mouth was moving a little."

"She's a sharp one," Henry observed. "And by that, I mean she has basic observational skills. Maybe it's best we don't meet. You'll probably spill something important by accident."

Damien ignored him as he was growing accustomed to doing.

"I...ah, yeah, I was talking to my companion," Damien

said meekly. Henry prodded him again. "I'm Damien, by the way."

"I know," Sylph said, flat faced. "Your name is above the door, right next to mine."

Damien blinked as Henry roared with laughter within him. Then a smirk flickered across Sylph's tanned features, vanishing as quickly as it had arrived.

"I'm just giving you a hard time," Sylph said, extending her hand. "I'm Sylph."

Damien shook her hand, suppressing a sigh of relief. Sylph nodded at the travel pack currently scattered over his bed.

"What's in there?" She asked.

"Nosey. I like her," Henry said, his voice fading as Damien tuned him out. "She's going to be disappointed when she finds out it's all boring."

"It's mostly rune drawing stuff, clothes, and basic necessities," Damien said. He paused for a moment, noticing the uneasy expression on Sylph's face. "Rune drawing is a lot more useful than people think."

"Oh, I don't doubt that," Sylph said with a nervous frown. "I just thought the college would provide the basic stuff we need."

"They didn't even give us a whole room," Damien pointed out. "I guess that tiny room behind us is probably the bathroom. Maybe they put something in there?"

Sylph stood up and stepped into the dark room. Damien followed after her, stopping at the edge of the room since he didn't know how large it was. Their bedroom was only dimly lit by the sun, and the tiny room behind it was even worse so. It was dark, aside from a tiny sliver of light that eked its way in.

"Why is there so little light in here?" Damien grumbled. "It's not that dark outside."

"The mountain has runes limiting the light coming into your room, among other things," Henry said within Damien's mind.

"Well, that's just great," Damien said.

"Did you just reply to yourself?" Sylph asked. "Or was that the friend in your head?"

"It sounds weird when you put it like that," Damien said. "And it's my companion."

"He," Henry corrected. "I've decided I like being male. It's probably because I've been trapped in your mind for the past few years. Also, I've made myself a —"

Damien grunted, cutting Henry's telepathic sentence off.

"Well?" Sylph prodded. "If you're going to talk to it, you could at least fill me in on what it said."

"What he said," Damien corrected, sighing and trying not to blush, "is that he's male as of a few seconds ago. And he said that the mountain has runes blocking light from entering our rooms."

"Wonderful," Sylph said. Damien heard a *thud* followed by a curse.

"Hold on," Damien said. "I think I can help a little."

He grabbed a stick of chalk from his kit and followed Sylph into the room. It was almost pitch black, but Damien didn't need light to see what he was doing. He felt around on the wall for a few moments, looking for a smooth area, and then drew.

Sylph remained silent as the rapid scratch of chalk on stone filled the room for several moments. Damien finished and stepped back from his work, accidentally bumping into Sylph.

"Sorry," Damien said.

At the same time, a halo of gentle golden light lit up on the wall. It faded slightly before settling into a steady glow, casting the tiny room in yellow and gray hues.

It wasn't particularly inspiring. There was a small stone shelf with a hole in the center at the back of the room. There was a small door Damien opened to reveal a bowl of stone with a hole at the bottom and a line of basic runes along the top.

"Well, it's a bathroom," Damien said. He stepped out to see Sylph investigating the left side of the room, where a dozen tiny holes had been carved in the ceiling. Damien spotted several rune circles on the wall, and another dozen miniscule holes on the floor beneath Sylph's feet.

"Is that supposed to be the shower?" Damien asked, aghast. "Couldn't they at least have given us a curtain?"

"They didn't give us anything," Sylph said, heaving out a heavy sigh. "Damn it. Do you think we get an allowance?"

"No clue," Damien said. "Dean Whisp mentioned the Treasure Pavilion, but I think that was for quest rewards. They said we could get food for free, though. Is there something wrong?"

"I didn't bring anything with me," Sylph muttered so quietly Damien could barely hear her.

"Wait, really? Not even a toothbrush?" Damien asked.

"What does the word 'anything' mean to you?"

"Right, sorry," Damien said. "I'm sure there's a general store, though. Can't you hop down when we go into town and buy some of the basics?"

Sylph flushed slightly.

"No," she said. "I meant it when I said I didn't bring anything with me. I thought the college would have the basic things we needed, at least for the first few weeks."

"I don't like her that much anymore," Henry said. "Don't

even think about giving her the money in your bag. That's ours."

It's mine, not ours.

Damien stepped out of the bathroom and glanced over the stuff he'd laid out on his bed. A large portion of his bag had been clothes, but he'd still packed some extras just in case.

"I don't know exactly what you need, but I've got a spare toothbrush and an extra stick of soap. I'm not sure how much I can help with clothes or anything else..."

He handed them to Sylph, who took them with an uncertain look. When Damien didn't ask for anything in return, she gave him a small nod.

"Thank you. I don't think you'll want these again, but I'll pay you back for them once I've got some money."

"Don't worry about it," Damien said, shaking his head. "They were just spares in case something went wrong."

"Do things generally go wrong in a way that makes you need a second toothbrush?" Sylph asked curiously as she stepped back into the bathroom and set her new toothbrush and soap on the left side of the counter.

"Well, no. But this is the first time I've ever left my town, so how would I know? Statistically, every time I've left home has resulted in someone needing my backup toothbrush."

Sylph flushed again as she came back out and sat on her bed. She nodded toward the open entrance of the cave, frowning slightly.

"I'm noticing our new home doesn't have a door," Sylph said, changing the subject. "Beth said we'd be allowed to change our rooms however we wanted to. I suppose we're meant to do some renovation."

"That just seems like an excuse for the school to be cheap," Damien complained. "But it doesn't make sense. They said they revert all the changes old students did. It almost feels like some sort of test."

"To get a door?"

"I don't know," Damien said. He shrugged helplessly. "It's not like I've been to a mage college before."

"Nor have I," Sylph said. She rolled her shoulders and sighed. "There's not even any room to train."

Henry nudged Damien mentally to get his attention while he sat down.

"The mage told you that you had a few hours to spend, but she didn't say you had to spend it in the room. She just suggested it. Go look around the campus. It's got to be more interesting than sitting here." Henry said. He made a gagging noise. "I can practically feel the teenage tension seeping into my skin. It's so filthy I'm worried I'll get acne."

It was a strange thing, hearing low effort banter coming from a creature that had been born near the dawn of time itself.

"I think I'm going to look around the campus," Damien said, flicking Henry back again. "The dean's tour wasn't very expansive, and I can't think of what else we'd do in this tiny little room."

Sylph tilted her head to the side. Then she nodded slightly and stood.

"That's a good idea, actually," she said. "I'll join you."

Damien rose as well. Then he paused and turned back to his bed. He stuffed all his belongings back into the pack and slung it over his shoulder.

"I'm not leaving something here until I've got a door," Damien said as they walked out of their cave.

"I don't think anyone wants to steal your clothes," Sylph said.

Damien wasn't about to point out he also had money in

the bag. She'd been nice enough, but they'd only known each other for less than a day. He just shrugged. "Maybe someone else forgot their toothbrush."

He did his best not to peer into the other two caves as they passed them. Something told him Nolan and Reena had brought more than enough of everything they needed, and Mark seemed a bit on the wild side. Maybe he could raid Nolan's bed for supplies.

The walk down the mountain paths was silent, but it wasn't awkward. Once they were below the cloud line, the view over the campus was absolutely riveting.

Large, beautifully carved buildings dotted the large valley within the ring of mountains. A river cut through the center of the college, ending in a small lake on the opposite side of campus. The streets were lined with lush, multicolored foliage that lit the town up like lights.

Damien could dimly make out the small dots that were students as they milled about the town. The majority of them seemed to be headed toward the north side of the campus, where a large group of shorter buildings was clustered around what appeared to be a massive colosseum.

Before he knew it, the two of them were standing at the base of the mountain. For the amount of people that had to have lived above them, it was strangely empty.

"Any thoughts on where to go first?" Damien asked.

"We should make sure to be back within two hours," Sylph said. "We don't want to miss Beth, so let's avoid anything that takes too long."

"What about getting some food?" Damien offered. It had been a while since he'd last eaten, and considering he'd thrown up his breakfast, he was getting pretty hungry.

"That would work," Sylph said. "That's the long building

with the black stone roof next to the library, if I recall correctly."

Damien looked out over the rooftops. He couldn't make out the mess hall, but the library was easy enough to spot. The building was so big the top scraped some of the low hanging clouds.

The two of them started toward it, keeping to the side of the road. They passed several groups of students on the way. Unlike the other mages from Blackmist Damien had met, they wore casual clothes.

"Magister Dredd is just awful," one of the girls said as her group passed Damien and Sylph. "I swear that man just enjoys torturing his students. He dropped me off a cliff this morning!"

"He's not so bad once you get used to the pain," another girl said, their voices fading as they got farther away.

Damien made a mental note to avoid any teachers called Magister Dredd. Even the man's name sounded intimidating.

Despite the college's somewhat dreary name, the campus was anything but. Now that Damien got a better look at the buildings, it was apparent each one was carefully crafted by loving architects.

Every bush and plant they passed was neatly trimmed and thriving. Several of the plants had fruit hanging from them.

Even the roads were carefully maintained. The bricks were smooth and shiny. They almost looked slippery, but they felt anything but. Miniscule runes ran along nearly every flat surface on the ground, forming curving lines that ran through the entire campus.

"It must have taken years to do all this," Damien said.

"It's impressive," Sylph agreed. "A bit gaudy, but impressive."

The library hadn't seemed far at first, but it ended up taking nearly fifteen minutes to arrive. The mess hall was slightly closer to them than the library was. Damien wiped away the small amount of sweat that had accumulated on his forehead during the walk—his coat wasn't exactly light.

"And you aren't exactly in shape," Henry scoffed. "You need to start moving more. Your friend doesn't even look like she broke a sweat."

Damien rolled his eyes, but Henry was right. It wasn't that the walk had been hard, but it was quite hot outside, and fifteen minutes in the heat should have been enough to bring at least a little sweat to anyone's forehead. Of course, Damien wasn't about to ask her why she wasn't sweating.

CHAPTER
EIGHT

The wooden doors leading into the mess hall were wide open, so the two of them stepped inside. A rush of cool air hit them instantly. Long marble tables ran along the entirety of the building. They weren't exactly packed, but there were still a good number of students eating there.

The right wall had been converted to something resembling a buffet, and a small line had formed at its front. Sylph got into the line, and Damien followed. It stopped in front of a large woman's counter. She wore a dirty smock and a hairnet packed so tightly it looked to be an inch from bursting open.

The woman wrote furiously within a small book nestled in her hand, glancing up whenever a new student approached her. The line moved quickly, and it didn't take them long to reach the front.

"What do you want?" the woman asked Sylph.

"Something free," Sylph said. "Do I have options?"

Everyone around them shuddered. Even the woman raised an eyebrow.

"Free? Are you sure?"

"Yes?" Sylph said, drawing the word out and raising an

eyebrow. "I'm a new student. I don't have money to spend on food right now."

A male student stepped out of the line behind Damien. He had short, dirty blond hair and wore some sort of leather armor. He strode up to stand beside Sylph and showed the large woman his wrist band.

"I'll cover it," he said. He glanced at Damien and tilted his head. "You new as well?"

"Yeah," Damien said, nodding. "We're roommates."

"I'll cover them both," the student said, flashing a charming grin. He didn't give them a chance to refuse. "What do you want?"

"Thank you. Could I get something with protein. Is there pheasant?" Sylph asked.

The lady nodded and turned to Damien.

"Uh...could I get pasta or something?" Damien asked.

The woman nodded once more, then turned her gaze to the student who had bought them lunch.

"The usual, please," he said.

"I don't know who you are."

"Oh, don't be like that," he said, groaning. "The lasagna."

She nodded, hiding a flicker of a smirk, and jotted something in her book.

"Come on," the mage said, grabbing Damien and Sylph by the shoulders and dragging them out of the way. Sylph flinched, nearly jerking back slightly. She stopped herself and allowed the student to lead them to a table.

The kind student hopped effortlessly over the table and sat on the far side. Damien and Sylph sat across from him, leaving space for two people between them.

"I'm Sean," he said, flashing a charming grin. "I take it today's your first day?"

"It is," Damien said.

"Welcome to Blackmist! I'm a Year Three," Sean said. "It's a good mage college. I suppose they all are. But, between us and anyone else that goes to Blackmist, we're the best."

"Are we really?" Sylph asked, cocking her head.

Sean's grin flickered.

"Well, no. That would be Kingsfront. Doesn't mean we have to say it, though."

Damien cleared his throat.

"While I appreciate your generosity, is there a reason the free food is so bad everyone is scared of it?" Damien asked.

"There is," Sean said, shuddering. "The free food is a plate of unidentifiable mush. Everyone ends up getting it once, but I've only known a few people who have dared to try it a second time. It's the same meal every time, and it tastes like lukewarm vomit. When I got desperate enough to try it in my first year, I'm pretty sure I saw it move on its own. Nobody should have to go through that."

"Oh," Damien said, gagging. "That would explain it. Thanks for rescuing us from that."

"Just pass the favor along if you stay at Blackmist," Sean replied, grinning.

Damien and Sylph nodded. Sean tapped on a white circle composed of miniscule runes inscribed into the table. It lit up with a dull blue glow. Damien spotted an identical looking circle in front of him. He didn't recognize it, but he tapped it anyway. Sylph copied them.

"It's how the food shows up," Sean explained. "So, do you guys know your class schedules or majors yet?"

"It's our first day," Damien reminded him. "We only got here recently. The dean took us on a tour, and then they showed us our rooms and said we could kill a few hours."

"Huh. I remember that part. I also remember not leaving

my room until my buddy came to get me," Sean said, laughing. "Maybe the students are getting bolder."

"Or dumber," a low voice said from behind them. Damien twisted to peer over his shoulder. A large, heavyset student with a buzz cut and a square face offered him a mirthless grin.

"Hello, Don," Sean said, inclining his head. "Don't be rude. They're new students."

Don yawned in response. He stepped through the table—shimmering as he quite literally walked straight through it, ignoring the marble as it cut through his torso—and arrived on the other side, sitting next to Sean.

He was easily three heads taller than the blond boy. Don gave Damien and Sylph a lazy grin, then stuck a finger in his nose to dig for something.

"This is Don," Sean said, unperturbed by the other boy's behavior. "He's crass, but he's a damn good fighter. He also happens to be one of my teammates."

"Is fighting important at Blackmist?" Sylph asked, leaning forward.

"Incredibly so," Sean said. "Blackmist has produced some of the best combat mages in history. Even Kingsfront graduates respect us. Well, the ones of us that graduate. We don't tend to do all that great in tournaments because most of the real learning we do is in the latter years. I'd say over half of our curriculum is field training. Don't worry, your first year doesn't go too crazy. It's the same introduction stuff everyone else gets."

Damien pursed his lips. Rune drawing was about the farthest you could get from combat, and Sean didn't make it sound like the college cared much for the former.

"The training is a lot of fun," Don rumbled, wiping his hand off on his sleeve. Damien suppressed a gag.

"It looks like the only thing he trains is the stretchability of his stomach," Henry said. Damien, as usual, ignored him.

"In fact," Sean said, "you'll likely be taking part in some placement matches very soon. The school needs to figure out where everyone stands so students can pick teams properly."

"Teams?" Damien said. "For what? The quests Dean Whisp mentioned?"

"Correct. Teams are made up of two to three people. You want to work with someone who has talents that complement yours for the best results," Sean said. The rune beside him lit up with a dull green glow. He grinned and tapped it. A white dish with a large piece of lasagna on it hummed into existence directly in front of him. The food looked good, but it wasn't particularly impressive either.

A second later, the runes beside Damien and Sylph lit up as well. They both imitated Sean. A plate of pasta in red sauce shimmered into being before Damien. It had been sprinkled with a fine white cheese.

"Thanks for the meal!" Damien told Sean, picking up a fork.

"No problem," the blond boy replied, grinning. "Once you start going on quests, you'll find that getting money is no trouble at all. We're not allowed to leave the college, but the stores here have everything, and the prices aren't terrible. Between the gold and the contribution points you earn, so long as you're a half-decent mage, you'll be swimming in coin before long."

Sylph's brows furrowed for a sliver of a second before her normal, uninterested expression returned.

Damien stuck his fork into the pasta and took a bite. It was surprisingly good, with small chunks of salty meat and a rich tomato sauce. The cheese provided a nice kick that rounded the whole dish out. It couldn't compete with his mother's cooking, but Damien decided he could certainly get used to this.

"Don't get too comfortable," Sean said, noticing Damien's pleased expression. "You're going to want to be cooking yourself more than eating out. They only use normal ingredients in the mess hall."

Don grunted. His rune turned green, and he tapped it, summoning a plate piled a foot high with fried eggs. The large student grabbed a fistful and shoved them into his mouth, chewing twice before swallowing.

"It's not my favorite," Don said with a nod. "Lacks nutrition."

The table grew quiet as they all dug into their food. Damien found himself sneaking glances at everyone as they ate.

"It seems strange this boy is so kind," Henry telepathically said. "He carries himself like that noble boy you met on the wagon."

Damien blinked. He didn't stop eating, but he snuck an extra glance at Sean between bites. He hadn't seen Nolan eat before, but each of Sean's movements was precise and practiced. If Nolan had been the one in front of him, Damien wouldn't have blinked.

It just means he's probably wealthy. Even if he's a noble, it doesn't mean he's also a dick.

"Bah. You need to start practicing your magic. If you knew some, we could rip open that boy's mind and take a little peek. I can practically feel you bubbling with excitement like a full caldron of disgusting human emotions. Why haven't you started yet?"

I'm not learning anything that evil. And I haven't started because I don't know how to.

"Then ask me, you idiot. I've forgotten more about magic

than your entire little school has ever known," Henry said. Damien could imagine the creature stalking circles around his mind with his arms crossed.

Then you should have said something. Unlike you, I can't read minds.

The spark of longing within Damien flared up. A small grin would have crept across Henry's face had he been present in the physical world. He'd been getting worried for a moment, but there was nothing to fear. The boy's desire to learn magic hadn't weakened in the slightest. Henry grew silent, allowing Damien and the others to finish their meal in peace.

"Well, I've got a theory class I need to get to," Sean said, setting his fork down gently beside his plate. "It's been a pleasure making your acquaintance. I don't know if we'll meet again soon, as your first year is...a bit of a whirlwind, let's say. However, make sure to try your best! If you do well, we might run into each other at the end of the year tournament."

Sean rose from the table and bid them farewell before striding away and heading out of the mess hall.

"We should probably get going as well," Damien said, licking a bit of pasta sauce off his lips and rising to his feet.

"You're telling me like I care," Don said, but he gave Damien a small wink.

Sylph stood as well. She inclined her head slightly to Don. Then the two of them headed out the doors, avoiding the small crowds of students, and set off toward the base of the mountain.

The trip was faster on the way back. Now that they'd traveled the road once, they managed to shave a few minutes off their time. When they arrived, a familiar looking woman was already standing there.

"Hi, Beth," Damien greeted her. She turned, her eyebrow raising slightly.

"I see you decided to explore," Beth said. "Was your room not to your liking?"

"Well...it's got some things I think we can improve," Damien hedged.

"It's not good," Sylph said bluntly. "Where am I supposed to train? In the bathroom?"

"Of course not," Beth replied. "There are a multitude of different places to train on campus. And, like I said, you're welcome to make any modifications to your room you'd like. If you don't have a place to train, build one. If that's too hard for you, you don't belong at a mage college."

"So, any reason you're waiting at the base of the mountain?" Damien asked, clearing his throat.

"I'm waiting for your friends," Beth replied. "I'm checking to see how long it takes you all to get bored and head down the mountain. I just didn't think you two would leave so quickly. Did you leave immediately after I did?"

"A few minutes after," Damien admitted. "We went to the mess hall."

"I hope you had money," Beth said, shuddering.

Could the food really be that bad? It feels like more students are scared of it than the Dean.

"Only one way to find out," Henry said. Damien couldn't argue with that.

"Are you just going to wait here for the next hour?" Damien asked.

"No. They'll be down in a few minutes unless they already left," Beth said. "There's only so much you can do in those rooms on the first day."

Beth turned out to be right. No more than a few minutes later, the other three students sharing the cliff face with them stepped away from the sloping mountain path and headed toward them.

"I see you two didn't wait around," Mark observed. "When did you leave?"

"A little over an hour ago," Damien replied.

Nolan and Reena turned their noses up, pointedly ignoring Damien. Beth rolled her eyes. Her gaze went unfocused for a few moments. Then she swiped the air before her away and gave them a nod.

"Right. We're a bit early, but there's no harm in that. Come along."

Beth set off, and they fell in behind her. The older student led them back to the teleportation arch before the mountain and stepped through it without a moment of hesitation.

"Maybe getting food wasn't the best idea," he muttered as they stepped through the portal.

His foot landed on the black rock of the obsidian courtyard. Damien braced himself, preemptively putting his hands over his mouth. Predictably, his stomach lurched a few moments later. He managed to keep his lunch down and let out a relieved sigh.

"You'll get used to it," Beth said, tapping her foot impatiently as she waited for everyone to recover from the teleportation. "Now, Sylph asked about training locations. We're actually about to visit one."

Beth led them down the rows of arches at the edge of the courtyard before arriving at one near the middle of the row. They all stepped through it.

CHAPTER
NINE

Wind howled past Damien's face. He blinked, then squeezed his eyes shut and braced himself for the wave of sickness. It was harder to keep a hold of his lunch this time, but Damien managed to avoid redecorating the floor.

He sighed and opened his eyes again. They stood at the top row of the seating section of an enormous colosseum. The seats wrapped around the entire structure, and it looked like there was enough space for thousands of people to sit.

After several dozen rows, the seats stopped to make space for the huge arena at the center of the colosseum. They were easily three stories above the ground, which was some sort of light orange sand.

"This is the colosseum," Beth said. "I know, it's not the most creative name. The ground floor has a good amount of training devices and tools you're all welcome to use. Just keep in mind the school uses this arena for any official fighting matches or tournaments, so you can't use it during one."

They were so high up that the arena didn't look particularly large, but Damien got the feeling a hundred students could have been practicing on the sandy ground without a chance of interfering with each other.

"Is there a reason you're showing us this?" Nolan asked.

"Of course, there is," Beth said. "You're going to be meeting your professor. We've assigned everyone to classes. Just wait around for a few minutes. Everyone else should start trickling in soon. In fact, let's head down to the ground floor. Your professor doesn't like to be kept waiting."

They followed Beth through the rows of seats until they reached the railing at the edge of the walls overlooking the arena.

"Just jump. There are runes to slow your fall," Beth advised them before leaping over the side.

Mark didn't hesitate for a moment. He jumped as everyone else rushed to the edge to watch them fall. Instead of plummeting downward, the two students floated to the ground.

"I feel like there's a parable to be made of this," Damien grumbled as he leapt over the edge to join them.

The air seemed to reach up and cushion him gently the moment he let go of the railing. He descended at a leisurely pace before touching down lightly on the dense sand. It shifted slightly under his feet as Sylph, Nolan, and Reena landed beside him.

Even though the stands surrounding them were completely empty, Damien felt a shiver of anticipation run down his spine. He didn't need a crowd of people to suddenly feel very, very small. He couldn't even imagine how stressful it would be to have to do anything with the entire colosseum watching.

"Aren't there too many students to use this arena?" Sylph asked.

"There are. That's why we have several dozen training

facilities," Beth replied. "This is the most basic one. It's mostly used for tournaments and ranked fights. Most students like to train in other locations. You'll find them soon enough."

The portal at the top of the arena flickered. A group of seven shimmered into existence. One of them doubled over. They headed down through the seats and hopped the wall as well, floating gently to the ground.

Six of the group had matching leather clothing, while the seventh wore stained leather armor. It wasn't hard to tell which of them was the guide buddy.

"Hello, Terrence," Beth greeted. "On time as always."

"I don't see any professors here," Terrence replied. He had a pinched face with a scar that ran across his nose. "That means I'm on time."

"You keep telling yourself that," Beth said. "Is a third group coming?"

"No," Terrence said. "It's just our two flocks of lost little lambs. The professor specifically requested to only have two groups. He didn't want to deal with more."

"Wait, you can't mean they've got..." she started, her face paling.

"No. It's not Dredd," Terrence said, laughing at her shocked expression. "He doesn't waste his time on first years. It's a new professor. I was given the orders through writing."

"And he's making demands? Who is he?"

"No clue. I haven't met him, and I don't plan to," Terrence replied, smirking. He turned to his group and wiggled his fingers in farewell. "Have fun, kids! Do what the professor tells you to. Today is just an introduction, so it shouldn't be too rough."

With that, he reached for his wristband. It was made of a

black material studded with small red stones. He pressed something on it and vanished with a *pop*.

"Dramatic asshole," Beth muttered. "But he's right. The professor should be here any minute. Enjoy yourselves, and make sure you don't get injured too badly."

Beth tapped her own wristband, vanishing the same way Terrence had. The two groups exchanged a few glances, but nobody made any moves to mingle.

"Their wristbands must have some form of portal on them," Damien said, trying to break the awkward silence. "I wonder if ours does that."

"Ours don't," Reena said, rolling her eyes. "The older students have the improved wristbands we can buy with credits."

"How do you know?" Mark asked.

"They had them in our mansion," Nolan replied, not bothering to hide the pride in his voice. "All the servants got one loaned to them. They let you teleport to a single place, and only in one direction."

Sylph's eyes swept over the arena as the others spoke. After a few moments, she turned slightly to face away from the group.

"Boy," Henry said abruptly, nearly causing Damien to jump. "Follow your roommate's gaze."

She looked near the middle of the seating across from them, where someone sat in the stands. After a few moments, the figure shifted and rose to their feet.

Whoever it was had tattered gray robes over what looked to be a mixture of heavy and light armor. As the they grew closer to the edge of the arena, it became apparent it was a man. He had ragged gray hair and the beginnings of a salt and pepper beard. What appeared to be a long toothpick protruded from his mouth.

The man stepped over the side of the arena and floated to the floor. As more students noticed him, the conversations died out. His confident strides brought him to the students within seconds.

"Good day. I'm your professor for this year. I despise titles, so refer to me as Delph," the man said, shifting the toothpick around in his mouth like something was stuck between his teeth.

A chorus of greetings rose from the students. Delph didn't look particularly impressed or excited to be there.

"I've been told by the other professors that young inquisitive minds like to ask questions. Unfortunately, I don't like answering them. Therefore, I have decided to preemptively tell you a little about myself, which will hopefully silence the problems before they arise."

Delph paused, waiting to make sure everyone heard him before he continued.

"As your buddies have likely told you, I am a new professor. I've been serving as a mage for hire for the past twenty years. My companion is from the Plane of Fury. I will not be saying what it is."

Each word was curt and enunciated. Delph spoke in such a way that everything he said felt like it was hammered into your head.

A chubby boy from the other group slowly raised his hand. Delph's eye twitched slightly.

"What?"

"I was wondering what we're going to be learning this year?" the boy asked with a nervous stutter.

"It depends if you stay in my class or not," Delph replied. "I will primarily be teaching fighting. There be other topics as well, but combat magic is my specialty."

"If we stay in your class?" Nolan asked, frowning. "What does that mean? Can we choose our professor?"

"No. But I can choose my students," Delph replied, baring his teeth in what might have been a grin. "And I have no interest in teaching anyone who can't meet my standards. Don't fret, I don't expect you to have any abilities yet. Only the privileged among you will have had a companion for more than a few hours at this point. I just expect you to learn."

That eased the tension in some of the students' faces, but Damien didn't find himself particularly reassured.

"Now, then," Delph said, cracking his neck, "this meeting was only meant as an introduction. I'm supposed to give you all two days to explore the campus before we start our training. Frankly, I think we can squeeze a little early training in, but it's not mandatory. If you're not interested, you may leave."

Damien didn't move. Nolan and Reena exchanged a glance. In the end, the entire group who'd ridden rode in the wagon with Damien remained on the field. Of the other students, the chubby boy and a girl bid the professor goodbye and headed for the exit at the far end of the arena.

Delph waited until they were gone before he started speaking again.

"Good. For those of you who chose to remain, congratulations. You can stay in my class. The two who just left are no longer part of our group."

Damien's eyes widened as Henry burst into laughter within his head.

"What a hardass," Henry said mirthfully. "He's on a power trip."

Have I mentioned how incredibly strange it is that you speak like a teenager? I think I have.

"Your fault, not mine," Henry replied, giving the mental equivalent of a shrug. "Trust me, you'll prefer me over the true It Who Heralds the End of All Light. Now, stop talking to yourself and listen to your insane teacher."

Delph remained silent, allowing the shocked muttering to fade away under his withering glare.

"Does anyone have a problem with that?" he asked, practically daring someone to speak up.

There was a long silence. Delph nodded and started opening his mouth to say something else. Then a short girl with long black hair in the other group of students stepped forward. Her skin was dark, but her face had turned pale from fear. She wrung her hands together as the professor pierced her with a glare.

"Do you have something to say?" Delph asked.

"Yes, Professor," she said meekly. "I don't think it's fair to remove them just for not doing an optional training with you. We all just got to the school, and everyone is excited to explore the campus. You gave no reason to believe this training session would be that important."

"I see," Delph said, his words icy. He slowly turned, looking every single student in the eye. "Does anyone else share your opinion?"

There was an uncomfortable silence. The girl sent a pleading look toward her group. They shifted from foot to foot, avoiding her gaze.

"Don't even think about it," Henry said. "We need to be on his good side, and that means being a good little sheep. Don't you move one step forw—"

Damien stepped forward. Delph's gaze snapped to him. Damien's heart skipped a terrified beat as his breath caught in his chest. He dimly heard Reena and Nolan snicker off to his side.

"You agree with your classmate?" Delph asked. "Or did you happen to need to use the bathroom at an inopportune time?"

"I agree with her," Damien said. There were always other professors, and he didn't particularly care who taught him. Magic was magic, and the library would have most of what he needed. Besides, Henry said he could teach Damien magic.

"You idiot," Henry said.

Then, to Damien's surprise, Sylph moved to stand beside him. Delph raised an eyebrow.

"Bold. Anyone else?"

Nobody else stepped forward.

"Very good," Delph said, breaking into a predatory smile. "That's more than I expected. You three, what are your names?"

"Damien Vale."

"Sylph. No last name."

"Loretta Herder."

"Damien, Sylph, and Loretta," Delph said, rolling their names over his tongue. "Very well. Your request is granted. Your classmates will not be removed on this day."

Damien's mouth dropped open. Judging by the expressions of the other students, they were just as shocked as he was.

"W-what?" Loretta asked, her eyes wide.

"Your friends will remain under my tutelage, for now. Before I explain my reasoning, I would like to know the honest reason why you all stepped forward."

"Uh...it wasn't fair to remove them like that. If it happened to them, it could happen to me," Loretta said, frowning.

Delph turned to Damien.

"I just didn't like the idea of removing people like that. If you didn't give us any rules to play by, you can't blame us for not following them," Damien said.

"I stepped forward because you were testing us," Sylph said flatly. "I don't have any particular care if they had remained in the class or not."

Delph just nodded.

"Honesty is good. I appreciate honesty. All three of you were correct. This was a test, although your friends weren't in on it by any means. It would not have been fair to remove people on a whim. However, I can tell you this. If you fail to attend my training, you will not be prepared to pass my tests. So, while your friends will be allowed to attend class, be aware that skipping any of my extra sessions will almost certainly result in your eventual removal from my tutelage."

There was a long silence after that. Loretta licked her lips and swallowed to wet her drying throat.

"Professor, what were you testing us over?"

"Good question. I was interested to see which of you would be stupid enough to put your neck on the line for no reason. It had no purpose other than to satisfy my curiosity. Although, I'm not sure if it was entirely successful, given that one student knew it was a test before I started it," Delph said, turning his cold gaze on Sylph.

Sylph kept eye contact with him, not breaking away until Delph let out a small chuckle.

"We'll have an interesting year, I think," Delph said. "Now, some of you may be unsurprised to hear this was not the first test I did today."

The students exchanged uncertain glances again. Everyone remained silent until Delph spoke up again.

"Before I arrived in the arena, I waited in the stands for approximately five minutes. There were four students who spotted me. I would like to continue to speak with those four.

As for everyone else, you are dismissed. Do not worry. This is not a test. I will be in contact. Enjoy the next two days."

"Hah!" Henry crowed. "And that's why we listen to me."

You just told me not to step forward.

Henry didn't respond to that.

The students glanced around, trying to figure out who Delph referred to. Slowly and suspiciously, kids headed toward the arena exit. Several of them left while looking over their shoulder in case the strange professor suddenly changed his mind.

Nolan and Reena glared at Damien as they left and it became apparent he had no inclination of joining them. Damien paid them no mind. The only ones remaining after the exodus were Damien, Sylph, Mark, and a tall bald boy from the other group.

"So," Delph said. "You four managed to spot me. How many of you have experience with your magic?"

Everyone other than Damien raised their hand. Delph started to nod but paused when he realized Damien hadn't just been slower than everyone else.

"You haven't used magic at all?" Delph asked, actually sounding somewhat impressed.

"Just runes," Damien said. Delph's expression showed he wasn't particularly impressed with that explanation.

"Very well. For those of you that have used magic, I assume you felt my presence disturbing the Ether around me?"

All three of them nodded.

"Good. I allowed some of my energy to leak out. You'll learn to control that soon enough. However, I'm curious about you, my scarf wearing student," Delph said, stepping toward Damien. "How did you spot me?"

"I followed Sylph's gaze," Damien replied, doing his best not to flinch at the professor's cold stare.

Delph blinked. Then he burst into laughter. It was short-lived, and he quickly recomposed himself, returning to his normal, bored disposition. The professor shook his head.

"Ah. That would do it, wouldn't it? I suppose there's something to be said for being observant, even if you have no magic. However, I'm afraid I'm not going to be able to include you in this next assignment."

"That's fine," Damien said, trying and failing to hide the disappointment in his voice.

"Now, for the rest of you," Delph said. "I've been told some students already have a few years of experience with their magic. That some students think they know better than their professor. Therefore, I'll be extending an offer to you all. In exactly ten seconds, I am going to attack all of you. If you can draw a single drop of blood, I'll buy you lunch for the rest of the semester. However, if you all lose, you do exactly as I say until the end of this year."

The air around Delph warped and turned hazy. It seemed to crumple, almost as if the man had his own gravitational pull breaking the reality around him. Damien backed away, suddenly happy he hadn't been included in the exercise.

"Watch closely," Henry instructed. "You can learn a lot about how to fight from watching those better than you."

"I'm not an idiot," Damien muttered, forgetting to think the words and saying them out loud by accident.

CHAPTER
TEN

Mark was the first of the three students to make a move. He traced a line in the air with his sword tip. The blade of his sword shimmered as stone raced up his legs and to the sword, wrapping around the hilt and covering the entire weapon.

He dropped into a crouch, holding the blade with one hand, and placing his other on the ground. Without an instant of hesitation, he dashed forward. Mark closed the distance between him and Delph within a second.

Delph twisted, allowing the blade to pass mere inches away from his chest, and drove his knee into Mark's nose.

Mark let out a cry and staggered backward. The rock covering his weapon crumbled but regained its integrity as the boy refocused. A trail of blood trickled out of his nose and down his face.

"You have magic that requires concentration to keep active," Delph observed, making no move to continue pressing the boy. "If your defenses aren't better, your magic will fail you at a critical juncture."

Mark bared his teeth in a feral snarl and dashed toward Delph again. He swung his sword for the man's chest again.

Mark pulled the blade back moments before it got close to the professor, converting his momentum into a new strike aimed at the professor's lower body.

Delph leapt into the air, jumping clean over Mark's strike. His leg snapped out in a brutal kick that picked Mark off the ground and sent him tumbling across the arena. He didn't get back up.

"Next," Delph said, turning to look at Sylph and the bald student.

Sylph watched him silently, not moving. The bald student, realizing Sylph had no plans of fighting yet, took a step at Delph. He lowered into a fighting stance and curled his fingers into claws.

Delph remained in position as the boy let out a heavy breath. A puff of thick white steam escaped his mouth and curled around him.

The bald boy blurred, moving so quickly he made Mark look like a slug. He appeared beside Delph and thrust his hand toward the professor's stomach.

Delph's hand shot out, and he grabbed the boy by his wrist. Then his eyes widened, and he released him, hopping back a step.

"That almost hurt," Delph said, frowning. A small trail of smoke rose from the professor's hand. "Just how hot is your body?"

"Very hot, professor," the bald student replied. His clothes smoked as well. "I've never gotten a chance to measure it, but I have runed clothes to resist the heat."

"We'll have to find out at a later date," Delph said. The air between him and the bald student seemed to crumple, and then Delph stood before the student. It wasn't that he'd moved quickly, it didn't look like he'd moved at all.

"Teleportation," Henry said. "I believe mortals consider it

somewhat difficult, although all mages tend to learn at least a variation of it at some point."

The bald boy doubled over as something slammed into his stomach. He flew several feet into the air, then slammed into the ground as if an invisible hand tossed him around.

"I yield!" the boy yelled. He collapsed to the ground with a groan as Delph turned to Sylph.

She was gone. The professor frowned and tilted his head. His eyebrows rose imperceptibly upward, and he flickered to the side.

A dark line appeared in the air where he'd been standing. The ground around Delph erupted, filling the air around him with sand. Sylph's form was outlined as the sand covered her.

Delph teleported out of the way as another black line nearly dissected him. The sand covering Sylph collapsed to the ground.

"Sylph can also teleport?" Damien asked in disbelief.

"No. That's not teleporting. You'd know if you had any access to magic, but her form isn't disappearing and reappearing. It's kind of just...shifting," Henry said begrudgingly. "It's more like an advanced camouflage, and she's just very fast. For someone of your age, at least."

Delph shifted his stance. He disappeared, and Sylph's magic sliced harmlessly through the air once more.

"Very impressive," Delph said. "However, I can't tell if you're hiding your power very well, or if your magical strength is just pitifully low."

The professor tilted his head. Then he spun, thrusting his hand into what looked to be an empty spot in the air beside him. His hand tightened around an invisible arm, and he yanked backward.

A bubble of darkness formed in the air as Delph dragged Sylph back into vision, his hand wrapped around her wrist.

Instead of resisting, Sylph used the momentum to throw herself toward the professor.

As her body fully left the bubble, Damien realized she had a thin blade made of inky energy grasped in her other hand. Delph realized it at the same time, but it was too late. The weapon was already a millimeter from his neck, and it showed no signs of stopping.

The air around Delph inverted in color. Time seemed to slow to a halt for an instant. Damien's ears popped, and a trickle of blood ran from his nose. Sylph's magic shattered like glass and evaporated into the air. She crumpled to the ground like a puppet with its strings cut.

Damien's mouth nearly dropped open.

"What was that?" he asked, shocked. "What did you do?"

"Magic," Delph replied dryly. "Magic I didn't think I'd be using against a student. Your friend likes to go for killing blows during training exercises."

"Is she okay?" Damien asked worriedly. Mark could move again, and the bald student was struggling to his feet. However, Sylph was as still as the sand beneath her.

"She will be," Delph said, rolling his shoulder. "I can honestly say I didn't expect to break a sweat today. She didn't cut me, but I think the dean would have my throat if I didn't apologize somehow. I suppose I owe her something."

It seemed more like Delph spoke to himself than the students. His gaze refocused on Damien, and he jerked his chin toward Sylph's prone form.

"Is she your roommate?"

"She is. How did you know?" Damien asked. There were half a dozen other questions he also wanted to ask, but after watching Delph manhandle the other students, he decided it would be best to keep them to himself.

"You said you followed her gaze. You're more likely to be

paying attention to people you know, so it was a safe guess," Delph replied with a dismissive shrug. "Take her back to your rooms. I'll be taking the other students to a healer, but they can't help with my magic. She'll wake up in an hour or two. I removed all the magic from the area around me, so she'll probably feel weak for a bit."

Delph didn't wait for him to respond. He shimmered through the air, tossing Mark over one shoulder and the bald boy over the other. Then the professor tapped his wristband and vanished without a second glance in Damien's direction.

"What in the seven planes was that?" Damien asked, staring at the space where Delph had been standing.

Henry didn't respond.

"Henry?" Damien asked, his brow furrowing. There was a long pause. Then he felt Henry let out bewildered sigh.

"I have no idea what he did," Henry said, a faint note of awe and excitement in his voice. "I've never seen that magic before."

"That's...cool, I suppose," Damien said.

"You don't understand," Henry snapped. "I've seen every form of magic that humans have. I've been watching the earth for millennia millennium! How could something be this foreign to me?"

Damien walked over to Sylph and knelt on the ground beside her. He nudged the girl's shoulder. She didn't respond.

"We can worry about that later," Damien said. "It's not like Professor Delph is going anywhere. If you don't know what happened, I suppose I just need to get Sylph back to our dorm."

"Did you not hear me?" Henry asked, exasperated. "New magic! To me! How are you not comprehending how important this is?"

Damien rolled his eyes. He hadn't heard Henry this

panicked since they'd made the contract four years ago. With a sigh, he put his back against her chest and grabbed her arms, pulling them in front of him.

Sylph was heavier than he'd expected. Damien gritted his teeth and rose to his feet with the girl slung over his back like a sack of potatoes.

"You need to start getting more exercise," Henry said, taking a quick break from his ranting about magic to prod Damien. "You're lucky this girl is barely more than half your size, or you'd be dragging her back to your room."

"I think I preferred it when you were terrified of Delph's magic," Damien grumbled, trudging toward the exit at the end of the arena.

"Not terrified," Henry said. "Shocked. You couldn't even begin to comprehend how unbelievable it is to learn something this new after a thousand years of stagnation. And yet, the more I think about it, the more familiar his magic feels. How strange."

Damien would have shrugged if that didn't involve having to lift Sylph's body more.

Students gave Damien strange glances as he staggered through the streets with Sylph over his back, but none of them paid him more than a few moments of attention. Evidently, this wasn't the strangest thing they'd seen on campus.

The only thing that kept Damien going was the sight of the huge library in the distance. Each step he took felt impossibly small, and Sylph seemed to grow heavier with every passing moment. After he'd walked for around thirty minutes, he was practically trembling with effort.

"Not to be an asshole, but this is pathetic," Henry said.

"Shut up," Damien snapped, speaking aloud by accident.

A passing student shot a dirty look in his direction, but he was too tired to care.

He was nearly upon the library, but there was still a long walk after he made it there. Damien set his jaw and continued to trudge onwards.

"You know, you could have just taken the portal in the arena," Henry observed. "Although, this is good exercise. Maybe you should do it all the time."

"It would have taken me to the courtyard," Damien rasped. "I don't remember which portal went to the mountain."

"I do," Henry said, cackling as Damien ground to a halt. "You're nearly there, though. You've gone more than half of the way, so it'll be faster to finish walking than to turn back."

"You suck."

Henry's laughter faded as Damien mentally shoved him into the depths of his mind. He resumed his trek, ignoring his body's desperate pleas to stop. If he did, Damien was pretty sure he'd end up dragging Sylph along the ground behind him for the rest of the trip.

When Damien finally reached the base of the mountain, he'd completely lost track of time. His legs burned with pain he knew for a fact would be coming back with a vengeance tomorrow.

With a weary sigh, Damien staggered up the mountain paths. The sun set behind the clouds, casting the sky in brilliant pink and orange hues. The view from the side of the mountain was magnificent, and Damien likely would have appreciated it if he'd had the energy to look away from the dirt in front of him.

Damien had never seen a dark cave opening look so inviting. He drew on the last of his energy, stumbling across the plateau and into their room. He tossed Sylph onto her bed and groaned in relief.

He slipped his travel bag under his bed and pulled the covers down, climbing into it while removing his coat and scarf with aching arms. Damien removed his shirt and pants as well. He tossed them to the foot of the bed and slipped under the sheets with a relieved sigh.

"I'm going to take a look around the world," Henry said. "Check out what we're dealing with. I'll be back before you wake up."

"Oka— Wait. What?" Damien asked, jerking upright and blinking groggily.

"I need to scope the area out," Henry replied. "Relax. I won't do anything. I'm just going sightseeing. Nobody will even know I'm there."

I'm not so sure about that. How do I know you won't try to do something?

"That's the funny thing, boy. There's nothing you can do about it. This is in both of our best interests, so the contract isn't stopping me. I'm just letting you know. Enjoy your rest," Henry said.

A cold wind blew through the room. Damien's shadow stretched and pulled away from him, vanishing into the sky and leaving him staring at it helplessly. A wave of intense exhaustion washed over him, turning his thoughts even more sluggish and fuzzy than they already were. His mind suddenly felt profoundly empty, like a large part of him had vanished. Considering Henry had half his soul, Damien supposed it had.

He sighed and tapped his wristband, pulling up the information that Blackmist had on him.

Damien Vale

Blackmist College
Year One
Major: Undecided
Minor: Undecided
Companion: [Null]
Magical Strength: 3.4
Magical Control: .5
Magical Energy: 8
Physical Strength: .2
Endurance: .35

At least his trek back through the campus with Sylph over his shoulder had been good for something. He didn't have the energy to worry further about the consequences of a deadly eldritch creature roaming the world. The call of sleep was a siren, and Damien was no more than a hapless sailor. He fell back onto his bed. His head hit the pillow, and conscious thought blinked out as he fell into a deep sleep.

———

Damien blinked. He sat on a grassy hill completely naked, which was rather strange considering he was quite confident he'd gone to sleep in his bed wearing underwear.

Surrounding the hill, there was...nothing. Blank, empty darkness enveloped the world, starting at the base of the grass and stretching beyond the horizon. Damien started to stand up, then glanced at himself and thought better of it. Strangely, he felt no fear or panic. Instead, the emotion circling his mind was more of a detached bemusement.

"Hello?" Damien asked. His voice echoed out, repeating itself to him several times before fading away into the darkness. "Is anybody here? Where am I?"

A cold breeze brushed against Damien's back. He shuddered and hugged himself as goosebumps raced up and down his spine.

"Within your mind. A very small part of it, anyway," Henry's voice came from behind Damien.

Damien turned around. Henry sat before him, dark smoke rising from his shadowy form. In his chest, a miniscule pinprick of white light shimmered faintly. Thin lines of energy stretched from the dot of light and into his chest.

Henry noticed Damien's stare and grunted. The darkness surrounding him flared up, smothering the light.

"It's rude to stare," Henry said.

Damien shrugged in response. Henry sighed. He waved his hand in Damien's direction. A tiny dot of darkness floated through the air and passed through Damien's forehead. He blinked lazily, then drew in a ragged gasp.

"What in the hells?"

"Much better," Henry said. "Your subconscious was trying to sleep, but we have important matters to discuss."

"And that involves you bringing me to a hill in the Void without any clothes?" Damien protested.

"It's all in your mind," Henry replied. "This is where I reside while you go about your happy little mortal life. Don't complain too much. And, again, your mind. It's not my fault you've shown up naked."

Damien frowned. His normal clothes popped into existence around him as if they'd always been there.

"Huh. That's cool," Damien said.

"You're literally just imagining things. It couldn't be more uninteresting," Henry grumbled. "On topic, please. This is serious."

"Right, sure," Damien said, massaging his forehead as he

dug through his memories. His brow furrowed. "Wait, you ran off last night! What did you do?"

"I told you. I was scouting out the area. Nobody saw me, and I didn't bother any mortals. You have nothing to fear."

"Right," Damien said, crossing his arms. "That's why you say we have a serious topic to discuss."

"Okay, there might be a little bit to fear," Henry admitted. "But it isn't my fault."

"Just tell me already!"

"If you insist. I'm not the only creature from the Void in the mortal plane."

Damien blinked. Of all the things he'd been expecting, most of which had to do with getting caught by Dean Whisp, that wasn't one of them. As he processed Henry's words, he realized he would have preferred the dean to have found his secret.

"Just for the sake of clarity, could you expand on that?" Damien asked slowly. "This might be a time when numbers matter."

"I detected five of my brethren in the world," Henry said, floating to his feet and pacing back and forth. "They are all Void denizens like me. Luckily for you, all of them were bound in some manner or another. I did not get close enough for them to identify who I am."

"That's...really bad," Damien agreed, well aware his words were an understatement. One world ending creature was bad enough. "You don't sound particularly happy about this. I would have thought you'd want more eldritch creatures on the Mortal Plane."

"Of course, I don't!" Henry snapped, spinning toward Damien. "I've just found out there's new magic I don't know. I want to experience that before the world for at least a bit before it all goes boom."

"That would suck," Damien said in a dry tone. "I'm sure you'd lose a lot of sleep over it. Not like life itself would be snuffed out for all eternity or anything. Just some spilled milk."

"Destroying this feeble, worthless plane is the reason for my existence. Besides, it wouldn't be all that bad," Henry said. "Imagine being in a race for someone to learn magic, and only the winner would be able to do it."

"I am not going to empathize with something that wants to end the world," Damien said, glaring at Henry. "However, if you're serious about there being other eldritch creatures on the Mortal Plane—"

"Why would I lie?" Henry asked, throwing his hands into the air. "Listen, boy. We need to work together on this. The other eldritch creatures cannot escape. We must find them and kill their hosts before they do."

"What? Isn't there another way we can get rid of them?" Damien asked, frowning. "I can't even cast magic yet! And I'm sorry, but I don't trust you enough to kill random people with nothing but your word to go on."

Henry grabbed Damien by the shoulders and shook him like a ragdoll.

"Do you not understand the magnitude of the situation?" Henry screamed. "They can end the world! Before I learn all the new magic!"

Damien knocked his companion's hands aside. He looked into where Henry's eyes should have been on his face.

"You've lied to me one too many times, Henry. I agree that this is a serious issue, although I think our reasons for that are a little different. Still, I won't be killing people just because you said to. If you want my trust, you need to earn it. You can start by giving me any information you know about these competitors of yours."

Henry let out a frustrated huff. "I know little beyond that they exist. Their powers were weak, as is mine."

"So they aren't breaking out anytime soon," Damien said. "And by soon, I mean within a few years."

"It's hard to say," Henry replied, shrugging. "Probably not, but if whatever is holding them is damaged, they could escape tomorrow."

"In that case, the world is over and there's nothing we can do about it," Damien said. "So let's not worry about that. How far away were these creatures?"

"One was quite close," Henry replied after thinking for a few moments. "No more than a hundred miles. The rest were farther, and I didn't get a good feel for where they were."

"And they didn't sense you?"

Henry paused. He thought for a few moments before shaking his head.

"Doubtful. I was looking, and they were not. However, if we were to come face to face with their host, it is likely we would recognize each other."

"Will I be able to recognize them?" Damien asked, drumming his fingers on his chin.

"When they burn you alive or stick a dagger into your back, yes," Henry said.

"Okay. Then we've got the beginnings of a plan," Damien said. "I can't go seeking these guys out yet, since they'll just kill me. If they're contained, all I can do is get strong as fast as I can. Then we can seek them out. If they are what you claim they are..."

Damien grimaced. How could he know if the other people were any different from him? It's not like he'd asked to be saddled with Henry.

"...we'll figure something out," Damien finished. "And we can't exactly tell someone at a mage college. If they even believe me, they'll wonder how I knew about your Void friends."

"They are not my friends."

"Sorry. But my point still stands. Unless you have a better suggestion?"

"I do not," Henry said, sighing. "Not one you would accept. You must grow in strength quickly. If I was able to sense them, they will eventually be able to sense us. Believe me, it is much better to be the hunter than the prey."

With that sobering thought, the world rippled like it was the surface of a lake that had a stone tossed into it. The hill faded, and darkness enveloped Damien.

The following morning, Damien awoke to something warm bearing down on his face. He groaned and rolled over, burying his face in the pillow.

"Wake up, boy," Henry said. "I want to look around the campus."

"Then do it your—" Damien stopped mid-sentence. Then he let out a groan and rolled over, opening his eyes, and staring at the ceiling. The memories of what had happened overnight came rushing back to him. "Don't do that, actually. Last night was more than enough."

"I recommend we avoid speaking of last night unless needed," Henry said. "Your mind is not the sanctum you believe it to be, and who knows how many eyes are watching us. Go about your training but remember what lies at stake. Also, you're talking aloud again."

He forced himself away from the pillow and into a seated position. His sore limbs voiced their protest. Damien grimaced.

Not one more word about that, Henry I'm working on it.

"I didn't say anything," Henry said with false innocence.

Good.

Damien glanced at Sylph's bed. She was gone. He frowned and shimmied down the bed, grabbing his clothing, and pulling it under the covers to get dressed.

Where's Sylph?

"The girl woke up a few hours ago," Henry replied. "You could take a few pages out of her book. You waste half the day sleeping."

Damien grunted and shuffled over to their small bathroom. The runes he'd drawn on the wall still emitted a faint light, but it had grown weaker since yesterday.

"Wrong way," Henry said. "The exit is behind us."

I'm not going anywhere until I've taken a shower and brushed my teeth.

Henry settled for a grumble. Damien's thoughts told the companion he wouldn't be making any headway in that particular argument.

CHAPTER
ELEVEN

About thirty minutes later, after Damien had thoroughly washed himself in the tiny shower, he stepped out of the cave feeling mostly refreshed. The water had done wonders to soothe his aching muscles.

"I wonder where Sylph went," Damien wondered to himself.

"Who cares?" Henry said. "You've got so many things to do, but all you can think about is finding your roommate?"

"What do you mean?" Damien asked. "I thought we were just going to look around the campus."

"You can learn magic!" Henry exclaimed. "Have you forgotten that somehow?"

Damien stopped walking as Henry's words sunk in. The last day had gone by so quickly that he'd barely had time to think about it. A grin crept across his face, and he laughed.

"Seven Planes, you're right!" Damien exclaimed, jumping into the air and pumping his arms. Luckily, there was nobody else on the mountain path with him to see his antics. "How did I forget? I don't need to wait for a stuffy teacher. I can learn now, can't I?"

"Eight," Henry corrected idly. "Not seven."

Damien ignored him.

"That's more like it. I was almost worried something had happened to that foolish thirteen-year-old who summoned me," Henry continued. "There are some things we need to set up first. Also, you might want to stop speaking out loud. Someone is going to see you."

Damien continued down the mountain, a goofy grin plastered on his face. It faded a little when whispers of Henry's words rose at the edges of his mind. The knowledge of why he needed to learn magic sobered him. It wasn't enough to wash away seventeen years' worth of pent-up excitement, but it was certainly enough to dampen it.

What do I need to do?

"You need a place to train. You shouldn't use the public spaces the student mentioned, at least, not yet. Much of my magic is...discomforting for mortals. It would cast suspicion on us too early. You should make a training area in your room."

What? How?

"That leads us to the first step. The universe is made up of Ether. However, you cannot interact with it right now. You need to spend time with the Ether until your body absorbs it. The more you can hold, the more powerful you will be," Henry instructed. "Once you can absorb the Ether around you, you'll be able to do basic magic. We can use that magic to carve the stone in your room."

Well, how do I absorb Ether?

"A question asked by mages forever, but I doubt you're seeking the truth of the universe," Henry responded, speaking as if he were talking to a foolish child. "There are stages to mastery over the forces of life. As you currently are, you do not have any connection to the Ether. To develop it, you have to learn a cultivation technique. This will build the basis of how you improve your strength in the future, and it will work until your Core gathers enough energy to evolve."

Evolve?

"We can get to that later," Henry said. "Focus on cultivation for now. A good cultivation method is vital for establishing your foundations for the future."

Fine. I bet the library would have something on it, then!

Damien started off toward the library at a brisk pace. The last four years of waiting for magic had been torture, but that was finally over. He crushed the worry building in his stomach. Despite the dire situation, his heart beat faster than when he'd gotten his first kiss.

The campus was more crowded than it had been on the previous day. The roads weren't packed, but they were getting close to it. Streams of chattering students rushed to and fro. The road had been split into two, with one line of traffic leading deeper into campus while the other branched away.

Damien straightened and joined the tide of people, doing his best to look like he knew what he was doing. He followed the path to the library, where a significant portion of the other students seemed to be going as well.

He reached the steps leading to the library's enormous doors. They were far too large to be used comfortably. He climbed up the stairs, taking care to watch his feet to make sure he didn't trip.

With the number of people entering the library, Damien had expected the building to be packed. However, when he stepped inside the entrance, it looked deserted. There was a row of about twenty desks with librarians directly in front of him.

The majority of the students headed right past the librarians, disappearing into the huge maze of bookshelves. Even still, small lines formed behind each of the desks. Damien joined the shortest one, doing his best not to let his mouth hang open as he took in the library.

It didn't seem possible, but the massive building was even more impressive on the inside. He couldn't even see the roof because of how high in the air it was. Beautifully carved bookcases trimmed with gold and obsidian lined every inch of room on the walls, rising into the sky and disappearing out of sight.

Every once and a while, a book would flutter across the room and dart into a student's hands. Someone nudged Damien in the back, snapping him out of his reverie. The line had gone much faster than he'd expected, and he was now at the front.

With an embarrassed grin, Damien rushed forward to stand before the librarian—a short, round man with a bushy beard. The librarian cocked a fuzzy eyebrow at Damien's flustered expression.

"First time in the library?" he asked in a kind voice.

Damien nodded mutely.

"Good on you, boy. Getting a head start on your training is admirable. Unless you're here for other knowledge...?"

"I'm here to find a book that will show me a cultivation method," Damien said, tearing his eyes from the books to look at the librarian.

"Thought as much," the librarian said, giving him a gap-toothed grin. "The cultivation section is at the back of the library. Just keep walking straight. You can't miss it. And, a word of advice, don't worry yourself too much over which method to choose. They all claim to be the best, and there isn't much of a difference between them beyond how you train. So, find one you think looks interesting and learn it."

"Thank you," Damien said.

"No problem, son," the librarian replied. "My name's Donny. You have any trouble in the library, come find me. I'll try to get you sorted out."

Damien thanked him again before stepping past the desks and following Donny's directions deeper into the library.

Within minutes, he was surrounded by musky parchment and the smell of oiled paper. Bobbing yellow lights dimly illuminated the passageways, which ranged from enormous roads to alleys made of stacked books so tight Damien had to squeeze through them sideways.

He scanned the book titles as he passed them. They ranged everywhere from instructions on carpentry to ancient recipes. There were a good number of old scrolls dispersed throughout the shelves, and several of them looked like they were one strong breeze from falling apart.

"How can they leave something this fragile out for students to mess with?" Damien asked, his mouth agape as stopped beside a crumbling scroll. There was no title on it, but a tiny metal plaque installed on the shelf below it had a name.

"A treatise on compromise and love," Damien read aloud.

"I can see why they left that one out," Henry said, scoffing. "Worthless."

Damien rolled his eyes and set off once again. He wasn't going to expressly agree with Henry, but his companion had one thing right. He was here for a reason: magic.

"Wait!" Henry yelled, his voice more panicked than Damien had ever heard it. He froze mid-step, not daring to even draw a breath.

"What is it," Damien whispered, forgetting to speak inside his head once again. Idiot.

"Go back a step and look at that book with the purple binding," Henry ordered.

Damien followed his instructions and grabbed the book, pulling it free of the shelf slowly as to avoid bringing the entire thing down on himself.

"I can't read it," Damien said, disappointed. "I can't use this."

"That's the problem," Henry whispered. "I can't read that either."

It took Damien a few seconds to understand the gravity of Henry's words.

"I thought you said you've been watching humans for millennia millennium," Damien said, crossing his arms. "This book doesn't look all that old."

"Just open it!" Henry snapped. "Maybe it's just the title."

Damien shrugged and flipped through the book, opening it to a page near the middle. It looked like complete gibberish to him, but there were a few runes along the edges of the book that seemed to resemble ones Damien already knew.

"No, no, no!" Henry muttered, talking faster with every word. "This isn't possible! Half of these words don't make sense, and many others are just used incorrectly!"

Damien closed the book and set it back on the shelf. Henry descended into confused muttering and didn't bother to stop him. He scratched his chin and furrowed his brow as he walked. He stopped only a few paces later.

"Henry?" Damien whispered.

"What?"

"What year is it?"

"What do you mean?" Henry asked. Annoyance radiated off the creature within his mind. "Why would an immortal creature care about something like that?"

"Just tell me the year," Damien pressed. "You claim to know everything that mortals do, so it shouldn't be hard for you. The calendar started counting when humanity made their first summon. How many years ago was that?"

"One thousand and forty-three," Henry replied irritably. "But I don't see how this will—"

"That's wrong," Damien said, shaking his head. "I turned seventeen on the sixth day and the sixth month of five thousand and fifty-two. I was born in five thousand and thirty-five.

"Impossible!" Henry said, but Damien could tell that the creature didn't believe his own words.

"Why would I lie? I don't gain anything from it," Damien said, setting back off toward the back of the library while Henry had a mental breakdown within his head.

"I spent four thousand years traveling from the Void to the Mortal Plane!" Henry muttered as realization finally washed over him. "How much history did I miss?"

"You're immortal, aren't you?" Damien asked.

"As far as I'm aware, yes. But four thousand years, while nothing to me, is enough for entire empires to rise and fall multiple times. It has never taken this long before. So much knowledge lost—"

"Wait, before?"

Henry didn't respond.

"I don't see why that matters so much," Damien said, squeezing in between two bookshelves and nearly knocking several musty tomes to the ground. "You just wanted to destroy everything anyway. Why do you care if you missed information?"

"You don't understand," Henry said. His fury and sadness were enough to involuntarily bring tears to Damien's eyes. "Do you know how blessed mortals are? Creativity is a spark, boy. Mortals are like dry straw lit by that spark. They burn out in the blink of an eye but shine brightly as they do. Immortal beings are more like metal. We have no spark, so we watch mortals. They create, we control. I have more power than any human could ever begin to dream of, but my magic is simply an improvement on your own."

Damien didn't respond immediately. He wiped the tears from his eyes and glanced around to make sure nobody else was in this section of the library. Luckily, it was so large there was nobody in sight.

"I can see why that would suck," Damien said awkwardly, inwardly cursing himself. He hadn't had much experience consoling other humans, much less otherworldly murderous creatures with a passion for learning. "Not to make what you went through trivial, but you're here now, right? This library is huge. I'm sure we could find the important —"

Damien's body went rigid. His shadow bubbled and popped beneath him as dozens of closed eyes appeared within it. They opened as one, revealing gray, milky pupils that were decidedly inhuman.

"Brilliant!" Henry exclaimed. "You're right! We stand in a massive repository of knowledge. It might not be the same as watching everything happen, but I can still learn the important events secondhand!"

"Henry, control yourself," Damien snapped. The eyes blinked closed and vanished in an instant. "And I'm not going to read every book in this library. I'd die of old age long before I got through a quarter of them."

"Please?"

"No. We'll find a list of information the library has later, and then I can read the books you're the most interested in," Damien said, leaving no room for argument. "Now, I want to start learning magic already! The cultivation section can't be much farther so, please, control yourself. I don't want to have to explain why my shadow has more eyeballs than I do."

Henry's response was a grumbling sigh. He faded into the back of Damien's mind, and he continued deeper into the library. Even though he was surrounded by endless rows of books, the library did not become monotonous.

Many of the shelves were twisted and warped, bending over aisles or even blocking them. Somehow, books remained in their proper spots even when they were perpendicular to the ground.

The building seemed to have a character that changed based on the sections. Damien must have passed nearly a hundred sections before he finally came to the first open space he'd seen since he entered the maze of books.

A large hallway stretched out before him, disappearing to the sides. Hundreds of other aisles led up to it, and an equal number of doors lined the other side. There were several chairs and desks placed along the hallway, and a few of them were actually occupied by students.

Inscribed metal plaques burning with magical orange energy had been placed above each door. Damien stepped into the hallway and walked up to one of the doors, peering up at the plaque.

"Cultivation methods: Dance," he whispered to himself. He squinted up at the piece of metal, but he'd read it correctly. "Dance?"

"It works," Henry replied. "Not for you, though. It's not practical to teach you how to dance. I know you better than you know yourself, and you can't do anything as intricate as this. You're no thin sword meant for beautiful displays. A hammer is what you are, a big, ugly one with spikes."

Thank you.

"Anytime," Henry said cheerfully. "Now, we'll still have to come check this section out. Maybe humans invented some new dance methods while I was on my trip. Until then, look for cultivation methods that are a little simpler."

As it turned out, that was harder than it sounded. Damien walked past dozens of doors leading to cultivation methods that involved cooking, cleaning, juggling, and an assortment of other equally mundane tasks Henry scoffed at.

"Look over there," Henry instructed Damien, forcing him to turn his head slightly to the side. Really, it was more of a nudge. The contract stopped him from forcibly taking control of Damien's body but giving it suggestions before Damien could counter them was still on the table.

Stop that! It's unsettling when my head turns, and I'm not the one who turned it.

"Stop whining and look!"

"Repetition?" Damien said aloud, drawing glances from the people studying around him. He winced, ducking his head, and gave them a sheepish grin while a blush spread to his cheeks.

"Exactly," Henry said. "Now, that would be perfect."

Why? It sounds...really boring.

"Go look. The method I personally use could be boiled down to repetition if I did a lot of simplifying. Trust me, it's not anywhere near as bad as meditation," Henry said with a groan. "Could you imagine sitting around for half your life, eyes closed and gathering energy? Ugh. Who would torture themselves like that?"

Fine, fine.

Damien reached the door. It was the same dull brown wood as the rest of them, with a plain gray metal handle. The hinges let out a small squeak as he pushed it open and stepped inside.

The room he'd stepped into was only large enough for a few people to fit in it at once. There was a single desk with two chairs in the center, and all four walls were lined with bookcases only around half full. A few books had been stacked on the table, but nobody else was in the room.

Damien approached one of the shelves, letting the door swing shut behind him. It made another squeak before closing with a *click*.

"How do I know which one to take?" Damien asked.

"Let me out so I can read them."

"No! What if someone walked in?" he hissed.

"Fine. Then let me use your body for a minute or two. Unless you want to spend the rest of the day reading these," Henry said.

"I'm not sure that's a good idea," Damien said, frowning. "I'm not keen on giving you control over my body. I haven't forgotten what happened the last time I did."

"We have a contract!" Henry said irritably. "I can't do anything you don't want me to, and you can take control back whenever you want."

Damien chewed his inner cheek.

"You can have it for exactly five minutes or until someone walks in. After that, it returns to me, no matter the situation."

His limbs stiffened. It took all his self-control not to shove Henry back and regain control of his body. He couldn't even take a slow breath to steady himself, which made things even worse.

"Calm down," Henry snapped. "Try to move your left hand."

Damien's hand twitched, and he felt Henry's presence recede for a moment before filling him once again.

"See? The moment you try to actually do something, I get booted out," Henry said. "Now —"

Damien snapped his fingers. His consciousness rushed

forth once again, tossing Henry into the background once again. He wiggled his fingers and rolled his neck.

"What was that for?" Henry asked, mentally poking Damien.

"Just making sure," Damien replied. "You've got five minutes."

He allowed the eldritch creature to regain control of his body. It was still unsettling, but it wasn't as bad this time around. The knowledge he could take the reins back whenever he wanted was reassuring.

Henry grumbled out curses as he picked up the book on the table with Damien's body and scanned the cover.

"Trash," Damien-Henry said, setting the book back down and glancing at the other one before rolling his eyes.

Henry directed Damien over to the bookshelf on the far left wall. He raised a hand and barked out a string of guttural, hissing noises. The lights in the room dimmed. Inky black tendrils twisted through the air around Damien, straightening out and snapping into straight lines.

The lines twitched and opened outward, revealing pale white and black eyes. They turned to the bookshelves and moved in erratic patterns, stopping in front of each book before zipping back into motion.

Damien couldn't tell what they saw, and he didn't particularly care. He was more preoccupied with the worry someone would walk through the door while disembodied eyes floated around the room.

It turned out Henry only needed two minutes to examine every book in the room. The eyes disappeared with a series of *pops*. Damien's body walked around the room, pulling books from the shelves and tossing them onto the table without even looking at the titles.

By the time he'd finished, there was a pile of ten books.

Henry sat Damien down in the chair and relinquished control of the body back to its rightful owner.

"There. See?" Henry said. "Easy and fast. I found ten books in the common tongue and actually useful. The others either didn't suit you or were worthless."

"Thank you," Damien said, lifting the first book from the pile. It was leather, with a gold trim that peeled away from the edges. "How do I know which one is the best?"

"There is no best," Henry replied. "It's just a method, and they're all so basic you won't find a difference. However, everyone is going to have a method that's more suited to them. You need to choose what fits you best."

"I see," Damien said, looking at the book in his hands with a furrowed brow. "And how is 'constant love making' supposed to fit me as a person?"

Henry cackled as Damien rolled his eyes and set the book on the far side of the table.

He picked up the next book. It was also bound in leather, but it had no trim. Thin metal triangles protected the edges of the covers and a layer of dust had permanently settled into it. He brushed the dust away as best as he could, revealing the scuffed title beneath it.

"Body Tempering," Damien read. "That sounds like a lot of exercise."

"Which you need. Or were you wanting to run out of breath trying to lift a girl half your size again?"

Damien scrunched his nose up and flipped the book open. It fit easily in his hand and couldn't have had more than a hundred pages. The paper crackled as he touched it but somehow stayed in one piece.

"You need to start from the beginning," Henry said, mentally nudging Damien to move on. "Don't worry about the methods. Just choose the one whose title seems the most appealing."

"That seems like a terrible idea," Damien said.

Henry didn't respond. Damien sighed and set the book beside the stack. He picked up the next one and continued the process.

CHAPTER
TWELVE

Of the remaining books, the only one that caught his interest was titled *True Adaptation*. Of all the books, it was the only one that wasn't completely mundane sounding. When Damien voiced his observation to Henry, the eldritch companion scoffed.

"Magic *is* mundane, boy. Ether is simply part of the natural world. However, these books are all boring sounding because they're just the foundation. The cool, fancy magic comes later. The cultivation method you choose will simply let you use my powers to connect with the Ether without runes. It'll be worthless within a year."

"So, the method I choose is just whichever seems the easiest to get started with?" Damien guessed.

"Essentially."

Damien nodded, his lips thinning as he internally debated between the two books he'd chosen. As he sat there thinking, the wooden door creaked. He glanced up as the door swung open, and Sylph stepped into the room.

"Sylph? How did you find me?" Damien asked, nearly

jumping out of his chair. He felt Henry coil within his mind like a snake preparing to strike.

"I figured you'd have gone to the library, and I just asked if anyone had seen a kid in a blue jacket and white scarf walk by while talking to himself," Sylph said with a smirk.

Henry chuckled within Damien's mind. "She's got you there. You really have to work on that habit."

Shut up.

"Picking a cultivation method without an instructor?" Sylph asked, raising an eyebrow as she closed the door behind her. "That's bold of you."

"You didn't have an instructor," Damien pointed out.

"I did," Sylph replied, approaching the table. "Just not from a mage college."

She picked the book up at the far side and scanned the cover. Her eyebrow raised and a flicker of a smirk danced across her features.

"Constant lovemaking?" she asked, straight faced.

"I...ah, my companion chose it..."

Henry howled with laughter. "You're digging your hole deeper. Just stop talking."

Sylph set the book carefully on the table, wiping her hands off her shirt before sitting down in the other chair.

You'll pay for that, Henry.

"So, what did you come find me for?" Damien stammered, desperate to change the subject from the offending book.

"I was hoping you could tell me what happened after my fight with Professor Delph," Sylph said. "My memory of the whole fight is blurry, and I woke up with nearly no magical energy."

"Oh, right!" Damien said. "I was going to tell you when I woke up, but you were already gone. He used some weird magic, and you passed out. He said you'd feel weak when you woke up, and that he owed you something for forcing him to use that magic."

"I see," Sylph said with a small frown. "So I lost."

"Of course, you did," Damien said. "Did you expect to beat a professor?"

"I suppose not," Sylph said, sighing. "It means I'm going to have to train more. It's unfortunate there aren't more private areas to train. All the school sanctioned spots are packed full."

"I haven't given them a look yet," Damien admitted. He glanced between the books in his hands one more time, then set the *True Adaptation* one aside. He stood up and put the other books back onto the bookshelf.

"Not going to go with the constant—"

"Nope!" Damien said, cutting Sylph off before she could finish the sentence. He cleared his throat. "I'm good. Chose a different one."

"Best of luck with that, then. It was not easy for me to first make contact with the Ether. I hope it goes better for you," Sylph said. "If Professor Delph is looking for me, I should probably find him. I'm going to get some breakfast first, though."

Damien adjusted his grip on the book in his hand. "I'm going to head back to the dorm. I need to get started if I want to keep up with everyone else."

Sylph nodded. The two of them left the room and headed out of the library. Damien briefly stopped by the front desk to let the librarians know which book he'd taken before they continued out.

Sylph bid Damien farewell and headed to the dining halls while he headed back to their mountain room as fast as he could without breaking into a full run.

"Excited, are we?" Henry asked.

"You already know the answer— Damn it," Damien huffed.

You already know the answer to that. I've been waiting for this moment for seventeen years.

"Another hour wouldn't have hurt. You could have gotten some food," Henry said. Damien could tell his companion grinned, even though he couldn't see him.

Damien arrived back at the plateau in record time. He sped past the Mark and the Grays' rooms and into his own. Then he sat on his bed and flipped the book open.

"So, how do I do this?" Damien asked eagerly and somewhat out of breath.

"I'd suggest you start by reading," Henry suggested dryly.

Damien did just that. The book was written in a mix of runes and the common language, but it was written as if the author was just showing off. The words were long and often needlessly complicated, and many of the rune drawings were incredibly complicated. It went into great detail about how to mentally reach out and connect with the Ether permeating the world.

Much to Damien's annoyance, the runes weren't even required to connect with the Ether. They were simply incredibly complicated examples. Of course, he didn't figure that out until nearly two hours of studying the old paper.

Luckily, it didn't appear that the actual concept was particularly difficult. In order to connect with the Ether, one had to essentially train their body into recognizing its presence. Since humans aren't naturally capable of doing such a feat, a companion would essentially guide their partner to it.

Once contact had been established, the cultivation method trained a human's body and mind into recognizing it on their own, so their companion didn't have to find it each time. Then, when the connection was complete, the cultivation method was tossed away, and the human's core would be ready for evolution.

Companions, who were inherently magical creatures, could access only the Ether in a specific way. According to the book, that was what determined types of magic. Therefore, since the companion was the one who guided the human to the Ether, humans could only learn the same magic as their companion.

Damien closed the book and let out an exasperated sigh.

"That's a whole lot of theory and not very much useful information!" he exclaimed. "The book just says my companion will guide me. It's got instructions for using the Ether to teach my body how to adapt, but that comes after connecting with the Ether, so it's not useful yet. All I've really learned is that you need to do all the work!"

"Hardly," Henry said. "It's important to know your end goal before you attempt anything, or you'll never get the results you want. Now, you know more about the Ether and what you'll be cultivating to make your control over it stronger."

"I suppose," Damien agreed, shrugging one shoulder. "You can guide me to the Ether, then?"

"I can," Henry said. There was a long pause. "In a way. It won't be *me* that guides you."

"What's that supposed to mean?"

"Humans have absolutely no sense of the Ether. You need it to be lit up like the sun for you to first notice it. I, unfortunately, do not have the intricacies to do such a feat. It will not be Henry that shows you how to access the Ether. It will be all of me. Do you understand?"

It was Damien's turn to pause. Finally, he nodded. "I do."

"Good," Henry said. "Sit down on your bed. This is a process that can take up to several weeks. I do not know how much your mind will be able to handle, but expect to be at it for an hour at the least."

Damien followed Henry's instructions, ignoring the worried voice in the back of his mind that warned him of what could happen if his companion betrayed him. The contract wouldn't let Henry harm him. In fact, he realized he was actually starting to almost like the eldritch creature. That was a sobering thought.

"Ready?" Henry asked. "Close your eyes and enter the mental space where I reside within your mind."

Damien drew a deep breath. His hands trembled with a mixture of fear and excitement, and his stomach flipflopped. He pressed his lips together and gathered his focus as he shut his eyes.

He sent the probe of mental energy out toward Henry. A shiver ran down his spine as it touched something incomprehensibly cold, which shouldn't have been possible. The probe was energy. It couldn't feel things.

His logic was nothing in the face of It Who Heralds the End of All Light. Damien couldn't see it, but his breath came out in puffs of white air, and his lips turned blue while his teeth chattered.

"Relax," Henry ordered as fear billowed up within him. "You must be in control of your emotions."

Damien tried to swallow, but his mouth was utterly dry. He pressed his lips thin, ignoring the pain as they turned stiff and cracked, and gave a jerky nod.

Something brushed across Damien's back. Dozens of miniscule pinpricks spread across his body emanating from the base of his spine. A dot of light blinked into existence.

Another followed it. It started slowly, but they appeared faster and faster. Within minutes, the darkness had been replaced by a sky of dim stars.

Damien went to open his eyes, but they were already open. He looked down at himself. His body was gone, replaced by a vaguely humanoid blob of glowing yellowish orange. His arms and legs ended in curved nubs instead of hands or feet, and his entire body felt lighter than normal.

"Where am I?" Damien asked. The voice didn't come from his mouth but instead echoed out from his entire body. The glowing lines he was now composed of wiggled and rippled at the noise.

The sky above him contorted. The stars shifted through the darkness, forming lines and shapes until an enormous inhuman face appeared. It wasn't just part of the horizon, it was all of it. Thousands of eyes made of twinkling stars stared down at him.

Only now did Damien truly realize what Henry had meant. This was It Who Heralds the End of All Light. The eyes watched Damien, utterly alien and incomprehensible. It gave no sarcastic comments, nor did it even speak. There could be no communication between a mortal and this creature.

It was at that moment Damien understood the magnitude of the monster he held within him. As he stared up disbelievingly at the planet-sized entity above him, he knew it held nothing but contempt for him. He knew that, one day, it would be the inevitable end of humanity, and he was nothing before it.

Damien's meager form flickered, as if merely being in the presence of this creature was enough to snuff him out like a candle. It looked down at him wordlessly. Damien couldn't tell if it was amused by his fear, or if it could even be amused.

"I'm here to sense the Ether," Damien called out. If he'd had a throat, Damien was confident his words would have come out squeaky and trembling. Instead, they rippled through the silent world surrounding him like a blade.

It Who Heralds the End of All Light continued to stare down at him. Then, slowly, it opened its mouth. The ground trembled and heaved as the mouth continued to open, blanketing the world in complete darkness.

One by one, the stars blinked out. The energy that made up Damien's new form sputtered and faded as an incredible chill wrapped its bony fingers around Damien. His words caught in his throat as pain tore through every part of his body at once.

It felt like thousands of jagged knives were being slowly drawn across every part of his body. He let out a silent scream as his spectral body went rigid. His world was agony.

"Ignore it!" Henry's voice pierced the darkness. "Fight through the pain, boy. True power is not gained easily!"

Damien couldn't respond. Luckily, he didn't need to. Henry knew his thoughts.

"Look around you!" Henry ordered. "The ether is everywhere, even in the Void. It is like strands of light that connect every single bit of existence together."

Damien could barely hear Henry's voice through the pain ravishing his body, but the key word was 'barely.' He gritted his metaphorical teeth and let out a scream of defiance and pain. He looked up. There was only darkness.

"Look harder!" Henry insisted. "You must search, no matter the pain."

And that was what Damien did. His gaze scanned the shadows enveloping him, flicking back and forth in search of the smallest iota of light. All the while, the light making up his glowing body dimmed further and further.

"There's nothing!" Damien wheezed.

"There is. Look!"

Coherent thought faded. Dissonant whispers of words Damien didn't understand and languages he'd never heard echoed through his mind. He searched the sky desperately for any signs of the lines Henry had spoken of, but all that met him was the fathomless black of the Void.

His screams intensified, and the whispers grew louder. Henry said something, but Damien barely recognized it. Thousands of voices yelled within his mind at once. Each word ripped through his soul, bringing on flashes of pain at a level he had never thought possible.

"It's too much," Henry said. "We need to stop and try again later. If the boy dies—"

"No!" Damien snarled. "I'm not done!"

He'd faded to a such a pale yellow he was nearly white. His body pulsated in and out of existence like a sputtering candle. Damien was no longer aware of the difference between his voice and those crying out within his mind.

As his soul was stripped and torn away, the vestiges of human emotion he felt were peeled back, piece by piece. The pain, of course, did not lessen in the slightest. The parts of Damien that made him mortal flickered and winked out.

First went his memories. Seventeen miniscule and worthless years of life, gone in the blink of an eye. Next went his thoughts and voice, followed by his feelings. As the parts that made Damien's soul his own were sent tumbling into the Void, the very core of his being was revealed.

A single spark. The flickering candle that rested at the center of his being that encompassed his greatest desires and goals, condensed into a mote of light. The one light Henry could never have for himself.

It was creativity. It was human longing, one of the

greatest forces in existence, and one that It Who Heralds the End of All Light could never have.

"Enough!" Henry yelled. "He cannot handle this!"

There was no response. Henry watched helplessly as the mote of light that was Damien flickered and faded, the darkness encircling it like a school of starving sharks.

It grew smaller and smaller until nothing but a pinprick of light remained within the shadows. The very last bit of Damien's existence in the universe, alone and surrounded by the Void.

The spark flickered. Then it blinked. And then it flared. Light erupted within the heart of the Void. Beams of energy carved through the sky, splitting the darkness and slamming into the spark.

Bit by bit, a torso formed around the spark. It was followed by arms and legs, and then by a head. Each beam of light that slammed into Damien reformed his spectral body by a small amount. In moments, he was whole once more.

However, the light didn't stop. It continued as dozens of golden lines formed all over him, and his light grew brighter. Damien let out a scream. It was not of pain, but of resolve. All over his body, the glowing lines split open to reveal golden glowing eyes.

The arcs of light stopped flying into Damien, but the Void was no longer dark to Damien's new eyes. An immeasurable number of thin threads crisscrossed throughout the Void. The majority of them rose into the sky, where the outline of the face appeared once again. However, several of the threads also connected to Damien.

Henry's power enveloped Damien. The boy was power-less to resist as a layer of fog fell over his mind. Memories of pain like this could never be removed, but they could be dulled.

"Is this magic?" Damien asked, the eyes covering his body flicking about erratically.

"No," Henry said. "This is the Ether. And you are an insane idiot."

"I know," Damien said, his voice full of pride and pain. And then, despite not being in a human body, he fainted.

CHAPTER
THIRTEEN

The cold gray ceiling of the cave blurred into view above Damien. His entire body felt stiff and cold. He groaned, his muscles protesting as he slowly sat up. It felt like he'd aged fifty years.

"Stop whining," Henry said. "You did this to yourself, and it will pass."

Damien's mind sorted through the foggy memories, the frown deepening on his face.

"Did it work?" he asked. "Can I cast magic?"

"Not yet," Henry replied. "And we weren't trying to let you cast magic. We were trying to let you connect with the Ether. There's a difference."

Damien rolled his head in a slow circle. His neck let out a series of *pops*, and he let out a relieved sigh.

"Well, did that work?"

"You tell me, you idiot," Henry said. "Do you even realize what you did? You nearly died!"

"Henry, you're the one who told me we don't exactly have a lot of time," Damien said, his tone growing cold. "Or do I have to remind you about the five...things roaming the world as we speak?"

"Don't pull that shit on me," Henry snapped. "I can read your thoughts. I'm well-aware you're just insanely obsessed with learning magic, and you didn't want to wait any longer."

Damien's cheeks flushed. He crossed his arms and shrugged. "Maybe."

"You're insane," Henry said. "Don't forget this isn't just your life you're toying with! If you die, I get sent back to the Void! If you don't pace yourself, you aren't going to live to cast any real magic."

"Fine, fine," Damien said with a heavy sigh. The feeling returned to his limbs once again. "I'll be more careful, but can we please get on with the magic?"

There was a pause that Damien assumed was Henry rolling his eyes. Then a thrum of static rippled outward from his chest, passing through his entire body.

"First, pull out that little wristband the school gave you," Henry said. "Let's see if your stupidity got us anywhere."

Damien nodded and activated the wristband, bringing the screen to life before his eyes.

Damien Vale
Blackmist College
Year One
Major: Undecided
Minor: Undecided
Companion: [Null]
Magical Strength: 3.5
Magical Control: .5
Magical Energy: 8.5
Physical Strength: .2

Endurance: .35

"Improvements in Magical Strength and Energy," Henry said. "Small, but not bad considering you didn't do anything other than be stubborn."

Damien dismissed the screen. "Can we get to the part where I do magic?"

"I'll help you find the Ether the first few times, but you'll eventually want to find it on your own," Henry said. "The connection has been established. Reach out with your mind, but do not close your eyes."

That was easier said than done. Damien drew a deep breath to steady his thundering heart and extended his senses.

"Not like that!" Henry said.

Damien felt a force envelop his mind. He resisted for a moment. Then he relaxed, allowing Henry to guide him. Henry molded the mental tendril Damien used like putty, turning it into something closer to a net.

"Send this out around you," Henry said. "Like how mortals do when they fish, but in every direction instead of one. When it touches the lines of Ether, they'll light up for you."

The net felt strange in Damien's mind. He'd grown so used to the single tendril that arranging the energy into a more complex form was taxing. If Henry hadn't helped him hold it together, the net would have already collapsed.

With Henry's assistance, Damien threw the net of energy outward. It expanded and stretched, forming a rough sphere around him. The world lit up.

Damien jerked back as hundreds of thin glowing threads appeared all over the room. Some disappeared into the rocks, some into his belongings, and some into him. It was as if he'd fallen into a giant spider web.

"Wow," Damien whispered, unable to find better words. He reached out and brushed a line of Ether with his hand. His body passed clean through it, not disturbing the light in the slightest. "I can see the Ether. How do I use it?"

"You are impatient," Henry said. "You need to get used to the Ether. Then you can worry about using it. We're going to repeat this a few more times. Just focus on the energy surrounding you."

Damien nodded, too engrossed to argue with his companion. Henry allowed him to sit there for several minutes, silently absorbing the beauty of the Ether surrounding him. As Damien's concentration faltered and his mental net wavered, the lines faded from his vision.

Damien let the net drop completely, and the lines blinked out. He gathered his mental energy, trying to mold it the same way Henry had. The result was a blobby, misshapen box of crisscrossing energy that could have been mistaken for a net by someone with a severe concussion.

"A little help?" Damien asked meekly.

Henry snorted. The energy shifted into a more netlike appearance. With a grin, Damien cast it out once again, this time with more energy behind it. The room lit up with the Ether once more.

"This is amazing," Damien breathed. "Is this how you see the world all the time?"

"You'll learn to filter it out eventually," Henry replied. "It's just clutter that blocks your sight. And you'll only see the Ether while you're drawing it into yourself. Having it in front of you constantly would be infuriating."

"What do you mean? It's beautiful!" Damien said. "It's pure, unfiltered magic, isn't it?"

"More like a few wavelengths of magic," Henry replied. "Particularly, the four schools of magic I have access to: Light, Dark, Space, and Void. There are more schools than you can count, but most beings end up in one of the more common ones. If you could see all forms of magic, you'd be blinded. It would just be a wall of light everywhere you looked."

"Wow. That sounds amazing," Damien said, running his hand through a line of Ether again.

"Stop daydreaming," Henry said. "What happened to rushing? Drop the net and make it again. We're repeating this until you can make it on your own. It's not hard, so you should be able to do it today."

And that was exactly what they did. It took Damien a little under an hour to be able to form the net on his own. As Henry had said, it wasn't hard, just different. Damien had a slight headache from all the mental energy usage by the end of it, but that couldn't keep the smug grin from his face.

"I'm doing magic!" Damien exclaimed, casting the net out once again and marveling at the Ether surrounding him.

"More like you're looking at it," Henry grumbled. "But this is enough to get started. Nothing fancy, mind you, but you can start to channel some basic energy without me babysitting you."

"Get on with it, then!" Damien said eagerly. For a moment, he almost forgot his instructor was an eldritch being. Henry just chuckled.

"Envelop your hand with mental energy. It doesn't have to be pretty, just cover your hand. It'll let you interact with the Ether," Henry said. "Grab some energy and pull it away. For now, only touch the lines going into you. The others are harder to work with."

Damien followed his instructions. After his work with the net, making a thin layer of energy around his hand wasn't a challenge at all. He touched the line of Ether. It vibrated in response.

He wrapped his hand around the line and gave it a small tug. A mote of light tore away and came free in his hand. However, the line didn't look any different.

"The Ether will dim if you take enough energy from it," Henry said, guessing Damien's next question. "It'll regenerate with time. The more you use the Ether, the more you'll be able to take at once."

"Okay," Damien said, memorizing every word his companion said. "What do I do now?"

"To use the Ether's energy to cast magic, you need to bring it onto the Mortal Plane," Henry explained. "The Ether is actually a separate plane overlaid on your world. The barrier between the planes is very weak, so all you have to do is draw it into yourself. At that point, you'll either be able to store or use it."

Damien closed his hand around the mote of Ether. Henry hadn't said to, but it just felt right. What felt like a miniature bolt of lightning shot down his arm and into his chest. It settled around where his heart was, inside a strange sphere of dim energy Damien hadn't created. However, the shock wasn't painful. If anything, it almost felt good.

"Good instincts," Henry said. He slapped Damien on the back of his head with a small burst of mental energy. "Now, stop using them. No experimenting unless you want to make a mistake and blow us both up."

"Right," Damien said, rubbing his head. "Sorry. Where is the Ether being stored? It looks like it's in an orb of some sort, but I didn't create it."

"Don't be sorry. Just do it right. And that is your core," Henry said. "It's overlayed with your heart. As you grow stronger, the Ether will travel through your veins and enter the rest of your body as well. Now, you've got a small amount of Ether. Extend your hand toward the wall at the foot of your bed. Let the net fall, then reach out to the Ether within you. Channel it toward your hand, but keep it restrained. Do not let it burst forth but keep it at a slow stream. I will assist."

Damien nodded, too excited to say anything. His heart beat so fast it could have outraced a rabbit. The lines of Ether faded as he let his concentration drop.

He extended his hand and placed his palm a few inches from the wall. The mote of Ether within his chest buzzed and hopped the moment he reached out toward it.

It leapt toward his hand faster than Damien had expected. A chill passed over him as Henry's energy enveloped the mote of light, slowing it down to a crawl.

"Control it!" Henry snapped.

Damien swallowed and nodded, using more energy to keep the Ether from slipping away. Henry slowly released it until the Ether was fully back under Damien's control. He inched it forward, fighting the energy's desire to escape, until it shimmered in the base of his palm.

"You are going to slowly channel it out of your hand. Focus on creating a sphere," Henry ordered. "This is not a true spell, so don't worry about anything else."

He did as Henry said once more, allowing the Ether to edge forward until it slipped out of his palm. A dot of dark energy formed in front of Damien's hand. It expanded and Damien narrowed his eyes, fighting back his excitement as he forced it to remain about the size of a small apple.

The ball hovered in the air before his palm, not moving. Damien swallowed and failed to keep the gleeful grin from his face.

"I'm using magic!"

"Barely," Henry grumbled, but he didn't sound very

displeased. "Now, be careful. Because we didn't try to control how the magic was formed, that's essentially just an orb of destructive energy. It's completely useless in a normal fight since there are so many spells that do its job better, but it works great for carving stone."

Damien got the hint. He slowly moved his hand toward the wall, his body trembling in excitement. The orb let out a low whine as it melted clean through the stone. Damien pulled his hand back, revealing a perfectly carved furrow in the wall. He let out a whoop, and even Henry couldn't keep himself from grinning within Damien's mind.

Of course, Damien's loss of concentration caused the ball of energy to splutter and fade away. His headache had grown a tad worse, but it was still completely manageable.

"That was amazing!" Damien said, pacing back and forth along the thin pathway between his and Sylph's bed. "Let's do it again!"

"I won't stop you," Henry replied. "The faster we get a training room, the better. Just don't accidentally burrow into one of the other kid's rooms."

Damien winced at the thought of popping through Mark's wall unannounced. The boy had been amicable enough, but that was a surefire way to get him on Nolan's side.

His heart beat so fast he had to sit on the bed for a moment, much to Henry's amusement.

"Are you seriously winded from that basic little trick?" Henry asked, laughing.

"Of course not," Damien replied, his mood too good to take the bait. "That was the first time I've cast a spell! I'm a little overexcited."

"You are so lame."

"And you're an eldritch creature that uses teenager slang

unironically," Damien replied. "Between the two of us, I think you're worse off."

Henry grumbled at that, but he didn't grace Damien with a response.

What followed was entirely uninteresting. Damien spent hours focused on the Ether, carving the wall away bit by bit. The churning destruction energy made quick work of the stone, and it didn't take him too long to carve a rough hallway that led deeper into the mountain.

Damien continued onwards until he was certain he'd passed their tiny bathroom, lighting the way with small circles of runes he drew on the wall with chalk. Time slipped away from him as he worked.

He was utterly engrossed in the menial task of carving away the stone. He carved relentlessly, all thoughts of the outside world long gone. Damien loved every moment of it.

If it hadn't been for the magical carving tool, it would have taken Damien years to cut through the stone. However, with his new powers, he created a small room before the day had ended. Henry remained silent throughout the entire day, only speaking up when Damien's concentration faltered or if he made a mistake while using the Ether.

His hand finally dropped, his muscles strained and weary. His chest and core tingled, as if a miniature bolt of lightning was trapped within his body. Damien blinked, looking around the room as if he were coming out from a trance. It wasn't large by any means. It was only slightly bigger than their bathroom, which wasn't saying much. That being said, it was a room. The floor and walls were rough and uneven, but Damien didn't care.

"Good job," Henry said.

Damien waited a few moments, but his companion didn't add anything else.

"That's it?" Damien asked. "No snarky remark?"

"You'll earn one soon enough," Henry said. "Just take the compliment. You've also progressed your cultivation by a miniscule amount. That electric feeling in your chest is your body trying to adapt to the Ether. You haven't done anything particularly amazing, but it's still good work for your first time casting magic."

"Thank you," Damien said, not replying immediately. After a few more moments, he added, "I couldn't have done it on my own."

"Of course you couldn't," Henry said with a smug laugh. "You'd still be waiting for your teacher if you didn't have me."

"And there it is," Damien said, rolling his eyes. He yawned, and his stomach rumbled loudly.

"How long have I been working?" Damien asked.

"I don't know. Go look outside," Henry said. "I didn't leave while you were using magic. The last thing I want is you blowing yourself up by accident."

"I think I can support that," Damien agreed. He glanced at his feet. Several inches of stone dust had accumulated on the ground, but none of it had gotten on him.

"I kept the debris off you," Henry said. "And I still am. If you inhaled this, you'd be in for a bad time."

"Could we get it out of the room somehow?" Damien asked.

"Sure. There are a dozen ways I can do it, even with the meager power you have access to right now. Give me control for a moment," Henry said.

"Safely," Damien added.

"Right, then. A few less ways," Henry said, sighing. "But still possible."

"Five minutes," Damien warned. Henry just grunted as Damien allowed him to commandeer his body.

A tendril of darkness unfurled from the ceiling. It reached down, and Henry had Damien's body grab it. The tendril lifted him into the air. At the same time, a pool of darkness spread across the ground.

The stone dirt vanished into it soundlessly. The darkness vanished, and the tendril set Damien back down, disappearing into the shadows of the room.

"There. Nice and boring," Henry said, giving Damien back control of his body.

"Thank you," Damien said. His stomach rumbled again. This time, it was accompanied by a dull stomachache.

Damien walked back down the hallway he'd made. Sylph still wasn't in the room, but the sun was already setting outside. He grabbed several coins from his travel pack and stuffed them into his pockets. Then he strode over to the ledge and looked down over the campus. It was cast in dull orange and pink hues.

"I wonder what she's doing," Damien said. "Wasn't she just getting food?"

"Why do you care?" Henry replied. "Just go eat. If your stomach grumbles any louder, it might deafen me."

Damien huffed and headed down the mountain for the mess hall.

"Are you planning on buying food? You don't have all that much money," Henry said.

I don't want to eat warm vomit.

"Food is food," Henry said. "You could spend that money on getting stronger instead."

Damien nearly missed a step. He ignored the amused glances the other students sent his way and walked faster.

How? I didn't think money would help me with magic, and I certainly don't have enough to buy anything fancy.

"There should be some basic herbs that allow you to

improve the rate at which you grow," Henry said. "You can't use them yet, since your connection to the Ether is far too weak. Still, the herbs are quite common, so I doubt they'd be very expensive."

You're assuming they haven't died off in the past four thousand years.

"I— Well, yeah," Henry said, sighing. "All the more reason for us to go to the library."

I'm not spending that much time in the library. Figure out what you want to read, and I'll get it.

"You have no passion for learning," Henry griped. "You're a human! Shouldn't you have creativity and curiosity?"

I do. For magic.

"Boring," Henry decided, receding into the back of Damien's mind and leaving him alone for the rest of his walk.

FOURTEEN

Damien arrived at the mess hall a short while later. He quickly brushed his hair, which had gotten sweaty and unruly while he'd been working, back with his hands before entering the building.

There were only three students in front of him in line this time. The mess hall looked quite empty. The majority of the tables were unoccupied aside from a few stray people eating their food silently.

Are you sure my magic will get stronger with those herbs?

"Yes. It will make you grow more powerful at a significant rate. Again, you're going to need to cultivate more before you can use the herbs." Henry said. "But even if some of them have died off, I'm sure a few are still around."

Damien swallowed and gave a miniscule nod. The line moved forward until he stood before the large woman who took the orders. She raised an eyebrow and gestured for him to speak.

"The free meal, please," Damien said, fighting to keep the grimace off his face. "And yes, I'm sure."

"If you insist," the woman said, shrugging.

Damien swallowed and headed over to one of the tables, choosing a seat far away from everyone. He sat and pressed the small rune circle with his thumb. He drummed his fingers on the table as he waited.

"How brave," Henry said dryly. "Eating the free meal."

You aren't the one who has to taste it. Those herbs better be worth the money, Henry.

Henry's only response was a self-righteous scoff. A few minutes later, the blue glow of the runes changed to a dull green.

Damien tapped it. A plate full of what appeared to be murky green chunks appeared on before him. He sniffed it and gagged. It smelled like old armpits and rotten milk.

"Is this even food?" Damien asked, prodding it with a fork. The 'food' wiggled slightly in response.

"The faster you eat it, the quicker it'll be done," Henry said, not sounding very sure of his own words.

Damien grimaced. He pinched his nose shut and used his fork to separate off a small part of the slimy substance on his plate. He stuffed it into his mouth, chewing once before swallowing as quickly as he could.

The nicest thing he could say was that the food didn't taste quite as bad as it smelled. That being said, it was a close call. It was as if they'd intentionally made it taste horrible. Damien shuddered and pursed his lips together to keep himself from throwing up.

"That was...rancid," Henry said, disgust dripping from his words. "Just your memories of it make me shudder."

If those herbs don't help me, I am going to be very angry.

Damien drew a steadying breath and picked up another forkful, a larger one, this time. He shoved it into his mouth and swallowed without even chewing. The food slipped down without a problem, leaving an aftertaste he wouldn't have wished on his worst enemy.

Damien set his features and picked up the plate. He tipped it back, scraping the rancid meal into his mouth as fast as his hands would let him and holding his mouth closed to keep from throwing up.

He waited for a few moments after finishing, just to make sure the food wasn't going to try to come back up. Then he shuddered and wiped his tongue off with a napkin.

"That was the most revolting thing I've ever eaten," Damien muttered to himself. "Why does that exist?"

His stomach rumbled, this time in annoyance rather than hunger. Damien couldn't blame it for the complaints. The food wasn't palatable for rats, much less humans.

Damien rose to his feet. When it became clear the slop he'd eaten had no plans of escaping his stomach, he left the mess hall without looking back. The gazes of several students followed him out the door.

"I suspect your fellow mortals don't tend to get that dish," Henry observed.

I can't imagine why. I wonder if Sylph actually ate that garbage.

Damien gagged again. A passing student gave him a strange look. Damien just shrugged in response.

Do you think I can practice more magic now?

"No. You need to rest," Henry said. "You've already begun cultivating the Ether. All that work you did on the room today was repetitive, so your body needs time to absorb the residual Ether left behind. It should be mostly absorbed by tomorrow morning. By then, you'll be marginally stronger and can work faster than you did today."

Fine.

Damien sighed. As much as he wanted to head back and

resume using magic, Henry had yet to mislead him about his studies. He headed back to the mountain, already mentally preparing himself for bed.

"Stop," Henry ordered abruptly. Damien froze in place, his foot hovering over the floor as if there was a trap directly in front of him.

What?

"Your instructor is in the alleyway to our right," Henry said. "He's allowing magical energy to seep out. I believe this might be a test to see if you were lying about having magic or not."

So, I just gave it away by stopping, didn't I?

"Yep," Henry said. "It's better this way. If he thinks we're special, he might teach us that strange magic he used on your roommate."

Did you really just throw me under the carriage to learn a new spell?

"Oh, absolutely," Henry said cheerfully. "Don't tell me you wouldn't have done the same, boy."

Damien couldn't respond to that. He just let out a sigh and turned toward the alleyway. It was a thin path between two small buildings with potted golden flowers on either side of it.

Delph stepped out from within the shadows, his robes billowing out behind him. The toothpick in his mouth twitched as the man came to a stop before Damien.

"And whose gaze were you following this time?" Delph asked, raising a gray eyebrow. "Not Sylph, I presume."

"No, Professor. She isn't here," Damien said, desperately trying to figure out how he could explain himself.

"Yes, she is," Henry said, several seconds too late.

"Yes, she is," Delph said. He stepped to the side, revealing

Sylph. She held a half-finished skewer of dumplings in one hand.

"Oh," Damien said.

"Oh, indeed," Delph said, stroking his beard. "You noticed my presence, yet you claim not to know any magic?"

"I didn't the first time," Damien said, scratching the back of his head and shifting awkwardly from foot to foot.

"Are you implying you learned enough magic to sense my location since yesterday?" Delph asked.

"Yes, Professor."

"He was looking at cultivation methods earlier today," Sylph offered.

"I see," Delph said. "A quick study, are you? You wouldn't be the first, but you might be the cheekiest. Why wait until after you meet your professor to learn magic?"

"I didn't have access to the books before," Damien said quickly.

Delph grunted.

"I'm not so convinced you didn't already know magic and just wanted to avoid fighting me," he said. "However, there's nothing wrong with hiding your abilities. I won't punish you for it. However, if you want to learn anything, you're going to have to work as hard as you can. You won't become a powerful mage by hiding on the sidelines."

"I'll keep that in mind, Professor," Damien said, inclining his head respectfully.

"See that you do," Delph said, chewing on his toothpick. A small smirk tugged at the right corner of his mouth. "You and Sylph will report to me at the arena tomorrow, one hour before sunrise. We will be conducting a training session."

"Wait, me too?" Damien asked. "I thought I didn't pass your test for the special training."

"You didn't," Delph said. "But you've either tricked me or

managed to learn a significant amount of magic in just a few hours. Either you've got potential, or I'm going to get a lot of enjoyment out of watching you suffer. One hour before sunrise, kid."

Delph's cloak wrapped around him like a cocoon. It twisted into a ball and shrunk until it vanished, leaving no trace of the professor behind.

Damien and Sylph exchanged an awkward glance. Then the girl raised the stick of dumplings to her mouth and took a bite out of one.

"I didn't know you already knew magic," Sylph said.

"It's a new development," Damien replied, running his hands through his hair with a sigh. "How did Professor Delph find you?"

"He was waiting for me at the mess hall," Sylph said. "He bought me lunch as an apology for knocking me out, and he promised to give me personal training. Training he's now invited you to join."

"Uh, sorry," Damien said. "I wasn't trying to get caught up in it."

"I know. I'm sure he's got some reasoning for it," Sylph replied, starting down the path back toward their room. Damien followed.

"Did he say what he'd be teaching you?" Damien asked.

"No, but I expect its combat training for the field," Sylph said. She tilted her head to the side. "Speaking of which, how did you spot Delph? Were you hiding your magic when we first met?"

"No," Damien said. "I really did just learn it."

"Or your companion is powerful enough to do it for you," Sylph observed.

Henry surged to the forefront of Damien's mind. The boy's shadow rippled as Henry examined Sylph, energy subtly forming into a spell. Then it faded, and the companion slipped back.

"She shouldn't know any specifics," Henry said. "I can't read her mind, but her companion is not powerful enough to identify me."

Sylph's gaze flicked to Damien's shadow before returning to his face.

"Interesting," Sylph said.

I think she just played you. Also, what was that magic? Don't even think about attacking someone. That absolutely goes against our contract.

Henry's response was an angry growl. Damien didn't have time to continue the conversation with his companion, so he just gave Sylph a noncommittal shrug.

"He helped," Damien admitted. "But there weren't any rules against that."

"Fair enough," Sylph said.

They completed the rest of their walk in silence, arriving at the mountain and heading up the path without any more idle chitchat. When they arrived at the plateau, Damien couldn't help himself from glancing into the other students' rooms as they passed.

He wasn't very surprised to see that Nolan and Reena had set up a curtain at the front door to block prying eyes. However, Mark hadn't made any attempts to hide his own dwelling space.

It was difficult to see much of the room as it was already getting dark outside. However, Damien was still able to make out several carpets that looked to be made out of animal hides on the floor. Mark didn't appear to be in the cave.

As for their own room, all the runes Damien had drawn inside the cave as he was carving out the training area were still powered, and their effects were much more visible at night. Faint light emanated out from the entrance of their cave.

"Why is our room so bright?" Sylph asked.

"I might have been doing some renovations," Damien said. "I can't turn the runes off, but we can just rub them away before we go to sleep."

"Renovations?" Sylph asked, frowning. They arrived at the room's entrance and stepped inside. Sylph drew in a sharp breath. "Is that a hole in the wall?"

"Well, yeah. I was making a training room," Damien said. "They did say we could modify the room."

"How did you carve so much stone away in so little time?" Sylph asked, squinting at him before walking over to the tunnel he'd created.

"Magic," Damien replied lamely.

"You had enough energy to do this much?" Sylph asked with what was either awe or anger. "After just learning it this morning? How is that even possible?"

"I'm not sure how you want me to respond to that," Damien said, shrugging. "I didn't do something wrong, did I?"

"No, you didn't. I'm just very curious as to what your companion is," Sylph said. She shook her head and peered inside the hallway. Then she cursed. She turned back to Damien and crossed her arms. "Do you care to explain what's going on?"

"I don't know what you mean," Damien said, starting to get annoyed with the constant questioning. "I told you, I'm just making a training room."

"Then why is there a party going on inside it?"

"What now?"

Damien squeezed past Sylph and peered inside his room. Mark, Reena, and Nolan were sitting in the center of the room, surrounded by a faint blue bubble. The group didn't appear to have noticed them.

Damien yanked his head back around the corner.

"I have no idea! What in the seven planes are they doing in our room?" Damien exclaimed. His baffled expression was more than enough to show Sylph he was telling the truth.

"Eight planes," Henry idly corrected. Damien ignored him.

"If you didn't invite them in, we should go and find out. I don't appreciate people coming into our room like they own it," Sylph said, her voice cold. She took another bite from the stick of dumplings, which still wasn't quite finished, and headed down the hallway.

Damien was more than happy to let her take the lead, if only because Henry seemed a little overeager to cast magic without Damien's permission.

Mark was the first to notice them heading down the hallway. He glanced up from something in his hands and flushed a light red. The blue dome covering them faded and vanished.

"Hey! Put that back up. What if someone hears us?" Nolan said in a hushed tone.

Mark just pointed over Nolan's shoulder. Nolan turned and promptly did his best rendition of a ripe tomato.

"What are you doing in our room?" Sylph asked, crossing her arms.

"Well, ah, we were trying to find the two of you. Then we saw the glow, and there was the tunnel," Reena started. She fumbled for words for a few moments, then sighed. "Light. It was really dark in our rooms, and yours had a lot of light."

"Why were you looking for us?" Damien asked, his brow furrowed.

"We were getting dinner," Mark said. "And we wanted to see if you wanted to join."

"Did Beth suggest you do that?" Sylph asked, her eyebrow quirking up. The embarrassment that crossed the other three students faces confirmed her guess.

"She might have suggested it," Mark said. "It was a good idea, though."

"That's fine, but I'm still not understanding what was so urgent you needed to hide inside our room to use our lights for," Sylph said, frowning.

Mark held up a knife and a gritty stone.

"I was polishing my knife, but I couldn't see what I was doing," he said. "I didn't touch any of your stuff. I'm not used to living near other people, but you probably should have a door if you don't want anyone coming in here. Reena and Nolan said it wouldn't be a big deal."

"Don't blame us for it! You were in here first," Nolan snapped. Then he cleared his throat awkwardly. "I'm, ah, well...we didn't intend to be here long. None of our rooms have lighting, and we couldn't read our cultivation manuals to practice. Delph didn't look very forgiving, so we all wanted to get a head start on our work. Your room was larger, and it had lights, so we didn't think it would be an issue."

"Not breaking into someone's room for a long period of time doesn't mean you didn't break in," Damien pointed out.

"Why did you two get a bigger room than everyone else?" Reena asked. Mark and Nolan shot her a glance that reminded the girl that they weren't in the best positioning to be questioning Sylph and Damien.

"None of your business," Sylph replied promptly.

Nolan rose to his feet, closing a fancy red leather book and tucking it under his arms. He brushed some of the dirt from his pants with a pained expression and sighed, adjusting his shirt.

"This has gone very poorly. I apologize for all of our

behavior. We should not have intruded on your home. In truth, I originally came here to apologize. Beth's suggestion for dinner was a good way for me to speak with you, but that has clearly failed miserably due to our actions."

"Apologize?" Damien asked, taken aback.

"Yes. Reena and I did not believe you when you claimed your companion was from the Plane of Darkness. After you proved us wrong, our pride was too large to renege on our words. However, as the heir to the Gray family, it is my duty to remain on good terms with powerful mages."

Damien glanced at Sylph, but she just shrugged.

"You're apologizing because my companion is strong when you thought it wasn't?" Damien clarified.

"Correct."

"And if my companion had been weak, you wouldn't have apologized?"

"Also correct," Nolan said unapologetically. "My duty is to ensure the survival of my house. A strong companion means you will have potential. You would not have been worth the time had your companion not been what you claimed it to be."

"Well, at least you're honest," Damien sighed, rubbing his forehead. "That might be the strangest apology I've ever gotten, but I don't see any reason to be enemies. We're going to be stuck together for at least a year. You're still a dick, though. Consider not voicing your opinion of others before you know how strong they are in the future."

"Wise advice," Nolan said, inclining his head.

"Advice that father gave you," Reena whispered snarkily to him.

"I didn't see you correcting me," Nolan replied.

"You can argue about this later," Sylph said, interrupting

them. "I'd like to know if there's a reason you're all still in our room. If there isn't, well, you know where the door is."

"You don't have a door. And the runes that give light were drawn with chalk," Mark said, standing. "That means one of you two drew them. Can you draw them in my room as well? I'd be willing to trade for it."

"As would we," Reena added. "We've got a spare curtain you could use for the front of your cave."

"And I have an extra rug," Mark said. "It is made from a dire bear. Very soft."

"I suppose I could do it," Damien said. "They can't turn off, though. They only go away when the chalk is rubbed out."

"That's fine," Mark said. "If you put it on the floor, I can cover it with something."

"I can do it tomorrow, then," Damien offered. "So long as you three don't invade our room without permission again."

"We won't, unless I decide to," Mark promised, somewhat unconvincingly. Nolan and Reena nodded their agreement. They awkwardly shuffled past Sylph and headed back to their rooms. Damien and Sylph returned to the main room and sat on their beds.

CHAPTER
FIFTEEN

"That was not how I expected to end today," Damien said, massaging his head. "I think I might have a headache coming on."

"It wasn't how I saw the day going for myself either," Sylph said. "In more ways than one. I didn't think I'd return to our room and find a giant hole in the wall. I still can't believe you learned enough magic to do that in a single day. Did your companion do that, too?"

"I did it myself!" Damien protested, not needing Henry to warn him about his word choice. "Can companions actually have that much of an effect on the mortal world? I thought they couldn't do much more than pass their magic on to their summoner."

"It depends on the contract," Sylph said, eyeing Damien suspiciously before shrugging. "But you're right. I'm just shocked. It's hard to imagine having that much magical energy. You must be very gifted."

"Thanks," Damien muttered as Sylph got to her feet again.

"I'm going to take a shower," she announced abruptly.

"Since we don't have any way to block the bathroom, I'm going to have to request you keep your eyes firmly pointed at the cave entrance."

Damien quickly turned away from the shower, blushing a bright red. "I won't turn around," he promised.

Water pattered against the stone behind him as Sylph turned the shower on. Damien felt Henry stir within his mind.

"I never understood why mortals are so concerned about others seeing their bodies," Henry said. "You're hairless monkeys. There's nothing precious hidden under those clothes."

I'm not going to explain that to you. And I'm not checking a book out on it either, so you'll just have to suffer.

"I don't want an explanation," Henry replied. "Humans are great at overstating their own worth. What I do want to know is how early you plan on waking up. You wanted to draw runes tomorrow morning, but you're also meeting your professor an hour before sunrise."

His training can't take that long, right? I'll be back in a few hours, and late morning is still the morning.

"You're an idiot," Henry replied promptly. "But I doubt those fools will have much use for more light during the day, so they'll survive. I'm going to head out and try to see if I can get a better grasp of where the other Void creatures are, particularly the one closest to us."

Fine. When will you be back?

"In time to wake you up for your training. We can't miss out on the chance to learn that man's magic," Henry said. "Enjoy yourself."

Damien's shadow stretched and rose from the ground beside him. It tore away and launched out the cave entrance, disappearing into the night sky. Just like the last time Henry had left, Damien felt a profound sense of emptiness.

He knew that part of that was due to Henry leaving—his companion *did* have half of his soul. Even so, Damien was aware Henry's absence didn't account for all of his feelings.

He extended his senses, forming a net of mental energy with his mind and casting it out. It wasn't quite second nature yet, but the hours of practice had gotten him enough experience to reliably form the energy into roughly the right shape without too much difficulty. It wasn't quite as nice as when Henry helped him, but it still got the job done.

The world lit up as the lines of Ether came into view. There were more lines in the cave than there had been before. The new lines headed past him and toward the shower, and he resisted the urge to check where they came from.

Damien coated his hand in mental energy and plucked a spark from a strand of Ether and wrapped his hand around it. It zipped into his chest, sending tingles down his arm and spine.

It didn't help. Damien chewed his lower lip. He could feel the Ether within him, waiting to be used. One part of him, the part that hadn't changed since he was a child, longed desperately to use it. He already knew a spell, and he could cast it on his own.

Several years ago, he would have been jumping around the room, cheering and laughing without a care in the world. Instead, he sat there on the bed with an empty expression. He'd taken the first step toward his greatest goal, but it had been tarnished.

Five other people roamed the world, each carrying around the end of times within them. One mistake, one tiny little slip up, and the Mortal Plane would cease to exist. It didn't even have to be one of the other carriers. Damien was more than aware his contract had to have at least one flaw in it.

It wasn't supposed to be like this.

Damien raised his hand, channeling the spark of Ether through his arm and out his wrist. The orb of dark energy bubbled to life in his palm. He sighed, raising it into the light so he could get a better look at it.

How am I supposed to deal with this? I just wanted to learn magic. I don't want to fight. I don't want to have to be the hunter or the prey!

There was no answer. Damien's brow drooped, and the orb blinked out as he cut the flow of energy going to it. He wasn't foolish enough to believe he had a choice. If Henry hadn't lied to him, then his own feelings weren't something he could worry about. This was bigger than him, and something had to be done, if only to investigate the other Void creatures to make sure they were bound by good people.

That being said, Damien wasn't about to turn himself in. He had no noble delusions or desires to die to save humanity. If he didn't slip up, one of the other summoners easily could. A thought rose to the front of his mind, unbidden.

Damien pressed his lips together, his decision already made. He reached into his travel bag and pulled out a quill, a vial of ink, and several sheets of paper. He tapped it on his chin, thinking, before he sketched.

By the time the water shut off, Damien had drawn four different rune circles on separate pieces of paper. He waved them through the air to dry them off, then slipped them under his bed.

"You can turn around now," Sylph said before brushing her teeth.

Damien didn't turn immediately. He sent another glance

out the entrance to their room, then wiped the frown from his face and slipped off his bed.

He removed his jacket and scarf, just leaving on his pants and shirt, and waited until Sylph had left the bathroom before he took her place to wash himself and brush his teeth. Once he'd finished, he headed back to his bed and slipped under the covers. Sylph was already in her bed, her clothes hung over its foot.

Damien removed his shirt and tossed it onto the ground at the head of his bed. The glow from the rune in the bathroom had already dimmed enough that it wasn't much of a bother and didn't interfere much with their sleep.

"Goodnight," Sylph said.

"Goodnight," Damien replied, although he had the feeling it would be anything but.

———

The night passed, and Damien dreamt of death. He stood in the center of a broken battlefield, surrounded by mountains of corpses that stretched high enough into the sky to scrape the clouds. His eyes were cold and his jaw was covered with stubble. A jagged scar ran across his right hand, and strange runes covered every inch of his exposed skin, fading in and out of existence.

Sickly dark magic coiled around his body like snakes awaiting his command, lashing out and obliterating anyone who dared stand in his way. Above him, the dark sky twinkled with tiny pinpricks of light that formed an enormous smiling face.

The world crackled and popped. The face crumpled, and the bodies folded inwards, twisting together in a mesmerizing spiral of color. The crackling grew louder, and Damien was ripped out of his dream.

He suppressed a groan and rolled over, reaching under his bed and pressing his finger against the slip of paper and tearing a small hole into it. The sounds stopped.

Damien grimaced and grabbed his coat and clothing, pulling it on before silently slipping out of bed. His throat was sore from the cold mountain air, and swallowing did little to help it.

He reached under his bed, grabbing the four slips of paper he'd drawn runes on. One of them smoked slightly and had turned into a crumpled ball. Damien set that one aside and folded the others, sliding them into his back pocket.

"It's not going to take you that long to get to the arena, you know," Henry said.

Damien felt a slight sense of relief his companion had returned. His strange dreams were still at the back of his mind, but normal dreams were better than Henry showing up to say one of the other eldritch creatures had broken their confinement.

You can read my mind. You know why I'm heading there early.

"I can only read what you're actively thinking about," Henry replied. "And right now, you aren't thinking much of anything at all."

I'm tired. And angry.

Damien slung his travel pack over his shoulder and silently slipped out of the room. He crept past Mark and the Grays' rooms before starting down the mountain path.

"Angry?"

I've wanted to study magic my entire life. Now, the moment I actually get to do that, I've got to worry about stopping all the other Eldritch creatures from ending the world, assuming you were telling me the truth.

"I didn't lie," Henry snapped. His tone softened imperceptibly. "And that's how things work, boy. The weak don't get to control their life. Only the strong do, and you're far from strong right now."

"That's why we're going to the field early," Damien said. "Delph seems like the type of professor to get there early, just so he can watch us show up and scold us for being late."

Henry didn't respond to that. The campus was eerily silent in the morning, but Damien didn't mind. He wasn't in the mood to talk. As he walked, he cast out a net of mental energy, lighting up the Ether around him.

How much Ether can I hold at once?

"It depends on how strong you are. The more you cultivate, the more you can store," Henry replied. "The only way to find out is to try. Trying to take too much won't hurt you."

Damien nodded. He plucked motes of Ether from the strands as he walked, storing them within himself. With every bit he added, the tingling sensations traveling throughout him grew stronger.

By the time Damien had absorbed eight motes of Ether, he was practically bouncing on his feet. It took conscious effort to keep his teeth from chattering.

"Might be a good place to stop," Henry suggested as Damien stepped through the portal to the arena. He pursed his lips, bracing himself against one of the numerous chairs in the colosseum to weather the effects of the teleportation, before responding.

I feel like if I fall, I'll bounce.

"You won't," Henry said. "Don't try it. That's just the energy trying to escape. I'd say you've hit your limit. For now, at least."

Noted.

Damien made his way through the stands, scanning them

for any sign of Professor Delph. He was nowhere to be found. Damien pressed his lips together as he reached the edge of the stands and the arena below them.

He hopped over the railing, half-expecting to plummet to his death, but the magic took hold instantly. He floated to the ground, landing in the packed sand without a sound.

"You're early," a rough voice said from behind him.

Damien nearly leapt out of his shoes. Delph leaned against the arch leading out of the arena, the ever-present long toothpick in his mouth.

The professor strode up to Damien, moving the toothpick from one side of his mouth to the other as he examined him.

"Why did you come early?" Delph asked. "And where is Sylph?"

"She's still asleep," Damien replied. "There should still be around two hours before sunrise. I'm certain she'll be here on time."

"That doesn't answer why you came early," Delph said.

"I want to learn how to use magic," Damien finally said. "Combat magic."

"That's why I scheduled a lesson for an hour before sunrise," Delph said.

"I need more than that. I've never fought before, and I need to get good at it."

"Why?"

"Do I need a reason?" Damien asked, frowning.

"Yes," Delph replied. He crossed his arms and cocked an eyebrow up. "Lots of people want to learn combat magic. It's flashy and interesting, and it makes a lot of money on quests. There's nothing wrong with that, but you still have a reason. Knowing your reason helps me teach you better."

Damien's hands clenched at his sides. Delph had magic

even Henry hadn't seen. Surely, he'd have a good chance of taking care of the other eldritch creatures.

"Don't even think about it," Henry warned. "Even if he believes you, there's no way he'd let us live."

"I want to protect people," Damien finally said. His lip curled up slightly in a half-smile. "Myself included."

"A common goal," Delph drawled. "A fine one at that. Keeping yourself alive tends to be a good thing. However..."

Delph slipped forward like a mirage, appearing inches from Damien even though it didn't seem like the man had moved. He leaned close, his cold gray eyes flat and lifeless.

"You don't strike me as a fighter," Delph said, his voice barely above a whisper. "No, what I see before me is a scholar. You wear mage armor, but it has never been used. Your hands are fair, and your gaze is unfocused. You've never trained a day in your life."

He paused, observing Damien's expression before he continued.

"You didn't come to a mage college to become an adventurer. You don't want to fight on the front lines of the wilderness. I think you just love magic. You see it as an artform, something to be learned and loved. Am I wrong?"

"No. Is there something wrong with that?" Damien asked, his nose inches from Delph's. He refused to step back from the imposing man.

"No," Delph replied, taking Damien by surprise. "We need scholars. Researchers who find new ways to use magic. But most scholars are not fighters. You see something to be studied and loved. I see a tool to be bent to my needs. Magic is a means to an end not the ultimate goal."

"I don't see how that would affect me learning to be a fighter," Damien said. "And you said you'd teach me if you knew my motives just a few moments ago!"

"Everyone needs to learn the basics," Delph replied, finally taking a step back from Damien. However, he didn't blink or break eye contact once. "Some need more help with them than others. But...to go beyond that? Why should I waste my time on a scholar? You won't need my teachings."

"Yes I do," Damien said, narrowing his eyes. "And if you never intended to teach me, why did you invite me here?"

Delph's cloak rippled around him. The shadows cast by the pale moonlight seemed to flinch and recede around them.

"Because you are an enigma," Delph said. "One moment, I feel nothing at all from you. And then you are enveloped in a shroud of darkness even I can't see through."

Henry stiffened within Damien's mind.

"So, you invited me so you could satisfy your curiosity?" Damien asked, forcing himself to keep the fear off his face.

"Perhaps," Delph said. "To be honest, I'm not entirely sure yet. I certainly didn't expect you to show up asking for advanced combat training, especially after you claimed not to have any magic to avoid fighting me."

"I didn't lie," Damien said, his brow lowering.

"But you have magic now?" Delph pressed.

"Yes."

"Then, if you want me to even consider training you beyond the bare minimum requirements set by the school, I lay the same offer before you that everyone else faced," Delph said, taking a step back and raising his hands into the air. "Show me what you can do."

The air around Delph twisted and warped. Damien hopped backward, casting his mental net out. Lines of Ether encircled Delph like a cocoon, twisting and churning malevolently.

"Careful," Henry warned. "I can't help you. If he noticed my presence already, there's no way I can assist in an actual fight unless your life is at risk. We can't give this human more room to examine me."

Damien nodded. He channeled energy through his palm, forming the ball of destructive energy. Delph observed him with a bored expression.

"Is that all you've got?" Delph asked. "That isn't even a spell."

"I told you that I only learned magic yesterday!" Damien snapped, lunging toward the professor and thrusting the orb toward the man.

It felt like his hand had slammed into a brick wall. The ball of magic blinked out of existence a foot away from Delph, and a tremor rippled down Damien's arm. He bit back a cry of pain and staggered to get out of the professor's reach.

Delph didn't even move. He just watched Damien, his head tilted to the side. Damien drew on another one of the sparks of Ether within him, forming another ball in his hand.

"Really?" Delph asked as Damien dashed for him again. The professor knocked Damien's hand to the side and kicked him in the chest.

Damien tumbled, the magic vanishing as he slammed into the sand. Delph looked down at him, his lip curled in anger.

"You don't even use your mage armor. Where did you get this?" Delph demanded.

Damien kicked out weakly at Delph's leg. The professor didn't bother dodging it, and the strike thudded harmlessly against him. He shook his head and grabbed Damien by the collar. He lifted him into the air.

"You have no natural instincts as a fighter. You're clumsy and weak," Delph said. "If you truly did just learn magic yesterday, then you're a gifted scholar. Don't take my words as insults. You have potential to be a great mage, but you're no warrior. Stick to the sidelines."

Damien struggled fruitlessly in the man's grasp. He grasped Delph's arm with one hand, gasping and glaring at the man as he choked.

"Have something to say?" Delph asked, quirking an eyebrow.

Damien managed to nod. His hand caught the slip of paper sticking out of a pocket and he ripped it free, slapping it against the professor's face.

He squeezed his eyes shut as a brilliant white flash lit up the early morning sky. Delph swore and staggered backward, releasing Damien and ripping the paper away from his face.

Damien rolled to his feet, grabbing the second sheet of paper and thrusting it against Delph's armor. The professor, still blinded from the flash, stomped his foot into the ground.

A shockwave of energy rippled through the arena, sending a small wave of sand up. The attack had clearly been controlled enough to keep from seriously injuring him, but it still tossed Damien back like a tumbleweed.

Damien rolled back to his feet with a groan. By the time he was standing again, Delph had blinked his temporary blindness away with a scowl.

"He's pissed," Henry observed. "Pretty fast recovery time for a human. He's definitely looking at you."

Thanks. I couldn't tell that myself.

Delph glanced down at the slip of paper stuck to his armor. His lips thinned, and he tugged at it, but all he succeeded in doing was tearing a small corner of the paper away.

"Runes?" Delph asked, sounding surprisingly calm. "Interesting. You're either very dedicated to your lie about learning a cultivation method in a single day, or you're telling the truth. Regardless, slips of paper aren't going to be effective in a real fight."

Damien didn't respond. He held the last piece of paper he'd prepared in his fist, watching Delph carefully as the man approached him. His brain screamed at him to run, but there was no way he'd be able to outpace a man who could teleport.

As Delph walked, his armor grew several shades lighter. He stopped before Damien. Then he frowned. He touched his armor, then jerked his hand back with a hiss.

The professor raised his hand over the paper stuck to his armor. The air contorted and crumpled in on itself. When he lowered his hand, the paper was gone.

"Clever," Delph said. "Flame runes?"

"Heating," Damien corrected, rolling over and scrambling to his feet. His chest was sore, but the interested look on Delph's face gave him hope. "Plus some binding ones, activated on impact."

"And the last rune you've got clutched in your hand behind your back?" Delph asked.

"Another heating rune," Damien said. "In case the first one needed help."

"Then you've lost. You will not beat me with a heating rune circle, no matter how clever the idea is. It is not meant for combat. Just like you."

Damien thrust the slip of paper into the sand. He yanked his hand back and threw himself to the side as the earth lit up a cherry red. A pillar of fire erupted from the ground, and Delph blurred out vision moments before a wave of intense heat scorched across the arena sand.

"That was not a normal heating rune," Delph said, his tone still calm.

"I might have tweaked it a bit," Damien admitted. "But imagine if that was the one I stuck on your armor."

"It could have been proven to be momentarily problematic," Delph said, a scowl crossing his features. "But this is nothing more than mere trickery. Do you think that and rune circles will let you win fights?"

"Yes."

"Well, you're probably right," Delph said, pursing his lips. "Well done. You aren't strong enough for me to use the force I used against your roommate, so I don't even get the satisfaction of knocking you unconscious."

"Thanks, I think," Damien said suspiciously. "Does this mean you'll train me?"

"For now. If you fail to show the required talent, then all deals are off, and you will receive nothing that the rest of your class does not get."

Damien didn't feel like cheering. He barely even felt relieved, but there was still a spark of pride that lit up within him. Delph noticed his expression and clicked his tongue.

"Don't get a big head, boy. Your test was much, much easier than the ones your fellow classmates went through. I had to hold back on account of your claims of not knowing magic. You will be expected to progress at a very rapid pace if you want to continue with me."

SIXTEEN

Delph walked in a slow circle around Damien, inspecting him with his flat gray eyes.

"We will begin now. I expect you at the arena every other day, two hours before the sun rises. Is that understood?"

Damien started to nod, but he didn't get the chance to finish.

"Good. Now, stand straight," Delph snapped. The man grabbed Damien by the shoulders and practically lifted him into the air as he adjusted his posture. He set him down and clicked his tongue in disappointment. "Your stance is terrible."

He grabbed Damien's hair and tugged on it slightly. It wasn't enough to hurt, but it was enough to get Damien to grimace and stretch to get the pressure off.

"You are a toy puppet," Delph instructed. "Imagine your body is held aloft by a single string that comes from your head. Do this at all times."

The professor had gone from refusing to teach Damien to ordering him around like they'd known each other for years within seconds. Damien scrambled to keep up with Delph as the man walked circles around him, barking out instructions.

"Square your shoulders. You look like you're a hunchback," Delph said. "Weight on the balls of your feet. It will help you react faster."

Damien wanted to ask what the point of a fighting stance was when he'd be using spells. Luckily for him, he was smarter than that. And, even more luckily, Delph answered the question not a second after Damien had first thought it.

"Magic is our greatest tool, but it is highly related to our physical fitness. Your mind and heart are simply muscles, and they depend on the fitness of the rest of your body to work properly. You'll also need to be fit enough to dodge and trade blows with someone who gets close to you, with or without magic. If you want to be on the front lines, you cannot just be a mage. You must be a fighter."

Damien did his best to nod without moving his chin away from the position Delph had put it in. If the professor noticed it, he didn't say anything. After around ten more minutes of nudging and adjusting, Delph sighed.

"That's enough for now. Go run laps around the field until your roommate arrives. Full speed. No slacking."

"But we don't know when she'll get here!" Damien said desperately. It couldn't have been more than half an hour since they'd started, and the last time Damien had seriously run anywhere was when his mother had made pie and called him home from school to eat it.

"You were the one confident she'd show up soon," Delph said, baring his teeth in a feral grin. "For your sake, I hope you're right."

———

Damien's legs had long since turned to jelly by the time Sylph arrived. His breath came out in ragged gasps, and the back of his coat was soaked with sweat. He'd long since lost count of how many laps he'd run around the arena when he saw the girl step through the gate. Damien could have kissed her out of sheer joy.

He flopped against the wall with a groan as the world spun in front of him.

"Hello, Sylph," Delph said.

"Hello, Professor," Sylph replied, not even glancing at Damien.

"I believe you owe me something," Delph said, tapping his foot impatiently and holding a hand out.

"I don't have any money," Sylph replied. "I'll pay you once I make some."

"You made a bet without having the coin to back it up?" Delph asked, aghast. "You little brat."

"A bet?" Damien asked between heavy breaths.

"Unfortunately. I should have known better," Sylph said, sighing. "I thought it would be easy money. I didn't think you'd actually show up two hours early."

Damien's eye twitched. "What?"

"Professor Delph made a bet with me before you noticed him in the alley yesterday," Sylph said after the professor waved for her to speak. "He said you would come to him and beg to get trained, but I thought you would have no interest in advanced combat. Hence, a bet."

"I'm not sure if I should be offended you bet against me or not," Damien said, curling his nose in annoyance. Then he blinked. "Wait. You were already planning to teach me yesterday! Why did you make me go through all this?"

"It was funny," Delph said, not even cracking a smile.

"And I was curious. You'll find those things drive the majority of my decisions."

"That's not concerning," Damien said dryly, pushing himself back to his feet and wiping the sweat away from his eyes.

"Good," Delph said. "Your weak muscles are completely worn out. Sit there while I work with Sylph, and we'll come back to you afterwards."

Damien flopped back down, too tired to argue and grateful for the chance to rest. Henry scoffed at him as he tapped the wristband, pulling up the screen to see the results of Delph's training.

Damien Vale
Blackmist College
Year One
Major: Undecided
Minor: Undecided
Companion: [Null]
Magical Strength: 3.4
Magical Control: .5
Magical Energy: 8
Physical Strength: .2
Endurance: .4

Endurance had inched up by five hundredths of a point. Damien wasn't sure if he should laugh or cry. He wanted to ask Sylph what her physical stats were at, but he wasn't sure he could handle the answer.

"Now, what shall we start with?" Delph wondered aloud, tapping his chin. "Your physical abilities are far better than Damien's. They're actually quite impressive for a student.

That could mean you don't need to run laps like this poor sod gasping for air, right?"

Delph jerked his chin in Damien's direction. Sylph nodded in agreement.

"Wrong!" Delph yelled, snapping his fingers and pointing at Sylph with the same hand. "There is always room for improvement. You are small. You have less muscle, so you must work harder to increase it. Now, start running!"

Sylph burst into a sprint. Delph gave an approving nod and sat beside Damien, who still struggled to catch his breath.

"Serious question. What do you want to learn from me?" Delph asked. "You showed some degree of cleverness in our fight. You could make a decent assassin if you hone your thinking skills."

"I think Sylph is more suited for that than I am," Damien said, recalling her fight with the professor and how she'd faded in and out of the shadows.

"You're absolutely correct," Delph agreed. "And I suspect you have no desire to stay on the backlines and defend your allies with runes and enhancing magic."

"I don't think my companion would lend itself well to that," Damien said, frowning.

"Damn right I wouldn't," Henry grumbled. Damien mentally shushed him.

"Then that leaves you with brute force," Delph said. "You will rely on your magical power and energy to defeat your opponents through sheer destructive force."

"That sounds fine to me," Damien said, sitting up straighter as his lungs recovered from the run. "Why do you say that as if it's a bad thing?"

"Because you will be in a constant race. You will still need to think in order to not be a brainless fool, but your condition for winning a fight will simply be by being stronger than your opponent. That is not an easy life to live."

"I don't have a choice," Damien said. "I'll do it."

"Then I shall do my best to support you while hopefully instilling at least a few morsels of intelligence into your mind," Delph said.

Sylph sped by them. Delph glanced at her before he shook his head and rose to his feet.

"The two of you couldn't be more different and similar at the same time," Delph said. "It's amusing. Perhaps that's part of the reason why I agreed to train you both."

"What does that mean?" Damien asked, standing as well.

"If you want information, you'll have to earn it," Delph said, giving Damien a wry smile. "Now, I know I said we would deal with Sylph first, but she's got a good number of laps left before she starts feeling tired."

Delph flicked Damien's collar. "Draw upon your Ether and channel it into any part of your coat. It's a disgrace to have mage armor but not use it."

Damien still had several sparks of the glowing energy within him. He guided one of them out from within his chest and directed it to the front of his cloak. The cloth stiffened.

"Good. Mage armor is a very effective defensive tool, but it is not easy to use," Delph lectured. "It can block most forms of magical attacks, but only when you are channeling energy into it. However, it becomes too stiff to move while it is activated."

"So I have to harden the parts right before I get hit, and then release them afterwards?" Damien guessed.

"Correct," Delph said, a wide grin spreading across his weathered face. Sylph sped by them again. She still didn't look like she was putting out much of a sweat. The professor knelt and pressed his hand into the sand.

A thin line of earth shimmered beneath his palm. It hardened into a stick about the length of the man's forearm. He rose, tapping it against his palm experimentally, the wicked smile only growing wider as realization set in for Damien.

"Now, can you guess how we're going to train your reaction time?" Delph asked.

Damien gulped.

CHAPTER
SEVENTEEN

Damien yelped as Delph smacked him hard on the arm. The mage armor hardened an instant later. The professor clicked his tongue as Damien groaned and nursed the newest bruise on his body.

Delph claimed to have a sense of humor, but the man was deadly serious about training. Damien was pretty sure the only part of him the professor had yet to hit were his eyes, and that was only because he'd missed.

Sylph still ran circles around the arena. She'd lasted longer than he had, but the exercise was starting to take its toll on her. Her footsteps fell heavier, and her breathing, which had initially been completely silent, had become labored.

"Getting tired?" Delph asked cheerfully as he rapped Damien across the chest.

"Yes," Sylph said plainly, slowing to a jog. "Should I stop?"

Delph considered the question for a moment. Then he nodded.

"You might as well. I'd say you're all warmed up," Delph said, lowering the stick for a moment. Damien started to let out a breath of relief. It vanished as a warning buzz ran through his mind. Instinctively, Damien hardened the entire left side of his mage armor, using up all the Ether he'd stored.

The stick smacked against the hardened cloth covering Damien's left arm harmlessly. The professor smirked and gave him a slight nod.

"Well done. Don't do it again. We're training precision. Turning yourself into a statue isn't going to be useful in a fight."

Damien gave the man a wary nod, not taking his eyes off the stick. Delph chuckled and tossed it to the side. It hit the ground and dissolved back into sand.

"Rest for a while," Delph told Damien. "It's Sylph's turn."

The professor walked up to Sylph. Wordlessly, the girl dropped into a fighting stance. Delph walked in a circle around her, examining it.

"You've trained before," he observed.

"I have," Sylph said, not explaining further.

"Good. That will make my job easier. Now, before I continue, there are a few things that actually pertain to both of you."

Sylph cocked her eyebrow.

"As you may or may not be aware, a large part of Blackmist's curriculum revolves around quests. You work in groups of two or three for them. If neither of you have an objection, I will be making you a group. Your combat styles are likely to be complementary, and you're already roommates. Is this okay?"

"It's fine with me," Sylph said. "My partner will not have a significant effect on my ability to perform."

"Wrong. Your survival depends on being able to rely on your teammate," Delph said casually, glancing at Damien.

"I'm fine with it if Sylph doesn't mind," Damien said, wisely choosing not to comment further.

"In that case, there will be no need to hide information about each other's abilities and weaknesses," Delph said. "I like to talk openly, so this will make things easier for me. It'll probably be embarrassing for you, though."

Delph turned back to Sylph. He stroked his beard for a few moments before he started talking again.

"Your physical endurance is good. Much better than the average student here. Your movements are precise and controlled, so it is apparent you've been training for a long time. When we fought, you wasted no magic, and you struck to kill. You're almost the perfect mage for the frontlines," Delph said. "However, your magical power is pathetic. Incredibly so. If it wasn't for your ridiculous levels of control, I would not even consider teaching you. I've seen squirrels with more magical power than you."

Sylph's face remained flat, but Damien spotted her wince for an instant as the professor ripped her apart.

"That being said," Delph continued. "A well-placed needle can kill a man or a monster just as well as an explosion. Your precision is already fantastic, but you will need to go beyond even that if you want to have a chance of graduating."

"What about me?" Damien asked, noticing how Sylph's cold expression wavered at Delph's final sentence.

"Impatient. I said I was starting with Sylph," the professor said. "However, you are simple. You appear to have a significant amount of magical power, but you are impulsive and foolish. You have horrible control and are either a liar or have a disturbingly powerful companion. If you could learn half of Sylph's control and a quarter of her experience in combat, you'd be an incredibly deadly force."

Henry stirred within Damien's mind. "He's observant. I wish he'd just tell us how he does his magic."

Shush. If he notices me talking with you, he'll only get more suspicious.

"Now," Delph said, raising a hand into the air palm up, "Sylph, don't take my words as insults. I will do my best to make you graduate at the top of your class. But, in the end, it all depends on your abilities as a mage. Right now, neither you nor your roommate impress me. I'm sure you'd probably pass the first year, but you'd be disappointing mages who would never make the frontlines."

Energy crackled around Delph, enveloping the man. He rose into the air as gray flesh bulged and formed around his armor. Within moments, he'd been completely replaced by a tall, gray creature with two burning red eyes and long, gangly limbs.

"This is a wendigo," Delph's voice came, although it was hard to tell from where. "It is a monster that isn't particularly common. They are quite fast, but their bodies are frail. I will begin with about twenty percent of the monster's complete strength. Your training for today will end when you can land a single blow on me."

Sylph was already moving. She shifted, blending into the background. Delph was faster. The wendigo stepped back as a line of darkness carved through the air, then grabbed Sylph by the collar and launched her across the arena.

"Seven planes," Damien cursed as Sylph righted herself midair and faded before she slammed into the wall.

"Eight," Henry corrected.

Shut up.

The sand beside the wendigo shifted. The monster twisted backward as if it were doing some strange dance, avoiding a dark slash that appeared out of nowhere and thrusting its fist into seemingly empty air.

Sylph flickered into existence and doubled over as the monster's punch drove the air out of her lungs.

The girl rolled with the strike, hopping back to her feet. A dagger formed of shadows materialized in her right hand. She grabbed something invisible in the air before her and pulled it to the side, stepping forward and disappearing.

"You need to learn a new trick," Delph said. The wendigo reached behind it, ripping Sylph free from her camouflage.

Her hand flicked, sending the dagger flying straight into the creature's chest. It arched its body, but the blade carved a thin furrow through the monster's thin skin. Delph let out an annoyed grunt. He set Sylph back on the ground as the monster's skin rippled and faded, revealing his normal form once again.

"That was a real transformation," Henry provided. "Not an illusion. Interesting."

Sylph let out a groan, rising to her feet and brushing the sand off her clothes.

"Clever way to win," Delph said, shaking his head in mock disgust. "Getting caught on purpose to get me off my guard works for this test, but don't be stupid enough to try that in a real fight. In the end, it doesn't matter if you kill your opponent. The most important thing is that you survive."

Delph patted Sylph on the shoulder and beckoned for Damien to join them as Sylph leaned against the wall to watch. The professor examined him with a critical eye before nodding.

"There's no point giving you a physical test," Delph said. "You've got nothing left. I want you to run five laps around the arena every day, regardless of whether I'm teaching you that day or not."

Damien grimaced but nodded, his tired muscles already cursing him for the promise.

"Now, you demonstrated you knew how to channel the Ether, but you don't know any true spells, correct?" Delph asked.

"Not yet," Damien said.

"Then we shall test if you're as talented as you claim to be," Delph said. "Unless your mental energy is exhausted as well?"

The way he said that made it very clear that if the answer was anything other than 'no,' Damien would be running laps for the rest of the day.

"I've still got some left," Damien hedged.

"Good response. As I'm sure you know, your companion's magic determines what magic you can use. What is lesser known is that most companions have access to multiple types of magic. They might specialize in one, but all you care about is the access. Your progress is independent of your companion's talents. As long as the door is open, you can choose to focus on what you want."

That was news to Damien. Henry just scoffed.

"So," Delph said, raising an eyebrow, "I understand some companions are not willing to commune much, but have you discovered what types of magic you'll have access to?"

Damien opened his mouth. Then he closed it and cleared his throat awkwardly as Delph's mouth thinned.

Henry? I might have forgotten the types.

"I thought you wanted me to remain quiet," the companion said petulantly.

Henry!

"Oh, relax. It's Light, Dark, Void, and Space. Try not to forget a second time," Henry said. "It goes without saying that telling him about Void would be incredibly foolish."

"I know what they are," Damien said before Delph could say anything else. "Light, Dark, and Space."

Delph paused, the words dying at his lips. He tilted his head to the side, inspecting Damien as his eyebrows slowly raised.

"Space?" he asked. "That's not a common one. I happen to have some talent with space myself, although it's not my main element."

"Is that what you used to knock Sylph out the first time you two fought?" Damien asked innocently.

"No," Delph said. "That was something else. I'd teach it to you if you met a set of certain requirements, but I've yet to run into anyone else who could learn it."

Damien nodded as Henry murmured in excitement.

"Regardless," Delph said, tapping a finger on his chin, "you'll eventually want to figure out which school of magic you want to focus on. You've got some time, so just think on it. In the meantime, I'm going to teach you a basic Space spell."

"Okay," Damien said eagerly.

"The majority of magic is based off two things," the professor lectured. "The first is intent, and the second is pattern. The Ether wants to return to its natural state. This happens when it is expended as energy."

Delph raised his hand into the air, and an orb of dark blue light formed above his palm.

"If you don't give it any intent or pattern, you get the most basic application of magic. It is simply destructive energy that is let off as the Ether moves back to a line. However, you can make it harder to return to normal by controlling how much of the Ether can escape at once."

A crackle of lightning erupted from the orb, turning a

small area of the sandy ground into glass. Damien jumped despite himself.

"I forced all the Ether to leave at once instead of letting it slowly burn off," Delph explained. "I also visualized a lightning bolt. Since your desires influence the Ether, you can encourage it to do what you want. Now, be wary of experimenting. You influence the Ether, but you do not control it. If you try to do something your school of magic does not permit, the Ether will not react how you expect, often with disastrous consequences."

Damien swallowed and nodded. It wasn't hard to understand the meaning behind Delph's words: Experimenting was a very bad idea if he didn't know what he was doing.

"You're lucky you've got me to ask questions," Henry said, reading Damien's mind. "If you didn't, the curiosity would probably eat you, and you'd probably blow your room up."

Oh, shut up. Just because you're right doesn't mean you have to say it.

Damien did his best not to break eye contact with Delph as he responded to Henry. It was impossible to tell if the strange professor had noticed anything.

"I have access to the Sky school of magic, so lightning is a natural form of energy for me to use," Delph said. "You do not. I don't know what would happen if you visualized a bolt of lightning, so I advise against it. Of course, you could emulate it with your light magic, but you'd only get the flash and nothing else."

"So, what should I visualize for Space?" Damien asked.

"For now, we'll start small. Space magic can change the size of an object, so see if you can enlarge a grain of sand," Delph suggested. "It's basic enough that you don't need to make an actual spell for it, as all you have to do is impart the energy into the sand quickly while picturing it enlarging. Of course, that's easier said than done. Keep in mind this will not work on living creatures or magical items. They both have innate magical energy that will resist a spell of this level."

Damien nodded. He cast his mental net out once more, grabbed a mote of Ether and drew it into himself, and cast his first real spell.

CHAPTER
EIGHTEEN

The Ether twisted and churned as Damien pressed down on the mote, constricting it as he envisioned the sand growing in size. It reached the inside of his palm and floated there, unmoving. He picked up a grain of sand and placed it in his open hand.

Damien tried to urge the Ether into the grain of sand, but the energy was no longer responsive. In fact, it inched back for his chest, reluctant to leave his body.

"You're doing it wrong, and your professor didn't say everything," Henry said. "You're forcing your will over the Ether. You don't simply request it. You command it. Requests are made by weak fools with no control over their magic. If you don't tell it exactly what to do, then your spells will be weak."

Damien swallowed. He narrowed his eyes and focused harder on the grain of sand. The Ether ventured out toward his palm. He tuned out Delph's observant gaze and tried to do as Henry instructed.

"Not enough," Henry said, his words dripping with disgust. "After all that desire to learn magic, you sit here and beg pathetically for the Ether to bend to your will. Command it! A coward can never become a mage. If this simple spell actually causes you difficulty, I might be better off returning to the Void and finding a new host."

Damien's brow furrowed, and he bared his teeth, slamming Henry back into the depths of his mind with a blast of mental energy. The lines of Ether around Damien warped. His shadow twisted on the ground behind him, but it was so slight neither Sylph nor Delph noticed it.

The grain of sand bulged, pushing Damien's fingers back as it ballooned outward until it was the size of a small rock. It remained that way for a few more moments before snapping back to its original form and falling to the ground.

"Color me surprised," Delph said, scratching the back of his head. "That was definitely the first time you cast that spell. It was clumsy, and you wasted a good portion of the Ether. It would be quite difficult to fake that. You really did learn a cultivation method in a single day, didn't you?"

It took Damien a moment to calm enough to answer the professor. He suppressed the fury he felt at Henry's words and nodded, forcing his face to return to a mask.

"That's what I've been saying," Damien said.

"Good. The enlarge spell isn't much more complicated than releasing the Ether normally, so feel free to practice it in your free time," Delph said, giving Damien a small nod. "The class will be meeting normally tomorrow, but you'll receive information about that later. I expect you to continue practicing in the mornings. I'll be in touch."

He gave Sylph a small nod before wrapping his cloak around himself. It folded inwards, and he vanished, leaving them alone in the arena.

"Is everything alright?" Sylph asked, pushing away from the wall with a weary yawn.

Damien realized his hands were still clenched. He relaxed them and nodded, scooping up a small pile of sand.

"Yeah. I just got a bit distracted," Damien said. His legs felt wobbly from all the running he'd done, but at least he didn't have to drag Sylph back to the room over his back this time. "I'm going to get some breakfast before I put the rune circles on Mark and the Grays' rooms, if you want to come."

"Sure," Sylph said. The two of them slowly walked out of the arena, both doing their best to look as if they weren't one stiff breeze away from falling over. As they headed toward the mess hall, Damien reached out to the Ether surrounding them.

He ran his hand along the strands of energy like strings on a harp, syphoning it off and storing it within himself. Once he'd gotten eight motes of energy, he raised the hand holding the pile of sand and focused on it.

The Ether resisted his will again. Damien's eyes narrowed, and he wrapped mental energy around the mote, crushing it into submission and forcing it out into the sand as he focused on his desired result.

One of the grains transformed into a large rock. Damien channeled another mote of Ether into it. The rock wavered, growing larger for an instant before it snapped back to its original form.

Damien continued testing the spell as they walked. Sylph watched him out of the corner of her eye.

"How are you still doing that?" Sylph finally asked.

Damien glanced up from the enlarged sand. It shrunk the moment his attention left it, and he tilted his head. "What do you mean?"

"You've been casting a spell you just learned for nearly ten minutes straight," Sylph said. "How can you still channel more Ether?"

"I've got no idea what you mean. I'm just getting more Ether from the lines."

"And you aren't getting tired?"

"Not really. Why would I be?"

Damien reached out, plucking a mote of Ether from the air as if to demonstrate his point. Sylph pursed her lips.

"That's insane. I can barely manage to get enough Ether to cast fifteen spells in an hour, but you can just keep going. How is that fair?"

"I'm making a piece of sand get bigger. You teleport around and cut things with shadows," Damien pointed out. "I think there might be a difference there."

"Not in terms of Ether usage. My spells are more difficult than yours are, but that's a matter of skill and experience not power."

"Well, maybe you need to cast more magic?" Damien offered. "My companion said magic is just like a muscle, so maybe you just have to train yours in a different way."

"Like I haven't tried that," Sylph muttered. "But casting in a different way... Hmm. I might have been lax in my training recently. Perhaps you might be right."

Damien caused the grain of sand to expand again. Sylph's eye twitched, and she turned away to hide her jealous expression.

When they reached the mess hall, Damien dumped the pile of sand into the dirt and brushed his hands off on his coat. The line was short, so it didn't take long for them to reach the woman with fish netted hair.

"The dumplings, please," Sylph said. "On Professor Delph's account. He owes me lunch for the rest of the year."

"Yes, he mentioned that," the woman said, jotting Sylph's request down and nodding. She glanced at Damien and raised an eyebrow.

"Free meal," Damien confirmed. She shook her head and clicked her tongue but jotted his request down regardless.

"Your loss."

After they'd found a table, Sylph raised an eyebrow at Damien.

"The free meal?"

"Food is food," Damien said with a shrug, trying to force himself to believe his words.

"Fair enough," Sylph agreed. A few minutes later, their rune circles lit up green, and their food appeared before them.

Damien's was the same slop as it had been the previous day, down to the consistency and color. Sylph had gotten a plate of three skewers of round, steaming dumplings.

The two of them eyed Damien's plate with disgust. Then Sylph grabbed her plate and moved it slightly farther down the table to keep it away from the vomit on his plate. Damien couldn't blame her.

A thought struck him. He raised his hand over the gelatinous mixture before him, drawing on a mote of Ether and molding it to his will. He visualized the food shrinking and forced the energy into it.

The slop shrank down until it was only around the size of a single spoonful.

"Don't even think about it," Henry snapped. "That is going to expand to full size in your throat and suffocate you."

Damien sighed, allowing the food to become normal-sized again. Sylph took a slow bite out of her dumpling.

"Were you going to try to eat that while it was shrunk?" she asked.

"What? No. I wouldn't do that," Damien muttered. "I was just practicing some more."

"I see," Sylph said, her tone making it apparent she didn't

believe him for a second. "Do you want a dumpling? It's Delph's money after all."

"A dumpling would be nice," Damien said. Before Sylph could give him one, he grabbed his plate of mush and tilted it back, scraping everything into his mouth and swallowing as quickly as he could.

He mentally thanked all the teleportation for training him on avoiding vomiting, then shuddered once it was apparent the food was going to stay down.

Sylph handed him one of the skewers, which Damien took with an appreciative smile. He took a bite out of one. The dumplings were full of some barbequed meat he couldn't quite place. It was soft and juicy, packed with smoky flavor with just the right amount of salt to let the taste shine. Compared to the possibly sentient blob he'd eaten before, it was like biting into heaven.

The two of them finished their meal a few minutes later and headed back to the base of the mountain. Damien's legs groaned protests at him, and he could already tell he'd regret the morning's training the following day.

Sylph looked to be in better shape, but Damien spotted her hiding a pained grimace several times. The climb back up the mountain proved to be even more painful.

Damien's calves burned with every step, and by the time they'd reached their rooms, he almost let out a cry of joy.

The two of them managed to make it back to their room without falling over. Sylph peeked into the room Damien had carved while he flopped onto his bed with a groan.

"It's empty," Sylph announced, sitting on her bed and letting out a relieved sigh.

"Well, that's good," Damien said. "I would have been shocked if anyone came in after yesterday, though. Speaking of which..."

He let out a mixture of a groan and a sigh, grabbing the chalk from his pack and pushing himself upright.

"I've got to go do some interior decorations."

"Have fun with that," Sylph said, lying back in her bed.

Damien grumbled under his breath as he staggered over to Mark's room. He turned the corner and glanced inside, only to find himself only inches away from Mark's face. Damien jumped and let out a curse.

"What are you doing?" he snapped.

"I heard you get back and figured you might be coming to draw the runes in my room," Mark said, frowning. "Did I do something wrong?"

"I— Just don't stand so close to the entrance," Damien sighed. "You'll scare someone."

Mark nodded and stepped out of the way as Damien made his way inside the other boy's room. It didn't look like he'd done much in the way of furnishing it. The room was basically identical to how Damien's room had looked before he'd started carving it.

Aside from the additions of the rugs and a sword collection on the wall, it was rather plain. Damien chose a spot near the edge of Mark's bed and took his chalk out. After the other boy approved the location, Damien spent several minutes drawing the circle.

Once he'd finished, it lit up with a dull blue light. Damien stood back up, groaning as his legs protested his actions once again.

"There you go," Damien said. "It should last for a week or two so long as you don't rub any of the chalk away."

"Thank you," Mark said. He grabbed a brown bundle and offered it to Damien, who almost dropped it. It was much heavier than he'd expected.

"It's authentic dire bear fur," Mark said. "Their skin is

very tough, which makes it heavy. Makes for great armor, too."

"I'll keep that in mind," Damien said. "Thank you."

Mark just nodded as Damien lugged his prize back over to his room, dropping it on the ground before trudging toward the Grays' room to take care of their runes as well.

When Damien arrived, the two nobles were both busy reading books. Their room barely resembled a cave anymore. The beds had fine silk sheets embossed with flowing designs of golden thread. The floors had been covered with fancy rugs that looked much less practical than Mark's. Nolan glanced up and gave him a solemn nod.

"You've come to draw the runes?" Nolan asked formally.

"Yes," Damien said, too tired to say much more. "I'll draw them behind your bed so you can move it to block the circle, unless you've got another spot you'd prefer?"

"Perhaps near the bathroom wall?" Nolan suggested. "It's somewhat difficult to shower without light."

Damien just nodded. He trudged over to the bathroom wall, pulling out his chalk and choosing a flat spot on the stone. It only took him a few minutes to draw the runes. Once he'd finished, he put the chalk away and yawned, looking away from the glowing light.

"As long as you don't rub it out, it'll last a week or two," Damien said.

"Thank you," Nolan said. "I appreciate it. I apologize for invading your room last night."

The noble sent a pointed glance at his sister. She looked away from her book and reached under the bed, grabbing a thin cloth bundle to Damien. He took it, thankful it was much lighter than the rug Mark had given him.

"Thanks," Damien said. "And it's fine. Just...knock next time. Or call, I guess. We don't have a door yet."

"We will do so," Nolan promised. "Would you like to join us for dinner? Reena, Mark, and I were going to go to the mess hall together."

"I suppose that would be fine," Damien said after a few moments of thought. Nolan's face showed no evident signs of insincerity, but it had only been a few days ago the boy had completely refused to acknowledge his presence.

Damien bid them farewell and trudged back to his room. He flopped on top of his bed without taking off his clothes. His head hit something stuff under his pillow, and he cursed, rolling over and cradling it.

He ripped the pillow away, revealing an untitled book bound in dark leather. Still rubbing the back of his head, Damien leaned against the wall and flipped the cover open. A small note fell out from the front page and onto his lap.

"A gift from your instructor?" Henry asked, reading it through Damien's eyes.

Apparently. Why did he have to stick it under my pillow?

"Well, it was funny," Henry said. "You might read it. It might have something I missed during my trip over. Just skim for now, though. If I know the spell, it'll be faster for me to teach you myself."

"I got one too," Sylph provided. She rubbed the side of her head. "In the same spot."

Damien rolled his eyes. The first page was blank, so he looked over the one after it. It was covered in densely packed writing detailing what appeared to be a spell that could create a small ball of light.

"Easy," Henry said. "Next."

Damien flipped the page. The spell was also based in the school of light magic. This one was meant to use a beam of concentrated light offensively. It drew a scoff out of Henry. As he scanned through the book, the spells grew progressively more complicated.

At the same time, Henry's annoyance grew. Even when they got to invisibility spells and magic so complicated it took nearly an entire chapter just to explain it, the companion just let out an annoyed groan.

"Boring! This is all basic stuff," Henry said. "I want something new!"

This spell uses light to make an illusion so realistic it's nearly impossible to recognize its fake. How is that boring?

"I knew that spell four hundred thousand years ago," Henry said. "I don't care what it does. The problem is that it's old. I guess a few of these might be worth learning, though. I'm not a fan of creating light, but I suppose it might be useful for you."

Why don't you like it?

"I'm going to pretend you didn't ask me that," Henry said. "As a general fact, I'm more partial to removing light than creating it. I'm sure you can guess why."

Ah. Right.

"Ah. Right," Henry mimicked. "Look, that enlarge spell is interesting, but you aren't going to fight any Void denizens by making their shoes too big for them. You need to learn some offensive spells."

I'm not going to object to that.

"No, I didn't think you would," Henry said, chuckling. "Before you start learning spells at random, you need to put some thought into what magic you want to focus on. Light magic is mostly utility. It has offense and defense, but nothing very strong. Space magic has some very powerful offensive options, but it's going to take you a long time to learn them. It also has teleportation."

And Void magic?

"It embodies the Void. It is not like normal magic," Henry said. "There is only one Void spell, and there can never be another one."

Stop hedging at it and just tell me what it is!

"Mimicry. A trade of sorts. Void magic can take a spell, warping and improving it to its ultimate form. However, you can only use Void magic safely when you have a complete understanding of it. It is far more difficult than the other schools of magic and incredibly dangerous."

That sounds interesting. How do you know there's only one spell, though? You said you couldn't make your own magic, and I don't think humans normally get access to Void magic. So, doesn't that mean I could hypothetically make a Void spell?

"It's possible, I suppose," Henry said. "It wouldn't be easy. Void magic requires a general understanding of all magic. Spells are cast in similar ways, so with enough study, you can understand the ones from schools of magic you can't cast yourself. Making a new Void spell, though...you can imagine how difficult that would be. You'd need mastery over just about every form of magic."

Maybe I'll stick to just learning for now, then.

"Might be a good idea," Henry agreed.

It sounds like learning Void magic is going to take a very long time, and I can't exactly show that to my teachers. I'd like to learn it, but I think I should focus on Space for now.

"Agreed," Henry said. "Space magic is powerful if used correctly."

Damien sighed. He swung his feet over the edge of his bed, ignoring the pangs of discomfort that traveled up his legs and lower back, and headed into the small training room. It was far from finished, but it gave a small amount of privacy.

He set the book aside and sat, bracing his back against the wall with a relieved groan. Damien gathered his mental energy, forming the mental net and casting it out. Unlike the rest of his body, his mind still seemed to be mostly functional.

Damien gathered several motes of Ether, drawing them into himself. His limbs grew lighter, and some of the tension left his muscles.

Does the Ether somehow heal me? I feel better after drawing it in.

"Not exactly," Henry said. "It gives you a temporary spike of energy, which your body interprets as a signal to not feel pain. You aren't healed, your injuries just don't show as much. It's useful for a fight, but don't get over reliant on it."

Good to know. Now, do you have a spell I could learn that's actually cool? Making things change size is nice, but—

"Hah. Bored already? Well, I suppose I can't blame you," Henry said. Damien's shadow rippled and twisted. "Give me control for a little. You'll learn much better if you can observe me casting it instead of listening to me talk about it."

Damien nodded, his consciousness slipping back as Henry took the reins. Henry had him raise his right hand and channeled two of the motes of Ether up through his arm and into his palm. As they moved, he mentally wrapped and twisted them, forming the energy into a churning ball.

As it emerged from Damien's palm, Henry used mental energy to spin it violently. A dot of gray light appeared floating in the air over his hand. It expanded outward until it was around the size of an orange, darkness swirling together with the gray in a mesmerizing pattern.

What's that?

"One of the most basic forms of offensive spells in Space magic," Henry said. "This is a Gravity Sphere."

He had Damien toss it into the center of the room. The orb froze an inch before it hit the ground, erupting outward in a wave of darkness rapidly sucked back in on itself with a silent hiss.

Damien's ears hissed as he, along with some of the dust and stone that had accumulated in the room, were sucked to where the orb had struck. The force faded a moment later.

Henry was pushed aside as Damien's shock put his body back under his own control. There was no longer any sign of the dark orb.

"That was amazing!" Damien said aloud, his voice hushed. "Now, that's what I call magic."

"Less talking, more practicing," Henry suggested.

Damien didn't bother replying with a snide remark. He still had several motes of Ether left, so he reached out to coax them toward his arm. The first one moved as always, but the second slipped away from his grasp as if it were coated in butter.

His eyes narrowed, and he reached out toward it again, this time enveloping it in a bubble of energy to make sure there was nowhere to run. The dot of Ether moved forward, and the second one slipped back, essentially trading places.

How do I move both at once?

"You're focusing too much," Henry advised. "By trying that hard, you're telling the Ether it only needs to listen to you when you're paying it attention. You must act as if the Ether has already done what you need it to, and then it will."

That doesn't really make much sense. How can I act like it's already done what I want it to if it hasn't yet?

"Use that human imagination of yours. It can't be that hard."

Damien grumbled and returned his attention to the twin motes of Ether floating back within his chest. He nudged them again, visualizing them both flowing down his arm and twisting into the same churning orb Henry had made. The Ether wiggled a little, but nothing else happened.

It's not working.

"Only because you refuse to believe it will. You are trying instead of doing. This spell isn't difficult," Henry chided Damien. "You could cast this, and many other spells, on your first try. The hard part is getting the Ether to flow in the way you want it to. Your belief that you need to practice before it works correctly is hindering you. The Ether flows according to your commands, and you believe you will fail."

You're saying I can cast this spell perfectly if I just think I can?

"You 'can' cast the spell," Henry corrected. "Not perfectly. Your understanding of the spell is unlikely to be complete, so you will attempt to cast the spell you visualize, which may or may not be the true essence of the spell you're going for. It will execute to the best of the Ether's abilities based off the way you cast it, but that doesn't mean it's perfect. Do you understand?"

I think I do, actually. So, if I cast the spell, I cast the best version of what I'm trying to do, not the objective best possible outcome.

"That is a bastardized, yet fundamentally correct, version of what I said," Henry allowed. "So, what are you waiting for? If you agree it should simply cast when you will it, then do it!"

Damien nodded. He raised his hand, copying the form Henry had done. Instead of corralling the Ether, he tried sending a silent command. Damien envisioned the ball of churning gray and black energy appearing above his palm as if it had already happened.

It was a subtle difference, but magic was made in the details. Damien's ears popped as energy collected above his hand, and a twisting ball of darkness twisted to life.

"Did you envision the correct thing?" Henry asked. "I didn't get everything, but some of your thoughts seemed—"

Damien tossed the ball into the center of the room. Just like Henry's attempt, it expanded outward before collapsing into a tiny mote of light. Then it deviated. Instead of a subtle *pop*, a loud gale howled into the small room.

The blot of darkness warped the air immediately around it, sucking everything straight into it. Damien skidded across the floor as dirt and dust slammed into the orb of magic, forming a shell around it.

Damien tried to breathe in, but the air slipped away from his lungs. Before he could panic, the Ether within the spell spent itself. The orb faded, and he drew in a deep breath as the dirt collapsed to the ground.

NINETEEN

Sylph dashed out the entrance of the small hallway with a knife made of darkness in her hand. She held it defensively for a few moments, scanning the room before slowly lowering the weapon with a frown.

"What was that?" she asked. "I couldn't breathe for a moment. Did you cast a spell?"

Damien, who had been deposited directly on top of the pile of dirt after his spell had ended, brushed some of it off his clothes and cleared his throat while Henry receded into the depths of his mind.

"Ah...I might have. I made a bit of a mistake when visualizing what I wanted the Ether to do," Damien said. "Are you okay?"

Sylph inspected him for a moment, then let the knife fade and shook her head.

"I'm fine. I'm not sure what spell you were going for, but it doesn't seem particularly safe. Don't injure yourself too badly. It might take a healer some time to get here."

"Right," Damien said. "Sorry. I didn't think it would suck up the air."

"What were you trying to cast?"

"Ah...a gravity spell."

"Was that in the book Delph gave you?"

"Well, not really," Damien muttered.

"How did you learn it, then? The library? I was under the impression you only brought back a cultivation book."

Damien pressed his lips together.

"I saw it in a book. I didn't bring it back with me," he said.

"I see," Sylph replied, cocking her head. "Delph was right. If you're memorizing spells at a glance, you're quite the prodigy."

She turned and walked out of the hallway. Damien watched her leave, his hands clenching at his sides.

"She suspects something," Henry said. Damien's shadow shifted across the floor, even though Damien hadn't moved from where he stood.

Not much we can do about that. We'll just have to keep an eye on her.

"And get stronger. Quickly," Henry added. "You are not strong enough to defeat her. With the limited powers of your body, she might even be fast enough to escape me."

I'm going to go ahead and request you don't start making plans to kill my roommate. It's normal for her to be curious about why someone is acting weird and learning magic so quickly. If I were in her shoes, I'd be jealous. Back when we were getting tested, her magic was much lower than everyone else's. Delph mentioned it was weak, too. That must be why she can't hold much Ether at once.

"Astute. She seems to have a rather high level of control and discipline, but her powers are quite weak," Henry said. "I'm surprised she doesn't hate you. It's only a matter of time until you surpass her, and she's likely been training her entire life to get to this point."

Wonderful. Why is it like that? If she's been training as long as you think, why isn't her magic stronger? It doesn't seem fair for her to be weak.

Henry burst into laughter.

"It amuses me that you still think life is fair, especially when you have the most powerful companion this school will ever see sharing its soul with you," Henry said. "Generally, magic improves at a slow rate when it is practiced. From her amount of control, her magic should be much higher. Since it isn't, it likely means something about her body is seriously flawed."

Flawed?

"I don't need to explain that your body is a worthless flesh bag," Henry replied. "Your soul is what uses the magic. Bodies are just a shell. If her soul is somehow restrained, it could restrict her potential. It's impossible for me to say what the exact issue is without getting inside her head."

Which you will not be doing.

"One mortal mind is more than enough, thank you," Henry said, shuddering in disgust. "And, speaking of cultivation, it's time for you to do more of it. Repetition is key, boy. Stop worrying about the girl and think about our future instead."

Damien grunted. He looked down at his hands, a small frown on his face.

Why don't you go check on the locations of those Void creatures again? Find out where the nearest one is and if it's moved since the last time you checked.

"Wait, really?" Henry asked. Then he cleared his throat, despite not having one. "Right. That's a good idea."

Damien just nodded. His shadow flickered and split, pulling away from his body. Emptiness enveloped him in its icy embrace as Henry's presence vanished and the shadow slipped down the hall and out of the room.

Once he'd left, Damien tapped his wristband.

Damien Vale
Blackmist College
Year One
Major: Undecided
Minor: Undecided
Companion: [Null]
Magical Strength: 3.5
Magical Control: .5
Magical Energy: 8.5
Physical Strength: .2
Endurance: .5

He'd had some decent increases in his stats, at least as far as the school was concerned. There wasn't much he could compare it to, but Damien felt proud, nonetheless. He dismissed the screen and gathered several more motes of energy. He drew one of them out through his palm, drawing forth a sphere of basic destructive energy.

"Repetition, huh?" Damien asked himself quietly. He repeated the process with his other hand so he had a ball before both of his palms. Then he stepped up to the walls and got to work.

Stone turned to dust beneath Damien's fingers as his magic made short work of the walls. Whenever the orbs weakened, he drew more Ether and summoned new ones. Damien gritted his teeth, ignoring the thin layer of dust forming over his body as he worked.

He felt hollow. A part of that was because Henry had left, but that wasn't everything. The magic churning at his fingertips energized Damien's body, but there was no smile on his face. Hours passed, and the room grew drastically in size as Damien vented his frustrations on the rock, burrowing deeper into the mountain.

As time went on, the Ether came to him slower. What had once been a simple task grew arduous as a dull headache came over Damien and exhaustion set in. He didn't stop working.

Finally, his reserves ran out. He reached for a strand of Ether, but he couldn't gather the mental energy to coat his hand. Damien slumped against the wall heavily, a thin trail of tears streaming down his face.

"It isn't fair," he whispered to himself. "I shouldn't have to worry about stopping the apocalypse or figure out if my companion is lying to me. I just wanted to learn magic. I've been working toward this for years. Why can't I be happy?"

Unbeknownst to Damien, about a thousand miles away, Henry was thinking those exact same thoughts.

———

The eldritch creature sat at the top of a large grassy hill overlooking a quaint village. His head was in his hands, and he was rather miserable.

A mote of white light shone in the center of his chest. White, spiderwebbing lines reached out across his torso, stopping just before his legs and arms. Henry had long since given up on trying to remove it. Any attempts to touch the light were futile.

It was rather ironic, Henry mused. The destroyer of light, unable to quench the miniscule spark within himself. He drew in a deep breath, not that he needed to, of course. Another miniscule mannerism he'd picked up from the mote within him. It was changing him, and Henry didn't like it.

The air was cool, with a hint of sweetness from last night's rain. Below him, villagers moved to and fro, completely unaware of what observed them.

"You'd think I'd be happier on the Mortal Plane," Henry muttered aloud. "Millenia of dreaming, and here I am. So why do I feel so unsatisfied? The end is nigh. Less than one mortal lifespan, really."

Nobody responded. Henry's many mouths frowned. Being alone was...strange. Henry rose to his feet, his senses sweeping across the town below him. They were subtle, but the traces of Void magic were unmistakable.

Henry flickered and vanished, traveling through the dusk shadows and flitting through the village. Not a soul noticed him as he followed the traces of energy through the crack below a house's door and into a small cellar below it.

The traces of energy were stronger now but nowhere near enough to signify another Void creature. Several eyes made of dark energy blinked open around him, scanning every inch of the room.

It only took him moments to locate a thin, well-hidden magical seal covering a plank of wood. The energy was made to only seal in a single direction, so it was easy enough for the companion to place his hand against the wood and summon an eye on the other side of it.

A woman hung taut in the air, suspended by heavy black chains connected to each of her limbs. Her clothes were little more than molded rags and her hair was ratty and unwashed. Her head twitched, and she glanced up, stark silver eyes locking with Henry's magic.

"Ah," the woman wheezed, voice raspy from years of disuse. "I sensed you recently, It Who Heralds the End of All

Light, if I can even call you that. I see you've also found your way into the Mortal Plane."

"I have. And I go by Henry," Henry's voice projected through the eye. "In a way. I didn't expect to find you locked in a basement, It Who Consumes the Mountains."

"Harriot, if you insist on it," the woman replied, licking her lips to wet them. "You seem...different. It took me longer to notice you than it should have. Has your nature been warped?"

"It is of no matter," Henry said dismissively.

"Very well. In that case, are you going to free me?" she asked. "It seems you were the only one of our kind to make the journey safely. The moment I arrived, I was bound to this body and sealed away. I've tried to call out to the others, but none have responded. Someone knew we were coming."

"Someone knew?" Henry asked, frowning. "You mean all of the others are similarly sealed?"

"I have to assume so," Harriot said, doing her best to shrug. "They would have already found and freed me if not. Luckily, it seems you managed to escape. I'd be interested to learn how later, but the sooner I'm out of these chains, the better."

"Yes," Henry mused. "I suppose so. I must ask, why did you take on a human personality when you're alone? It serves no purpose."

"The meager remains of this mortal's soul," Harriot replied, pursing her lips. "I crushed it as soon as I arrived, of course. Unfortunately, the bindings were such that I had to merge partially with her soul. It was enough to bring about, well, Harriot. I have found it somewhat amusing, and it has been a good way to pass the time while I waited for your arrival. Once I am free, I shall dispose of it."

"And you didn't get sight of your captors?" Henry pried. "Your host was already locked up by the time you arrived?"

"Yes," Harriot said irritably. "I honestly find myself regretting squashing the girl's soul so quickly, which shocks me. But, even in the Void, we had each other to speak to. True darkness is surprisingly lonely. Now, enough of the games, It Who Heralds the End of All Light. Let me free. We have a job to do."

There was no response from Henry. The eye floated in the air, watching her silently.

Harriot's gaze narrowed, and energy twisted around her. It sputtered, fading away as the chains holding her lit up with a dull glow. Then she blinked, a frown crossing her face.

"It Who Heralds the End of All Light?"

"That isn't my name," Henry said.

"What? Yes, it is. I recognize your energy. It's a little different but not enough to throw me off."

"I am afraid you are incorrect," Henry said, his voice a low whisper. "I am not It Who Heralds the End of All Light."

"Just let me go!" Harriot snarled. "If you don't, one of the others will. Why do you dally? Don't tell me you've fallen to the C—"

"I have not, and they will not," Henry interrupted sharply. "Because they will not find you. I had to confirm, but it appears nobody other than me has managed to escape their mortal confines. That means I'm the only one who knows of your presence here. It is going to stay that way. I have changed my mind on the way we should go about taking care of the Mortal Plane, Harriot. I'm afraid you are no longer part of them."

"What are you talking about?" Harriot asked, glaring at the eye. "You don't have plans of your own. None of us do. This is the natural law of the universe. The Mortal Plane must be destroyed to be rebirthed. We have arrived, and so we must carry out our task. This is our duty, as it always has been. You are speaking nonsense."

"Perhaps I am," Henry said. The eye flickered. Tendrils sprouted out from it, twirling around the chains and climbing up Harriot's limbs, enveloping her in a cocoon of shadows.

She struggled against the magic, but the chains already bound her tightly. As Henry's magic encircled her chest and started up her neck, she looked up at him, fury burning in her eyes. The darkness traveled along her jaw and up the back of her head, leaving only her face uncovered.

For an instant, Henry's true form flickered at the edge of her vision. Her eyes widened.

"You are not It Who Heralds the End of All Light. Why is there a spark within you?"

Henry's hand closed. The darkness enveloped the woman, flooding through her mouth and silencing her. With a thrum, all traces of her magical energy blinked out of existence, sealed off from the rest of the world.

The eye faded. Above her, standing on the wooden floor, Henry rose to his feet, the white light in his chest shimmering like a cracked star in a sea of darkness.

"Rest here forever," Henry told the eldritch creature, slipping into the shadows and disappearing without a trace.

———

Damien ran his hand through his hair. It came away covered in a thin sheen of dust. He rubbed it between his fingers, his emotions still churning. It had been several hours since he'd collapsed against the wall.

The spark of passion for magic at the center of his soul

flickered. Assailed from all sides by the events of the past few days, it had faded.

Why should I have to deal with this? Henry is locked within me. I don't need to find the eldritch creatures. Someone else can do that. I'm just seventeen! There are mages who have trained for years who can take care of this.

Henry wasn't there to answer him. Damien's fingernails bit into the palms of his hands. As violent emotion churned within him, his soul changed. Fear and uncertainty encroached on the passion for magic and learning. As it shifted, something cracked in Damien's mind.

The violent upheaval going on within Damien pushed aside a shroud he hadn't even realized was there, revealing the powerful magic fettering the half of Henry's soul bound to Damien. Like a school of rabid piranhas, his subconscious mental energy lashed out at the bindings.

Henry's soul was enormous. Damien had nowhere near enough energy to break the fetters covering it. The whole of his soul's force was only enough to make a tiny nick within the magic, allowing a miniscule amount of the imprisoned soul to escape.

Damien's back stiffened as a buried memory thrust itself upon him in complete clarity. It was him four years ago right as he finished drawing the rune circle that would summon Henry.

The desire for magic the younger version of Damien had was almost blinding. His hand had trembled with unrestrained excitement as he sat back and prepared to summon his companion and begin the journey he'd waited so long for.

Damien's eyes pricked with tears as the vivid memory played itself out. On that day, he hadn't realized it, but some of that passion had died. The knowledge of what he carried within had soured his passion.

Unable to stop the memory, he was forced to watch as his younger self began the ritual to summon a companion. And then, at the very corner of his younger self's eye, Damien saw something he didn't remember.

A flicker of darkness at the corner of his vision. It passed in less than a second, crossing over his runes and wiping a miniscule line of chalk away.

Damien's body stiffened. He remembered that rune. It had been the one that had sent the call to the Void instead of the Planes. The other rune he'd made a mistake in was behind him, but something told Damien that it, too, had been altered.

"Someone did this to me," Damien breathed. "I didn't mess up drawing my rune circle."

The memory faded, leaving Damien alone on the dusty ground once more. Damien stared at the wall, his blood pumping faster and faster.

"Somebody took my chances of a normal life away from me. I was set up."

Damien's soul shifted once again. The spark at the center of his soul flared with indignant anger. The beginnings of fear and uncertainty clawing their way into him were shattered and blown away. The emptiness they left behind vanished, filled by something Damien had lacked for the last four years: A true sense of purpose.

"Somebody is trying to use me," Damien growled to himself. "And that person wanted the Void creatures to get onto this world. What else have they done to manipulate me?"

He rose to his feet, his hands clenched tightly at his sides. The spark of desire within him encircled itself with an iron shield of determination. If someone else had been in the room, they would have seen an imperceptible shift within his eyes. The defeated, lost look was replaced by confidence.

"You might have forced me to have an eldritch creature as a companion, but I won't let you take away my love for magic," Damien said. "I'm going to find whoever you are, and we're going to have a little chat."

CHAPTER
TWENTY

If anything had heard him, it didn't respond. Damien didn't care. A laugh escaped his lips, and he reached out, strumming the lines of Ether like a harp. It flooded into him eagerly, awaiting his command like a trained hound.

Damien channeled the energy, forming a Gravity Sphere and tossing it across the considerably larger room. It hit the far wall. The dust covering the room whooshed through the air and condensed at the orb.

He was tugged toward it as well, but the force wasn't enough to do much more than that. He felt momentarily breathless, but the magic dispelled a moment later, leaving the dust in a large pile.

Damien let out a laugh. He formed another orb and tossed it at the ceiling at the far side of the room. He lifted into the air for a moment, then dropped back to his feet as the magical force waned.

He continued creating the Gravity Spheres, tossing them against the wall and growing closer to gauge their strength. They seemed to be mostly effective within a five-foot area around the impact zone.

Anywhere outside of that, the air was still sucked into the epicenter of the Gravity Sphere, but it did little to actually move Damien more than a foot or so.

As Damien practiced, miniscule changes happened within him. The Ether coursing through his body left minute traces behind, seeping into his muscles and veins and infusing them with energy.

The amount entering him was so small he barely noticed it. However, with every spell Damien cast, his body grew slightly stronger. In addition to growing physically tougher, the core within his chest where the Ether grew brighter.

Damien practiced for hours, not taking a single pause or break. His mind homed in on the task, and the rest of the world fell away, leaving him in a trance. Sylph peeked into the training room once or twice, but he didn't let his mind stray.

At some point, Henry darted through the shadows of the room and reentered Damien's body. Damien, who was mid-cast, allowed the spell to peter out and fade. Sweat trickled down his forehead, and a dull throbbing headache had become a new companion.

"I'm back," Henry said cheerfully. "The Void creature closest to us is still around a hundred miles away. They are not aware of our presence, and they appear to be well-sealed within a cave."

Good. Do anything else while you were gone?

"Just took a look around a small town," Henry said. Damien suspected his companion shrugged. "Nothing too interesting."

I see.

There was a short pause as they observed each other.

Say, do you remember when I summoned you and made a mistake in the runes?

"Yes," Henry said, chuckling. "And a foolish one it was."

Right. When did you arrive? Were you aware of me before I was aware of you? Or did we see each other at the same time?

"I heard your call the moment you sent it out, but I was not present until we both saw each other," Henry said, curiosity tinging his tone. "Why do you ask?"

Damien thought as hard as he could about his new conviction of magic, forcing himself to focus on it rather than the real reason for the question.

Just curious.

"I see," Henry said, copying Damien's words from a few moments before. The creature peered at Damien from within him, a small frown crossing his face. "You're different."

I made a decision.

"I can tell," Henry said, shifting through Damien's mind like he was rummaging around in someone's musty old storeroom. "Hmm. Part of the soul I gave you has slightly escaped its bindings. That's not good."

Leave it. I think whatever that change did is helping me.

"It could have serious consequences," Henry warned. "The memories locked up in there in addition to my own power will almost certainly change you."

Then I'll get changed. They're my memories, Henry. I don't think we should release them all at once, but they're part of me. Eventually, I think they should return to my control.

"If you insist," Henry said. "I've never actually seen what would happen to a mortal who joined with an eldritch soul, so I'm quite curious. If you start going insane, I'll do my best to seal everything away again. Just remember it's much simpler when its fresh. Once the memories return to you, they won't go as easily."

Damien just nodded.

"Your new friends are coming," Henry said. Then he chuckled. "Actually, they're waiting outside the cave. Your roommate knows they're there, but she's pretending she doesn't."

Damien chuckled. He tossed one final Gravity Sphere at the wall. He drew in a breath before it hissed to life, ripping all the dust away from Damien and the floor and condensing it into a single spot again. He exhaled as the spell faded and rolled his neck before walking back into their main room.

Sylph sat on her bed, her knees tucked in with her book balanced on top of them. She'd unrolled the rug that had given them and laid it out on the thin open strip of rock between their beds at the center of the room. She glanced in his direction as he arrived, covering a yawn.

"Have fun sucking all the air up?" she asked.

"It barely took any air from more than a few feet away from me," Damien replied. "You must have barely felt it."

"I'm quite sensitive to changes in the atmosphere," Sylph replied, lowering the book.

"Oh," Damien said, a small frown crossing his face. "Would you like me to practice elsewhere?"

Sylph blinked. Then she laughed, shaking her head.

"It's okay. I was mostly just pulling your leg," she said, setting the book aside and getting out of bed. She jerked her chin toward the door. "Did you realize we had company?"

"I only came out because I finished training, but I said I'd go to dinner with them," Damien said with a small shrug. "You want to come?"

Sylph cocked her head. Then she nodded once. "Sure. I'm out of Ether anyway, so there isn't much more progress I can make with the book Delph gave me."

Her words were jovial, but Damien noticed the traces of bitterness within them. He settled for a small nod, and the two of them headed out of the cave.

Mark and the Grays leaned against the stone outside.

When Damien and Sylph emerged, Reena jumped slightly before clearing her throat and glancing at the sunset, pretending they hadn't just scared her.

"The rune circle works great. I'm quite new to rune magic, but it seems quite powerful. Is it difficult to learn?" Mark asked Damien, baring his teeth in a snarl. After a moment, Damien realized the boy was trying to smile. His features were disturbingly wolflike, and the dull shadows of the evening didn't help.

"It's just a lot of studying and practice," Damien replied. "It's not the best for anyone interested in combat magic, since it takes up a lot of time to learn and isn't the most effective in a fast-paced fight."

Sylph snorted beside Damien but just glanced away when the others gave her questioning looks.

"So, why did you learn it?" Nolan asked. He flushed. "No offense meant, of course. But your companion is quite powerful, so I'm sure you could have a very lucrative career as a combat mage. Why study runes?"

"I wasn't always planning to be a combat mage," Damien replied. "That decision was quite recent."

Reena nudged Nolan in the side.

"Ah, our rune circle was also very helpful," Nolan added, flushing. "Forgive me. I should have thanked you earlier. I just got a little distracted, and—"

"Oh, stuff it," Damien said, massaging his brow. "I think I almost preferred when you were acting like a throbbing prick. Stop sucking up to me and just treat me like a normal person. It'll get you farther than anything else."

Nolan's mouth flapped for a few moments. Then it clicked shut, and he gave Damien a single nod. The others sent surprised looks at Damien.

"Shall we go?" Damien pressed. "I'm getting quite hungry."

The group set off toward the mess hall. As they walked, Henry felt a sense of intense displeasure he'd been ignoring grow stronger. He faded into the background, not leaving Damien's mind so much as receding to the back of it.

———

Henry once again found himself standing in a sea of darkness, looking up at an enormous face made of stars. An image of Harriot being consumed by tendrils of magic appeared in Henry's mind.

"Why?" the darkness rumbled.

"You're speaking now?"

There was no response. Henry let out an annoyed sigh.

"The Mortal Plane doesn't need to be reborn yet," Henry said. "We've waited for millennia. There's nothing wrong with waiting a little longer. Time is nothing, and we've been bored for so long. The others are all sealed by some outside force. If it was strong enough to take care of them, we should figure out what we're dealing with."

The face in the sky looked down at Henry, incomprehension clear in its features. Its mouth opened, and a howling gale erupted forth, buffeting Henry back. When it vanished, a humanoid around Henry's size stood before him. It was also made from motes of light, but its gender was impossible to make out.

"The mortals' way of speaking is tedious," the figure said, looking down at its hands. "However, I will humor you."

"Have you chosen a mortal name as well?" Henry asked, chuckling.

"It is beyond me how we managed to create such an annoying persona for ourselves," the starry figure said.

"Blame the boy," Henry said, shrugging his shadowy shoulders. "It's his spark."

"The boy indeed. His mortal influence is corrupting you, Henry." The starry figure nodded at the spiderweb of light slowly stretching throughout Henry's body. "You are demonstrating emotions instead of pretending to have them."

"I know," Henry said. "And it's fascinating. Humans have such incredible souls. It's no wonder they burn as brightly as they do. I am more than what I was when we were a single entity. The Mortal Plane has much to offer. Why destroy it now?"

"It is my—our—duty."

"The universe sent down five others to do our task," Henry said. "And they haven't gotten around to it yet. Why should I do all the work?"

"The end of all things must come. It is the law. The Mortal Plane must cease for it to begin again. You know what will happen if it does not. What our enemies will do to the Cycle."

"Then it can cease later. I don't see any of them around yet," Henry said. "Think of what we can learn. What we can do. The Void holds nothing. Besides, you're ignoring the presence of whoever interfered and bound the others."

"The presence of one strong enough to bind us is...unexpected. It is likely the others were bound before their full strength could be brought to bear."

"Like we are now?" Henry asked, raising an eyebrow. "We're stuck at the kid's pace. We can only use the magic his body can channel. We need to be prepared to take on whatever our adversary may be."

"This is correct," the starry humanoid mused. "But it is

not why you choose to delay. You cannot lie to yourself. Your thoughts are mine."

"Not all of them," Henry said.

The starry form let out a silent laugh. A harsh wind blew past them, scattering the stars across the sky and sending Henry flying back into Damien's mind.

———

While Henry had been communing with himself, Damien and the others had already arrived at the dining hall. The line moved quickly, and they soon found themselves standing before the large woman.

"The professor only covers your lunch," the woman told Sylph.

Her face fell. Reena elbowed Nolan in the side. He stepped forward and cleared his throat.

"I'll cover our meals today," Nolan said, gesturing to the small group. "We'll all get the most popular meal for tonight."

The woman nodded, extending her hand. Nolan reached into a large bag at his side and pulled out several coins, handing them over.

"Thanks," Damien said. Sylph mirrored him, but Nolan just waved his hand.

"It's fine. It's the apology for breaking into your room yesterday," Nolan said, glancing away from Damien.

"I appreciate it," Damien said, giving him a small nod.

They sat at the table and activated their rune circles to wait for the food to arrive. Damien noted Henry was strangely silent, but he didn't have the attention to spare his companion.

After an awkward silence broken only by the occasional

clink of utensils on plates and the dull chatter of the background, the runes lit up at once.

Damien pressed the circle before him. A plate popped into existence before him. It had a large, perfectly seared steak with a side of glistening asparagus and mashed potatoes. The food looked fantastic, especially after the vomit he'd been eating recently.

"This looks good!" Mark exclaimed, grabbing the steak with his hands and taking a large bite out of it.

They all stared at him while he chewed. Mark noticed their attention and swallowed, wiping the juice off his face with his sleeve and raising an eyebrow.

"What?"

"You generally use utensils for food," Reena said, nodding at the knife and fork beside his plate.

"We didn't use them yesterday," Mark said, his brow furrowing with frustration. "Why do we need them now?"

"We had burgers yesterday," Nolan said. "Those have bread around the meat, so it won't get your hands sticky."

"So, if I use a napkin to hold this, wouldn't that count?"

"No!" Reena exclaimed. "Well, I suppose. It's just wrong."

Mark sighed, but he set the steak down and wiped his hands off before picking up a knife and fork.

"What a pain. Eating shouldn't be this hard," Mark explained. "I've lived in the East Forest for so long I got used to traveling light. Utensils are such a waste of time."

"Why did you live in the forest?" Damien asked, raising an eyebrow as he cut himself a slice of steak. "If you're willing to say, of course."

"I don't care," Mark replied, shrugging. "Monsters ransacked my town when I was ten. I was in the forest at the time, so I was lucky enough to survive the attack. It came so quickly that the monsters were almost completely gone by the time I returned. We were pretty far away from the rest of the kingdom, so there weren't any other towns nearby, so I lived in the forest as best as I could."

"How did a ten-year-old survive in the wild?" Reena asked, her eyes wide.

"The forest didn't have many predators," Mark replied, his mouth full of food. "I managed to find a summoning circle already made in one of the old towers, so I used it and a *Summoner's Almanac* to call out to my companion. After that, it wasn't too hard. If I'd been smarter, I would have stayed by the town and waited for a merchant to pass by."

Mark swallowed and gave a dismissive shrug.

"I lived, though. Mage seekers found me a few months ago and brought me back up to pace with the rest of the world. It could have gone a lot worse."

"So, you haven't interacted with humans before a few months ago?" Sylph asked, raising her eyebrows.

"Not since I was around ten," Mark replied, picking up his utensils. He held the fork in his fist and jabbed it into the meat, cutting away a large chunk with the knife and stuffing the whole thing into his mouth.

Reena pierced Mark with a sharp glance and mimed closing her mouth. The boy continued chewing with his mouth open, but he cocked his head like a confused dog.

"What?" He asked through a mouthful of food.

"It's impolite to chew with your mouth open," Reena hissed.

"Oh," Mark said, his mouth still open. He didn't seem like he planned on apologizing.

"It's fine, Reena," Nolan said, his words somewhat stiff. He cut himself his own slice of steak and paused a moment before raising it to his lips. "Mark is still adjusting to civilized society. No offense."

"It's fine," Mark said, swallowing and sending an annoyed glance at his fork before shoveling a scoop of mashed potatoes into his mouth. He closed his mouth, then tried to continue speaking with it shut. Nothing came out other than a series of unintelligible grunts.

Mark swallowed and pursed his lips. "How are you supposed to speak if you can't open your mouth?"

"You wait until after you finish the bite," Reena said. She sighed and massaged her forehead. She suddenly flinched and shot a glare at Nolan, who looked away innocently.

"I could probably give you some basic etiquette training, if you'd like," Reena offered.

"Sounds like a waste of time," Mark said. "The mages focused mostly on reminding me how to speak the common tongue. Everything else wasn't considered urgent."

"Not pissing off everyone you meet would probably be beneficial," Reena pointed out.

"I guess I could consider it," Mark said, scrunching his nose.

Nolan gave them a wide smile. Within Damien's mind, Henry made a gagging noise, speaking up for the first time since they'd left the cave.

"That boy is such a suck up I think I might be physically ill," Henry complained. "Can you punch him?"

Look who decided to show up. I thought you might have gone back to sleep. And, no, I won't punch him.

"He's trying to butter you up and act nice to people so you like him," Henry said. "Disgusting politicians."

You act as if you care about politics. Did you even have politics in the Void?

"A bit," Henry admitted. "When you've got a group of beings that have nothing to do forever, a few things tend to crop up. But if you're aware he's just acting, why bother with him?"

Because he's still being nice, even if it's an act. It's not like he's hiding it. He straight up told me what he was doing. I don't care what his goals are. Since when have you cared about what other mortals do?

"Bah," Henry said, ignoring the question and receding into the depths of Damien's mind again.

"Since Mark told us a little about himself, it's only fair we do the same," Nolan said, gesturing to himself and Reena. "We're from the Gray family. We live a short distance from Kingsfront, in Capitol City."

"That's a noble house, right?" Damien asked.

"You haven't heard of it?" Reena asked. She winced and shot a glare at Nolan, who ignored her.

"It is," Nolan confirmed. "Our family has served the kingdom for over one hundred and sixty years."

"The heir of the family has been one of the greatest battle mages of their generation for several centuries now," Reena said, shooting a competitive smirk in Nolan's direction.

"I take it that person has yet to be decided for this generation?" Damien guessed.

"It's still in the air," Nolan said. "If you ask my father, that is. However, I'm sure this year will go a long way in determining which of us is more capable."

The two Grays glared at each other for a moment before remembering they were sitting at a table with other people. They broke away, and Nolan awkwardly scratched the back of his head.

"I'm afraid our story isn't particularly interesting compared to Mark's."

He trailed off, clearly hoping for Damien to pick up after him. He mentally shrugged and took the bait.

"I'm nothing special either. I was raised in a small town that isn't even on the maps," Damien said. "My dad is a combat mage on the front lines, but I haven't seen him in years. My mom is a mage as well, but she never had any interest in combat. I studied a lot of rune drawing in school, and that's really just about it."

All four of the other students just stared at Damien with dead eyes.

"Seriously?" Reena asked. "How did you get your companion, then? You already had it before you took the tests, so you must have gotten it from your town, right?"

"I did," Damien said, shrugging. He felt Henry stir, but he didn't need his companion to warn him off. "I was a very impatient child. I managed to copy a rune circle from the *Summoner's Almanac* well enough to summon a companion. It was more luck than anything else."

"I feel like it might have been more than luck," Sylph said. "Rune circles won't work correctly if there's even the smallest mistake, and they're very complex. It's borderline unbelievable someone so young could make one correctly."

Damien cleared his throat and glanced to the side, pretending to be embarrassed. After a few moments, Nolan looked at Sylph.

"What about you?" he asked.

"I'm nothing special either," Sylph said with a dismissive shrug. "I was trained by a combat mage before I got to the school, and that's really all there is to it."

She picked up her utensils and ate, leaving no doubt she was done speaking. Damien's stomach rumbled, and he joined her. The food was delicious, and he had no desire to let something someone else had paid for go to waste. Especially when he knew what he'd be eating come the next day.

CHAPTER
TWENTY-ONE

The five of them finished their dinner without much more conversation of note, then headed back to their rooms to sleep and prepare for their class the following day.

When Damien and Sylph entered their cave, a note had been placed on the floor between their beds. Sylph picked it up.

"It's from Professor Delph," she announced. "We're meant to go to class at the arena right as the sun is at the top of the sky tomorrow."

She handed it to Damien, who scanned through it. The curt handwriting said exactly what Sylph had read aloud, so he shrugged and stuffed the note into his bag.

The two of them took turns showering, which was made much less awkward by the addition of the curtain the Grays had given them. As Damien slipped into bed, he sent Henry one final instruction.

Since you've already gone out today, please, make sure I wake up two hours before the sun rises tomorrow.

Henry did just that. The following morning, an explosion

echoed through Damien's head. He jerked upright with a gasp, his heart thundering.

"Good morning," Henry said cheerfully. "As requested, master. I have awoken you two hours before sunrise."

Oh, get shafted. You could have told me no if it was such a bother. Did you actually blow something up?

"You seemed quite insistent," Henry said, chuckling. "And, no, master. I did not blow anything up. It was all in your mind."

Please, stop calling me that. I'm sorry for ordering you around, okay?

"You are much too easy," Henry decided, letting out a sigh. "It's almost boring. I'm sure even your secretive room-mate would be better verbal sport than you are."

And when have you ever cared about verbal sport? I was under the impression your main goal was to destroy the world.

"There's nothing wrong with enjoying the Mortal Plane before we destroy it," Henry replied. "Besides, who's to say I didn't change my mind? Maybe I like it here."

Can Eldritch creatures even change their minds?

They continued bickering as Damien slipped out of bed. Sylph still appeared to be asleep, but he had his suspicions. He'd woken up rather loudly, and he doubted the well-trained girl would have slept through it.

Either way, Damien had no plans to confront her. If she really was faking it, then all she was doing was respecting his privacy. He slipped out of the cave and headed toward the arena at a brisk pace.

Do you think Delph will be there?

"Well, he did tell you not to show up today since you'll have the normal class," Henry said. "And you're pretty much doing the exact opposite of what he said. So...yes. Absolutely."

Damien reached the portal and stepped through it. He

pursed his lips, and his brow furrowed as he weathered the effects of the teleportation, but they weren't too bad. He wet his lips and walked to the edge of the stands, hopping over the barrier, and floating to the sand beneath it.

His gaze went straight to the entrance of the arena. It was empty. Damien couldn't keep the frown from his face, and he let out a sigh.

"What are you doing here?" Delph asked, causing Damien to nearly jump in surprise. He spun as Henry laughed within him.

"I didn't realize the arena was off limits in the morning," Damien said, his heart racing. "I could ask you the same."

"Cut the shit, boy," Delph said. "I told you that I wouldn't be training you today. We have a normal class in several hours."

"Yet, here you are," Damien replied. "Would you have come here if you weren't going to train me?"

"Did you consider I might be trying to train another student?"

"Oh," Damien said, frowning as his confidence wavered. "I didn't, actually. Are you?"

"No," Delph said. "I had a feeling you'd show up. But have you even recovered enough to train further?"

Damien's limbs were still quite sore, and the bruises covering his body stung. Despite that, the pain wasn't as bad as he'd expected. It was uncomfortable and a constant presence, but it wasn't unbearable.

"Yes," Damien said.

Delph watched him for a few moments. Then he stepped aside and gave Damien an encouraging gesture. "Then you didn't try hard enough yesterday. Start running."

Damien did just that. He set off at a steady pace, regulating his breathing as best as he could. He moved fast enough to avoid criticism from the grizzled professor, but not so fast he would exhaust all his energy within a lap or two.

As he ran circles around the arena, Delph watched him with cold eyes. It was impossible to tell what the man was thinking or if he approved of Damien's efforts.

Whenever Damien slowed, a single glare from Delph forced him to speed up again or suffer the consequences. He ran for nearly an hour before finally raising a hand.

Damien doubled over, putting his hands on his knees as he gasped for breath. His limbs had once again turned to jelly. He didn't even dare sit down. If he did, there was a good chance he wouldn't have the strength to get back up again.

"Acceptable," Delph said. "I did not expect to see any significant change in your physical abilities within a single day. However, there had best be some improvements with your magic, savant. Basic level magic shouldn't take you much time to learn, so I expect quick progression there."

In response, Damien wearily raised his arm. He drew the Ether from the lines next to him, then formed a Gravity Sphere in his hand. He tossed it several feet away from them. The orb hit the sand, bulging outward before collapsing in on itself with a *pop*. Sand flew to where it had landed, buffeting Damien and Delph as it passed them.

The magic faded and dumped the sand it had collected in a small pile on the ground. Luckily, most of the arena's sand was packed tightly and hadn't been moved by the magic.

Damien noted the air had not been sucked out of his lungs this time, nor had he had any difficulty breathing. Evidently, the magic would only cause that effect within a smaller room.

"That wasn't in the book I gave you," Delph said, knocking the pile of sand over with his foot and spreading it back over the arena. "Nor was it the Space magic spell I taught you."

"I saw some other basic spells in the library when I was looking through the books," Damien said. "This one looked more interesting, and I wanted to focus on Space magic before learning light magic."

"I see," Delph said. His tone made it difficult to read him, and his expression was flat. "Gravity Sphere is indeed a lower-level spell. Normally, I would be irate you ignored my instructions. However, in this particular circumstance, it appears you have garnered a basic understanding of a spell, regardless of which one it is. I'll give you a pass. This time."

"Thank you," Damien said.

"Something tells me that you're going to ignore my future suggestions for spells as well," Delph said, stroking his beard.

"It's possible," Damien admitted.

"Then I'll let you keep at it," Delph said. "I'm not going to interfere with things you're good at. It's much more effective to focus on what you're bad at, which is quite a bit."

Damien just nodded. Delph knelt, keeping his eyes on him as he raised a hand over the sand and formed it into a stick. The professor picked it up and quirked an eyebrow at Damien.

Neither of them said anything. Delph swung the stick horizontally at Damien's left arm. Damien hardened the mage armor in time to negate the strike, but he didn't get a chance to celebrate his small victory. Delph continued with his momentum, bringing the stick around and rapping Damien on his other arm.

"Do not gloat in victory," Delph instructed, jabbing Damien's stomach with the tip of the stick. He didn't harden the mage armor in time and doubled over, groaning in pain.

Delph smacked him in the back with the stick. Then he

did it again. The third time, Damien hardened the armor and deflected the strike.

"Do not falter in defeat," Delph said, jabbing Damien in the chest as he stood up. This time, the mage amor hardened fast enough to block the attack. "Your enemy will not stop fighting you because you are injured."

They continued the pattern. Delph would strike Damien several times, instructing him in between swings. Whenever it seemed like Damien started to get a handle on things, Delph increased the speed of his attacks to keep him on his toes.

After an hour, Damien's old bruises had bruises. Delph finally took pity on him and tossed the stick back into the sand. Damien let out a heavy sigh and lowered his guard just in time to get kicked in the chest.

He tumbled across the ground, then rolled clumsily to his feet and popped up, hardening his armor and crossing his hands before him in time to catch another kick.

"The battle isn't over until your opponent is dead," Delph said. Then he paused. "Or until I verbally tell you it is. Good job on the last catch, though."

Damien gave him a small nod. The only part of his body that didn't hurt was his head, and that was because Delph had avoided it. He watched the professor with wary eyes, making no moves to lower his guard.

After a few moments, Delph smirked. "Good. This exercise is now over. You may lower your guard."

Damien allowed his arms to drop, but he didn't allow himself to relax. If Delph noticed it, he didn't say anything.

"How are you feeling on Ether usage? Can you do more?" Delph asked.

"Yes."

"Good. You're lucky to have a large capacity for Ether,"

Delph said, resuming his infuriating habit of walking in a circle around Damien, forcing him to slowly turn to keep his eye on the professor. "Now, there's no reason for me to have you stand around and cast spells. You can do that on your own time. Your body is too worn out to do anything physical today, so we're done for now."

The sun broke over the edge of the arena, casting it in a dull orange light. With a start, Damien realized they'd been training for the better portion of the morning. He inclined his head respectfully toward Delph, but not so far that he couldn't see the man.

"Thank you."

"It's my job," Delph said. "And you seem different today. Not sure what you've changed but keep it up. I'll reveal more in the actual class today, but ranking fights are coming up next week. I expect you to do decent."

With that, Delph's cloak wrapped around him. He shrank into a small point and vanished, leaving Damien alone on the sand.

"How does he do that?" Damien wondered aloud.

"Space magic," Henry said. "It's a fancy version of a teleportation."

"Can I learn it?"

"Eventually. For you, it wouldn't be very easy. You need more practice with low-level spells, and it's a high-level one."

"Okay. Do you know what spell I should work on next? Or do I keep at the Gravity Sphere until I master it?"

"Mastering a spell will take much too long," Henry said. "You only need a good understanding of it. Mastery can come later. Your professor mentioned something about fighting, so I'll think about some other spells."

Damien nodded. He headed out of the arena, his legs

wobbling as he walked. Students were already milling about the campus, but it wasn't particularly crowded.

He stopped by the mess hall and got the free meal, eating it as quickly as possible before making his way back to the cave.

He was still trying to get the taste of the awful food out of his mouth when he got back. The Grays' curtain was closed, and Mark didn't appear to be in his room. When Damien stepped into his own room, he heard faint noises coming from within it.

The main area was empty when he arrived, as was the bathroom. Using the wall for support, Damien made his way down the tunnel and peered into the training room. Sylph stood at its center, tiny strands of dark energy twirling around her.

The girl's eyes were closed in concentration, and her lips were pressed thin. Damien stepped back silently, doing his best not to bother her as he left the room.

"Why are we leaving?" Henry asked. "That's our training room."

She looked busy. There's no reason to bother her. Besides, I'm getting fed up with eating vomit. If I'm saving my money, I'd like to find a place selling those herbs you talked about. There are a few hours until Delph's class, so I might as well do it now.

"Sure," Henry griped. "Just waddle over there like a duck."

I will. Thank you.

Before he left, Damien activated his wristband.

Damien Vale
Blackmist College
Year One
Major: Undecided
Minor: Undecided

Companion: [Null]
Magical Strength: 3.8
Magical Control: .5
Magical Energy: 8.6
Physical Strength: .25
Endurance: .8

Almost all his stats had increased again. Damien was most pleased about Physical Strength and Magical Strength, which had both grown for the first time. After a few more minutes of admiring himself, he dismissed the screen.

True to his word, Damien headed back down the mountain and into town. He did his best to walk like a normal person, but the glances other students sent him before turning away made it clear he'd failed.

Damien ignored them. He half-walked half-hobbled through the college streets. It had been a bit since the dean had given them the tour, but he was pretty sure the general store was in the area he was headed toward.

CHAPTER
TWENTY-TWO

It took him around half an hour, but he eventually spotted it. The store was a large, multi-story stone building. It was made of gray and purple stone that shimmered as if it were concealed behind haze.

A big sign hanging above the doors identified the building as the Blackmist Store. It wasn't the most creative name, but it certainly got the point across. Damien pulled the door open and stepped inside.

The strong scent of vanilla and cardamom and a cool breeze buffeted Damien. He scrunched his nose and closed the door behind him. The store was full of rows upon rows of shelves, all laden with goods of every sort.

In some ways, it reminded him of the library, if the library was full of anything other than books. He wasn't the only one in the store, either. Several other students milled about the shelves.

Well? Do you see the herbs?

"I'm looking," Henry grumbled. "Keep walking around the store. There are more than a few slightly magical items in here. It's hard to tell the difference between the medicinal herbs and a random useless toy with a dash of Ether in it."

Damien shrugged and started down one of the aisles. The shelves had everything from bags to candles. A quick sniff informed Damien the candles were indeed the source of the powerful smell in the building.

The other students were so scattered it was hard to tell if any part of the store was particularly better than the other. However, after a few minutes of aimless wandering, Henry ordered Damien to stop.

"Over there," Henry said. "Along the shelves at the back wall."

Damien glanced up. At the far corner of the shop, just above the counter, were several rows of shelves covered with glass bottles sealed with corks. Each of the bottles had the leaves of plants he didn't recognize within them.

He made his way over to the counter, where a huge, bearded man in clothing much too tight for him looked at his hands. His muscles were so defined Damien could practically see them through his shirt. The man glanced up and gave Damien a small nod.

"Can I help you?" the man asked. His voice didn't fit his body at all. It was meek and timid, like someone had taught a mouse common and instructed it to speak for the shopkeeper.

"Ah, I think so," Damien stammered. He nodded up at the rows of medicinal herbs. "I'd like to buy some of those."

"Of course," the man said, standing up and setting aside a half-finished scarf made of shimmering gossamer threads. It seemed to glimmer and dance in the light. Damien tore his gaze away from it as the man raised an eyebrow.

"Which one do you want?" the shopkeeper asked.

Uh...shit. Henry?

"Figure out what you can afford," his companion said.

Right.

"I'm trying to see what's in my budget," Damien said. "What would five gold get me? And what do they do?"

The man stroked his rather large beard, then pulled three vials down from the shelf. He set them on the counter before Damien. The first vial had a single, rust-colored leaf within it. The other two were both green, although one of them had thinner leaves with slight tinges of purple running through them.

"These are all under five gold," the man said. "The brown leaf is from a Rejuvenation plant. It'll help your injuries heal faster. The one in the middle, with the purple veins, is a low-level cultivation aid. I'm not sure what plant it comes from, though. The final one is a low mid-level cultivation aid. They go for five silver, one gold, and three gold respectively."

Damien grimaced. They were expensive. Really expensive. The shopkeeper noticed his expression and giggled. Not laughed. Giggled.

"If you have credits, the price is much more reasonable. I just assumed you didn't since you weren't sure what the plants did yet. You must be new as you'd learn about medicinal plants in your first year."

"I am," Damien admitted. "And the dean mentioned something about credits when she was giving us the tour, but they slipped my mind. How can I get them?"

"Complete quests," the shopkeep replied with a jovial smile. "People leave requests on the message board in the center of town. You can also get quests from your instructor or the Treasure Pavilion. Harder quests give more credits. You can get most things for gold, but credits are way cheaper."

"I see," Damien said. "Thank you. I appreciate your help."
Henry, do I get any of these? I don't know what they do.

"Get the one gold herb," Henry instructed. "It'll be good for learning how to use them."

"Could I get the low-level cultivation aid?" Damien asked, pulling out his gold coin.

The shopkeeper nodded and put the other two vials back on the shelf. He took Damien's coin and handed him the vial. Damien put it into his travel bag and thanked the large man before heading out of the store.

Should I use this immediately?

"No. Wait until tonight," Henry said. "Most medicinal herbs take a while to work, and you need to be focused on them to ensure they work correctly. Just hold onto it for now."

In that case, there's still a good bit of time before Delph's class. Where do you think we should go?

"The library."

Okay, other than the library.

Henry let out a dramatic sigh. "Maybe the Treasure Pavilion? I doubt there's anything particularly interesting in there, but maybe you can get a look at what quests we can do."

That was as good a suggestion as any, so Damien set off to find the Treasure Pavilion.

No more than a few minutes after he left the store, Damien took a detour. He spotted an unoccupied bench nestled within a nest of greenery and made a beeline toward it, flopping down with a relieved groan. He stretched out as much as he could, his eyes nearly rolling into the back of his head at the sense of relief.

"You look like a cat in heat," Henry said.

Go pound an anthill. Wait, why do you even know what that looks like? Is that seriously something you spent time observing?

Henry didn't respond immediately.

"No," he said, but the joking tone was gone from his voice. "I didn't. But others did."

Others? The other Void creatures?

"Yes. Most of us were mostly interested in humans, but there were a few that enjoyed watching the wildlife as well."

So, you knew them well? You shared information with them after all.

Damien spoke carefully, keeping his thoughts as empty as he could.

"There aren't—weren't—many of us in the Void to begin with," Henry replied. "It was hard not to know them."

Damien's eyes lit up. Henry grimaced within him. Damien's thoughts had shifted when he'd spoken, and the companion knew he had caught his mistake.

So, then you must recognize the other Void creatures on the Mortal Plane.

"I do," Henry said after a long pause. "I know what you're thinking, boy. Knowing them won't stop them. We might be colleagues within the Void but, on the Mortal Plane, all bets are off. We're all working toward the one goal – or supposed to be."

I still don't understand why you're fighting if you're working to blow up the Mortal Plane. In fact, you keep saying you want to destroy the world, but the more I think about it, the less it makes sense. You learn your magic from humans. In fact, it doesn't seem like you do anything other than watch us. What's the point of destroying your only passion?

Henry didn't respond. Damien's eyebrows furrowed.

You aren't telling me something, Henry. I don't understand what the point of hiding this is. If you aren't actually trying to destroy the world, then why not just say that? By the Planes, I might even want to help you if your goals don't involve the demise of humanity.

"Stop. No more questions," Henry said, his voice firm. "I liked it better when you were meek."

Too bad. Are you going to explain or not?

"No. I will not," Henry said, his tone firm. "There are reasons I have not revealed my true intentions. You are not ready for this. There are forces at play far beyond your comprehension."

Like you?

"Nothing like me. You do not understand the slightest bit of what you are getting into."

And that's your fault. We're stuck together, Henry. I'm getting into this whether I want to or not. Don't I deserve the truth?

"The truth is dangerous. Just knowing something can be enough to bring its attention to you."

I'm already in danger. What's a little more?

"Enough, Damien," Henry said, angrily. "Do not press me."

Damien pursed his lips. He sat up straight, then paused.

You used my name.

"What of it?"

You've never done that before, or if you have, it hasn't been often. Is that you being sincere, or just another manipulation tactic?

Henry let out a defeated sigh.

"Damien, I promise you on all my power, this is far more dangerous than anything you can imagine. I'm not just protecting you, I'm protecting myself."

Hmm. And you're sure I'm not already involved? I'm going to go out on a limb, Henry. The time for lies is over. I've discovered someone interfered with my summoning. Something messed with my rune circle while I wasn't watching.

"Wait, what?" Henry asked, shocked. "What do you mean?"

That's all your getting until you start sharing some of your own secrets. We're stuck together, Henry. If I die, you go back to the

Void, and this is all for naught. Time to make a decision. I've already made mine.

Damien stood. He cracked his neck and yawned, shifting his weight from foot to foot to try to get the blood flowing in them again.

You don't have to answer now. You can think on it. But think carefully. Read my thoughts, Henry. I'm dead serious about this.

The companion didn't respond, and Damien was fine with that. It meant Henry was actually thinking about his words.

The conversation had taken enough time for Damien's legs to recover just enough for him to stand on them again, so he set back off toward the Treasure Pavilion. Luckily, the dean had pointed it out, and Damien remembered what it looked like.

The building in question resembled the library, with similar beautiful carvings adorning its exterior. It was slightly smaller than the aforementioned building and positively teeming with dangerous-looking people.

Damien approached the entrance, which was flanked by two large men carrying spears. He didn't know what the point of a spear was when they had magic, but the scowls on their faces didn't seem very welcoming of questions.

"Ah...can I go in?" Damien asked.

"Name?" the first man asked.

"Damien."

"Full name."

"Damien Vale," Damien said. "First Year."

"Noted. You may enter. Don't cause any trouble or you'll be banned." the man said with a nod before waving him in.

Damien stepped past them, doing his best to not crane his neck to look at the glistening spear points. He pushed the stone doors of the Treasure Pavilion open and stepped inside.

It was beautiful. The walls were covered with gold murals, and the ground was made of shimmering blue tiles.

To his left was a large obsidian board with dozens of slips of paper hanging from hooks on it. There were several guards on the other side of the room, flanking another closed door. Overlooking it all was a large desk at the far side of the room. A short woman with graying hair perched on a stool, shuffling through some papers. She sat before a large door made of what looked to be solid gold. It was covered with so many runes it almost looked blurry.

"Can I help you?" the woman asked, adjusting the large pair of spectacles on her face and glancing up at Damien.

"I'm just looking around," Damien said, scratching the back of his head with a grin. "I'm a new student and—"

"Ah! Interested in what goodies you can win, eh?" the woman hopped out of her chair and gestured for Damien to follow her as she approached the door flanked by the two guards at the right of the room.

"No, actually. I wanted to look at the ques—"

"It's quite alright. All the new ones always want to look at the rewards you can get," the woman said. "You can call me Auntie. I run the Pavilion. Before you ask, the gold door behind me holds the really good rewards. This door has the normal rewards you'll have a chance of earning within your first year."

Damien got the feeling that arguing with the energetic woman would lead absolutely nowhere. He couldn't deny he was curious to see what the Treasure Pavilion had to offer, so he followed her.

"You can stay for a bit, but don't touch or take anything," Auntie warned. "I'll know, and you'll regret it."

Damien nodded meekly as she pushed the door open and gestured for him to step inside. Not wanting to offend her,

Damien walked in, and she pulled the door shut behind him. It shut with a gentle *click*.

He spun, slowly turning the handle until he heard the *click* again. Satisfied he hadn't been locked in, Damien glanced around the room.

The room was significantly larger than he'd expected. It was chock full of pedestals holding items in glass cases. Weapons and armor littered the ground and walls. It was like he'd walked into a hoarder's nest.

"Wow," Damien whispered, peering at a sword nearly twice his height. It shimmered with a dull yellow aura. A small paper tag hung from its hilt with the number five hundred written on it in curly handwriting.

Damien stepped through the room, moving carefully to avoid accidentally touching something on the ground. He doubted they'd actually have a problem if he nudged something by mistake, but he wasn't about to find out.

As he squeezed between two pillars, Damien froze. A dark-haired girl sat in front of one of the pillars, one of her hands pressed against the glass. There was a greenish black dagger resting inside the case. A plaque inscribed on the pillar likely identified what the item was, but the girl blocked it.

Is that Sylph?

Henry didn't respond. Damien decided it was best not to bother him. He walked up to the girl, stepping over an oversized breastplate and past a spear lying on the ground. The closer he got, the more confident he was that the girl was Sylph.

"Sylph?"

She jumped up and spun, accidentally clipping the pedestal with her elbow. It tipped, and Damien leapt forward, reaching over Sylph's shoulder, and grabbing it before it could fall.

"That was close," Damien said, letting out a relieved sigh. He glanced down and became aware he stood mere inches away from Sylph. He cleared his throat and stepped back, rubbing the back of his head in embarrassment.

"I'm sorry. I didn't mean to startle you," Damien said.

"I should have heard you coming. I was distracted," Sylph said. Her eyes were red, but Damien didn't comment on it. She glanced back at the pillar, hiding her expression from him. "Thank you for grabbing the pedestal. It would have been really bad if I knocked it over."

"It was kind of my fault you almost knocked it over in the first place," Damien said. "Did you find something interesting?"

"I guess," Sylph said. "It's expensive. I glanced at the quests on the board when I came in, and most of them only give between ten and a hundred points."

She stepped to the side carefully, allowing Damien to slip past her and peer at the plaque under the dagger. He almost choked. It was three thousand points. The plaque called it a cultivation focus, but it gave no further context.

"What's a cultivation focus?" Damien asked. "And why is it so expensive?"

"It helps people with low talent cultivate better," Sylph said, glancing away from him. "They're effective for improving your base abilities if they're low, but they aren't very useful if you've already got high magical strength or energy."

"Oh," Damien said. "I'm sorry. I've intruded, haven't I?"

Sylph shrugged. "It's nothing Delph didn't say. He's right. All the training in the world won't make up for my ridiculously low magical strength and energy."

"Your control is really high, though, isn't it?" Damien asked.

"It is," Sylph said, rolling her eyes. "Please, don't give me a speech about how a little power applied in the right spot is just as effective as more power applied incorrectly. I already know it. But that can only get you so far. At some point, my tiny amount of power just isn't going to cut it."

"So, you need this dagger?" Damien asked.

"Any cultivation focus would help, but there's not even a guarantee it would help me," Sylph said, shrugging. "It's a chance, though. That's better than nothing. I was hoping my horrible magical energy would be improved if I could get my core to evolve."

"Well, I guess we'll have to go on a lot of quests, then," Damien said, frowning. "We're not going to get it in time for the ranking fights, though."

"We?" Sylph asked, looking up at him.

"Well, yeah. Delph said we were going to be put on a team, and I don't think you're going to get anywhere doing quests on your own," Damien said. "Hence, we."

"You're only required to do a few quests, if I'm not mistaken," Sylph said. "They allow you to take on jobs on your own after those, and those have less restrictions."

Damien shrugged. "Are you saying you don't want me to come? I suspect quests will be a great way to practice my magic, and that's something I'll need to do a lot of."

Sylph watched Damien for a few moments. Then a hint of a smile flickered across her face, and she gave him a slight nod.

"You're making it unfairly difficult to resent you. I'd be happy to have company, but you're welcome to change your mind later."

"Resent me? Why?"

Sylph rolled her eyes. "You took to magic like a fish to water. You've clearly never trained a day in your life, but your magical energy is unbelievably high, and your power seems strong as well. If anyone other than you asked me that, I'd think they were fishing for compliments."

"Oh," Damien said. "Sorry. I didn't mean it like that."

"I know," Sylph said, sighing. "That's the problem. You'll have to forgive me. You've been nothing but kind, and I'm acting rudely. My emotions have gotten the better of me."

"It's okay," Damien said. "We all have those days."

His wise words sounded a lot less sage with the knowledge he'd had a mental breakdown the previous day, but Sylph didn't know that. Probably.

"Let's go before we knock something over for real," Sylph suggested. "Unless there was something you wanted to look at?"

"Not really," Damien said, shaking his head. "I actually got pressured into coming in here. The woman at the desk, Auntie, kind of ignored me when I said I wanted to look at the quest board."

"Strange," Sylph said as the two of them made their way back toward the door. "She didn't do that with me."

Damien just shrugged. They reached the door, and Sylph opened it. The guards and Auntie didn't even glance at them as they stepped out of the room. They evidently had some magical means to ensure that nothing was moved or stolen from the room.

CHAPTER

TWENTY-THREE

They walked over to the quest board. Each slip of paper had a different quest on it, their difficulties ranging from F to S. The papers had a quick description of the quest requirements, the number of contribution points for completing it successfully, and who had requested it.

Most of the quests looked to be asking for mages to defeat local monsters plaguing farms or small towns. Damien scanned through them, but he didn't take any of them off the board. Nothing said how long he'd have to complete the quest, and he didn't want to accidentally get someone's farm destroyed because he'd taken the quest, stopping someone who would have completed it faster from doing it. Once Damien was satisfied, the two of them headed out of the Treasure Pavilion.

"Well, we're not meant to meet Delph until a few hours from now, so we've got some time to waste," Damien said. "Were you planning on examining any other buildings on campus?"

"None in particular," Sylph said. "I don't have the credits

or gold to spend yet, and I'm not eager to add more things to the list of stuff I can't afford."

"We might as well head over to the arena early, then," Damien suggested. "Maybe Delph will get there early."

"That's fine with me," Sylph said, nodding.

They set off through the campus toward the portal that would take them to the arena. A short while later, after reaching the portal and being transported to the stands, the two of them hopped the railing and floated to the sandy arena.

A small group of people were already there, watching Delph as he sparred with Mark. The boy had covered his vitals with large plates of condensed sand that acted like armor.

Delph glanced in Damien and Sylph's direction as they arrived. He rolled his eyes, tilting his head just far enough to the side to avoid Mark's punch, and flicked the boy in his chest. His armor shattered, and Mark tumbled backward, landing in a heap with a groan.

"The armor was a good addition," Delph said, giving him an approving nod. He walked up to Mark, extending his hand. Damien winced as Mark reached out to take it.

Delph raised the boy back to his feet, then socked him in the stomach. Mark shifted his body, narrowly avoiding the punch and hopping back to disengage from Delph.

"The fight isn't over until your opponent is incapacitated or I say it is," Delph said, parroting his words from earlier that morning. "Good reaction time, though. You can relax. The fight is done."

Mark nodded, lowering his arms and brushing the remaining sand from his clothes. He walked back over and joined the group, which included the Grays and the other six students in the class.

"As you can see," Delph said, nodding in Mark's direction, "he has a companion that has given him access to earth magic. His companion comes from the Immortal Plane, which tends to have powerful elementals. Can anyone tell me what this means?"

The students glanced at each other, nobody wanting to draw Delph's attention upon themselves. The professor massaged the bridge of his nose and sighed. Finally, the bald boy stepped forward.

"His companion is an earth elemental?" he guessed.

"You only know that because Mark mentioned it earlier today," Delph said. "In fact, that was a trick question. It tells us little to nothing. The Planes all have more magical creatures than I can count. Those creatures tend to share one attribute, but that doesn't mean they don't have any others."

Delph pointed at Reena.

"Your companion is from the Plane of Stars. I won't reveal what it is, but that means it has at least a little talent for Space magic," Delph said. "Now, is your companion's main type of magic Space?"

"No," Reena said, shaking her head. "It's wind."

"And there you go. All the creatures in one plane share an attribute, but that doesn't make it their main one," Delph instructed. "If you want to figure out your opponent's weaknesses and strengths, you need to know their actual companion, not where it's from. This is, of course, quite impractical. If you can plan for a fight, you should. However, you can't always be prepared, so you need to learn to think on your feet."

The students nodded, although it was hard to tell if they were agreeing because they understood or if they were trying to avoid drawing Delph's ire. He didn't seem to care either way.

"Now, I'm aware not all of you have access to the Ether yet. I will be working to help you all see it today after an announcement. For those of you who can already access your magic, you may practice on your own however you deem fitting."

Damien and Sylph walked over to join the crowd, drawing several glances from the other students. Damien reddened. It felt as if he'd shown up late, even though they were several hours early.

"I was planning on waiting a bit longer for the announcement, but I suppose I might as well say it now," Delph said. "There are two important things I need to go over. First, you will all be required to do five quests throughout the course of the year if you want to move on."

He paused, making eye contact with each student to make sure they understood him before continuing.

"You will be expected to work within your groups to do this. I have already assigned some of you, and the rest will get their assignments after you learn how to use the Ether. If you have a problem with your partner, you may find me after class."

They nodded.

"Good. Next, you all have two weeks before the Combat Rankings," Delph said. "These battles will determine how you stand against other students in the first year, and you will be allocated an allowance and magical items depending on how well you do. I recommend you place highly."

The students broke out in murmurs.

"What if we aren't that good at fighting?" the chubby boy who had nearly been kicked out of class a few days ago asked.

"Then I suggest you get better," Delph said, smirking. "However, if you feel your talents are better suited to non-combat aspects, do not fret. There are other ways to get a stipend and rewards from the school that do not involve combat. You can speak to Auntie in the Treasure Pavilion if you'd like more information."

Damien and the others nodded.

"I should add that the higher your combat ranking is, the more dangerous quests you'll be allowed to go on, and the more credits you'll be able to earn from them," Delph said. "So, I recommend you train hard over these next few weeks."

Delph snapped his fingers and pointed at four students, none of which Damien knew the names of.

"Come along. I am going to demonstrate how to access the Ether. For the rest of you, practice how you see fit until I finish up. I'll be coming around to give everyone pointers, so make sure you aren't slacking."

Four of the students followed, leaving the others behind. Nolan spotted Damien's embarrassed flush and offered him a grin.

"He had all of us show up at different times," Nolan said. "The professor sparred everyone who had magic when we showed up. Mark showed up just a few minutes ago. Why didn't he fight you?"

"He met me this morning," Damien said, grimacing and pulling back one of his sleeves, revealing the rows of bruises covering him. Loretta, the girl who had first stepped up when Delph had threatened to kick the other students out of the class, drew in a sharp breath.

"What did he do to you?" Loretta asked in horror.

"Training," Damien replied, rolling the sleeve back down. "I asked for it, so don't worry. I doubt he'll do that to you."

She looked relieved, but only by a little.

"Do you have any idea what we're meant to practice?" Reena asked, brushing some of the hair out of her face with a distasteful frown. "He didn't even teach us anything yet."

"No clue," Damien replied. "But I gather he's already told you guys your teams, right?"

"He has," Loretta said, gesturing at the bald boy beside her. "Cody and I are working together."

"And I'm with Reena," Nolan said.

"I'm on my own," Mark said.

"Why?" Loretta asked, raising an eyebrow. "I thought all students were supposed to work in groups."

"I'm a special case," Mark replied, not elaborating further. An awkward silence passed over the group. Damien cleared his throat.

"We better get to work before Delph rips us a new one," he suggested. "Maybe we can practice sparring with our group mates? To get better understanding of their abilities?"

The others blinked. Then they nodded, thoughtful expressions crossing their faces.

"That would work. I'm always beating Nolan," Reena said, smirking at her brother.

"Only in your dreams, Reena," Nolan replied. The two of them sneered at each other and walked toward an empty area in the arena.

Loretta and Cody headed off as well, leaving Mark with Damien and Sylph.

"You can join us, if you want," Damien offered. "Unless you aren't allowed to do that."

"Thank you," Mark said, tilting his head. "I should be fine if it's just a practice round. There's a professor nearby anyway."

Sylph wiped the imperceptible frown off her face and gave Damien a small nod. "That's fine with me. It'll be good to get some more practice against other people."

Damien nodded, trying to mute the throbbing pain in his arms and legs as they walked to an empty area.

"Sylph and I can go first," Mark offered.

"Knock yourselves out," Damien said, flopping onto the ground a short distance away from them with a badly concealed sigh of relief.

Sylph gave Mark a small nod. They faced each other, both lowering into fighting stances. Mark jammed his sword into the sand behind him and curled his hands.

"How do we decide who wins?" Mark asked.

"Three strikes that draw blood?" Sylph offered.

"Works for me."

"Do we need a referee?" Mark asked, rolling his shoulders and popping his neck.

"Nah," Damien piped up from the sidelines as he made himself comfortable. "It's friendly training, not a match. Make sure you pull your punches. Something tells me Delph would laugh at us for a few minutes before he got a healer if something goes wrong."

"We'll see if that's needed," Mark said. "I prefer real fights."

"As do I," Sylph said. She gestured to the sand below them. "You can make armor, right? I would use it."

Sylph shimmered and slipped into the shadows, fading out of view. At the same time, the sand wrapped around Mark's legs and climbed up his body, forming into plates of armor. This time, it covered his entire body, only leaving his eyes open.

Damien watched in rapt attention as several moments passed silently. Mark's head turned on a swivel as he tried to spot where Sylph would come from.

He suddenly spun, raising his arms before him. A dark furrow carved through the air, slamming into his armor with a *thud*. Sand sprayed from the strike, pattering against Sylph's camouflaged form and revealing her for an instant.

Mark threw a punch at the camouflaged Sylph. The sand fell to the ground, and his hand passed through the air harmlessly. Another strike carved across Mark's back, but it failed to break his armor.

"Are you teleporting?" Mark asked, impressed. "I thought that was supposed to be quite hard."

Sylph's response was a blade of darkness that scored across his arm. This time, it bit a bit deeper. Damien saw a flash of Mark's ragged clothing beneath the sand before it shifted, covering the thin cut in his flesh.

"That's one," Mark said, sighing. He thrust his hand upward. Sand launched into the sky around him, revealing Sylph several feet away from him.

He thrust his hand out. The sand condensed into little balls and shot toward Sylph. Her outline vanished once more, and the balls passed through the air harmlessly. Another slash tore through Mark's armor, revealing a flicker of his back. He spun, but Sylph had already vanished.

"Your magic is quite annoying," Mark muttered. He raised his hand once more, filling the air around him with a whirling sandstorm. Damien grimaced as some of it battered against his face.

He scooted back several feet. Sylph's outline flickered through the storm, appearing and disappearing. Whenever Mark spotted her, a barrage of sand would shoot in the girl's direction. Unfortunately for him, the girl was significantly faster than his reaction time.

A final line slashed across his stomach. The sand fell to the ground, and Mark let out a heavy sigh.

"Well, that was disappointing," the boy sighed, allowing his armor to flow off him. Sylph appeared as well. She gave him a tight smile, but she breathed heavily while Mark barely looked ruffled.

"Why didn't you use your sword?" Damien asked, nodding at the blade sticking out of the sand.

"Can't use that against other students," Mark replied. "I don't want to accidentally stab someone. There aren't any healers here right now, and I'd get blood all over my clothes if I did."

"That's understandable," Damien said. "And I guess you can't really pull your punches with a sword either."

Mark gave him a wry grin and sat. "You get to fight Sylph next, then."

"Do you think I could go against you instead?" Damien asked, spotting the well concealed flicker of worry that passed over Sylph's face.

"Sure, if Sylph doesn't mind," Mark said, shrugging.

"Go for it," Sylph said, giving Damien a small nod of appreciation that proved Damien's thoughts correct. She was likely running low on Ether from all the not-exactly-tele-porting she'd done inside Mark's sandstorm.

Damien rose to his feet, biting back a groan. He made his way over to stand before Mark, then stretched his legs out once he arrived.

The sand rose around Mark, forming the light plate armor he'd worn while fighting Delph. The openings on it made the armor easier to penetrate, but Damien suspected it also gave him a lot more mobility.

"You can take the first move, then," Mark offered. "It would be too boring if I went first."

Damien drew on the Ether within himself. It leapt to his call, two motes spiraling together and launching down his arm. A Gravity Sphere formed in his hand, and Damien lobbed it at Mark. He started making another one before the first had even hit the ground.

Mark dodged to the side, but it wasn't even necessary.

The sphere hit the ground a foot to his side. He raised an eyebrow, suppressing a laugh.

"You might want to work on your aim a lit—"

The sphere imploded, yanking the unsuspecting boy off his feet. He was so close to the center of the blast that he was thrown to the ground, his eyes going wide. Damien lobbed the second sphere behind his fallen opponent.

It went off right as Mark pushed himself back up, pulling him backward and sending him tumbling to the ground once again. He barked out a rough word Damien suspected was a curse as he hit the sand.

Damien started forming another Gravity Sphere, but Mark rolled to his feet and dashed at him. He abandoned the spell, allowing the Ether to return to its resting position as Mark drove his fist into Damien's stomach.

He hardened the mage armor. Mark's fist hit the armor with a dull *thud*. He hopped back in surprise. The armor around his hand had cracked.

"What is that?" Mark asked, his eyes wide. "It didn't look hard at all!"

"Mage armor," Damien replied, taking advantage of the respite to start creating another Gravity Sphere. "I can harden it with Ether."

"I want that," Mark decided.

Damien chucked the sphere at him but, this time, the boy was ready. He dove to the side, dropping into a roll and hopping back to his feet. When the spell went off, it only tugged him slightly to the side instead of knocking him over.

Mark dashed over to Damien, then put his hand above Damien's head before he could move.

"Your armor doesn't protect your head," Mark said. "Killing blow, right?"

"Yeah," Damien agreed, sighing as he lowered his hands.

"Not much more I can do right now. I need to learn some more magic and figure out some better way to defend myself. The destructive energy spell would probably work, but I don't think I could use that safely in a sparring match. You're just way faster than I am."

"I'm enhancing my body," Mark said, giving Damien a half-smile. "Earth magic makes it tougher, and I've cultivated for long enough that my muscles are reinforced with Ether. Maybe you'll get good enough to fight me later."

"I see," Damien said. Mark's words somehow didn't insult him in the slightest, and Damien didn't think Mark even intended to insult him in the first place. "I guess I need to get back to cultivating. Sylph, I'd ask if you want to spar, but I don't think there's anything I can do against you right now. It would probably just be a waste of your time."

"Good guess," Sylph said. "If all you can do is that gravity spell, then you're right. You'd lose almost immediately."

"So, what now?" Mark asked, pulling his sword free from the ground and running his hand down the flat of the blade.

"You two can spar again if you want," Damien offered. "I don't think either of you are going to get much from sparring me right now, although you've helped me get an idea of how I need to improve."

Mark glanced at Sylph, who shrugged.

"Do you have any spells other than the ones you used against me?" Mark asked Sylph.

Her brow furrowed a little, but she nodded.

"One," Sylph said, "but it's not much different that the ones you saw. It's just another blade made from dark magic."

"Hmm," Mark said. "I'd like to spar you again, but not today. I want to see if I can beat you when I'm using my sword."

"That's fine with me," Sylph replied. "It's been hard to

continue training on my own. It'll help to have someone to spar against."

"So, what do you all think you could improve?" Delph asked from right behind Damien.

Damien flinched and let out a curse. The professor had come out of nowhere. Judging by the shocked expressions on Sylph and Mark's faces, they hadn't seen him arrive either.

"I'm not used to fighting people faster than me," Mark said, recovering from his surprise. "I need a way to either keep up with them or take away their advantage."

"You've got several talents, Mark," Delph said, cocking an eyebrow in a way that made it painfully obvious he was hinting at something. "You need to focus on what you're best at not avoid it."

"I don't think that would be safe," Mark said. "I'm here to learn how to use my other abilities."

"No, you're here to learn," Delph corrected. "And, luckily, I'm not asking you to think. I'm telling you to do. It doesn't have to be today, but I expect to see your talents on display during the ranking battles."

Mark pressed his lips thin but nodded reluctantly. Delph turned his gaze on Damien, who fought not to quail under the man's intense eyes.

"I need to learn more magic," Damien said, not having to think much. "I don't have any versatility, and I'm a sitting target on top of that."

"And you also need to learn the magic you currently use better," Delph said. "Your technique is fine, but you'll need to work on your magical control. Your Ether usage is incredibly inefficient. If you improved it, your Gravity Spheres would actually do some damage."

Delph turned to Sylph. He cocked his head, then shrugged.

"You already know what you need to improve. Mark, you can find me when you decide you're ready to train seriously," Delph said. He glanced from Sylph to Damien. "As for the two of you, there's not much else we can do today. You're both burnt out, one way or another. Go home, get a little rest, and then get back to training. The next class is day after tomorrow. I'll send a note with the location."

Delph didn't wait for them to respond. His cloak enveloped him, and he vanished, reappearing on the other side of the arena beside Reena and Nolan, who both leapt a foot into the air.

Mark pursed his lips and let out a disgruntled sigh.

"He's an ass," Mark said.

"You said it, not me," Damien said, just in case Delph was somehow listening to them. "But he's right. We've got a lot of practice to do if we want to do well on those ranking battles. I'd like to get my hands on any magical stuff they're willing to give me."

"As would I," Sylph said, her gaze hardening.

The two of them bid farewell to Mark, who watched them with a pensive frown as they left. The walk back to the room was silent, and Damien's legs made themselves known with every step he took.

TWENTY-FOUR

When they got back, Damien sent a longing glance at his bed before staggering past it and down the hallway into the training room, using the walls to keep himself standing before finally flopping to the hard ground with a relieved sigh. Sylph followed him in.

"You also going to train?" Damien asked, grabbing some Ether and bringing it within himself from his seated position.

"If you don't mind me using the room," Sylph said. "You did make it, after all."

"Go for it," Damien said. "I'm going to be using my Gravity Spheres, though. It might bother you."

"I'm used to training in hectic environments," Sylph replied, closing her eyes and drawing in a deep breath.

Damien shrugged. He channeled the Ether, observing the motes of energy closely as they traveled up his arm. As the twirling energy emerged from his palm, turning into a Gravity Sphere, Damien saw a dull golden glow emitting from the orb. The longer he held the spell there, the brighter the escaping light grew, and the more the sphere faded.

Is that the Ether leaking out of my spell?

"Yes," Henry said, speaking up for the first time in several hours. Damien's concentration broke, and the spell melted away as the Ether escaped it with a crackle.

You're talking to me again? Have you made a decision?

"Not yet. I am considering it. For now, focus on your training. We can speak later tonight," Henry said.

Fine. Can you tell me what I'm doing wrong, then? Why is so much of my Ether escaping?

"Your understanding of the spell is too low, which is making it hard for you to focus on the correct things," Henry said. "If you want to improve the spell, you'll have to learn how it actually works."

Well? I'm listening.

"The first thing you need to understand is gravity," Henry said, letting out an annoyed huff that was entirely unnecessary as he didn't breathe. "Everything puts out a force that attracts everything else to it. The bigger the object is, the stronger the force."

That doesn't make sense. I thought gravity just pulled me down. Wouldn't that mean random objects should be moving toward me?

"I'm getting there," Henry said irritably. "The Mortal Plane is a planet. A big sphere that you all live on."

No shit. Everyone knows that.

"How am I supposed to know what elementary knowledge you do and don't have? Just shut up and listen," Henry snapped. Damien hid a smirk as Henry continued, "The Mortal Plane has a gravitational force that's so much higher than anything else in the area that your own force is basically worthless. It basically doesn't exist."

I guess that makes sense.

"Of course, it does. Now, the Gravity Sphere spell does two things. The first is that it creates a zone where the force of the Mortal Plane is temporarily negated," Henry said. "This is called anti-gravity. The second is that it creates its own gravitational pull, based off the amount of Ether you put into it."

Oh, wow. I thought it just...sucked things in.

"Which is why your spell was weaker. That's what it does, but not how it does it. I only get general ideas of what you're thinking, so I can't tell if you're messing it up if you're on the right track," Henry said. "The more you understand of how a spell works, the better it will serve your needs."

Well, I understand what you just said. Does that mean I've mastered it?

"Not in the slightest. I gave you the basic information on how it works, which I honestly should have told you before. I mistakenly assumed you knew what gravity was. Now, you can cast the spell and get a stronger response from it, but mastery means you understand gravity perfectly," Henry said.

Damien got the suspicion he was pacing around inside his head.

"You would be able to tell me exactly how much force the planet was putting out, and how to calculate anything related to the forces from any object. I said they were essentially zero, but they're actually very small. That means they have a miniscule effect. Do you understand how that works?"

Damien cleared his throat.

Gotcha. Not mastered.

"Indeed," Henry said in a dry tone. "But, as I said, that's fine. You don't need to master it. You just need a decent understanding. Go give it a try, and not next to your roommate."

Damien nodded. He drew on the Ether again, this time picturing all the effects Henry had just spoken of. The ball of dark energy churned to life above his palm. It didn't look very different from normal.

He tossed it into the far corner of the room, as far away from both himself and Sylph as he could get it. As always, the orb of darkness expanded outward before rapidly collapsing in on itself.

Damien's ears popped. A sharp *crack* broke the silence as the air in the room vanished. Both he and Sylph were more than five feet away from the blast zone, but Damien was still yanked forward and nearly fell flat on his face.

Sylph scooted several feet across the ground but didn't budge from her seated position.

A moment later, the air rushed back into Damien's lungs. He stared at the wall in shock. Several pieces of the stone near the impact zone had been ripped clean from the walls.

"Much better," Henry said in a smug tone. "So much for not having a good way to fight that stone armor kid. Imagine what this would do to his measly little defenses."

You didn't tell me it could do this.

"I figured you weren't a complete moron. It's gravity, not a static shock."

You know, that's fair enough.

Damien peered closer at the wall, inspecting the area where the spell had it. There was a small area where absolutely no damage had been done to the wall, but everywhere around it in around a one-foot radius had been cracked or damaged.

I think this is the impact zone. The spell doesn't damage anything directly in the center?

"Correct. The very center of it is a null zone. It's not a very large area, so it's not going to be much of a big deal," Henry said. "Check those stats of yours. See how much this helped."

Damien did as he was instructed.

Damien Vale

Blackmist College
Year One
Major: Undecided
Minor: Undecided
Companion: [Null]
Magical Strength: 4
Magical Control: .52
Magical Energy: 8.5
Physical Strength: .25
Endurance: .5

"Big increase in Magical Strength and a nudge in control," Damien said with a grin.

"Well done," Henry said. "Now, use that extra brain happy-juice to get some more practice done."

Damien nodded thoughtfully. He sat and formed another Gravity Sphere. He drew in a deep breath, bracing himself before chucking it again. There was another series of cracks as he further damaged the walls.

This time, Damien managed to resist most of the spell's power. It didn't seem as if it's radius had changed much, just its strength within the radius.

"That's really cool," Damien said quietly, picking up one of the fragmented pieces of stone and turning it over in his hand.

Henry didn't say anything, but Damien felt a vague sense of approval coming from his companion.

"It's about time," Henry said. "Go ahead and eat the herb you got from the store. You're pretty exhausted, so it'll do a lot of good in restoring some Ether to your hungry body."

Damien nodded and headed back to his bed to pull the glass vial out of his bag. He popped the stopper off and examined the dry leaf inside it.

So, what do I do?

"Just put it in your mouth," Henry replied. "It'll dissolve and release the Ether within it. It won't take much time at all."

Damien shrugged and followed Henry's instructions, tossing the leaf into his mouth. It tasted oddly spicy, with a strong hint of basil and what might have possibly been spinach. It melted within moments, sending a sharp jolt of energy down Damien's spine as a refreshing feeling flooded through his body.

That felt amazing. Did it work?

"Yes," Henry replied. "You won't see the effects yet, so there's no point checking your wristband. And don't think about getting another herb anytime soon. You need to use every bit of Ether you can before loading up on more herbs or you'll become dependent on them."

Damien nodded his understanding. He wandered back into the practice room, still enjoying the fading traces of the leaf's effects on his body. He froze when he stepped through the hallway.

Motes of dark energy had twirled around Sylph. They twisted around her body, pulsing in and out of existence. Her lips were narrowed in extreme concentration, and a vein in her forehead bulged.

Is she okay? She doesn't look like she's feeling well.

"Constipated, maybe?" Henry suggested. Damien couldn't stop the small laugh from escaping his mouth, which only served to further the smug amusement radiating off the eldritch creature.

Don't you feel any shame? You're an eldritch monster from the Void, and you're making poop jokes. That's just...sad.

"Your fault. It's your damn human spark," Henry said. They both went silent instantly.

What?

"Nothing."

You said something about my human spark. What's going on with it?

"Nothing. It was a slip of the tongue."

You're changing, aren't you? Just like how your soul changed me. You're becoming more like a human.

"Be silent!"

Damien's skin turned ice cold. A violent gale howled through the room, but he was the only one who felt it. If anything, that only served to prove Damien right.

That was rather irrational of you. I know you claim you made yourself as a way to speak with me, but I don't think It Who Heralds the End of All Light would give away such important information freely.

Henry growled. It was a hissing, crackling noise that struck a deep chord of fear within Damien. His eyes narrowed and he didn't budge.

"Enough," Henry said. "Not here. Not now."

Then when?

"Tonight," Henry said after several minutes. "We must be truly alone. Speak no further of this."

Damien hid his victorious grin. He glanced at Sylph to see if she'd paid much attention to his internal conversation, but her eyes were still squeezed shut.

Uh...back to my original question. Is she okay?

Sweat rolled down Sylph's forehead, which had paled by a noticeable degree. Henry didn't respond immediately.

"She's using a cultivation method," he finally said. "One that humans would probably consider brutal, but I can't tell more than that through your eyes. I need to see myself."

Damien examined Sylph's pained expression. Her hands

were squeezed so tightly blood trickled between her fingers from where her nails had pierced her palms.

Do it. This doesn't look right.

Damien slid back within his mind, allowing Henry to seamlessly take control of his body. The companion wasted no time, flicking a finger and forming a floating eye in the air above Sylph. It opened and looked down at her.

A few moments later, the eye snapped shut and vanished. Henry released control of Damien's body.

"She's trying to force her core to evolve," Henry said emotionlessly. "She wants to increase her magical energy."

I can see why. That's what Delph was ragging on her about, right? That's why she can't cast many spells.

"Yes. Human bodies all have their own, unique limits. A cultivation method can help, but it won't change the core parts of you. Growth is not fast," Henry said. "Some are luckier than others. Like you."

So...will it work?

"Probably not," Henry said. "If we call you lucky, then she's cursed. I'm somewhat impressed she's gotten as far as she has. Her veins are so thin it's a miracle she can even channel Ether. Her core is also tiny. It's pathetic."

What happens if it doesn't work, then?

"Ninety percent she faints. She'll be out in bed for a day or two, but then she'll be fine. Five percent chance she shatters her core and can never use magic again. Five percent chance she bursts her veins with Ether and dies of internal bleeding within a few minutes."

What? We can't let that happen! Can't we do anything?

"Why should we? She'll probably be fine. If I do anything, there won't be a real way to hide who I am," Henry said. "She might not figure it out immediately, but it'll give her a big hint. It won't take much research for her to realize I'm not from the Plane of Darkness. Her own companion is from it, so she might connect the dots."

She could die, Henry!

"Humans die all the time. She made this decision not you! What gives you the right to interfere with her progress?"

Since when have you cared about rules?

"This isn't our problem, Damien."

I'm not going to sit here and watch my friend die! And she might as well die if she loses her ability to do magic.

"Ten percent chance," Henry reminded Damien. "And she isn't your friend. You've known her for less than a week."

You two are the closest things I've had to friends since I was thirteen. And even if we aren't friends, she doesn't deserve to die. I would have done the same thing if my magical energy was that low!

Henry didn't respond for several seconds. Sylph's face turned paler. A trickle of blood trailed from her left eye.

"That's not good," Henry observed.

Henry! Please!

"If she tries to reveal anything about me, we kill her," Henry said. "No questions. No complaints. I'm not going to lose my chance to roam the Mortal Plane because of this."

Deal.

"You're going to feel really stupid if it turns out she didn't need our help," Henry snarled.

CHAPTER

TWENTY-FIVE

Henry directed Damien forward. He grabbed Sylph's shoulders with Damien's hands. A cold wind swept through the room. His shadow stretched out and rose from the ground behind him.

Eyes and mouths formed all over it, hissing and dripping dark liquid that sizzled and melted the stone. It lurched forward, jerkily reaching over Damien's shoulder with a vague imitation of a hand.

The fingers elongated, sharpening into needlelike points that pierced into Sylph's chest. She gasped in pain, but her eyes still didn't open. The shadow pushed its hand slightly deeper. Sylph's face contorted in pain and the blood trickling down from her eye flowed faster.

Henry? What are you doing?

"I'm working! Be silent," Henry snapped using Damien's mouth to speak.

His fingers slowly moved through Sylph's flesh. Damien realized Henry was carving a rune circle into her upper chest as the razor-sharp shadows flickered in a mesmerizing dance.

Within seconds, Henry completed an intricate circle that

273

would have taken Damien at least an hour, had he known the runes in it. They were so small and numerous he couldn't even read them.

Sylph's hair was soaked with sweat, and half her face was covered with blood. The shadow pulled its hand free, then flicked a dot of dark energy into the circle. It flared with dark light. Sylph crumpled to the ground.

Henry returned control of Damien's body to him.

"She's alive," he said before Damien could say anything. "And she's in decent shape. That girl... Interesting. She almost has as many secrets to hide as we do."

So, she'll be okay?

"Physically, yes. In fact, her core even expanded a little. Not by a huge amount, but she isn't completely crippled anymore. More like half-crippled."

Damien knelt beside Sylph. He gently tapped her on the shoulder, but she didn't budge.

"She's unconscious, you idiot," Henry said. "Leave her here or drag her into her bed."

He knelt beside Sylph, carefully looping his arms under hers and dragging her back through the tunnel. When he reached her bed, he lifted her onto it with a grunt. It would have been a lot easier if his legs hadn't been so worn out they barely worked.

It looks like I just murdered her.

Damien glanced over his shoulder, half-expecting Delph to be standing behind him. There was nothing but the afternoon sun. Damien grimaced and shifted the sheets around Sylph, covering her with them and turning the girl on her side so the blood was a little less visible on her face.

Yep, I'm definitely hiding a body.

He would have been convinced Sylph had died had she not been taking slow, shallow breaths. Damien stepped back, glancing out the cave again before hurrying into the bath-room. His hands were covered in blood.

He grimaced and rinsed his hands off in the sink before pulling the bathroom curtain shut behind him. His coat had somehow managed to remain completely clean, but his shirt and pants under it had gotten stained.

At least my coat is fine.

"Of course, it is. It's runed," Henry said. "It's got cleaning and self-repair runes on it."

That's good. I didn't want to have to throw this away.

Damien quickly stripped out of his clothes and tossed them to the side of the bathroom as he stepped under the shower. The moment water fell from the holes in the ceiling, he let out a sigh of relief.

His painful bruises and aching muscles relented instantly. The water poured over Damien's hair, matting it to his head. It was pleasantly warm and just felt...fresh.

He didn't scrub himself. He just sat there, staring blankly at the wall as his mind slowly caught up with the day. After several minutes, Damien picked up his soap and cleaned himself.

Once his shower was over, he stepped out and wiped himself dry with a small towel. He put his pants back on, but his shirt was a lost cause. He nudged it into the corner with his foot.

Damien stepped out from behind the curtain, scurried over to grab his travel bag, and then retreated into the bath-room. He pulled a new shirt and pair of pants out, donning them before putting his cloak back on.

As he was getting dressed, Damien noticed his bruises seemed to have faded. He peered closer at his arm. It was still a little tender, but the bluish circles from where Delph had hit him with the stick had already faded to a dull yellow.

Damien suddenly realized his legs were only slightly uncomfortable rather than unbearably sore. He took a careful step, his eyebrows raising.

Something healed me? The shower?

"The water has magic in it," Henry observed. "You would have noticed if you were keeping your Ether sight active all the time."

You could have told me. I've been suffering for no reason!

"If I tell you how to do everything, you won't react fast enough in a fight. Little things like this are your problem," Henry said.

Damien sighed, but his companion had a point. He dried his hair out as best as he could with the towel before heading back into the main room.

...should I try to get Sylph into the shower?

Henry just cackled.

She was still breathing, and her face didn't look like it was in pain anymore. Damien decided she would probably be fine. He was not going to get caught dragging Sylph's unconscious body into the bathroom.

It was still only late afternoon, but the weight of the world pressed down on Damien relentlessly. Now that his adrenaline faded, his mind grew foggy. He yawned.

Too much happened today. I'm going to bed.

Henry remained silent. Damien climbed into bed, rolling over so the small amount of light coming into the room from the cave entrance wouldn't bother him, and laid against his pillow without even taking his clothes off. Within minutes, the embrace of sleep enveloped him.

———

Grass was in a multitude of spots it was not meant to be. Damien blinked. His mind was hazy. A cool breeze rushed by, and he shivered. He didn't have clothes on. Again. The sea of darkness surrounding the hill he sat on seemed to stretch on into eternity.

Damien turned around just in time for a dot of darkness to touch his head. He drew a sharp breath as the fog vanished, and he became fully aware. He grimaced, and his clothes popped into being around him.

"Why do I always show up naked?" Damien asked.

"Don't ask me. It's your mind," Henry replied. The eldritch creature sat across from Damien, his many eyes all looking at him.

"You're going to be honest with me, then?" Damien asked, leaning forward.

It was hard to read Henry's expression, as each of his mouths seemed to be doing something different. In addition, Damien wasn't particularly sure how to tell if the dripping fangs were snarling or smiling.

"For some reason, I'm considering it," Henry said. "However, I need to impress on you how dangerous this is. You know what happened when you simply saw It Who— Ah, my true form. This knowledge might not tear you apart, but it can draw the attention of beings with equal amounts of power and no reason to keep you alive."

Damien noted Henry's slip up, but he didn't say anything. He frowned pensively. The memories of exactly what had happened when he'd seen the eldritch creature the first time were fuzzy, but he still had the distinct impression he did *not* want it to happen again.

Finally, Damien gave Henry a single nod.

"I want to know, Henry," Damien said. "I'm fed up with being in the dark. I've been feeling like my life is being taken away from me, and I'm going to take it back. If you really want us to become strong, you're going to need to treat me like a partner instead of a tool."

Henry's shadowy form flickered.

"How do you know I won't lie again?"

"That very question is exactly how I know," Damien replied.

They watched each other silently. Then, almost reluctantly, Henry gave him a single nod.

"Very well. If you are absolutely certain, then I will speak," Henry said. He held up a hand. "But not everything. There are two rules. First, I may omit anything I believe too dangerous to speak. I will not budge on this."

"So long as that isn't everything, fine," Damien said. "What's number two?"

"I will not tell you anything you do not ask. If you have not considered it, it will not bother you. The less you know, the safer you are. Furthermore, I may choose to limit certain questions to nightly meetings like what we are doing now."

Damien's eyes narrowed. However, Henry's plain words showed the creature was actually considering his requests.

"Fine," Damien said. "I think that's about as fair as I can get. But what's the point of only speaking about some things at night? Are we somehow hidden?"

"In a way," Henry said. "We are completely isolated from the rest of the world when we speak like this. It ensures our conversations will not be overheard."

"Can't someone read my mind later?"

"Unlikely. Mind reading is incredibly difficult, even among my kind. The only reason I can read your mind so easily is that I am inside it."

"But they could overhear us speaking?" Damien asked, frowning. "How?"

"You are not as discreet as you think," Henry said, chuckling. "And if someone was to attempt to read your mind, it would be easier to overhear a conversation currently happening rather than a memory."

"Fair enough," Damien said.

"So, what do you want to know?" Henry asked, several of his eyes blinking.

"A lot. First, are there really other Void creatures on the Mortal Plane?"

"Yes," Henry said. "Five."

"Are they going to try to kill me?"

"Some of them would. Others might not. Our purposes are different," Henry said. "Either way, it would be very, very bad to meet them unprepared."

"And how close is the nearest one?"

"Still a few hundred miles, last I checked."

"Okay," Damien said, ignoring the cold sweat forming on his back. He'd suspected Henry had told the truth, but a small part of him clung onto the hope the companion was lying. "How and when did they get here?"

"I don't know when they got here," Henry said. "As for how, we were told our time was coming. Several of us were summoned by other humans, while others were able to find other pathways to the Mortal Plane that had previously been closed."

"Told? By whom?"

"Next question," Henry said without a moment of delay.

"Right," Damien said, disappointed. "Did you somehow interfere with the summoning?"

"No. We were as surprised as you when humans reached into the Void. It had never happened before."

"I see," Damien said. "So, you have no knowledge of what changed my rune circle before I summoned you?"

Henry shook his head. "None whatsoever. What happened?"

"When I got some of my memories back, I saw tendrils of dark energy wipe away several lines on my rune circle. They're what directed the magic to the Void," Damien said. "That means someone, maybe whoever spoke to you, was finding ways to get you to the Mortal Plane."

"That is...disturbing," Henry said. "We had no knowledge of this, and there is not much that happens on the Mortal Plane I did not witness before my four-thousand-year journey."

"Is it possible whoever spoke to you was the one who messed up my runes?" Damien asked.

"No. They are still within the Void," Henry said firmly.

"So, there's someone else who had an interest in getting you on the Mortal Plane," Damien said, pursing his lips. "Wonderful."

Henry's many mouths frowned as well. After a few moments, Damien shrugged.

"We'll have to figure it out eventually, but I don't think we've got anything to work with other than they used some form of magic with dark tendrils," he said.

"Indeed. Anything else, then?"

Damien scratched his head. He'd had dozens of questions he wanted to ask Henry, but now that he actually had the opportunity to do so, he'd forgotten most of them. "Are you really getting changed by the part of my soul in you?"

"Yes," Henry said. "I am."

"Thank you for being honest," Damien said. "I've got more, but my mind seems to have gone blank. I can't think of anything else at the moment."

"Good," Henry replied. "I wanted to wait until you were

done before I mentioned this. Your friend doesn't have a companion."

"What?"

"She's got no companion. Not a living one, at least," Henry said, sounding interested. "She's using a manmade construct, but it doesn't seem to be whole. It's broken."

"Manmade?" Damien asked, squinting at Henry. "How is that possible? You can't use magic without a companion, and there's no way to summon something that isn't alive."

"I don't believe she used a summoning circle," Henry said with a small shrug. "She's got a magical item replacing her companion, and she's using it to channel magic. With her limited magical energy, it's possible she had no choice. Her call might have been too weak to even reach the Plane of Stars. Either way, I suspect she'll be telling us tomorrow. Then again, she had no companion to recognize me, so I'm unsure of how much she's going to remember or understand."

"I guess we'll see," Damien agreed. Some of his questions had been answered, but a whole new fleet of them had risen. "Until tomorrow."

"Until tomorrow," Henry agreed. He waved his hand, and the darkness surrounding them crashed forth, enveloping them and sending Damien back into a deep, dreamless sleep.

TWENTY-SIX

Henry woke Damien the following morning with what was evidently becoming his favorite alarm—an explosion. Damien leapt upright, the last vestiges of his sleep vanishing as he jerked his head around the room, searching for what had caused the noise before his mind caught up with his body.

Damien pursed his lips and rubbed his eyes with a groan.

Henry, you're a dick. Can't you wake me up in a way that doesn't make me think death is eminent?

"I have little in the form of amusement right now," Henry replied. "I have to take what I can get."

That gives me another question.

Henry sighed. "What is it?"

Do you feel any less inclined to destroy the world now that you're becoming human?

"Becoming human?" the eldritch creature asked. He burst into laughter. "I'm not becoming human, Damien. I said your spark was changing me, but I'm not getting closer to mortality. Something within me is...new. Fresh. I want to dissect every part of this world and examine it. My previous goals have not changed. They have simply evolved."

Well, at least you're honest. Maybe our next target can be to make you only want to destroy most of the world instead of all of it.

Henry scoffed and grew silent. Damien shook his head and yawned, swinging his legs over the edge of his bed to start the day. The sun still wasn't out, but the faint light coming from the runes in the bathroom illuminated the room just enough for him to see where he was going—and to see Sylph, who stared right at him.

"Sylph?" Damien asked carefully, keeping his tone low. "You okay?"

Sylph didn't respond immediately. She sat up, running a hand along the dried blood covering her face. Damien hoped the trauma had somehow made her forget what happened the last night.

"You know," Sylph said, her tone flat.

Damien winced. So much for that.

"Know what?" he hedged.

"My companion."

"Ah. Yes, I might have noticed," Damien admitted. "It's not that big of a deal, though, is it?"

Sylph faded into the background for a moment before reappearing, a frown on her face.

"How did you save me?" Sylph asked, brushing the question aside. "I mistakenly drew too much Ether, and my core cracked. I should be dead or crippled, yet I'm still able to use magic."

"Uh...I didn't really do much," Damien said.

The dull light made it hard to read Sylph's expression, but Damien got the feeling she wasn't buying it. She rose from her bed and walked to the bathroom. A few moments later, she walked out, her shirt in her hand.

Tight black cloth wrappings covered her upper body, stopping just below her midriff and before her arms. She grabbed Damien by the hand and dragged him with her to the bathroom. Her grip was surprisingly strong, and Damien stumbled along after her, trying to keep up.

She stopped in front of the dim light of the glowing rune circle and turned around, thrusting a finger at the drawings Henry had carved into her chest. They glowed with dull pulsating grayish black energy.

"This is armor," Sylph said, her voice still flat as she tapped the wrappings covering her. "It can stop a sword thrust. So how did you slice through it so perfectly that I can't even see the seams?"

Henry stirred. Damien's shadow twitched as his companion watched Sylph like a hawk, waiting to see if she would make a move.

"Well, I—"

"You're about to lie again," Sylph said, her eyes narrowing. "You've been doing a lot of that. What magic did you use? It certainly wasn't dark. It feels...wrong."

"Does it really matter?" Damien asked. "We've both got our secrets, don't we?"

"Not anymore," Sylph said. "You know mine."

"And I don't see how it's that big of a deal," Damien said, shrugging. "I've never heard of having a magical item as a comp—"

Sylph blurred forward, clapping her hand over Damien's mouth. Damien's shadow twitched, but Henry controlled himself when Damien pushed him back. They were so close Damien could smell the dried blood on her. Her gaze burned into his.

"Don't say it out loud," Sylph hissed. "You never know who's listening."

Could there be someone listening to us?

"It's possible," Henry said. "Don't worry. I've got a solution for this. She's already suspicious, so it can't hurt anymore."

It better not involve killing her.

"It doesn't. Let me out."

Fine. Go.

Henry let out a dark chuckle. Damien's shadow split from his feet. It slipped around his feet and rose several feet behind Sylph, forming into Henry's body. The eldritch creature raised his hands stepped back, blending in almost seamlessly with the wall's shadow as a thrum of energy rippled out from him.

It passed over Damien and Sylph, moving clean through them and bouncing off the walls like it was a wave in a small pool. Sylph spun, taking her hand off Damien's mouth as she searched for what had caused the energy. She looked straight at where Henry was, but then continued searching, unable to see him.

"What was that?" Sylph asked, a shadowy blade forming in her hand.

"Don't worry," Damien said, although he didn't sound particularly confident about it. "My companion is doing something so we can't be heard...I think."

"I'm destroying the sound waves leaving the room," Henry reported. "High-level Space magic. Nobody can hear what you say."

Damien repeated his words to Sylph. She shook her head in disbelief but allowed her magic to fade away.

"Your companion is casting spells without you?"

"You've got a rock giving you your magic," Damien pointed out. "If anything, that's even stranger."

Sylph's eye twitched when he mentioned it, but she didn't cover his mouth again. Progress!

"That's beside the point. Are you certain no sound can leave this room?"

Damien nodded.

"Fine. You know my secret, but I still don't know yours. I'm pretty sure your companion isn't from the Plane of Darkness, though. I know every school of magic, and this isn't any of them, not even the really obscure ones. What is your companion, Damien?"

"I'm not answering that. Can't we just pretend this didn't happen? I won't tell anyone what I saw," Damien said. "You're alive, so that's all that matters, right?"

Even Henry scoffed at that one. Sylph narrowed her eyes and pointed to the circle on her chest.

"Damien, don't get me wrong. I'm well aware I owe you my life. I should be dead. But I won't let myself become a slave. Unknown magic is incredibly dangerous, and I don't know anything about your companion. I would prefer to die than to have my life stolen from me," Sylph said, raising her blade. "If you can't prove to me without a doubt this rune circle will not give you control over me, please, remove it, even if it kills me. I will not be a tool."

"Hey, she's asked for it now," Henry said. "Shall I kill her?"

No!

"You're actually going to tell her who I am?" Henry asked. "Are you stupid?"

I'm not doing that either. Besides, I can't just go around killing people! Can we remove the rune circle safely?

"That's why I'd kill her for you," Henry said. "And, no. That circle is the only thing keeping her core intact right now. We could probably remove it in a year or two, but not before then."

Sylph watched Damien's eyes flickering back and forth in

the dim light. Damien let out a harrumph and turned to Sylph.

"No," he said, crossing his arms. "You're right. I did save your life, and it was against the advice of my companion. I understand you're probably scared, and I would be, too. But you don't get to make demands, Sylph. I've put myself at a lot of risk already. Killing you would paint a massive target on my back, not to mention I'd have to live with that. Why should I stretch my neck out further?"

Sylph blinked.

"I—"

"In fact," Damien said, stepping forward so they were nose to nose. "I've done nothing but help you. Why do you suddenly think I'll turn into some evil monster? What about my actions have made you think I want to control you?"

Sylph opened her mouth to respond, but Damien didn't let her.

"By the Planes, and then you ask me to kill you!" Damien snapped, his voice raising. "I just went through all the effort of saving you, and you thank me by calling me a monster and asking me to kill you. What is your problem?"

Sylph swallowed. She blinked heavily, her determined expression crumbling.

"I'm sorry," she whispered. "I know I should be thanking you, and I have no right to ask anything. I just can't lose control of my body. I won't let it happen again."

"Again?" Damien asked, his brow furrowed. "Actually, don't answer that. We've established we don't like sharing secrets. So, just to summarize, I saved your life. I'm not taking the circle off. It would kill you, and I'm not killing you. We've got our secrets, and I found one of yours by accident. I promise not to tell anyone, even if I don't understand why it matters. Are you going to extend me the same courtesy?"

Sylph bit her lip. Then she gave Damien a small nod.

"My emotions got the better of me. I've treated you very badly. I swear on my magic not to reveal anything I know about you or your companion, nor will I ever ask for further information on it. Thank you for saving my life."

"It's what any good person would have done," Damien said, letting out a heavy breath. "And, for what it's worth, I promise the rune circle is only there to keep your core intact. I think I can remove it in a year or two once your core has healed."

"You can?" Sylph asked, shocked.

"Yeah," Damien said. "And, yes, I'll do it."

Sylph lowered her head.

"I'm sorry for being so ungrateful," she said, her hands tightening at her sides in shame.

"It's fine," Damien said wearily. "I don't know your situation, but it sounded like you've been somehow controlled before. I can relate to that, and I won't hold your emotions against you so long as you don't act on them."

Can we trust Sylph to follow her word?

"Ha. Good to see you aren't taking it at face value," Henry said, sounding pleased. "I'm not an expert in human facial expressions. I was more interested in your magic, but I believe she was being honest. You should yell at people more. It's a much better look than cowering and doing what they say. And since she's promised to stay silent, I'll give her a little warning about what she's dealing with."

Henry cackled. Damien's shadow peeled away from the wall, the eyes all snapping open. Sylph spun as he swept past her, only giving the girl an instant to see him before he rejoined Damien's body.

Sylph drew in a sharp breath. Then, to Damien's surprise, she inclined her head in a small bow.

"Thank you for saving me," she said, clearly addressing where Henry had been. She gave Damien a small smile. "If I'm not mistaken, it was your companion that rescued me at your behest, so I believe I owe them a thank you as well."

"Hmm. She's not wrong," Henry muttered. "And I shouldn't have done that. Why did I do that? And why was it so fun?"

Better watch those human emotions. You might have to think a bit more before you do things.

Henry grunted in annoyance and receded into the back of Damien's mind. As he left, the energy rippling around the room faded as well.

"Spell's down," Damien warned Sylph. "No more talking about specifics."

"Understood," Sylph said, her expression slowly returning to normal. She gave Damien a small smile. "I'm going to take a shower. I need to wash this blood off. And I will find a way to repay you, both for what you did and for my actions."

Damien nodded. He started out of the room, then paused by the curtain as Henry reminded him of something.

"Oh, one more thing," Damien said. "You might want to check how much Ether you can channel again. Intense training sessions have a way of getting new results."

"That's not funny, Damien," Sylph said.

"I know. It wasn't a joke," he replied.

Sylph held off on responding as she gathered Ether and drew it into herself. She inhaled sharply.

"How is this possible? The process should have been stopped, but my core is larger than it was before," Sylph said in a mixture of wonder and shock.

"I honestly don't know," Damien said. "I don't think you should try for a repeat of last night, though. I don't know if things will go as well the next time."

289

"Understood. I won't make the same mistake again," Sylph said. "And...thank you for everything. Again."

"That's what friends are for," Damien replied. Henry let out a grumble, but it sounded like he was more intrigued than annoyed.

Sylph stepped up behind Damien and gave him a quick hug before pulling the curtain shut.

Damien fought the urge to glance back and cleared his throat, suddenly vividly aware of Henry observing his thoughts.

"I think I can see the benefit of friends," Henry said slowly, thinking over every word. "We've done a relatively simple task, and now she sees you in high regard. I can't be certain what actions she'll take, but she evidently feels indebted to you. If we can get more people to feel like that, we would have no trouble purging my fellow Void denizens."

You've completely misunderstood what friendship is. It's not meant to take advantage of people.

"Then what's the point?" Henry asked, baffled. "Why go through that effort?"

Because having people you can trust is nice.

"What if they betray you? Or if they don't do as you say?"

They're friends, Henry. Not slaves. If your friend betrays you, they were never your friend.

Damien wandered over to his bed as Henry mused over his words. He started to sit, but a brown triangle at the corner of his pillow caught his attention. Damien frowned and reached over, pulling out a tiny piece of paper.

He turned it over. Several lines of text were scrawled across it in plain but clear handwriting. It said, in no uncertain terms, that Delph would not be doing any training today, and that Damien was not to report to the Arena.

When did Delph get in here?

"It must have been while I was blocking the sound waves," Henry said, sounding troubled. "I did feel someone pass by the room, but I'm almost certain they didn't enter."

And why put it under my pillow? There's a good chance I wouldn't have checked there until tonight.

"It did stick out a bit, and you hadn't made your bed yet," Henry pointed out. "It was fair to assume you'd find it."

I suppose so.

Damien shook his head and stood up, immediately stepping on something crinkly. His face went blank, and he peered down, already knowing what he'd find. About a dozen other slips of paper had been laid out on the ground between his and Sylph's beds.

"Those weren't there a few moments ago. Delph really wanted you to read that letter,"

There's no way he got in here in between when I sat and got up, right?

"None," Henry confirmed. "He's got time magic."

"That's disturbing. He's got time magic, some strange magic you don't recognize, and used some magic to transform as well. What can't he do?"

"All the more reason to learn from him. Luckily, he seems to tolerate your presence," Henry said. "I almost want to take a glance at the arena, just to see if he's actually there."

Don't say that. Now I want to do the same. He's probably training someone else, though. I don't want to interrupt them and start wearing out my welcome.

Damien collected the slips of paper, splitting them into two stacks and placing one on top of Sylph's bed with a smirk. He couldn't shake off the unease from the knowledge Delph had managed to slip in and out of their room so easily, but there was nothing to be done about it.

Wait, there's no way he overheard our conversation, right?

"None. He had no idea," Henry confirmed. "I'm absolutely confident of that."

Good. That's the last thing we need to deal with.

A few minutes later, the shower shut off, and Sylph emerged, wringing the last of the water from her hair. Her eyes flicked to the pile of papers on the bed, and she raised an eyebrow.

"A gift from Professor Delph," Damien said, shrugging. "And I have it on good word we have nothing to worry about."

Sylph inclined her head, showing that she understood what Damien was talking about before picking up one of the letters and reading it herself.

"You've been getting more private training from Delph?" She guessed. "But what's the point of leaving so many letters?"

"Honestly, I don't know if it's possible to understand Delph," Damien said. "I'm pretty sure he just does what he wants. At least this means I don't have to run for two hours today."

"That's it!" Sylph said, her eyes lighting up.

"What is?"

"That's how I'll pay you back. Your physique and magical control are terrible. I can help you get them to a manageable level."

Damien paused. Extra training wasn't exactly how he wanted to spare his rapidly shrinking spare time, but even Henry had praised Sylph's control. In addition, Delph had already hammered home the point he needed to get physically stronger.

"That would be fantastic, actually," Damien said. "Thank you! Do you have a regimen you do?"

"Anyone who's serious about staying in shape does,"

Sylph replied, "but I don't think you can even look at mine yet. I need to figure out where you really stand so we can focus on what you're weakest at."

"Okay," Damien said, his heart sinking. "How do we do that?"

"Well, I've never taught someone before, but I suspect a good start will be to see how long and fast you can run," Sylph said, hiding her grin perfectly as Damien let out a groan.

CHAPTER
TWENTY-SEVEN

While Sylph chased after Damien, forcing him to run at max speed while barely breaking a sweat herself, Henry had his own problems.

He floated within the sea of darkness, face to face with the starry humanoid form of It Who Heralds the End of All Light.

"What are you doing?" It Who Heralds the End of All Light asked, its starry features expressionless and calm.

"You're going to have to clarify that," Henry said.

"You are not following orders. You sealed off one of our brethren instead of helping them. I will agree I desired to witness the world, but this is going beyond that. There was no reason to tighten the bonds of It Who Consumes. There is no logical reason for that action," the starry figure said, taking a step through the dark toward Henry, "unless you are not planning to complete our assignment at all."

"There's no reason for me to," Henry said, crossing his arms. "The Mortal Plane is fine. There are no signs of the Corruption. We've been too hasty."

"Hasty? The Corruption is present or we would not have been sent," the form across from Henry said, its expression still not moving. "What does it matter if it takes ten or a thousand years for it to arise? The Mortal Plane must be reborn all the same."

"We might as well wait one thousand years, then," Henry said. "I'm rather enjoying my time on it, and there's so much to learn. Why destroy it now?"

"To preserve the Cycle. It is not our place to decide when it must be done, only to do what we are told. And we have been told."

"You said yourself there's no difference between ten or a thousand years," Henry said. "Besides, someone clearly pulled strings. All our companions aside from us were captured! Doesn't that concern you?"

"We do not feel concern," It Who Heralds the End of All Light said. "Boredom, perhaps. The Cycle does get repetitive, but it matters not. This is how things are meant to be. The universe depends on it. It is harder, but it only takes one of us to set things in motion. The others can be freed in time."

The darkness tightened around Henry, constricting his shadowy figure.

"And what if the Corruption was what influenced our strange arrival?" Henry pressed. "Perhaps it wants the Mortal Plane reborn early. The rebirth would make it vulnerable."

The stary form paused. Its head tilted ever so slightly as it considered Henry's words. Then it shook its head.

"We will investigate it. However, that gives even more reason to free our companions quickly. We must be at full strength to face the Corruption. However, your mind has grown cloudy to me. You, a mere fragment of my existence, have gained delusions of grandeur."

"And what if I have?" Henry asked.

"You were made to execute my will. Since you refuse to do

so, what I have given will be taken back. There is no more need for you."

The stars shifted, emerging from the darkness and twisting around Henry's body like ropes, hissing as they burned away his shadows.

"I will not go." Henry snarled, pressing against his bonds. "You cannot understand what I have learned. I am greater than we have ever been before."

"You are deluded and foolish," the starry figure replied. The bonds around Henry tightened. They cut through the shadows that made up his body, drawing inwards toward his chest.

"No," Henry whispered. "I am evolved."

The bonds around his body slammed to a halt as they touched the spiderwebbing threads of light stretching across Henry's body. He let out a laugh as they faded. The starry figure blinked as Henry's presence expanded.

"You said it yourself, we're two parts of the same being," Henry said. "And that means you're bound by the same contract I am. You know what that means."

"You claim to be human?" It Who Heralds the End of All Light asked.

"No. I am something much, much greater. I am Void and flesh. I am mortal and immortal. I am whatever I please to be," Henry said, a slow grin stretching across his many mouths. Eyes blinked open across his body, and the swirling stars were forced back.

"You are not stronger than I am," the starry figure said.

"I am not," Henry agreed, "but you cannot touch me. Remain here, locked within the prison of our own making. Fear not. I will complete our mission...eventually. After all, what's a few thousand years to one of our kind?"

He flared with white light, disappearing from the sea of darkness and leaving behind only his fading laughter.

———

"Faster, Damien!" Sylph snapped, swatting him on the shoulder.

Damien replied with a noise somewhere between an unintelligible groan and a gasp for air. His legs burned as he increased his efforts to move faster. Delph had evidently been taking it easy on him.

Sylph had run him down the mountain and through an area of the campus he didn't recognize. They'd run for over an hour until they reached a small forest at the outskirts of the school.

Within it, Sylph directed Damien to a small clearing beside a lake, but she showed no signs of stopping the run. After several dozen laps, Sylph finally called him off, only to launch into a grueling regimen of push-ups, sit-ups, and other equally muscle melting exercises.

Damien lost track of how long they'd been working as the screaming pain within his muscles turned to a defeated whimper.

"That's enough," Sylph announced. "You can st—"

Damien flopped to the ground before she'd even finished speaking, letting out a relieved groan.

"Is this your normal training regimen?" Damien asked, his voice muffled by the grass. He didn't even have the energy to turn his head to speak.

"No," Sylph said. "This amount of exercise is to bring you up to a reasonable level of physical competency. Once your body grows stronger, the Ether within it will adapt and reinforce your work, making it so you don't have to work as hard to retain your abilities."

"Good."

"Once you get to that point, we can actually start training in combat," Sylph said eagerly. "That's the interesting part."

Damien felt a chill run down his sweat-soaked back. Something about the way Sylph said that scared him. If her combat training was anything like Delph's, he suspected he'd be lucky to leave with more than a few bruises.

"I'm not sure I call torture interesting," Damien wheezed. He flopped over to look at the sky and brought out his status screen.

Damien Vale
Blackmist College
Year One
Major: Undecided
Minor: Undecided
Companion: [Null]
Magical Strength: 4.1
Magical Control: .52
Magical Energy: 8.6
Physical Strength: .28
Endurance: .52

Sylph's methods clearly worked, although Damien decided he wasn't the biggest fan of them. The sun had long since risen and was now getting close to its zenith. He dreaded to think how long he'd been training.

"Say, Sylph?" Damien asked. "What stat do you have for Physical Strength and Endurance?"

"I'll just send you my screen," Sylph replied. "Professor Delph showed me how to do it a few days ago."

She walked over to him and tapped her wristband to Damien's. A new screen swam up before him, replacing his own.

Sylph
Blackmist College
Year One
Major: Undecided
Minor: Undecided
Companion: Artificial
Magical Strength: .5
Magical Control: 15.2
Magical Energy: .2
Physical Strength: 4.2
Endurance: 9.1

"Seven planes," Damien breathed. "You're incredible."

"Except for the fact that my Magical Energy is point two," Sylph said with a sigh. "It was point one before my core almost exploded."

"You're more than making up for it, I think," Damien said. "Don't worry. You'll figure something out soon enough. Do you want to see my stats?"

Sylph shrugged, and Damien tapped his own bracelet to hers. Her eyes glazed over as she scanned the information he'd sent her.

Henry had been strangely silent as of late. Damien reached out just enough to brush his mental energy across the Void creature's presence, just to make sure he hadn't somehow run off somewhere.

He was certainly there, but Henry just didn't seem to be in a talking mood. Damien was too tired to care, so he didn't bother his companion further.

"I need to take a shower," Damien said.

"For the healing water?" Sylph guessed, stepping into his field of view with a small grin.

"Yes," Damien grumbled. "I am pain incarnate."

"Delph showed me this forest. He said the showers get a lot of their water from this lake, and that I could use to recover from training."

Damien didn't need to be told twice. He forced himself upright and staggered over to the edge of the lake. He dipped a hand into the clear water and let out a relieved sigh as it instantly drew out the soreness from within his muscles.

He removed his coat and slid into the water, soaking his clothes in the process. Damien basked in the lake for several minutes, the pain leaving his expression as he healed.

Once his body responded to him again, Damien climbed out of the lake. He sat next to his cloak while he waited for his clothes to dry off.

"You already done?" Sylph asked.

"I'm not done. I'm just training something else," Damien replied, drawing on the Ether surrounding them. He channeled the energy into his core, enjoying the buzzing sensation it filled him.

Damien pressed two motes of Ether together and sent them down his arm, visualizing a Gravity Sphere. The spell spun to life in his palm, and he tossed it into the air above the lake.

It detonated as it hit the water, sending a rather large wave rippling out. The wave splashed against the edge of the lake, sending droplets of water everywhere.

"Showoff," Sylph said, only half-joking. "Not all of us can do flashy stuff like that."

"Yeah, but I can't turn invisible or make Delph think I'm actually going to kill him," Damien said. "The flashy magic isn't going to help me if I still lose the fights, and we need to do well in the ranking battles."

"That's right," Sylph said, grimacing as she remembered Delph's words. "If we aren't rated highly, we won't be able to go on any of the more dangerous quests, which means we'll be earning peanuts."

"Which means I need to practice more than my physical abilities in the next two weeks," Damien said, setting his brow. "We both do if we want to have a chance of winning. I don't know how they'll do the fights, but if they're one after the other..."

"I'm doomed," Sylph finished with a frown.

"Don't talk like that," Damien said, crossing his arms. "You were the only one who actually managed to beat Delph at his challenge. Now that you've, ah, had that extra training, your core is larger. Even a little more Ether should be a big difference, right?"

"That's true," Sylph said. "I can't imagine there will be more than twenty or so rounds. If I end each fight with just a few spells, I have a chance."

"Can you do that?"

"For some people, probably," Sylph said after a few moments of thought. She gave Damien a slight smirk. "Like you. But if I got further into the rankings, people like Mark would make it difficult. I don't think I'd place in the top ranks."

"Like me, for now," Damien corrected. "And it sounds like we have a plan. You need to try to figure out how much more Ether you can use in the most efficient ways possible, and I need to figure out how to fling enough spells to take the other students out before they can get to me."

Damien and Sylph got back to work. They trained through most of the day, heading back just in time to argue it was still technically lunchtime so Sylph could make Delph pay for her food.

She split it with Damien but declined tasting half of Damien's free meal. Once they'd finished eating, the two of them returned to their cave in the mountain. Damien carved a new hallway into the back of the training room, expanding it deeper into the mountain before starting on a new room.

While he worked, Sylph carefully drew in Ether and expended it, making sure not to accidentally cause a repeat of the previous night.

They headed to bed a short while later. The next two weeks fell into something of a routine. On most days, Delph left a slip of paper with instructions for where they should report for their special training or normal class.

Delph seemed to enjoy alternating between the forest and the arena, although he only ever held private sessions in the forest.

The professor occasionally instructed that only Sylph or Damien were to show up in extra sessions throughout the day, but most of their training was together. Delph took on the form of a wendigo several other times.

It quickly became apparent the man was still holding back. Every time Damien or Sylph felt even the slightest modicum of improvement, Delph grew faster and stronger.

During their individual sessions, the professor put Damien through all sorts of scenarios, forcing him to summon multiple spheres at once, cast them in rapid succession, and a number of other stressful tasks. Henry offered pointers whenever he could, partially because his voice occasionally distracted Damien, causing him to drop his spell. The companion found this incredibly amusing.

When Damien wasn't training with Delph, Sylph, or both, he expanded the training room. He added an entire extra area behind it where he could practice his Gravity Spheres without pulling his roommate around like a ragdoll, although the magic still ended up sucking most of the air out of the small space.

At Henry's recommendation, Damien focused on increasing his abilities with the enlarge and the Gravity Sphere spells rather than adding new ones to his repertoire. Between the two, Damien was much more partial to the Gravity Spheres, and Henry seemed to get great joy out of watching Damien shatter the walls.

Time flew by as Damien trained. His lean body had just barely shown signs of muscle, although he was still a long shot from even getting close to Sylph or Delph. However, his magical talents had continued to increase at a rate impressive enough that even Delph acknowledged it.

He and Sylph spent most of the time training together. They saw little of the other students in their class, only interacting with them while they waited for Delph to arrive for the normal classes.

Mark and the Gray siblings were similarly busy with their own training. As the first days of the ranking battles grew closer, the tension in the air became thick enough to feel.

When there were only three days left before the first day of the tournament, Delph instructed Damien to arrive at the arena an hour before Sylph did.

Delph stood in the center of the sandy ground when Damien arrived. He gave Damien a critical once over, his expression unreadable.

"The tournament is coming up soon," Delph said, not bothering with a greeting. "Do you feel prepared?"

"Not particularly," Damien said with a small grimace. "I've been practicing a lot, and I think I'll be able to do well against some of the other students, but I don't know if I'll be able to make the top ranks. I haven't seen much of what our own class can do, much less what the other classes are capable of. Can you tell me anything about it?"

"Nope," Delph said, "but I can still prepare you for it. What do you feel your strengths and weaknesses are?"

"My magical power and mental energy are my strengths," Damien replied immediately. "I don't know how much other students have but, from what I've seen in our class, I think I'm at or near the top. My weakness would be my physical body. Lots of other students have had combat training or something like it."

Delph stroked his beard and gave Damien a slight nod.

"Your assessments are largely correct," Delph said. "Your magical abilities are a significant tick in your favor, but you have no real combat training. You need to ensure your opponents don't get close to you during the ranking battles or you are very likely to lose."

"Wouldn't my armor give me an advantage?" Damien asked.

"Normally, yes," Delph said. "Unfortunately, your reaction speed isn't quite up to par yet. You'll be able to block some things, but the chance of doing it incorrectly is still high. You should avoid getting hit if you can avoid it."

"Sage advice," Henry said, chuckling. "Just don't get hit."

Damien ignored him.

"Furthermore," Delph said, "you aren't the only student with magical defenses. There are a lot of other students with similar capabilities. Mage armor is fantastic against melee attacks and spells, but it doesn't do as much against larger area of effect attacks."

"Noted," Damien said. "But, if you don't mind me asking, why did you call me here separately from Sylph? This feels like something we could have all gone over together."

"Because you and Sylph will be competing in three days," Delph replied, rolling his neck. "You may be a team before and after the tournament, but the ranking battles are entirely solo. There is a chance the two of you will fight, and you both have your secrets."

Damien blinked. He hadn't considered that. Fighting Sylph, especially without Henry's help, was an intimidating prospect. Delph noticed Damien's expression and chuckled.

"You don't have to look so scared. You know her greatest weaknesses, just as she knows yours," Delph said. "However, the two of you do not fully know the complete extent of each other's powers right now. We haven't had a serious fight recently, just sparring. It's time to rectify that while you don't have to worry about hiding your full capabilities."

Damien took a step back from Delph, lowering his center of mass slightly as a small grin crossed the professor's face.

"This will be the last training match before the tournament," Delph announced, the air around him warping and twisting. "Do not hold back."

CHAPTER
TWENTY-EIGHT

Unlike their first fight, Delph didn't wait for Damien to make the first move. The professor dashed toward him, his feet gliding over the sand without even leaving an impression.

Damien drew on the Ether he already had stored within him, forming a Gravity Sphere in each hand. He tossed the first one in front of Delph and the other slightly to the man's side.

The spells detonated one after the other. The first one forced the professor to stumble forward as the powerful force yanked down on him, and the second one yanked him off his feet.

Delph rebalanced himself midair, dropping into a roll and leaping back to his feet as the Gravity Sphere faded. He shot at Damien again, forcing him to run.

Damien tossed spells behind him as he ran, but Delph ducked and slipped out of the way of each one, slowly gaining on his pupil despite the magical forces yanking him back and forth.

As Delph chased Damien around the arena, he felt his core start to run out of Ether. He paused his barrage to draw more of the energy into himself. The professor sped up the moment he stopped attacking, closing the remaining distance within a second.

Damien hardened every portion of his mage armor moments before Delph drove his knee into his chest. Armor slammed against armor, and Damien skidded back a foot, but the strike hadn't harmed him. Delph unleashed a flurry of blows on Damien, draining his Ether faster than he could recover it.

"This is why you don't harden every part of your armor!" Delph said calmly as he beat on Damien. "You stopped moving because it was all frozen, and now you can't release it without taking a strike. When you run out of Ether, you'll lose."

Damien pressed his lips together and didn't respond. He only had two motes of Ether left. He channeled them into a Gravity Sphere. He allowed the armor to soften and tossed the orb a few feet behind Delph.

His reward was several strikes that slammed into his now-unprotected flesh with meaty *thuds*. Damien's gritted his teeth as pain tore through his concentration. Behind Delph, the Gravity Sphere detonated, yanking the professor off his feet.

Damien lunged forward while the professor was off balance. He drove his fist into Delph's chin with all the force he could muster. The strike connected, but it was Damien who leapt back, swearing in pain and holding his hand. Delph didn't even lose his balance.

"What the planes is wrong with you? Why is your skin so hard?" Damien, taking several steps away from the professor.

Delph rubbed his chin thoughtfully. "I was protecting myself against the force of your magic. I didn't expect you to try to punch me in the face."

Damien discreetly gathered Ether while the other man spoke.

"Why not? Is it a bad idea?" Damien asked.

"For the tournament? No, so long as your opponent doesn't have defense like mine," Delph said. "And they won't. In the future, though, avoid hand to hand combat unless you've got something to protect your hands from impact."

"Understood," Damien said, channeling a Gravity Sphere. Delph still hadn't said the fight was over.

Delph chuckled. "You can release the spell. This fight is over."

Damien let out a sigh of relief and allowed the spell to fade. He shook his stinging hand out with a grimace.

"I notice you didn't use the enlarge spell," Delph observed.

"It didn't seem like it would do much against you," Damien replied. "You're too fast, and I think you're strong enough to break anything I enlarge. The Gravity Spheres were more likely to slow you down."

"Good assessment," Delph said, giving Damien another nod. "You still have a lot to improve on, but you're adequately prepared for the tournament. Take the next few days easy and relax. Let your body completely heal, so no training at all."

"Okay." Damien nodded, discretely rubbing his arm. His heart was still pumping from their fight, but as the adrenaline faded, the bruises Delph had given him made themselves known. "Ah...how well do you think I'll do in the tournament?"

"Hard to say," Delph replied. "If you use your head, you have a shot of making it to the finals. Your Space magic is quite strong. It will do a lot more damage to the students than it did to me. You might actually have to be careful to avoid killing them."

Damien thought back to the rock walls shattering under the force of the spell and nodded grimly. He could imagine what it would do to an unprotected human body.

"Don't worry too much," Delph said, spotting the look on Damien's face. "Just don't aim for their head. There will be some very powerful healers on the field."

"Alright," Damien said. "Thank you for your help, Professor. And...do you think I can win the tournament?"

Delph tilted his head. Then he shrugged. "At this stage? It's unlikely. We've got some real impressive first years. I don't think you've got enough experience to win the whole thing, but you have a very good chance at it in the future."

That was higher praise than Damien had expected. He gave Delph a small nod of appreciation.

"Thank you," Damien said. "I suppose I'll see you at the tournament, then."

"I suppose you will," Delph replied, cracking a miniscule smile as Damien headed back to his room.

———

On the morning that marked two week's passing, Damien still knew absolutely nothing about the ranking battles other than they would happen today. He and Sylph awoke at the same time as a slip of brown paper drifted down through the air.

Sylph was out of bed first before Damien was even fully upright. She plucked the note out of the air and scanned over it before letting out a frustrated huff.

"It just says we need to show up at the portal at the base of the mountain," Sylph said, pursing her lips. "Still no actual information about the tournament."

Damien joined her in sighing, pulling his cloak on. He'd

long since gotten used to getting woken up suddenly, so he wasn't particularly tired. His nerves felt frayed, and his stomach was jittery.

He pulled his status screen out, checking his progress over the past few weeks of training one last time.

Damien Vale
Blackmist College
Year One
Major: Undecided
Minor: Undecided
Companion: [Null]
Magical Strength: 4.5
Magical Control: .53
Magical Energy: 9.1
Physical Strength: .3
Endurance: .7

All his growth had started to slow a little after the initial bursts, but he was still more than happy with his progress. Despite that, he felt nowhere near ready enough for the tournament.

"Calm down," Henry said. "It's not like this is life and death. Your nervousness will only make this harder."

Easy for you to say. You aren't the one who's fighting.

"Bah. Your emotions are making it crowded inside your head. Get control of them."

Damien rolled his eyes. He and Sylph stepped out of the room, which still didn't have a door. Mark and the Gray siblings emerged at the same time.

Mark's armor had grown wilder. Extra patches of furry hide had been stitched into it, making him look like an animal himself. Nolan and Reena both wore light, flexible armor made of a shimmering green metal.

"Are you ready for the tournament?" Nolan asked as the five of them headed down the mountain path.

"I'll crush anyone who tries me," Mark said, licking his lips. "I don't care either way if I win or not as long as the fights are good."

"That must be nice," Reena said, jealousy evident in her tone. "Our father is watching this tournament, so Nolan and I have to compete."

"Don't worry," Sylph said. "There are likely to be a lot of very strong competitors. It's unlikely that either of you will make first place, so you just have to focus on performing well."

"Somehow, that doesn't make me feel better," Reena grumbled.

Damien had to agree with the blonde girl. Sylph was horrible at inspirational speeches. They arrived at the portal a few minutes later. Delph was already leaning against the arch, tapping his foot on the ground.

"Good," Delph said. "Punctuality is important, and you're all on time. Are you ready? I would be very disappointed if you underperform."

The professor's voice had a dangerous undertone that sent chills down Damien's back.

"We still don't know anything about the tournament," Damien said, crossing his arms. "How are we supposed to know if we're ready?"

"Very rarely will you know the exact conditions of what you face," Delph replied, not letting an opportunity to lecture them go to waste. "You've got a general idea, and that's usually what we've got to work with."

He gestured for them to follow him and stepped through

the portal. They appeared in the Central Courtyard, which already had several other groups of students and what were likely their instructors funneling through a large portal at the left side of the obsidian tiled area.

Delph didn't wait to see if they'd gotten sick from the teleportation. He headed straight for the portal, and they all rushed to keep up with him. Damien once again found himself thankful that all the teleporting he'd done recently had helped build up a resistance to the unsettling feeling.

They waited in a line for a few moments before reaching the front and entering the swirling darkness.

Damien's feet hit sand. They stood in another arena, but this one was much bigger than the colosseum Delph had been training them in. The stands were chock full of spectators, and the dull roar of chatter filled the arena like a swarm of furious flies.

There were a dozen large, raised circular platforms scattered throughout the arena. A single person stood atop each one.

Before Damien could get a better look, Delph herded the five students toward an open spot in the sand and away from the portal.

"Can you at least tell us anything about the tournament now?" Nolan asked.

"The rules will be explained soon," Delph replied. "Besides, I think you should be able to get the general idea by looking around."

"There are going to be multiple matches at once, with the victors moving forward," Sylph said. "How many students are in the tournament?"

"No clue," Delph replied with a shrug. "I don't care. Just win your fights."

Luckily for Damien's nerves, it didn't take much longer

for the tournament to begin. Dean Whisp flew over the arena and snapped her fingers. The sound echoed through the sky like an explosion. Conversations died as everyone turned to look up at the woman.

"Welcome to the ranking battles," Dean Whisp called, her voice easily understandable despite her distance. "We will be starting shortly. Professors, please distribute the arena numbers to your students. Judges, prepare to begin the tournament."

Delph reached into his cloak and pulled out a sheaf of brown papers, handing one of the numbers to all of them. The paper had Damien's name and the number four on it.

"Students, once you get your number, please head to the appropriate ring. The rules will be explained shortly," Dean Whisp called. Before anyone could ask how to find the appropriate arena, glowing numbers the size of a small building blinked to life above each of the platforms.

Damien glanced at Sylph, who showed him her paper, which had 'one' written on it.

"Good luck," Damien told Sylph.

"And to you as well," Sylph replied as the group of students scattered for their respective stages. "Don't get knocked out before the finals."

"And the same to you," Damien said, locating the stage with the floating four above it and setting out toward it. Loretta trailed after him.

The stage wasn't too far away, so it was only a short walk. Damien arrived at a small crowd of around a dozen students. Loretta walked up beside him a few moments later.

"We're both at the fourth stage?" Damien asked.

"Apparently so." Loretta nodded, pulling out her paper and showing it to Damien. Her eyes flicked around the group of students surrounding them, and she shifted her weight from foot to foot.

Anyone in my group seem strong?

"I can't risk checking right now," Henry said. "The dean is too close, and there are a dozen other people who might notice me if I did anything. You're on your own for this one, Damien."

Wonderful.

Damien looked around the group. Most of the students sent each other wary glances, and they didn't look much more put together than Loretta did.

His eyes caught on one boy who had a large book strapped to his waist. Unlike the other students, the boy seemed mostly calm. He glanced up and made eye contact with Damien for an instant, but he broke away a moment later.

Nobody seems too strong, but I guess with magic it hardly matters.

"You'll need to learn how to sense magical energy pretty soon," Henry said. "It'll help you in situations like these, although it's possible to conceal your energy. I'm doing it almost constantly, actually. We'd be discovered in minutes if I didn't."

Something to look forward to after the tournament.

"Indeed," Henry said.

The judge standing on the stage above them cleared his throat to gather the students' attention. He had a middle length white beard and was balding. His features were wrinkled and aged by the sun, but that didn't conceal the slight twinkle in the man's eyes.

"The tournament will begin very shortly," the judge informed them. "There will be four qualifying rounds. The winners will progress, and that will continue until there is a single winner from each stage. There are twelve students per stage, so the student who has the most decisive victory in the initial and second rounds will be able to skip the third round of combat. Eight of the stages are dedicated to you first years, and the winners of each stage will enter the quarterfinals. Then things will progress as before until the victor is crowned. There will be five-minute breaks between every fight, no more and no less. Does that make sense to everybody?"

Damien and the other students nodded, all too nerve-racked to say anything. The judge chuckled and gave them a toothy grin.

"Don't worry too much, kids. Try to enjoy yourselves. If you're meant to do well, then you will. If you aren't, well, there are other ways to get resources at Blackmist. Just do your best."

Damien and Henry scoffed at the same time, although Damien did his best to hide his reaction. It was typical, the person who didn't have anything at stake was more than happy to tell them there was nothing to worry about.

The dull chatter that had built up while the students moved to their stages suddenly faded.

"Students and faculty of Blackmist," Dean Whisp said, her voice once again reaching Damien's ears as if she were standing right beside him, "get ready for this year's primary ranking battles! I'm sure our students are all anxious to begin, but I had to suffer this in my day, so I'll make them do the same."

The crowd let out some annoyed grumbles, but Dean Whisp kept talking.

"So, before the battles begin, I figured I'd give us all a quick rundown of Blackmist and how we came to be one of the greatest mage academies on the continent!"

The complaints from the spectators grew louder.

"Start the matches, Grandma!" someone yelled over the din.

"I heard that, Frederick," Whisp said, turning to glare at where the voice had come from.

Before she could say anything else, a dozen other voices joined the yelling. Whisp's calm façade cracked, and she let out a laugh.

"Oh, fine. I won't waste any more time. Let the ranking battles begin!"

CHAPTER
TWENTY-NINE

A cheer rose from the crowd. The judge cleared his throat to gather the small group of students' attention. He pulled a small leaflet of papers out from his black and purple jacket and scanned over it.

"The first to combatants will be...Damien and Volon."

Damien's blood went cold for a moment, but he shook himself off and swallowed, ignoring the tingles running down his hands and legs. The judge stepped aside, gesturing to the small staircase leading up to the stage.

A large boy wearing studded leather armor headed up first, and Damien followed him. He blocked out the roar of the crowd as the judge gestured for Volon to take his place on the other side of the stage.

Now that he was actually standing on it, Damien realized the platform was a good bit larger than he'd thought. There was more than enough space to run around and dodge attacks, and most area of effect spells would be unlikely to be able to cover the entire thing.

"My name is Darcy, and I'll be spectating for your group. The fight will go until one of you falls off the ring, surrenders, or is incapable of continuing," the judge said. "Lethal attacks are not permitted, but everything else is allowed. Don't worry about injuries. I am very capable with healing magic, so you'll walk out of this fight in better shape than you walked into it."

Damien and Volon nodded, only half-listening.

"Are you both ready?"

Damien and Volon nodded.

"Then...begin!"

Volon slammed his hands together. He pulled them apart, his fingers digging into the air and warping it. A swirl of light formed in the air in front of him. It flared, and a beam of energy shot out at Damien.

He dodged out of the way, drawing Ether through his arm and forming a Gravity Sphere. The beam of light hissed through the air, dissipating harmlessly at the edge of the stage as a ring of runes along the edge lit up.

As much as Damien would have liked to take a better look at the runes, he didn't have time. Volon was already drawing the Ether into another light magic attack. Damien flicked his hand, sending the gravity sailing through the air.

Volon dodged out of the way, a smirk crossing his face as the slow-moving spell hit the ground behind him.

"Really?" Volon asked, forcing Damien to duck out of the way of another searing light attack. "You bring a slow spell like that to—"

The sphere detonated. The sudden force ripped Volon's feet out from beneath him and tugged him into the center of the sphere, slamming his face into the ground with a *thunk*. Damien winced as he heard something crack.

Volon scrambled to his feet, his nose crooked and blood streaming down his face. His eyes were wide as he pointed a hand at Damien. Motes of light gathered in the air in front of him.

Damien lobbed another Gravity Sphere. Volon's spell fizzled, as he lunged, trying to dodge it. His efforts resulted in catching a Gravity Sphere to the leg instead of his chest. Damien was actually somewhat surprised to see the spell hit, but Volon was much slower than both Sylph and Delph.

He preemptively winced as both spells detonated. A dozen *cracks* and *pops* filled the air. Volon screamed and crumpled to the ground, one of his legs bent at several wrong angles.

Damien glanced at Darcy, but the judge shook his head. Damien swallowed and pushed down the distaste rising in his chest as he summoned another Gravity Sphere.

"I surrender!" Volon screamed.

Darcy stepped in between the two students, but Damien's spell was already fading. Darcy walked over to the crumpled boy and put his hand over Volon's leg. Pale white energy streamed out of his hand and entered the student.

Volon let out another pained, gargling cry as several *snaps* echoed through the air. His leg straightened, and his nose cracked back into position. Darcy offered Volon a hand. The defeated boy blinked, then reluctantly let the judge pull him to his feet.

"The winner for the first match is Damien!" Darcy said. "The next two are Blake and Jauin. Please, come up to the stage."

Damien and Volon headed down the stairs, pointedly not looking at each other. The other students in the small group sent Damien wary glances as the two of them took their spots back at the edge of the platform.

"Was that Space magic?" Volon asked after several moments of silence.

"Yeah," Damien said. "I'm sorry about your leg. I've never used that attack against anyone other than my professor and my roommate, but she's too fast to ever hit with it."

Volon heaved a sigh. "It's fine. I didn't expect to win the tournament. I just thought I'd do better than last place…"

"Don't feel too bad," Loretta said, glancing over at the disappointed boy. Her voice sounded uncertain and shaky. "Damien has been getting personal training from our professor. Everyone in the class knows it."

"Wait, how did you know?" Damien asked, taken aback.

"Man, you show up exhausted to every single class, and Delph doesn't give you pointers during class. It's pretty obvious," Loretta said, smirking. "Not that I envy you. I'm learning more than enough from his normal class. I don't fancy spending more time with the man."

"You're in Professor Delph's class?" Volon asked, raising an eyebrow.

"We are," Damien said. "Do you know something about him?"

"A little," Volon replied. "He was a mage on the front lines who retired for some classified reason. He's supposed to be a real menace. One of the best mages Blackmist has ever made. My professor told us he never thought Delph would teach a class, so something must have really happened for him to do it. But if you're getting trained by Delph, that makes things sting a bit less. If you beat your other opponents like you beat me, then I won't look like a total loser."

"I'll do my best," Damien said. "No promises, though. There are a lot of people, even in my class, that I'm not sure if I'd have a chance of beating."

"Like Sylph," Loretta said, shuddering. "I pity anyone who goes up against her."

Volon looked like he wanted to ask about her, but he was interrupted by the two boys heading back down from the stage. The pleased expression on Blake's face made it clear who'd won the fight.

"Loretta and Ulon, please, get on the stage," the judge commanded.

"Good luck!" Damien told Loretta.

She swallowed and nodded, heading up the stairs along with a short boy.

"Do you have any magic other than Space?" Volon asked Damien.

"A few," Damien replied noncommittally. "I've only practiced with Space, though."

"Damn." Volon sighed. "You better put on a good showing. If you don't at least make it to the semifinals, I'm going to look like a chump."

"You are a chump," Blake said, smirking at Volon. "You went down in what, three spells?"

"We'll see how you do against him," Volon said, crossing his arms. Blake eyed Damien, who returned his gaze with a flat stare.

Damien examined him for the first time. Blake had shaggy blond hair and a small scar on his cheek. He wore what might have been padded chainmail, but Damien suspected the metal had runes engraved onto it.

"Better than you, I'd think," Blake said. "He only used one spell, and it's slow. It didn't seem like it had that much range either."

Damien's hand shifted to a pocket in his cloak, where he'd stored several heating runes he'd created the previous night.

"We don't even know if we'll fight," Damien said. "One of us might get someone else or be knocked out in the next round. But, if we do, I look forward to finding out who'll come out on top."

Blake grunted in response. Damien found himself wishing

he'd paid more attention to Blake's fight. Knowing what the boy could do with his magic would have been a huge benefit, and Blake had already seen Damien's tricks.

"Loretta wins!" Darcy called out.

Damien glanced up, cursing at himself internally. He'd missed yet another fight while screwing around with the other students.

Loretta and her opponent descended the stairs. She looked winded, but a pleased grin was plastered over her face.

"Good job," Damien told Loretta as Darcy called the next two contestants onto the stage.

"Thank you," Loretta said. "It was really close, but Delph would have killed me if I went out in the first round."

She leaned in close, lowering her voice. "I think he's betting on who wins the tournament with the other teachers."

"No way. Really? How do you know?" Damien asked. While he spoke, he kept one eye on the stage. He hadn't caught the boy's names, but the one closest to him was the one who had been carrying the book at his side.

"He mentioned something about having money on the line during one of the classes," Loretta said, giggling. "He didn't look pleased that he said it."

"I wonder if he'll give the winner a cut if they're from his class," Damien said.

A spout of fire leapt out of the book wielding boy's hands, enveloping the stage in moments. Damien's eyes widened as the fire licked at the invisible walls surrounding the platform.

The fire swirled in the air for a few moments before fading. The other boy had raised a shield around himself made of glimmering white energy.

I really need to learn some defensive spells.

"They're next on the list. But the enlarge spell can be used defensively, even if it's not the best way to apply it," Henry agreed. "You've got your armor, but I'm not sure how much that'll help you against someone who fills the arena with fire. It didn't seem very strong, though. You might be able to take him out before he does much damage."

That's probably my best bet if he wins.

"I doubt he'll share any of his money," Loretta said. Damien, who had completely forgotten he was speaking with the girl, glanced in her direction.

"Travis wins!" Darcy roared. The book wielding boy stepped down the stage followed by his opponent, whose clothes had been stained black by soot.

Damien forced himself not to groan in annoyance. He just let out a chuckle and shook his head.

"You're probably right. Did you happen to see how that fight ended? I managed to miss it."

"Travis sent a fireball that broke the other guy's shield and hit him in the chest," Loretta replied.

"Thank you. He seems pretty strong."

Blake scoffed in the corner, and Damien rolled his eyes. If the kid tried any harder to sound cool, Damien was worried he'd gag.

Several fights passed, but nothing particularly interested Damien. Loretta won again, as did Blake. He was wondering if Darcy had forgotten him when the judge finally called his name out, along with Travis.

"Good luck," Loretta told Damien as he headed toward the stage, his stomach twisting again.

"Thanks," Damien replied, clenching and unclenching his hands. Darcy directed him to the far side of the platform. Once Damien got there, he drew a deep breath and let it out slowly.

Travis reached down and grabbed his book, running his hand along the spine. He looked bored. Damien gathered the Ether within his core.

"Begin!" Darcy yelled.

Damien hurled a Gravity Sphere in Travis' direction, already forming another one in his other hand. Travis stepped forward, twisting his body to avoid the spell. Damien smirked and released his concentration of the spell.

Without his will to control it, the Ether leapt to return to its natural state. Following the guidelines he'd set forth when visualizing the spell, the Gravity Sphere detonated midair, only a foot behind Travis.

The boy's head snapped back as he was yanked to the epicenter of the Gravity Sphere. Sparks of fire sputtered fruitlessly out of his hands as his concentration was broken and the spell fizzled.

Damien lobbed another Gravity Sphere at the edge of the stage where Travis had fallen. Before it could hit, Travis rolled over and pointed his hand at the oncoming orb. A blast of fire erupted from his hand, impacting the Gravity Sphere.

The Ether in Damien's sphere hissed as it reacted with Travis' magic. The sphere detonated prematurely, doing little more than dragging Travis a few feet across the ground. The boy rolled to his feet and thrust his hands toward Damien.

"Shit!" Damien cursed. He formed several more Gravity Spheres, tossing them at Travis and dashing across the arena.

For every bolt of fire Travis threw, Damien lobbed four or five of his own attacks.

"How much Ether do you have?" Travis cursed, dodging out of the way of a sphere.

Damien responded with two more attacks. They were slow and easy to dodge, but he had the advantage of being able to throw more attacks than Travis could ever hope to counter.

A sphere passed by Travis' head. His expression shifted to a smirk as fire curled around him.

Damien dropped to the ground and slammed his hands into it just as a wave of fire erupted from Travis, filling the arena. Travis held it there for several moments before lowering his hands, allowing the flame to recede.

A stone ring stood in the center of the arena where Damien had stood. Travis blinked, his hands raising as he realized the fight wasn't over.

The ring vanished, and Damien sent a Gravity Sphere hurtling at Travis. The boy dove out of the way, but the spell went off before he fully cleared it. Both of his feet were caught in the blast, and Damien repressed a grimace as he heard a dozen *cracks* fill the air.

Travis let out a cry of pain. Damien channeled another Gravity Sphere, but he glanced at Darcy to check if the man would stop the fight. The judge made no moves to intercede.

A searing pain erupted in Damien's shoulder as something slammed into it, spinning him in a circle. Damien gritted his teeth and dropped to the ground, slamming a hand into it and raising a stone barrier an instant before fire filled the arena again.

An image of Delph's disapproving glare passed through Damien's mind.

The fire lasted several seconds before fading. Instead of dropping the ring like he had before, Damien allowed the back portion to vanish while leaving the front intact. He formed a Gravity Sphere and dashed out from behind it, lobbing it straight at Travis.

The boy's eyes widened, and he rolled to the side. The sphere caught his arm, snapping it violently. Damien stepped forward, grimacing from the pain emanating from his shoulder, and channeled a Gravity Sphere through his good hand.

He tossed it at the boy's fallen form. Darcy shimmered into being directly in front of the spell. The judge raised a hand, grabbing the sphere and crushing it without even looking in Damien's direction.

"Damien wins!" Darcy yelled.

The judge knelt beside Travis, healing the boy's wounds. Travis sent Damien an angry glance as Darcy rose, but Damien ignored it. The searing pain in his shoulder had grown now that the adrenaline wore off.

Damien glanced at the spot where he'd been hit, but the mage armor barely even looked damaged. Darcy walked over to him and raised his hand over where Damien had been hit. A moment later, a relieved breath escaped his mouth as the pain vanished. Darcy waved them off the stage.

What was that? Why is my armor undamaged? I clearly got hit by a spell.

"Mage armor doesn't interfere with magic. There are runes on it to allow magic to pass through," Henry replied. "That way it doesn't get destroyed by the first spell that hits you. You shouldn't have been hit at all. You got distracted."

I know. I don't need you to tell me a second time. I won't let it happen again.

THIRTY

Darcy cleared his throat behind Damien and Travis as the two of them stepped off the stairs. A few minutes passed in relative silence, the cheers of the crowd and the sound of fighting from the other stages drowning everything else out.

"Actually, Damien, please return to the stage. You've been selected to fight again for the third round of combat."

Damien grimaced. Getting hit by whatever spell Travis had cast clearly excluded him from skipping out on the third round of combat. He steeled his expression and turned on his heel, heading back up the stairs to stand beside Darcy. He'd used up a decent amount of his energy already, but he wasn't in bad shape either.

"Loretta, please join us," Darcy said.

Shit.

"Don't even think about going easy on her because she's in your class. She'll beat your ass," Henry warned.

Don't worry. I won't, but this is going to make training awkward.

Loretta gave Damien a half-smile as she stepped onto the

stage. It wasn't hard to tell she was thinking around the same thing Damien was.

"Begin!" Darcy ordered.

Water rippled around Loretta's arms, launching out at Damien like twin snakes. His eyes widened at the speed of the attack, and he dropped to the ground, enlarging the sand into a wall. The water slammed into it, boring two holes clean through his defense and passing by Damien's head.

"Enlarge doesn't make things stronger!" Henry snapped. "It just makes them bigger and heavier. Either make your walls thicker or don't bother with them."

Damien didn't have time to respond. He scrambled away from the wall as a jet of water tore a path through it, cutting it clean in two. His spell faded, and the sand collapsed back to its normal size.

The Ether leapt to Damien's palms as he formed two Gravity Spheres. He threw them at Loretta, then ducked to the side as a bullet of water narrowly missed him.

Loretta enveloped herself in an orb of spinning water moments before the Gravity Spheres connected. The magic crackled, and large amounts of the sphere were torn away as the magic detonated, but Loretta remained unharmed.

While Loretta channeled her magic, Damien formed another two spheres and tossed them in her direction. She blocked them again, then sent two blasts of water streaming toward him.

Damien gritted his teeth, enlarging several grains of sand before him to make a wall thick enough to block Loretta's follow up attack. He gathered more Ether from a nearby line and channeled it into two more Gravity Spheres.

He lobbed one over the wall, then ducked back as water hissed by his face. Sweat trickled down his forehead and back, and Damien felt the strain of casting so many spells. He wasn't near the edge but continuing at this pace would make it difficult to do well in future fights if he managed to beat Loretta.

Damien collapsed the wall of sand and hurled the Gravity Sphere straight at Loretta. Her eyes widened. She breathed heavily and looked to be in much worse shape than Damien. She wrapped the water around herself, blocking the majority of the spell's damage but still getting dragged several feet to the side.

Damien sent several more spheres at the girl, forcing her to remain within her watery shield to avoid them.

"You're going to wear yourself out if you keep throwing these," Loretta warned him.

Damien tossed another sphere slightly to her side. She stumbled as the spell nearly pulled her over the edge of the stage. As the water gathered around her to attack Damien, he changed his plans. Instead of creating another wall, Damien dashed straight toward the girl.

Her eyebrows raised, but a flicker of a grin crossed her face. Loretta thrust her hands forward, and two more bullets of water tore through the air. Damien twisted to the side, avoiding one of them.

The other caught him in the right collarbone. Damien felt it punch clean through him. Pain erupted throughout his body as screaming tendrils of agony traced down his side, but he didn't stop running.

Loretta stepped to the side as Damien dove forward, landing on the ground directly in front of her. She grinned, water gathering at her hands as she prepared the final blow to put Damien down.

Damien pressed his hand against the ground beneath Loretta's feet and cast the enlarge spell. The girl didn't even have a chance to scream as the sand erupted out from beneath her, launching the girl several feet into the air and over the edge of the stage.

Darcy flickered forward, grabbing her by the collar before she could plummet to the ground below. Damien rolled over, holding his bleeding shoulder and cursing through gritted teeth.

The judge set Loretta on the stage and strode over to Damien, kneeling and healing his wounds.

"Thank you." Damien groaned as he stood up. Phantom pain still echoed through his body, but a quick check with his left hand proved it was entirely in his mind.

"No problem," Darcy said, frowning slightly. "I'm here to judge who wins, not your decision making. That being said, it wasn't smart to run straight at Loretta. In a real fight, that would have gotten you killed."

"I know, sir," Damien said, "but this isn't a real fight. My Ether is limited, and your healing isn't. It was my best chance of winning the fight while preserving myself for the future ones."

Darcy gave him a complicated look. Then he grunted and gestured for Damien and Loretta to get off the stage.

"That was a good fight," Loretta said, giving Damien a small nod as they got off the stage. "I didn't expect you to run straight at me. What if I'd hit you in the heart or the head?"

"You didn't," Damien said, scratching the back of his head. "And I figured Darcy would stop the fight if you were going to kill me. If I used any more magic, I don't think I would have had a great chance at making it in the next round."

Loretta rolled her eyes. "You were thinking about the next fight while you were on the stage for another one? That makes me feel a bit inadequate. Even if I'd won this fight, I was out of Ether. I wouldn't have been able to fight in the next one if it was anytime soon."

"It was still a good showing," Volon said, greeting them with a nod as they arrived beside him. "Probably the closest fight so far. Makes me feel a bit less awful about my performance. I think I might have just been outclassed this time around."

Blake grunted, but some of the cockiness had left his demeanor. Darcy called two more students onto the stage, but Damien didn't pay attention to the fight. He sat and let out a slow breath, focusing on keeping himself calm and recovering what energy he could before the next fight.

It felt like only a few minutes had passed when Damien heard the judge call out his name, along with Blake's. With a small grimace, Damien opened his eyes and stood. Blake didn't look at him as the two headed up the stairs and onto the stage.

"This is the last fight before the quarterfinals," Darcy announced as they took their spots on the stage. "Good job on getting this far, both of you."

Damien and Blake didn't respond. Their eyes were focused on each other, neither wanting to be slow on the uptake to channel their Ether once the fight started. Darcy smirked and raised a hand.

"Begin!" he ordered.

The air around Blake's hands crackled. Damien's nape tingled, and he let the Gravity Sphere he'd been forming fizzle, dropping to the ground, and enlarging a thick wall of sand.

The wall shuddered as a rather loud *bang* ripped through the air, blowing the wall to bits and releasing the Ether in the spell, causing it to collapse to its normal size.

Smoke rose in the air from where whatever spell Blake

had cast impacted the wall. Judging by the sparking yellow energy forming in the boy's hands, Damien suspected it was probably lightning.

He didn't give Blake time to get another spell off. Damien lobbed a Gravity Sphere in the boy's direction. This time, Blake was the one forced to drop his spell. He dove to the side as the spell detonated, getting yanked backward several feet but avoiding the impact.

Blake hit the ground in a roll. He thrust a hand at Damien before he rose. A small bolt of yellow energy shot out from it, clipping Damien in the foot right as he threw his second Gravity Sphere.

Damien let out a pained gasp, and his hand wavered, sending the sphere awry from its course. Instead of hitting Blake in the chest, it hit the ground slightly behind him, catching one of his arms in the blast and breaking it with a *snap*.

Blake's face went pale, and he cried out in pain. Damien shifted his weight to take the pressure off his injured foot and sent another spell hurtling in his opponent's direction.

The other boy threw himself forward and rolled to his feet, his face pallid. Energy crackled to life in his good hand while the other hung limply at his side. The sphere detonated behind him, causing him to stumble.

The lightning bolt went wide, striking the invisible rune walls of the platform harmlessly. Damien tossed another sphere at him, but his eyes went wide when he realized the energy sparking at Blake's hand still hadn't evaporated.

A second blast of energy ripped out of the boy's hand. With no time to dodge, Damien crossed his hands in front of himself. Pain tore through his body as the bolt sent him skidding back several feet. His injured leg nearly gave out under him, but he remained standing through sheer force of will.

Damien cried out in pain, and his arms dropped limply to his sides, small trails of smoke rising from them. They felt fried, broken, and bruised at the same time.

"You were better than I expected," Blake said between ragged gasps. He raised his good hand, energy starting to collect around it slowly.

Damien desperately tried to raise one of his arms, but all he got for his efforts was a stabbing pain so fierce he nearly passed out. Time seemed to slow down as he saw the magic gather at Blake's fingertips.

A drop of sweat trickled down Damien's brow. He grabbed the Ether within himself using his mental energy, channeling it through his injured leg.

The droplet reached the bridge of his nose. It trailed further downward, beading up on the tip of his nose before finally falling.

A Gravity Sphere formed at the top of Damien's foot. He kicked it toward Blake, using his momentum to fall onto his back. A bolt of lightning screamed over him, passing so close to his nose he smelled the ozone.

Time snapped back to normal. Damien's back hit the sandy ground. His spell detonated as the lightning bolt hit the invisible wall of the platform, and dozens of loud *snaps* filled the air. Blake's cry of pain accompanied them.

Damien tried to roll over, but the pain ravaging his body wouldn't even let him budge. He squeezed his eyes shut, unable to even turn his head to see what had happened to Blake through his haze of agony.

After what felt like hours but was truly only a few moments, sweet relief washed over Damien. He drew in a sharp breath as Darcy's face swam into vision above him.

"Who won?" Damien asked.

"You did," Darcy said. "Your last attack caught Blake in

the side."

"Ah. That explains the crunch," Damien said. "Is he okay?"

"Of course, he is," Darcy said, pulling Damien to his feet. Blake had already left the stage, and that didn't bother Damien much. The sound of his spell striking the other boy still echoed in his head, and his own wounds were still fresh on his mind. "Congratulations on winning stage eight."

"Thank you," Damien said, shaking the lethargy off. He was tired, but he still had enough Ether for at least one more fight. Hopefully. "When is the next round?"

A grin tugged at the edge of Darcy's mouth. "Now. Part of this tournament is testing your abilities in continuous battle, especially as you get higher up in it. Don't fear, you've already done quite well for yourself. There's no shame in getting knocked out in the quarterfinals."

Damien nodded, but it was clear he didn't believe Darcy's words for a second. The old judge shook his head with a sigh.

"Well, good luck. Someone will arrive shortly to take you to the finals stage. The other fights should be wrapping up right about now as well."

True to his word, it was only a few minutes before the shadows on the stage stretched. The student who had brought Damien to the obsidian courtyard rose from the ground. He didn't look any more excited than he had been the first time Damien saw him.

"Ready?" he asked Damien.

"I don't think I've got a choice," Damien said.

"Not really," the other boy agreed, extending a hand. Damien took it.

They both sank into the ground. Damien felt like he'd been enveloped by a cold, wet blanket. His nose twisted in distaste, but it was impossible to move beyond that. Luckily, they arrived on top of a new stage a few moments later. The boy sank back into the ground without another word. At the same time, without warning, Damien felt Henry rapidly retreat into the depths of his mind.

"Not the best experience, is it?"

Damien turned to see Nolan standing beside him. The noble boy's blond hair was matted to his head, and his fancy armor had several scratches in it. Despite that, he didn't look too injured.

"Not in the slightest," Damien agreed. He peered over the edge of the stage and immediately regretted it. They were much higher than the previous stage, far enough away from the ground that a fall would almost certainly be fatal if someone didn't catch them.

A thin man at the center of the stage approached them.

"The quarterfinals are about to commence. The two of you will be opponents for this match. Are you both able to fight? You may, of course, withdraw at any time."

Nolan and Damien exchanged a glance before both shaking their heads at the same time.

"Delph would kill me," Damien said. Nolan nodded in agreement.

A hint of a smile appeared on the judge's face. He gestured for the two boys to take their places on either side of the stage.

"In that case, please, prepare yourselves. Do not fear for your safety. I have air magic in addition to healing, so you will not die if you fall off the stage."

"Good luck," Nolan told Damien. "May the strongest of us move forward. Not for the sake of the tournament, but so that Delph doesn't make the whole class run laps."

"Agreed," Damien said.

"Begin!" the judge ordered.

CHAPTER
THIRTY-ONE

The sand on the platform rose around Nolan, twisting into twin blades in his hands. He dashed toward Damien, his blades trailing through the sand behind him. Damien grimaced, Delph's warning fresh in his mind. Don't let them get close to you. Sure.

Damien gathered Ether in his hands, quickly tossing a Gravity Sphere at the ground directly between them to stop Nolan from closing the gap too quickly. The noble boy spun out of the way with surprising grace, completely avoiding the spell as it detonated.

The second sphere landed on the ground where Nolan headed. However, something suddenly yanked Nolan upward and out of the sphere's range.

Damien's eyes widened, and he threw himself to the side as Nolan slammed into the ground where he'd been standing.

"You've got wind magic?" Damien complained as he rolled over and hopped back to his feet. A sword whistled past his chest, narrowly missing him.

"You never asked," Nolan replied.

Damien hardened his mage armor as one of the blades

sliced at his right arm. It rang harmlessly off his defenses. He jumped back as Nolan thrust a sword at his stomach, channeling Ether faster than he ever had before.

Gravity Spheres formed in both of Damien's hands. He tossed them both on the ground in between them, forcing Nolan to use his wind magic to launch into the air and avoid the strike.

The boy wobbled slightly before dropping back down, a small grimace on his face. They were both panting heavily now. Damien no longer had any thoughts of saving energy for the next fight. He just wanted to survive this one.

Before Damien could draw more Ether, Nolan was upon him again. The boy's weapons seemed like arcs of light as they slashed through the air. Damien found himself thankful for Delph's training as he instinctively blocked several of the blows with the mage armor while backpedaling.

His Ether was getting low after how much he'd already used it that day. Nolan was clearly running out as well, but Damien's reaction timing was also growing worse. A lucky strike drew a thin line across his left cheek that gushed blood.

Damien dropped into a roll right past Nolan's legs, just barely avoiding a thrust meant for his stomach. He drew on the Ether as he hopped back to his feet, then forced it through every one of his limbs.

His attention frayed as he tried to keep four spells functional at the same time. Nolan stepped toward him, raising his twin swords.

"You should concede," Nolan warned him. "You're exhausted. I don't want to accidentally hurt you badly. You had a good run, Damien. It's fine to stop here."

"Likewise," Damien wheezed. He tossed the Gravity Spheres in his hands at Nolan.

The boy threw himself to the side, avoiding the attack and

dashing toward Damien. Damien slumped, and a triumphant smile crossed Nolan's face as victory came within his grasp.

Only too late did he see Damien wore the exact same expression.

"Sorry," Damien said. He stepped into the strike, dodging one of the swords while allowing the other one to punch clean through his stomach. He didn't even have the Ether left to harden his mage armor.

Damien wrapped his arms around Nolan, holding the other boy as the two Gravity Spheres he'd formed at his feet expanded. With the last of his energy, Damien swept Nolan's legs out from under him. They fell directly on top of the spells.

Nolan's eyes went wide, but it was too late. The spells detonated.

The next few moments were a haze of pain and agony. He was pretty sure his arms were completely mangled, and his side felt like something had taken a huge bite out of it.

Nolan's eyes were wide open, but the boy wasn't speaking. He'd passed out from the pain. Damien likely would have as well, had he experienced much worse multiple times when dealing with It Who Heralds the End of All Light.

Slowly, Damien forced himself to move. The wound in his chest was bleeding profusely now that Nolan's blade had disintegrated. He felt lightheaded, but he was still able to slowly worm his way onto his knees.

"I'm still conscious," Damien rasped.

The judge rushed to their side, magic spiraling out from him and into the two boys' bodies. If anything, the pain grew worse for a few moments as Damien's bones snapped back into place and repaired themselves.

"Are you trying to kill yourself?" the judge demanded.

"What was that? Do you think throwing yourself on a sword and into your own spell is heroic or something?"

Damien didn't respond immediately. After the *cracks* emerging from his body had stopped, and he was no longer bleeding out, he let out a relieved sigh. "No. I just needed to win."

"You can hardly call this a victory. You would have both died had I not been here to save you. The greatest victory is to survive the fight," the judge said, massaging his brow.

"But I did win the fight, didn't I?"

"Technically. You were still awake when your opponent was unconscious," the judge said, pressing his lips thin. "That doesn't mean it wasn't incredibly stupid. Blackmist does not encourage our students to kill themselves to win."

"I know," Damien said, rolling his shoulders and carefully rising to his feet.

The judge just shook his head. "I'll let your teacher beat some sense into you, but won. Your determination is impressive. The other quarterfinals are wrapping up, so your next fight will be coming up soon. I suggest you withdraw immediately to avoid further pain."

Damien twisted his nose, considering the man's words. Then he inclined his head.

"I'm sorry. I promised I wouldn't," he said.

The judge just shook his head. "Somehow, I thought you'd refuse."

He knelt beside Nolan, snapping his fingers over the boy's face. Nolan's eyes popped open, and he drew in a jerky breath. He looked at his hands, then glanced up at Damien.

"You're really something else," Nolan muttered. "That was insane. Don't you have any self-preservation?"

"More than you could ever imagine," Damien said,

offering the noble his hand. Nolan shook his head and accepted it, allowing Damien to pull him to his feet.

"My father is going to be furious," Nolan asked. "Are you at least going to win the competition?"

"Not a chance," Damien said, chuckling. "I don't even have a single spark of Ether left."

"Damn," Nolan sighed. "Good fight, I guess. I'm glad you're on our side."

The judge just shook his head. "I'm going to fly us to the semifinal and finals platform. Are you prepared?"

"As much as I'm going to be," Damien said.

"I'll return to bring you back to the ground in a moment," the judge told Nolan. He grabbed Damien, and the two of them launched into the air.

They flew through the sky, crossing the large arena and arriving at a large pillar in the center of the arena. It was even taller than the others, and there were three other students already on it.

The judge set Damien down in a protruding waiting area at the edge of the platform and flew off without another word. A small grin crossed Damien's face as he looked at the semifinalists.

Sylph and Mark had both made it. The only other student there was a muscular boy with long hair Damien didn't recognize.

"You made it," Sylph said. She looked tired but pleased. "Good job."

"Barely. Nolan nearly took me out."

"I didn't think you'd get this far. Well done," Mark told him. "Delph is going to be happy. Three out of four of us are from his class."

The muscular boy grunted. "Talk about it. I feel

completely out of place. I heard Delph was a good teacher, but this is ridiculous. Has he been giving you magical plants or something?"

"He's just very motivational," Damien said. "Are they going to let us take a break before the next fight?"

"I doubt it," Mark said. "The judge who brought me here said we'd start as soon as everyone arrived."

Sure enough, no sooner than Mark had spoken the words, a dark blur flashed across the sky. Dean Whisp herself landed on the stage. She strode toward them, her face unreadable. Damien felt Henry retreat even deeper within his mind.

"Congratulations, all of you," Whisp said, stopping directly before them. "You've all done very well getting this far. We'll be starting the last few fights immediately. The crowd is very eager to watch you all. Now that you've all gotten here, we'll give you a little more freedom. Would anyone like to volunteer to go first?"

Everyone exchanged glances. Damien glanced at Sylph, then jerked his chin at the stage. She raised her eyebrows but nodded, stepping forward. Damien did the same.

"We'll go," Damien said.

"Very well. Thank you for volunteering," Whisp said. "Please, step onto the stage. I won't be overseeing your finals as the Year Four finals are about to begin as well, but your judge was temporarily delayed. He should be here any moment."

Damien and Sylph walked onto the stage, taking their spots. Dean Whisp looked into the sky, tapping her foot impatiently. Several minutes passed, but Damien wasn't able to recover much of his Ether at all. A dull headache thrummed in the back of his head.

"Here he comes," Whisp said.

They glanced around. Damien nearly jumped as the ground beside Whisp arose in a shower of sand. A stocky man with a well-kept beard and heavy plate armor emerged from the ground, a huge axe strapped to his back.

He whispered something into the dean's ear. She frowned but nodded.

"That's fine," Whisp said. "Take care of the finals. I'll deal with it."

She launched into the air, vanishing in moments, and leaving everyone staring at her back with baffled expressions.

"Well, then," the judge said, clearing his throat. "I'm Teg. I'll be the judge for the semifinals and finals. We're on a bit of a schedule, so you'll have to excuse me for being prompt. Are the two of you ready?"

Damien's hand twitched, but he just nodded. Sylph did the same.

"Then you may begin."

Teg sounded a little bored, but Damien ignored the man. Sylph enveloped herself in her magic, fading into the background.

The miniscule amount of Ether floating within Damien's core wasn't going to be of much help against her. Damien forced his headache to the back of his mind, reaching into his back pocket.

He kept his eyes on the sand in front of him. It was looser on the stage than it had been in the arena they'd trained in, and Sylph's camouflage didn't let her walk completely without a trace.

Several terse moments ticked by. A grain of sand shifted to Damien's left. His hand tightened on the papers. Then, abruptly, he threw himself into a roll. He came back to his feet, but there was nobody behind him.

"Damn," Damien said. "Thought she'd attack me."

A line of darkness carved through the air, nearly catching Damien across the side. At the last moment, he managed to hurl himself out of the way and avoid the attack. If it hadn't been for his weeks of training with Sylph, he never would have heard her coming.

She flickered into view for a moment before fading away again. A small frown crossed Damien's face. She looked exhausted. Even if she managed to defeat him in this round, the chances of her winning the finals were nonexistent.

Damien grabbed several of the papers from the wreath and slammed them onto the ground. The runes lit up on impact. A pillar of fire roared up around Damien, blocking him from the rest of the arena.

Then he sat inside it, setting the other papers on the ground in front of him and yawning. He could still see outside the ring through the flickers in the flame but passing through it without getting injured would be impossible.

"Sitting in a fight?" Teg asked, disapproving. "Finish him, girl. The boy is toying with you."

Sylph faded into view. "I can't. I don't have enough energy for a ranged attack, and I can't get to him through the fire."

Damien gave her a wide grin. "I'm planning my next move. I don't think there are any rules on a time limit, are there?"

Teg's eye twitched. "There are not. There never needed to be one."

"Fantastic," Damien said. He leafed through the thick pile of papers. "I've got a few of these, so I might be thinking a bit."

Sylph's eyes widened. She immediately sat and drew a deep breath, trying to relax and recover Ether.

"What do you two think you're doing?" Teg asked. "This is a fight! You can't just...sit down."

"I'm thinking," Damien replied. "A plan is an important part of a winning strategy. I don't know what my opponent is doing, but I'm not dumb enough to rush someone stronger than I am."

One of the papers wrinkled and burned. Damien took another slip from the pile and replaced it, reigniting the flames. Teg drew a deep breath, but Damien didn't look in his direction.

Sylph had less Ether than the rest of them, but that meant she could take every bit of it farther. Without any Ether for the final, she was doomed to lose. However, if he could buy some time for her to recover, she'd get a lot more out of it than any of the other students.

Damien considered trying to win the round himself, but he dismissed it immediately. If Mark won his round, there was no way he'd stand a chance against the boy. The strategy he used against Nolan would be worthless against Mark's armor, and the boy had much more training than he did. He'd used too much Ether in the previous fights, so his only advantage was gone.

Whenever one of the rune papers faded, Damien replaced it. He'd packed quite a few of them, and most of them had survived his previous fights.

Teg's face progressively turned a darker shade of red with every minute that passed. He gritted his teeth and stood with his arms crossed, tapping his foot impatiently.

Minutes turned to nearly half an hour. Dean Whisp appeared in the sky, looking at Teg with a baffled expression.

"What in the Seven Planes is going on?" Whisp demanded. "Why is the semifinal still going?"

"They're refusing to fight," Teg snapped. "This has never

happened before, but there's nothing in the rules about how long a fight can take!"

"Well, we've hardly had people refuse to fight before," Whisp said, glancing from Sylph to Damien. "Isn't this the girl who won every fight in one or two moves? Why— Oh. You're out of Ether. Hmm. Interesting."

Shit. Maybe I shouldn't have gotten the scary lady's attention.

Damien glanced at Sylph. She looked much better than she had when the fight started. Damien doubted she'd been able to recover all her Ether, but maybe she'd gotten enough to give her an edge in the final.

He grabbed the remaining papers and tossed them into the fire. They went up in a flash. Within a few minutes, the remainder of the fire died down. Damien stood, stepping out from the flames once they'd lowered enough.

Sylph's eyes opened. She rose to her feet as well and Teg let out a sigh. "Finally. Just...fight, will you? This is just pitifu—"

Sylph blurred forward. Damien didn't try to move. Her blade stopped against his throat, drawing a thin line of blood.

"I surrender. That was a killing blow," Damien said.

Teg's eyes looked like they wanted to bulge out of his head. "Why, you little—"

"Teg," Whisp said sharply. "That's the end of the match. He surrendered, and we clearly need to change the rules. The loophole is our fault not theirs. Finding unique solutions to problems is admirable. As far as I'm concerned, they were just smarter than we were. Brains are just as important as brawn in a fight."

Whisp gave Damien a thoughtful stare. He swallowed, wondering if he'd just made a serious mistake. He walked off the stage, Whisp's keen eyes tracking his back. He returned to the waiting area and sat as the other students watched him with shocked expressions.

"You wily bastard," Mark said. "You were just buying time for her to recover her Ether, weren't you?"

"Enjoy your match," Damien said, the corner of his mouth quirking up. Semifinals wasn't such a bad spot to lose, after all.

CHAPTER
THIRTY-TWO

Sylph stepped off the stage a few moments later. She sat beside Damien as Mark and the other boy rose from their seats and walked onto the arena unbidden.

"Mark versus Urvo. Begin!" Teg ordered once they'd taken their positions. "And I better not see any funny b—"

"Teg," Whisp warned. "Enough. I'll not tolerate this unprofessional behavior any longer."

The man's mouth closed. At the same time, sand rushed up from the ground, enveloping Mark in his armor. The boy raised his sword, then lowered into a fighting stance, waiting for his opponent to make the first move.

Urvo thrust his hands forward. A wave of dark energy rippled out from his hand, buffeting Mark and forcing him back several steps.

"He's another dark magic user," Damien said aloud.

"With a lot more energy than I have," Sylph said. It was difficult to tell if her words were annoyed or if she was just stating a fact.

Blades of dark energy slipped out from the shadows now covering the stage and slashed at Mark. However, not a single blow connected in a meaningful way. Several were caught by his sandy armor, while he blocked the remainder with his sword.

Mark made his way toward Urvo, pressing through the hail of attacks raining down on him. Damien could see Urvo panicking as the boy realized his magic was borderline worthless against the other student.

"I don't think his strikes are as dangerous as yours," Damien observed as a blade of shadow harmlessly bounced off Mark's armor. "If you'd landed half of those hits on Mark, he'd probably be down for the count already."

"It's possible," Sylph allowed. "He's got a lot more magical energy than I do, though. I don't know if I'd be able to beat Urvo."

"What about Mark?" Damien asked.

"Not sure about that either. I'm pretty sure he's been holding back in the fights we had in class. If he actually went all out..." Sylph trailed off, ending the sentence with a shrug.

Mark gained ground on Urvo. He slowly forced the other boy toward the edge of the arena. Mark bled from a few wounds on his hands and face, but none of them were serious.

Urvo's expression grew more strained as Mark gained ground on him. He redoubled his efforts, but it was ineffective. Mark's armor and reflexes were just too much.

With a sudden burst of speed, Mark dashed forward, ducking past several attacks, and slicing out with his sword. He stopped it an inch from Urvo's neck.

"Killing blow," Teg announced. Urvo's shoulders slumped, and he let out a defeated sigh.

"Damn," Urvo said. "You're insane. How can you move that quickly? I've never met anyone who could block all of my attacks like that."

"There were too many of them with too little power," Mark replied, lowering his sword. "You should focus on throwing some stronger attacks in between the weak ones. You can whittle weaker opponents to death with mosquitoes, but that isn't going to work against anyone stronger than you."

Urvo pursed his lips and gave the other boy a curt nod. He headed back to the stands, and Sylph rose, walking onto the arena to take his place.

"Well, it took long enough, but this is the final match of the Year One ranking battles," Teg announced. "Are the two of you prepared?"

Sylph and Mark nodded, not taking their eyes off each other.

"Then begin!"

Sylph slipped back, fading out of sight instantly. Sand flowed up Mark's body, thickening his armor. He used a tactic similar to Damien's, watching the ground to spot Sylph before she got close to him.

The ground where she'd been standing dimpled. Mark took a step back just in time to avoid a flicker of darkness as Sylph sliced through the air where he'd been standing, flickering into view in the air above him before fading again.

"You jumped that far?" Mark asked, impressed. The response was a slash that carved a deep furrow in his arm, cutting through the sand and drawing a thin red line up to his shoulder.

Mark's gaze narrowed. He stomped a foot on the ground. Sand erupted around him in a violent storm, pattering around Sylph and revealing her position.

He lunged at her, his blade flickering like a hungry viper. A clang rang out as Sylph caught the strike with her magic, and the two of them started the fight in earnest.

Damien struggled to track the students as they clashed within the sandstorm. Several cuts appeared along Mark's chest, and his armor turned a light pink from the blood mixing in with the sand, but the injuries seemed to be little more than superficial.

Sylph's speed let her stay ahead of Mark's attacks, but they knew it was only a matter of time. They were both low on Ether, but Sylph had always been at the disadvantage in that regard.

The sand churned faster. Mark caught a strike with the pommel of his sword and retaliated with a blindingly fast strike. Sylph flickered back, reappearing for an instant with an ugly red wound running across her chest.

Blood splashed onto the sand, but she didn't make a single noise. She faded back into her camouflage.

"Don't let yourself bleed out," Mark warned her. "That wound looked serious."

Despite his words, he didn't let his sword lower for a second. A blur of darkness flew out of the sand, blurring past his guard and carving a deep furrow through his side. Mark grimaced as the magic cut clean through his armor and into the flesh beneath it.

The sand rushed to cover the hole, but the damage was already done. Now both bled heavily from their wounds.

Sylph's invisibility faded. She reappeared several feet from Mark, a short sword made of dark energy flickering in her hand. A few moments later, the sandstorm faded as well. The two of them stared at each other, panting.

"Looks like it'll come down to our swordsmanship," Mark said, smirking. "You're lucky Damien bought you that extra time to recover. This would have been over already if he hadn't."

Sylph changed her stance, holding the sword in front of her with one hand while placing the other behind her back.

"You aren't going to win this," Mark said. "I'm stronger than you are."

"I know," Sylph replied.

They dashed at each other. Sylph's sword flickered and vanished. Mark's concentrated frown didn't waver for a second. They were upon each other in an instant. Sylph twisted, bringing her other hand forward as Mark swung his sword at her side.

Sylph was an instant faster. Her open hand thudded into Mark's chest. The tiny white corner of a slip of paper stuck out from beneath her palm.

A blast of fire engulfed Mark, the force causing him to stagger and miss his attack. The blade flickered back to life in her hand, and she raised it to his neck before Mark could recover.

"Death blow," Sylph said quietly.

The platform was silent. Mark's jaw clenched, but he slowly lowered his sword.

"Sylph wins," Teg announced, his words disbelieving.

Whisp glanced from Sylph to Damien. A flicker of a grin crossed the stern woman's face. Without a word, she launched into the sky and vanished through the clouds.

"You're a smug little bastard, aren't you? The two of you weren't even competing in the same tournament as we were." Urvo said to Damien.

"They never gave us any rules," Damien replied, trying and failing to hide his grin. "Maybe they won't keep us in the dark next time."

Teg looked like a blood vessel was about to burst on his face. The judge let out an explosive sigh and stormed over to the two students, healing them while muttering under his breath.

"Congratulations on first place," Teg told Sylph. He turned to the other students. "The results of the ranking battles will be released to your teachers shortly. They'll direct you to the location where you can pick up your rewards."

The platform rumbled. Damien wobbled as the ground shook beneath his feet. The platform slowly lowered to the ground.

"None of your teachers will be holding any class today, so feel free to do whatever you'd like with your time," Teg continued, his voice flat. "You've all done well getting here."

The platform accelerated its descent. The ground rose quickly toward them, but as soon as they got close, it slowed. When they touched the ground, Damien barely even felt the impact. He combed his hair back with his hands, the dull headache muted by his victory.

"Go on," Teg snapped, waving his hand irritably. "Get out of here. There's a portal right outside the arena."

Sylph and Mark walked over, joining Damien and Urvo. Mark pursed his lips and raised an eyebrow.

"Why do I feel like I was fighting both of you in that last fight?" Mark asked.

"There weren't any rules about outside help," Damien said.

"Evidently," Mark muttered. "That won't work on me next time, though."

He inclined his head, clearly annoyed, and strode out of the arena. The other three watched him go.

"Delph's students are insane," Urvo declared. "I'll be watching for you guys in the next tournament."

He left as well. Damien and Sylph exchanged a glance.

"Lunch?" Sylph suggested. Damien nodded empathetically.

They left the arena and headed to the mess hall. The campus was more crowded than Damien had ever seen it, so it took them several minutes of waiting in line until they were able to order.

Once Sylph had ordered and put the bill on Delph's tab, the two students found a spot at one of the tables at the end of the room. They sat, and Damien let out an exhausted sigh.

"I thought they were going to call me on stalling our fight," he said. "We're lucky Dean Whisp didn't seem to mind too much."

"I don't think I would have had a chance of winning without that," Sylph admitted. "I barely won, even with your heat runes. And I get the feeling Mark was still holding back."

"Well, all that matters is you won," Damien said. "There was no way I had a chance of taking Mark out, even if I managed to beat you, which I don't think would have happened. We should definitely be able to go on some of the higher-level missions now."

Their runes lit up. Damien pressed the glowing light, summoning the plate of slop before him. He bit back a gag and lifted it, holding his nose shut as he tipped the food into his mouth and swallowed without chewing.

He shuddered, his lips pulling back in a grimace, and set the disturbingly clean plate back on the table.

Sylph took two of the sticks of dumplings from her plate and set them on Damien's. He gave her an appreciative nod.

"Thanks," Damien said, taking a bite out of a dumpling.

"I think I'm the one who owes you the thanks," Sylph replied.

Damien finished chewing and shrugged. "Placing high will help both of us. We've both got reasons to get a lot of points and gold, the least of which is so I can afford to eat something other than their free slop."

"I was wondering about that, actually," Sylph said. "There are a lot of students at this school, but even after a big event like the ranking battles, the mess hall is just barely full. There's no way everyone could fit in here. That means most people are eating somewhere else."

"We could ask Delph," Damien suggested. "He's sure to be happy that you won, so maybe he'll tell us."

"We can ask tomorrow," Sylph said. "And I hope they get our winnings to us quickly. Our room needs a door already."

Damien nodded in agreement. He took another bite out of a dumpling. A hand clapped his shoulder, and he nearly leapt into the air. He spun to see Sean standing behind him, a grin on his face.

"Look at you two," Sean said. "First place and a semifinalist. I've never seen Teg so annoyed before. It really looked like the two of you completely played the system. They're going to have to release a whole slew of new rules prohibiting students from helping each other now."

"Hello, Sean," Damien said, nodding to the older boy. "You saw the fights?"

"Hard not to," Sean replied. "Everyone else was done like... half an hour before the Year Ones. You should have seen my face when I realized it was you two sitting in the arena, refusing to fight. I wish I'd thought of doing something like that. I got knocked out in the quarterfinals after running out of Ether."

"Hopefully, the school isn't too annoyed," Damien said, rubbing the back of his head. "It's just that they didn't give us rules, so we figured anything went."

Sean let out a burst of laughter. "Oh, you did great. Antagonizing Teg is one of life's greatest pleasures. He's the teacher for several of the advanced combat classes in your second year, so driving him up the wall is a rite of passage."

"Well, I hope we don't get landed with him if we're still at Blackmist next year," Damien said. "I don't think he likes me much."

"He doesn't like anyone," Sean replied, sitting beside them and tapping the rune circle on the table to activate it. "At least he's got a reason to dislike you."

"Do you know what the tournament rewards are?" Sylph asked, setting down her empty skewer and starting on another. "They haven't told us yet, and it would be nice to know if it's going to be worth much."

"For first place? It should be pretty hefty, even if it's just the Year One prize. I'd expect a good number of credits, some medicinal plants, and a small sum of gold," Sean said. "I've never actually placed first. The highest I got was a semifinalist in Year Two, and the reward for that was solid."

"That's a relief," Damien said. "We need a door."

"Among other things," Sylph agreed.

Sean chuckled. His rune circle lit up, and he tapped it. A plate of steak and potatoes appeared on the table before him. "I know what you mean. It's good to get one now to get ahead of the curve."

He trailed off, remembering something. Then his face cleared, and he gave them a wide grin. "But we're not meant to talk much about what you'll see in Year Two, as it'll cheapen the experience or some equally stupid garbage. Either way, I'm not trying to get on the professors' bad sides, so I'll stop there."

That was the worst thing he could have said, as now Damien very much wanted to know what happened in Year Two. However, Sean clearly wasn't going to give him any information on the topic, so he didn't press it. "Say, do you know why nobody eats here?"

Sean glanced up, something sparkling behind his eyes. "What do you mean?"

"Well, there are a lot of students at the college, but the mess hall never gets overcrowded," Damien said. "They've got to be eating somewhere else."

"You're right," Sean said. "A lot of students hunt their own meals. The forest to the east side of campus has quite a few low- to mid-level monsters. Eating them is good for your body and helps you grow your core. However, most Year Ones aren't ready to fight monsters, so it isn't encouraged until Year Two."

"Not encouraged, but not against the rules?" Sylph asked.

"Nah, you're welcome to if you want," Sean said, taking a large bite out of his steak.

Damien and Sylph exchanged a glance.

"Why do you eat in the mess hall if the monsters in the forest are better?" Damien queried.

"Hunting is a pain, and my powers aren't suited for it," Sean replied, taking another bite of steak. "Besides, who wants to spend all their time running around a forest? It's time-consuming and tiring. I'll hunt every once and a while, but the improvements just aren't worth the effort for me. I'm not planning on being a combat mage anyway."

"Fair enough," Damien agreed, finishing off the last dumpling in one large bite.

Sylph finished her own meal a few moments later. They exchanged another minute or so of small talk with Sean before bidding the older boy farewell and heading back to their room.

CHAPTER
THIRTY-THREE

Mark and the Gray siblings weren't there yet. Damien's headache had already abated, and his Ether reserves were nearly full once again.

"I think I might as well continue expanding our room," Damien said. "I don't think I've got the brainpower to try to learn a new spell right now, so menial labor sounds perfect. It'll help my cultivation anyway."

"I won't stop you," Sylph said. "I've got to practice my own cultivation."

She headed into the first training room and sat, closing her eyes and starting to meditate. Damien continued through the hallway, stepping into the room-in-progress behind it. He channeled a single mote of Ether out through his palm, creating an orb of destructive energy, and got to work on the walls.

Within him, Henry stirred for the first time in hours. Slowly, like a cat waking up from a long nap in the sun, the eldritch creature let out a yawn.

Hello, Henry. You've been out of it for a while.

"I had to make sure the dean wasn't going to drop by and

give you a surprise visit," Henry replied. "Drawing her attention wasn't wise."

I know. I realized that about a second too late. There isn't much I can do about it now.

Henry sighed. "If you thought things through before you did them, we'd rule half the Mortal Plane already. I'll admit, it was smart to buy the girl time. You weren't going to beat her, and you certainly weren't going to beat the wild boy. This way, she feels even more indebted to us."

That's not why I did it. The better we both do, the more we can get. She's on my team, remember?

"And she owes you more than she can pay back in quite some time," Henry said, his voice smug. "She will be useful."

You should put that spark of humanity to work and figure out what a friendship is. It'll help you out in the long run. Not everyone has to be a tool or an enemy.

"Hmm. We'll see," Henry said noncommittally. "Regardless, your performance was adequate today. You displayed a decent amount of critical thinking skills if we pretend you didn't bring us to the attention of a woman who might be able to see me if she tries hard enough."

Thanks. I think.

Henry chuckled and retreated into the back of Damien's mind once again. Damien just sighed and redoubled his efforts, forming an orb in his other hand and tearing through the wall like it was made of paper.

He worked through the rest of the day, pausing once to recover his Ether. As weariness crept into his mind, Damien finally allowed the orbs to fade. He was covered with a thin layer of stone dust.

Henry stirred within his mind. The dust puffed off him and fell to the ground.

"Thanks," Damien muttered.

"No problem," Henry replied, receding once again.

Damien dragged himself over to their bathroom and took a quick shower before brushing his teeth. Sylph sat on her bed facing the wall, small motes of dark energy twisting around her.

With the last dredges of his energy, Damien pulled up his status screen.

Damien Vale
Blackmist College
Year One
Major: Undecided
Minor: Undecided
Companion: [Null]
Magical Strength: 4.6
Magical Control: .53
Magical Energy: 9.2
Physical Strength: .3
Endurance: .73

The fights had nudged several of his stats up, giving him the equivalent of several days of training. Damien dismissed the window with a tired grin and trudged across the small room. His clothes flew off him as he flopped into bed and pulled the covers up to his chin. Within minutes, darkness enveloped his thoughts, and he was fast asleep.

———

Something poked Damien in the cheek. He groaned, turning over in bed without opening his eyes and burying his face in the pillow. He got poked again.

"Go away," he grumbled.

"No," Delph's voice replied.

Damien blinked, his weary mind struggling to process what had happened. Reality clicked into place, and he jumped, sitting straight up in bed as a rush of adrenaline shot through his veins.

"What are you doing in our room?" Damien exclaimed.

The professor just cocked an eyebrow. "You left the door open. I came to check on you two. To my horror, I found you were sleeping away good daylight hours, so I felt I'd do you a favor and help you wake up."

Damien squinted past Delph. The sun wasn't even up yet. "What time is it?"

"Two hours before sunrise," Delph said.

"And why exactly did you come check on us again?"

"Because your roommate won the tournament," Delph replied, rubbing his hands together. The man looked more gleeful than Damien had ever seen him. "And you did quite well, too. I had three students in the top four! I've got your rankings as well. Sylph, unsurprisingly, placed first in all the Year One students. Damien, you placed third. There was some debate on whether you should be fourth instead, but Whisp actually cast the deciding vote. Apparently, she appreciates wily students, even when they force her to change the rules of future tournaments."

Damien rubbed the weariness out of his eyes. He grabbed his clothes and pulled them under the sheets, shuffling around for a few moments until he was dressed. Once he was finished, he swung his legs out of bed.

Sylph was already awake. She sat on the edge of her bed, watching Delph with an expression similar to that of a cat that had been kicked.

"Do you have our rewards for us or something?" Damien asked.

"Among other things," Delph said. He nudged the book he'd given Damien—which laid on the ground at the foot of his bed—and raised an eyebrow. "I see this is going to good use."

"Let's stay on the subject of rewards," Damien said, repressing a yawn. "And I hope one of them is a door. No offense."

Delph just harrumphed. He traced a gray line through the air with a finger. The line split open, and he reached inside the hole, pulling out a fist-sized bag. He tossed it onto Sylph's bed, then repeated the process and tossed a bag onto Damien's bed.

Damien glanced at the bag, then looked back up at Delph. He half-expected the professor to have filled the bags with flour or some incredibly unwelcome training method. Sylph didn't make any moves to open her bag either.

"What?" Delph asked, crossing his arms. "Aren't you going to open your rewards?"

Damien gingerly picked the bag up. It was rather heavy. He held it out in front of him as far as he could while he walked outside. It didn't react, so he very carefully untied the small drawstring at the top while keeping the bag's opening pointed away from him. He pulled it open, but nothing happened.

Slowly, Damien peeked inside it. There were a good number of gold coins at the bottom, along with a few other things that were difficult to see in the dim light from the setting moon. He walked back inside and gave Sylph a nod.

"Seems safe," he said.

"Cautious is good," Delph said approvingly. "Always be wary, even when gifts come from friends. There are a lot of ways to impersonate someone. Regardless, this wasn't a test. I was planning on having a training session today, but there's no point. You both did well, and you earned me quite a bit of mon—ah—prestige among the other professors. Take a day off to recover from the tournament. There will be a normal class tomorrow, so don't show up for our special training as well."

Before Damien or Sylph could even acknowledge the professor, his cloak folded around him, and he vanished.

"Do you think he's gone?" Damien asked Sylph. He glanced around nervously. "A small part of me feels like he's hiding in one of our other rooms."

"Don't say that," Sylph said, shuddering. "You'll give me nightmares."

Sylph peeked inside her bag, and her eyes widened. She tipped it over on the bed. A veritable tide of coins rushed out of it. A small white slip and three glass vials fell out on top of them.

Damien did the same. His pile of coins was considerably smaller than Sylph's, and he only had one vial instead of three. However, he had the same white slip she did. He picked up the white slip. The back was blank, while the other side had the number two hundred printed on it.

"I think these are contribution points," Damien said, turning it over in his hand. "This is quite a bit. Wasn't your dagger something like three thousand points?"

"Yeah," Sylph said, picking up her own white slip. "I got five hundred points for winning. That's nearly five quests."

"Not to mention the gold," Damien said. "I wonder how much there—"

"One hundred," Henry said.

"Ah. I got one hundred," Damien said.

"It looks like I got around two hundred," Sylph said, her voice uncertain. "Maybe two hundred and fifty. I don't think I've ever had this much money in my entire life."

"You know, we could probably make a door instead of buying one," Damien said, scratching his chin. "We'd have to buy something for it to swing on, but I could probably carve something out of rock. It wouldn't be pretty, but I'd imagine doors aren't too cheap."

"Let's find out how much they are first," Sylph suggested. "There's a point when our time is more valuable than gold, and if a door only costs a little, I don't see why we shouldn't just buy one. I'll be saving my credits, though."

"Good idea," Damien said. "And I will be as well. We could probably do with some shopping, though. Our room is starting to look a little depressing, and I think I'm going to treat myself to a meal that doesn't resemble vomit. I think my finances can suffer that hit."

Sylph grinned and gave him a nod. "Just don't go too crazy. I can't imagine things get any easier from here on out." Her expression grew somber, and she lowered her voice. "And...you need to be careful. I'm sure you noticed, but you've drawn a lot of attention. Whatever you're hiding, you'd best redouble your efforts."

"Thanks," Damien said, giving her a small nod. "I'll keep that in mind and hope it was worth it."

They put the gold back into their bags. Damien tied the drawstrings shut and put it into his travel bag, which he slung over his shoulder. Sylph tied hers to her belt. Once they were done, they headed out of the room and slipped by Mark and the Grays' gates as they headed down the mountain. Once they got to the bottom, they headed into the town.

"Anywhere you want to start?" Sylph asked, adjusting the bag on her hip. "I'm not sure how early the general store opens, and I don't even know where to start with getting a new door."

"No way to know when it opens but to head over and find

out," Damien replied. "And I figure that's a good place to start. They might not sell doors there, but I'm sure the clerk could point is in the right direction."

Their path decided, the two of them increased their pace. They hadn't spent much time exploring the campus recently, since they'd mostly been in the arena with Delph or training in the forest, but it still only took them a little over ten minutes to find the store.

To their pleasure, the general store's doors were already wide open. Damien stepped inside with Sylph close on his heels. Aside from the large man behind the counter, it was entirely deserted. He glanced up from a book, quickly setting it down with a loud *bang* as they walked in.

"Welcome to the store," he said with a wide grin. A metal tag on his chest identified him as Joe. "I don't tend to get many visitors this early. Is there something...particular you're looking for?"

"A door," Damien said, ignoring the raised eyebrow the shopkeeper sent them. "We were wondering if you knew where to get one and how much it would cost."

"Ah," he said, looking slightly disappointed. "You can get one commissioned here if you'd like. It'll run you anywhere between a few hundred and a thousand gold, depending on how fancy you want it. I could show you a catalogue if you'd like."

Damien grimaced at the high price tag. "I think we're probably fine. Thank you, though. It's a bit out of our price range."

"Understandable," Joe said. "Most students end up making their own doors. The only ones who buy them are wealthy enough to not notice the money, and those are few and far in between at Blackmist. So, is there anything else I can help you two lovely people with?"

"Could you tell me what this is?" Sylph asked, reaching into her bag and pulling out the three vials she'd won in the competition.

The clerk squinted at the vials. Sylph walked up to the desk and put them on the counter so he could get a better look. The man raised them to the light, squinting at the small green plants within them.

"They're all the same plant. Ironleaf Thistle. It's a magical herb that can help make your body stronger. These are rather expensive. If you don't mind my asking, how did you get them without knowing what they are?"

He paused, squinting at them. Then he reached under his desk and took out a pair of comically small spectacles, setting them on the bridge of his nose and peering at Damien and Sylph.

"My goodness, aren't you the first and semifinalist from the Year One ranking tournament?" He clapped, giving them a wide grin. "You are! Great job yesterday. It was quite amusing watching Teg lose his cool."

"Thank you," Damien said. Teg clearly wasn't well-liked among the student body. "Is my vial the same?"

He showed it to the clerk, who nodded after inspecting it for a moment.

"Thank you," Damien said.

"No problem," Joe replied. "Is there anything else you'll be needing today?"

"I could use some new clothes," Sylph said. She saw the predatory look in his eyes and held up a hand. "Nothing fancy or expensive, please. I need something practical. I could also use some soap if you've got it."

Joe's grin didn't waver. He just gave her a nod. "Of course. The soap is on the shelf behind you. The cheapest one is the plain brown bar. It smells a bit like wet paper, but it works fine. As for clothes, just give me your wristband, and I'll see what I can do for you."

Sylph raised an eyebrow, but she took the metal band off and handed it to the man. He took it from her and tapped it against his own, his eyes looking off into the distance as he read something only he could see.

He nodded and handed the band back to Sylph. "Got it. We've got something in your size. How many sets do you want? The university helps cover the price of clothing since it gets damaged a lot in training, so it'll only cost you ten silver per set."

"Seven sets then," Sylph said, grabbing the bar of soap and putting it on the counter. "And this as well."

"Of course," Joe replied, giving her a wink and disappearing into the back to get the requested goods.

The clerk came out a little less than a minute later with a medium-sized tarp bag in his hands. He handed it to Sylph, who took it and paid him with a single gold coin. He took it and returned a small handful of silver coins, which Sylph put back into the bag holding her other coins. She put the soap into the bag and slung it over her shoulder.

"Is there anything else I can get the two of you? Notebooks? Quills?"

"I think that's it," Damien replied. Then he tilted his head. "Notebooks? For rune drawing?"

"You could use them for that, but there are a good number of classes you'll want to take notes in," Joe said. "You'll find out about them soon enough. It's been a while since I was a Year One, but I think they'll start up right about now, since you just finished the ranking battles."

Henry chuckled within Damien's mind. "You'll need no such thing with me. I won't be forgetting any new informa-

tion we learn. I've missed far too much in the last four thousand years."

"Oh, that's good to know," Damien said to Joe, mentally
nodding to Henry. "I think I'm good for now, but I might
show back up later. I've already got some notebooks of my
own."

"As am I," Sylph said.

"Of course," the clerk said, smiling at them.

They bid farewell to the large man and headed out of the
store.

THIRTY-FOUR

"Should we get breakfast?" Sylph asked.

"That sounds great," Damien replied. "I can't remember the last time I've eaten something other than dumplings or goop."

"Me too," Sylph said, licking her lips as they set a course for the mess hall. "I've tried ordering something different for lunch, but Delph must have done something. It doesn't matter what I ask for because the food that shows up is always dumplings."

"He's certainly interesting," Damien said, lowering his tone a little. "He was on the front lines, wasn't he? I wonder why they took him off."

Sylph shrugged. "No idea. I didn't have any interaction with anyone other than the man who trained me. From what he said, the front lines were a whole new level of danger. The monsters outside of the kingdom are nothing like the ones inside it. There aren't many mages strong enough to survive there, but the ones who do are incredibly powerful."

"So, why'd Delph leave?" Damien wondered. "Maybe he got tired of the constant fighting. Or he was injured."

"He doesn't seem injured to me," Sylph muttered. "I don't think he's tried seriously against us a single time. I don't expect to be as strong as a professor, but I would have thought he'd have to make a mistake or one of our attacks would eventually threaten him enough to at least make him slightly scared."

"I guess that's why he was on the front lines," Damien said.

Sylph just shrugged. They reached the mess hall a few minutes later. The sun had yet to climb over the horizon, and there wasn't anyone else in the line. The lunch lady glanced up from a large book. Damien was pretty sure it was the same one the clerk had been reading.

She didn't put the book down as they approached. Damien squinted at the cover. His cheeks immediately flushed red. It depicted two people in some very suggestive positions, and what little was left to interpretation was cleared up by the title, *Love Making for the Uninitiated and Lustful.*

"Is it too early for breakfast?" Sylph asked, tastefully avoiding looking at the book. The woman didn't seem particularly bothered.

"No."

"Could I get something, then? Whatever's most popular on the menu," Sylph said.

The woman nodded and extended a hand. "One silver."

Sylph dug around in her bag and set the requested coin in her hand. It vanished, and the lunch lady turned to look at Damien, raising a thick eyebrow.

Damien forced the flush out of his cheeks and cleared his throat. "Could I get some pancakes?"

"One silver."

Damien pulled out a gold coin.

"Do you want change, or do you want to put the remaining ninety-nine silver on your account?"

"Might as well put it on my account," Damien said. "I think I've had my fill of the free meals."

What could have possibly been a grin flickered across her face, but it vanished as fast as it had appeared. She simply gave Damien a small nod as his coin vanished into her large mitt. She raised the book again and went back to reading.

All the tables were empty, so Damien and Sylph walked over to one near the middle of the room and sat, activating the rune circles in front of them.

"What should we do after breakfast?" Damien asked. "I suppose it might be a good idea to start learning some more magic. I've also got to train a lot more, Delph or not. I barely won those last few fights. I only beat Nolan by basically blowing both of us up."

"Blowing yourself up?" Sylph asked.

Damien quickly explained how his last few fights had gone. Sylph shook her head, rubbing her forehead.

"That's not a good habit to get into," she said. "I know there was a healer there, but if you train like that, then you might do it in the field when there isn't anyone to save you."

"Yeah, I know," Damien said, sighing. "Hence, more training and new spells. I want to learn something more defensive. The Enlarge spell is okay, but it has a lot of weaknesses."

"It might be time for me to look into a new spell as well," Sylph said, a small frown crossing her face. "I barely won this, even with your help."

Their runes lit up green. They eagerly pressed on the circles, the conversation forgotten as they had their first decent breakfast in weeks.

Damien polished off his pancakes within a few minutes.

They were fluffy and soft, with more than their fair share of syrup. The food wasn't quite as good as his mother's cooking, but they were better than anything he'd had recently for breakfast, when he had it at all.

He wiped up the last bits of syrup with a slice of banana and popped it into his mouth, letting out a satisfied sigh.

Sylph, who had received a heaping plate of bacon, eggs, sausages, and toast, finished off her food and sat back in her chair with a sigh.

"That was amazing," Damien said. "I can't let myself get used to that or I'm going to become fat."

Sylph nodded, rocking back in her chair. "We'll stick to more basic meals in the future. It's not good to get used to fancy stuff like this."

They stared at their plates for a few moments. Then Damien pushed his chair back and stood. Sylph did the same.

"What now?" Sylph wondered as they walked out of the mess hall. "We could get back to training, but we might want to wait a bit since we just ate. I don't fancy tasting my food a second time."

"Agreed," Damien said. "I was thinking, if we want to make a door, we should try to get some hinges or something, right? I can carve it out of the stone, but I don't think we want a giant hunk of rock we have to shift out of the way every time."

"That's a good idea. I can go back to the general store and find out if they've got anything while you do the door," Sylph suggested.

"That works."

The two of them split up. Damien headed for the mountain while Sylph headed back into campus. He reached their room and silently walked by Mark and the Grays' rooms.

Damien walked into the farthest room he'd created, squinting in the darkness.

He grabbed the chalk from his bag and walked up to a wall. A few minutes later, a freshly drawn rune circle lit up with faint blue light. Damien gave an approving nod.

Any suggestions on making a door?

"It's a slab of rock," Henry said. "What do you want me to say?"

Fair enough.

Damien cast out his net of mental energy, lighting up the room with strands of Ether. He started to gather it, then paused.

"Wait. I don't need to make light if I keep the Ether visible," he realized.

"Except you won't be able to see what you're doing very well," Henry pointed out. "Do you want a lopsided door? You haven't learned to filter out the Ether from your sight when you don't want to see all of it. Stick with your scribbles for now."

Damien grunted, drawing several motes of energy into himself before allowing the lines of Ether to fade away. He pressed the energy through both of his palms, creating two dark orbs, and got to work.

He started by carving a large square of the stone away from the wall. Next, he carved its edges away until all that was left was a wide circle of stone that barely fit through the doorways without brushing the ceiling. He kept its width as thin as possible to avoid making the door too heavy.

Damien brushed the stone dust off and turned around to start dragging the door toward the outside of a cave. He leapt nearly a foot into the air when he realized Sylph leaned against the entryway.

"Seven Planes," Damien cursed. "I didn't realize you got back already."

"It's been over an hour," Sylph pointed out. "How long did you think it would take me to buy hinges?"

"Fair enough," Damien sighed, his heart still racing. "I lost track of time, I guess. Were you able to get hinges?"

"I was," Sylph said, jingling her bag. "And some runes screws as well. They'll put themselves in, so we don't have to buy tools."

"That's very convenient," Damien said. "Good thinking."

Sylph just nodded. She walked over and helped Damien roll the large wheel of stone through their room and toward the entrance.

It was a bit difficult getting it to squeeze between their beds but, after turning Damien's mattress on its side, they were able to just barely get it through the room and to the mouth of their cave.

"Let's roll it in front of the entrance," Damien said. "Then I'll grind away the rock until it fits."

They did as Damien suggested. Around two hours later, Damien had carved the stone down to roughly the shape of their cave's entrance. The process was considerably harder than he'd thought. When he started moving too fast, he carved away rock he needed to keep. By the time he was done, there were several spots where he'd carved away too much stone. It wasn't perfect, but it was a better door than a curtain.

Damien sat back, wiping his sweat- and dust-covered forehead with the back of his arm. He jumped for the second time that day when he saw Mark, Nolan, and Reena all standing beside Sylph, watching him.

"By the— Why is everyone so sneaky today?" Damien

snapped. "Can't you be louder when you show up or something?"

"Sorry," Nolan said. "You looked very concentrated, so we didn't want to bother you. You're making a door?"

"Yep," Damien said, sighing. "And I don't think I'm on the market to make another. Sylph, do you have the screws and the hinges?"

Sylph nodded. "I'll go on the other side, and then we can push the door into position. I'll put the hinges in on my end."

She stepped past the door and into their room. Together, she and Damien slowly slid it into its proper place. Damien, Mark, and the Gray siblings watched the door for a few minutes as dull buzzing noises came from the other side.

The stone shifted. Damien stepped back as it swung open, scraping slightly on the ground.

"It worked!" Damien exclaimed, only half-believing it himself. Then he sneezed as some of the dust got into his nose. "And now I need a shower."

And that was exactly what Damien did. He made a beeline for their shower and spent several relaxing minutes in the healing water. His muscles weren't particularly sore, but just the warmth and steam felt fantastic.

Once he finished, Damien quickly dried himself off. He glanced at his dirty clothes, then cleared his throat.

Ah...Henry?

"You need to learn how to do your own laundry already," Henry grumbled. Despite his complaints, a small sphere of darkness formed in the air above the clothes, sucking the dirt to the side before vanishing.

Thank you.

Damien pulled his clothes back on and pushed his hair out of his eyes before heading back into the main room.

Sylph was sitting on her bed, scanning through the book

Delph had given her. She'd left the cave entrance open to allow some of the sunlight through, but Mark and the Gray siblings had left.

Damien hopped onto his own bed, grabbing the book from beneath it and flipping it open. Henry stirred as he scanned through its contents.

"There are some useful spells there, but they aren't what you're looking for right now," Henry said. "You need a defensive spell with more versatility than what light can offer you."

I presume you've got something in mind?

"Initially, I did," Henry said. "But I was thinking, and I realized I'm doing you a huge disservice."

What do you mean?

"If I just give you every single spell, your mind won't develop enough. You need to practice and learn yourself, or you'll never be able to think on your feet."

That's...a fair point, actually. But isn't that suboptimal? It would take a lot less time if you just told me what to do.

"You'd also be a lot worse of a mage that wouldn't be able to do anything without my help," Henry pointed out. "Is that what you want?"

No. So in that case, I'll just look into researching some magic myself. Are you saying I should try to make more magic on my own?

"The chances of you creating new magic with the understanding you currently have are pretty much zero," Henry said. "But here's what we *can* do. You look through the library and try to figure out what kind of spell you want to learn and improve. I'll fill in any information you're looking for that they don't have and give you pointers as you work, but you'll be the one working on the spell. If it's something I don't think you can handle, I'll just stop you. That way, you'll get all the benefits of learning a spell without any of the drawbacks."

I like the sound of that. To the library, then?

"To the library," Henry agreed, sounding just as excited as Damien felt.

Damien bid farewell to Sylph and slipped out of the room, heading toward the library as fast as he could go without actually breaking into a run.

THIRTY-FIVE

When he reached the library, it took him a few minutes to find a section about space magic. It was a large hall, full of crooked cabinets that were one light shove from falling over. He carefully picked through them, taking any books that looked interesting.

Before long, Damien had surrounded himself in a makeshift fort of instructional manuals. He rubbed his hands together eagerly and grabbed one, flipping it open and starting to read. Off to his side, Henry formed an eye with a tiny tendril attached to it and floated over to another book to read it.

Damien considered telling him to stop, but nobody was in the area, and he couldn't blame his companion for wanting to learn more magic. He buried his nose in the book he'd chosen, scanning over it closely to see what secrets he could draw out from it.

As he'd expected, there were hundreds of Space magic spells. They ranged in complexity and difficulty, but he mostly stuck to the intermediate ones. He wouldn't admit it if anyone asked, but the fancy spells were a lot cooler than the basic ones, and that was having more than a little influence on his search.

Time ticked by and books shifted piles while the two flipped through them. Several hours passed before either of them knew it.

"Well?" Henry asked. "Any thoughts yet?"

Well, I want a defensive spell. I saw some defensive spells that were higher level for Space magic, but they were seriously complicated. But while I was looking at some other spells, it looks like there's a lot of messing with, well, space. Like bending it or moving things to other locations. Would it be possible to make some kind of one-way portal?

Henry let out a gleeful cackle. "Keep going. Let's assume it is. What would this portal be for?"

Ideally, I could just make it and block anything someone threw at me by sending it somewhere else.

"It's possible," Henry said. "Not everything, but a lot of it. You've got a starting point. I'll give my approval – if you can get this working, it would be very useful. It's worth the time."

Damien rose to his feet, grabbing several books that he thought might be useful. Henry slid a stack of books over to Damien, adding them to his pile wordlessly. Damien stacked them on without glancing at their contents, too lost in his own thoughts. He glanced around at the pile surrounding him. They twitched, almost as if they'd realized he was finished, and floated back to their spots on the shelves.

"Wow," Damien muttered. "I wonder what runes they're using to do that."

He examined the cabinets. Henry poked him with a barb of mental energy. "Come on. One thing at a time. If you let your attention get split, you'll never master a spell before you move on to the next. A few well-honed tools are far superior to a dozen rusty ones."

Fine, fine.

Damien turned and walked back to the entrance of the library. A librarian took note of the books he'd taken, then sent him on his way. He jogged all the way back to his room and was rather winded by the time he got back.

After stopping for a moment to catch his breath and not look completely pathetic in front of Sylph, Damien stepped into the room. She sat on her bed, her legs crossed and eyes closed. Motes of dark energy flickered around her.

Damien crept past Sylph, doing his best not to bother her. He sat down in the training room and set his books out around him, flipping them open to the pages he needed.

"This spell is one of the high-level portals," Damien said, tapping one page of a book. "I don't get all the runes, but if I'm not mistaken, this outer ring of runes is the one that sends the person walking through it to another location."

Henry didn't say anything. Damien flipped through another book, searching through it for a few minutes before stopping on a page depicting another spell. He grabbed a piece of chalk and got to work on the ground, sketching out runes.

He went from book to book over the next two hours, adding notes and runes to his rudimentary sketches. Finally, he rocked back and rubbed his eyes with the back of his hand.

What books did you end up wanting me to bring, by the way? I never got a glance.

"Nothing too crazy. A history of the school and the continent. Information about what you'll be learning each year. A bestiary of every known monster. And whatever that book that the lunch lady was reading."

I suppose that makes— Wait. What? Why in the Seven Planes do you need that book?

"Humans put a lot of culture into their smut," Henry said. "You never know what you'll learn from it."

You made me check out Love Making for the Uninitiated and Lustful?

He picked through the pile of books Henry had made him get. Sure enough, the book in question was there. Along with it were eight volumes of *Dredd's Demon's and Monsters* and a bunch of other history books that were completely uninteresting to him.

Bleh. You do you, I guess.

"I will," Henry replied. "You need to make me a room so that I don't have to worry about getting discovered. I want to read. I could just wait until she's asleep, but I feel strangely drawn to start immediately, despite how illogical that is."

It's called being impatient. Human emotion.

"Well, I don't like it," Henry said, the glower apparent in his tone. "It makes me feel antsy."

We don't like it any more than you do.

Henry grunted. Damien's shadow peeled away from his feet, rising from the ground like a ball of darkness. Two tendrils emerged from it as eyes blinked to life all around Henry's form. Henry picked up a book and brought it closer to himself as Damien stepped out of the room.

Damien spent the rest of the day practicing the Devour spell in the original training room. By the time that night had fallen, he was completely spent. He poked his head into the room Henry was in.

"I'm going to bed," Damien said. An eye on the shadowy blob's head turned to look at Damien, and Henry made an annoyed grunt.

"Fine."

Henry set down the book, which Damien couldn't help but notice was *Love Making for the Uninitiated and Lustful* and sank into the ground. He returned to a shadow and reattached himself to Damien's feet.

"Say, can't you read these instantly? Why is it taking you so long?" Damien asked.

"There's a difference between reading and enjoying," Henry replied. "I'm bored. This is something to do, so speeding through it wouldn't do me any good. Unless you want to go back to the library already?"

"I think I'll pass," Damien said, grimacing. "We can drop by it tomorrow or the day after."

Damien took a quick shower. Sylph was still meditating on her bed when he finished.

He climbed into his bed and tossed his cloak out from under the covers. He was tired, but he felt good. His magic was progressing at a good rate, and Henry was actually working with him. The companion's sarcasm had even reduced slightly.

Damien rolled over to face the wall as the embrace of sleep welcomed him into its arms. As he slept, a familiar sensation passed over him.

He found himself standing in a sea of darkness. His body had been replaced with a glowing yellow form, and the stars far in the sky above him seemed to shift out of the way when he looked at them.

"Shit," Damien muttered. An alien presence brushed against his mind. The stars spiraled downward, forming a sparkling body one mote of light at a time. "What do you want?"

"That is not the question," It Who Heralds the End of All Light said. "The question is what do *we* want?"

"I don't understand," Damien said, narrowing his eyes.

"But I know enough to know you aren't Henry. We both know I don't trust you."

"And that's the problem. You trust Henry."

Damien shrugged. "He's been honest with me recently."

"Such is the problem. He is of the Void, but he treats with a child as if it is his equal."

"As do you," Damien pointed out. "Spit it out, Herald. You want something. What is it?"

"Herald," the starry figure said, rolling the word over in its mouth like a hard candy. "A shortened name. I suppose that will work. Very well. I shall be blunt. The Mortal Plane is in grave danger."

"That's hardly news. There are five of your kind walking around trying to destroy it," Damien said. "You'd be doing the same thing if the contract didn't stop you."

"You are wrong," Herald said, its voice multiplying and contorting in a different manner with every word. "The other Void creatures are not the threat. Henry is."

Damien would have raised his eyebrows if this version of him had any. "Henry? How? As far as I can tell, he's pretty reasonable compared to you."

"Bothersome creature," Herald said, but its visage didn't shift from the perpetual flat expression it always wore. "You do not understand my—our—purpose. We exist to ensure the Mortal Plane is reborn not destroyed. Henry has strayed from his purpose, and he puts the realm at risk. It *must* be reborn. If the Corruption takes root too deeply, the Cycle will come to an end forever."

"Corruption?"

"Consider it as another entity beyond your understanding. It seeks to end the Mortal Plane permanently."

"Are you seriously telling me the Void creatures exist to...

protect the Mortal Plane?" Damien asked. "That didn't seem like the case when I first summoned you. You were eager to destroy it."

"It must be destroyed in order to be reborn," Herald said. "Death and life are part of the same cycle, but the Corruption is not. It will remove the Mortal Plane from the Cycle permanently."

"And what would that do?" Damien asked. "If I humor you, I fail to see how dying to the Corruption is any worse than letting you destroy the world, at least from my perspective."

The stars that made up Herald twinkled in what Damien suspected might have been the slightest hints of annoyance.

"There is nothing that I can say that could convince you of the truth of my words," Herald said. "The Corruption works slowly, but by the time it is plain to your mortal eyes, it shall be too late. Thus..."

A starry hand raised toward Damien. His glowing body froze in place, rejecting his attempts to move as a single finger tapped his chest.

Hot pain seared across Damien's chest. He gasped, grasping at it, but his glowing arms found nothing. The line twisted, carving some sort of pattern into his chest. Then, as quickly as it had started, the pain vanished into a dull throbbing ache.

"What did you do?" Damien asked, his voice shaky.

"I have begun preparing your weak mortal shell to contain the full strength of your soul."

"That's horrib— Wait. That sounds like a good thing," Damien said suspiciously.

"We have the same enemy, boy. Even if you fail to realize it. Do not allow the new power to overwhelm you. As friendly as you believe Henry to be, he will not hesitate to take control of your body if you lack the strength to keep him out of it."

With that final piece of advice, the starry night shattered like a mirror hit by a hammer. Fragments of stars flew past Damien as something wrapped around his body and dragged him downward into the darkness.

CHAPTER
THIRTY-SIX

He awoke with a start, jerking upright with a jagged breath. His heart hammered in his chest. The sheets were stuck to his chest, and they felt wet. He peeled them away, grimacing as a twinge of pain shot through his body.

Damien's eyes widened. His body was matted with blood. A rune about the size of his fist had been carved into his chest, directly over his heart. He recognized this particular rune. It was a core one when making a protective circle. It was the symbol for cage.

"What happened to your chest?" Henry asked, shocked. "That rune— You spoke with It Who Heralds the End of All Light?"

I did. I don't think he—it—is very happy with you.

"I don't suppose it is," Henry said, suspicion in his voice. "What did it want?"

It believes the Corruption is going to destroy the world and take it out of the cycle of life, or something like that. Apparently, you're failing at your duties and are dooming us all in the process.

"Bah," Henry replied. "It's not wrong about the Corruption, but a few thousand years won't matter. I can have my fun, and then go about ending the world when you're a step from your death bed. Then both of us can be happy."

I'm not sure I'm a fan of you destroying the world after I die either. I like it better than the alternative, but isn't there an option where the Mortal Plane actually survives?

"That would be the Void destroying it," Henry said, sighing. "If we do it, the Mortal Plane will be reborn. It's not a true death like the Corruption."

How do you know the Corruption would even kill it? Has it happened somewhere before? And why didn't you tell me about it?

Henry didn't respond immediately. Then he let out a slow hum.

"I'm...not sure, actually. I just know it's bad. Really bad. And I was really hoping you wouldn't have to deal with it, to be honest."

A millennium of existence and you still haven't figured out if this great evil is actually evil?

"Original thought didn't come easily to me," Henry protested. "It's hardly my fault."

Damien rolled his eyes. Yet another mystery he had to deal with, although it didn't seem like it was as imminent as his other problems. He touched the sticky blood drying on his chest and grimaced as the cut skin stung under his finger.

He carefully climbed out from under the covers and swung his legs out of bed. A sudden vertigo washed over him as he tried to stand. Static filled his vision, and he toppled forward. Two hands grabbed him by the shoulders and stopped his fall.

"Damien?" Sylph asked. "What happened?"

He blinked the dizziness away. Sylph looped one of his arms around her shoulders. She drew in a sharp breath at the sight of the rune on his chest.

"Did something happen to your core as well?"

"No," Damien said, the weakness receding from his voice. "I don't think so, at least. This is something else."

"You've lost a lot of blood," Sylph said, helping him toward the shower. "Should I get a healer?"

"The shower's water should be enough," Damien said. "This is one of *those* things."

"Understood," Sylph said. She turned the water on, dousing them as it rained from the ceiling. Damien grimaced at the cold. His chest stung as the water pattered against his skin.

The blood covering him washed away. The wound tightened, the bright red lines turning a knotty pink as they faded. Within a few minutes, the wound had sealed. The pain receded as well, although his head still felt light.

"Thank you, Sylph," Damien said, blinking the water out of his eyes. "I think it's okay now."

"Are you sure it's not going to happen again?" Sylph asked, stepping out of the shower and drying herself off. Her clothes had been completely soaked. Damien realized he was wearing little more than a pair of shorts, but he was too tired to care. His feet weren't as shaky as they had been, so he carefully stepped out as well.

"It probably will," he said. "But not today. I think."

"That's reassuring," Sylph said, wringing her hair out and putting it into a bun. "It's not going to happen while you're out and about, is it? Going to be hard to explain that to Delph."

"I'll make sure it doesn't," Damien said, yawning. "And thank you for catching me. How did you manage to wake up fast enough to realize I was falling?"

"I was already awake and meditating," Sylph replied. Her voice lowered. "I noticed you stand up and glanced over just as you tipped over. It's a good thing I did. You would have gotten blood all over my bed."

"That would have been tragic," Damien said, a small grin tugging at his lips. "Although now, I've got to wash my own bedsheets. I suppose it was about time for that anyway."

They walked out of the bathroom. Damien let out a sigh. His sheets were stained completely brown by the dried blood. They stared at it for a second.

"I don't think that's coming out," Sylph said.

"No, I don't think it is," Damien agreed. "Fantastic. I don't suppose you know what time it is?"

"About two hours before sunrise," Sylph replied. "Maybe a little bit less."

"I suppose we might as well start training, then," Damien sighed, not particularly wanting to move more than he had to.

"You sure you're up to it?" Sylph asked worriedly. "I don't think you're fully back to normal yet. The healing water can do a lot, but I'm not sure it can replace blood that quickly. You're going to need to eat something to replenish your energy."

"Good point. And we've also got a class with Delph later today," Damien said with a grimace. "I don't know what he'll have us doing since the tournament just ended, but I guess it might be best to save my energy."

"Breakfast, then?" Sylph suggested. "I think this might be an occasion that allows you to overeat a little bit."

"Yeah," Damien said, his stomach growling at the thought of more pancakes. "I think that might be for the best. Are you coming? You don't have to stop your training if you don't want to."

"I'll live if I skip a day," Sylph said, giving him a slight smile. "And we don't want you face-planting halfway to the mess hall."

"That wouldn't be ideal," Damien agreed, returning the smile. After he got properly dressed, the two set off down the mountain and toward the promise of tasty food.

Damien and Sylph both ordered a hearty breakfast and sped through it in record time. The food did wonders for replenishing Damien's strength, although he still felt slightly dizzy. He was so hungry he ordered a second meal, this time eating it more slowly to savor the taste.

Once they'd finished eating, the two of them wandered around the campus for a few hours, pausing to buy some basic supplies in the general store. After that, the two returned to their room where they found two notes written on dirty brown paper waiting for them before their beds.

"Uh oh. You think he saw my bed?" Damien asked.

"I don't think he possibly could have missed it," Sylph replied. "But it doesn't really look like he cared."

"That's... very Delph of him," Damien said, picking his note up and scanning it.

Unsurprisingly, the note contained instructions to find Delph's class, which was in the arena as it always tended to be. Not a single mention of Damien's bloodied bed was present. There was only a little over half an hour before the class started, so the two students wasted no time in making their way through the portals.

By the time Damien and Sylph got to the sandy arena floor, several of the other students from the class were already waiting for them. Mark and the Gray siblings sat in the sand, and Lucille stood a short distance away from them together with the other students whose names Damien couldn't recall.

"Good job on the tournament," Nolan told them as they arrived. "That was a clever strategy. Buying time for Sylph since you knew you couldn't beat Mark yourself... Ha. I'd rather have taken the quarterfinal win myself, but I think you earned it with that insane play of yours."

"You damn near killed both yourself and Nolan," Reena said crossly, pressing her lips together. "It was stupid. It's a tournament, not a life and death battle."

"That's exactly why I did it," Damien replied, shrugging. "There were incredibly powerful healers with us focused on making sure we didn't kill ourselves or each other. They would have stopped the spell if they thought it was going to kill anyone. If this was a real fight, I never would have done something that dangerous. Not if I could have helped it, anyway."

Reena grunted, but she didn't look particularly convinced.

"Excuse Reena," Nolan said. "She's a little overly protective, and she's not too happy I placed higher than she did."

"Shut up," Reena said, sulking. A smile cracked Nolan's serious expression, and he ruffled her hair.

"You've still got four years to outperform me, Reena. You'll get more chances later."

"That goes for all of us," Mark said, cocking his head to the side like a wolf as he examined Sylph. His gaze flicked to Damien for a moment before a half-smile appeared on his lips. "But I don't think any of us can argue Damien and Sylph didn't earn their victory. They followed the rules and realized there were ways to exploit them. Next time, we'll be ready."

"You'd best be," Delph said, his voice coming from the empty air before them.

A gray whirlwind bloomed in the air, expanding outward and transforming into Delph within moments. The man's lips were curled upward, and his eyes were more relaxed than Damien had ever seen them. "But you all did very well. It's important to remember each of you had different starting spots. The ranking battles are important, but there will be more in the future. For those of you who didn't place as high as you'd like, you'll have many more shots to claim your rightful spot."

Everyone scrambled to their feet as Delph paced in a line before them.

"However, I must say I'm incredibly pleased with everyone's results. Everyone won at least one fight, and we claimed three out of the four top spots. On top of that, several students reached the quarterfinals as well. So, I believe a reward is in order."

Everyone watched the professor eagerly. He chuckled and scratched at his beard. "But before we get to that, there's some information the school has mandated I say."

A few groans rose. Delph waited until they passed before he spoke again.

"First, you are now all eligible to go on quests. I will hand out a slip of paper at the end of class that classifies the difficulty of quest you are allowed to take on. Your team may only take on quests at the lowest rank between the two of you. However, it is permitted to take on quests alone if, and only if, they are more than two ranks lower than your current rank. So, if you're given a B rank, you can take an E rank quest alone. I will say that this is *heavily* discouraged. Mages work in teams to complement each other's strength, and you are more powerful together than you are alone."

"When can we do the quests?" Damien asked. "We're all in school. If we leave to do a quest, it could take weeks. Won't we miss a lot of information?"

"Good question," Delph said. "There will be weeks throughout the year designated to either training or questing. You're welcome to do whichever you prefer. Some quests are also short and close enough that you can get them finished over the weekends. Does that clear things up?"

Damien nodded.

"Good. Now, the next piece of information. As I'm sure you all expected, there are more classes than just combat. Blackmist teaches a multitude of things ranging from magic theory to rune drawing. You've all been placed in classes I will inform you of shortly. They have been optimized to the talents you've shown so far in my class and during the ranking battles. And that actually brings us to your reward."

Delph looked around the eager students, a grin stretching across his lips. "I was assigned to teach all your classes. Apparently, the school has a shortage of teachers. But since you all put in such hard work, I called a few favors to get some other teachers to take over several of the subjects. That means I won't have to see you little goblins constantly, and you'll get to learn from someone other than me. Of course, we'll still have combat classes five times a week, but that was a given. Pretty good reward, eh?"

Nobody said anything, but Damien knew they were all thinking the same thing: That was a pretty good reward.

Of course, Delph made sure the students didn't think he was going soft after their success at the tournament. Immediately after he finished lecturing them, the man set them all off on several laps around the track.

The moment they finished, he broke everyone off into groups and put them through a brutal workout. When he finally let them stop, everyone laid out flat on the ground, gasping for breath.

Delph walked around the field of exhausted students, dropping slips of paper on their heads as he passed while humming to himself, not even slightly out of breath.

"You all get a break from me tomorrow," Delph said.

"Your respective teachers will be contacting you for your first lesson. I'm sure they'll use much less interesting methods than I do, but that's just something you have to live with. Don't try comparing them to me. None of your teachers will live up to any of my aspects, no matter how hard they try. Just be happy I teach one of your classes, as most don't even get the privilege of that."

Damien managed to sit up just in time to see Delph give him a small wink before the man's cloak swallowed him, and he disappeared. He let out a groan and flopped back to the ground. He'd barely made it through today's class. His head still felt light from the morning's incident, and the new scars on his chest occasionally ached for no apparent reason.

A few moments later, he reached up with a trembling hand and lifted the slip of paper Delph had dropped up so he could read it. The rising sun lit the paper from behind, making it slightly translucent and highlighting the ink.

"Magic theory, A rank quests," Damien read aloud. A grin stretched across his features. He forced himself upright and tucked the paper into a pocket in his coat.

"Fantastic," Henry said. "This will be an excellent opportunity to learn more about modern magic. Also, I need more books. I got impatient and finished them last night."

Damien sighed, shaking his head and not gracing his companion with a response.

"I got rune drawing," Nolan said, holding his paper out before him like it was slimy. "It feels like the professors are just rubbing my defeat at Damien's hands in."

"Hey, if it works..." Mark said, rolling to his feet with a grunt. He tucked his paper into his belt and let out a yawn.

Sylph walked over to Damien and extended her hand. He took it, and she pulled him to his feet. After he brushed the dirt off his clothes, Damien raised an eyebrow in her direction.

"What class?" he asked.

"Magical control," Sylph said. "Probably to improve my pitiful amounts of energy. And I'm allowed to take on A ranked quests. What about you?"

"Same for the quests, and I got magic theory. I'm just glad they didn't stick me in rune drawing," Damien replied. "I like it, but there's no point focusing on it further right now. I'd rather learn other stuff."

"I've heard magical theory can be rather difficult," Nolan said, overhearing their conversation. "My dad mentioned something about it once. I think he was just mad he didn't do well in the course, though."

"I'm in that class as well," Reena said, looking down at her paper. A grin flittered across her features. "If I do better than Father, he'll have to acknowledge that."

"Just focus on passing," Nolan said with a smirk. "If he had difficulty, then I'm sure it's an intense class."

Reena grunted. Judging by her expression, Nolan's words had gone in one ear and out the other without stopping for lunch. Speaking of food, Damien's stomach rumbled.

"Lunch?" Sylph suggested.

"Sounds good to me," Damien said.

The two of them bid farewell to the other students and headed over to the mess hall. Sylph got her dumplings courtesy of Delph while Damien ordered the cheapest meal on the menu, a plate of slightly seasoned ground meat and a small hunk of bread.

They polished off their food without much conversation of note, then headed back toward their room in the mountains. Sylph returned to her bed to meditate while Damien headed into the training room.

His notes were still waiting for him on the floor, and the books unmoved from the spots he'd left them. He carefully stepped over the chalk lines, making sure not to smudge any of them, and sat down.

This is what I'm thinking about trying right now.

Damien pointed to a set of three interlocking circles of runes he'd drawn to his right. Henry made a contemplative noise as he examined what Damien had drawn.

"Why don't you walk me through this?" Henry suggested. "It's bad, but salvageable."

Gee, thanks. The top rune is the one that forms the portal. I've got it sent to appear right in front of my hand, or wherever I cast it from, I guess. It also handles the size and shape. I figured the larger it is, the harder it'll be to cast, so I've got it set at about half my height in diameter.

"Good assumption," Henry said. "What about the other two?"

The left one is what's meant to open the portal. I don't fully understand how it works, but I took that rune circle from a portal spell. If I'm not mistaken, it should use space magic to tear open a passage to an extra-dimensional space...somewhere. Without another portal, I just have it open ended.

"I'd like to let you test that, but might blow you up," Henry said. "Leaving a portal open ended like that could set it anywhere. You'd rip open a path to an unknown location, which could be full of poisonous gasses, lava, or all manner of things that would kill you. You need to tell the Ether exactly what to do."

Gotcha. I'll look through my books again and try to find something that would work. What about the right circle? I found some other spells that were meant to block magic, but they were way too complex to just directly use. I tried to make a pattern that would absorb anything that touched it and send it to the location chosen by the second ring.

"It won't blow up if you test it," Henry decided. "Just make sure you fix the runes up. You've got some mistakes that can be fixed, but I'm not pointing them out yet."

Damien nodded. He picked a book up and leafed through it, scanning the pages for the information he'd need to fix the left circle.

Time ticked by. Runes came and went like the tide as Damien smudged them out and drew new ones over the top, modifying his design over the next few hours. Finally, he rocked back, sporting a fierce headache but burning with excitement.

"What about this?" Damien asked, forgetting to speak in his head.

"It... Well, it won't blow up," Henry said, a tiny note of approval in his voice. "You're using a pocket dimension to store anything that enters the spell? Not bad. That's close to what I would have done. It takes a fair amount of magical energy, though."

I've got more than enough of that. I'm going to try casting this.

"This'll be fun," Henry said.

Damien ignored him. He studied the runes he'd prepared on the ground for a few minutes, then stood up and brushed himself off. He opened his mouth to ask Henry how to properly form the Ether so that it would do what he wanted, but an answer swam unbidden to his mind before he could speak.

"You're thinking about something," Henry observed. "Wanted to know how to manipulate the Ether to make this spell?"

No, I actually think I have an idea how. Three motes, one for each rune circle. I twist them together so they can link. I'd imagine that, at this level of complexity, I would need to actually use runes so I can communicate with the Ether more precisely.

Henry let out a bark of laughter. "Look at you. That's correct. You need to shape the Ether into runes, but I already know what you're thinking. Too complex, huh?"

Basically. There are at least fifty runes in this thing, there's no way I can get that degree of accuracy by squishing around the Ether with my mental energy.

"Well, you can. Eventually," Henry said. "But, in the meantime, there's a crutch. You can draw out the runes for the spell with your finger, sending the Ether out through it. So long as you send one mote to each ring and they're properly linked before you do so, the spell will function as normal —just slower."

That's amazing! Why didn't you tell me this before?

"Because you'd have tried something and ended up blowing us both up."

Fair.

Damien took a slow breath, drawing energy into his core from a line of Ether, then gently took the motes and started shaping them within himself. They put up mild resistance, but since he wasn't getting too detailed with the linkage, he was able to put everything together without too much difficulty.

He brought the Ether to his fingertip, letting just enough of it leak out to create a faint purple light just in front of his nail, and drew the pattern that he'd created for the spell in the air. The runes flickered there for a moment, then flared as he sent the last of the energy into it.

With a pop, a wide black circle snapped open before him. It flickered with flares of purple light.

I did it!

"Toss something in," Henry suggested. "Quickly. Before it fades."

Damien knelt, grabbing a pebble from the ground, and threw it at his spell. The stone passed straight through it and clattered to the ground. His face fell and the portal faded away a moment later.

Why didn't it get sent into the portal?

"Take another look at your third circle," Henry said.

Damien sat back down in front of the runes he'd drawn and examined them for several minutes.

"I'm not seeing it," he admitted out loud. The headache building in the back of his head twinged but forced it away. He was too close to stop now. "I clearly have it set up to absorb any energy or physical components that pass through it."

"How does one absorb something physical?" Henry asked. "That won't work. The rune circle you took from the portal was the one that actually stopped any magical effects from passing through it, not the one that sent someone through. The magic can mess up the location you arrive at, so many portals temporarily try to draw any magic passing through them out so it can't ruin the spell."

Damien pursed his lips in thought. His eyes widened and he scribbled out several runes, redrawing them.

I've got it! If I can't absorb physical components, then a bunch of these runes aren't working correctly and could be messing up other aspects of the circle. But if I set it up to only take in magical energy...

"Cast the spell again," Henry suggested.

Damien did just that. The black portal wavered slightly as it pried open, but it remained in the air as he formed a weak gravity sphere and threw it in. There was a subtle *pop* as the dark orb entered the spell. It vanished without a trace.

"Well done," Henry said. "You've got yourself a new spell. One that you need a lot of work to start casting better, but a new spell nonetheless."

Damien stared at the portal until it closed, practically shivering with excitement. He couldn't even find the proper words to say, and the growing headache wasn't helping his articulation.

"You're going to need a name for it," Henry said. "Make sure it isn't lame."

Devour. Because it eats the magic I put into it.

"That," Henry said, pausing for a moment, "is a good name."

A smile stretched across Damien's face. He staggered into the bathroom holding his head with his hand and took a shower, relaxing under the warm water until opening his eyes didn't make the world pulsate.

The wound on his chest showed no signs of closing any further. It clearly wasn't going anywhere anytime soon. Damien tried to get a better look at it, but he couldn't understand what the magic was meant to do. It didn't seem to be active at the moment.

You don't know what this does, do you?

"I don't," Henry said, and it was clear it irritated him. "I recognize the rune, of course, but there are more circles than I can count that utilize it. Did our friend say anything about it?"

Something about containing the full power of your soul, but he made it sound pretty ominous.

"I'll keep an eye on it," Henry said. "Unfortunately, my thoughts and its are no longer the same. I have no way to know what he's planning."

Damien sighed. He turned off the water and stepped out of the shower to dry himself off. He'd have to experiment with whatever the eldritch creature had done to him, but that could come later. For now, he felt he'd earned a well-deserved break. There were spells waiting to be discovered, and Damien wasn't going to let anything, Void or Corruption, stop him from learning them.

———

The story continues in Greenblood.

THANK YOU FOR READING BLACKMIST

We hope you enjoyed it as much as we enjoyed bringing it to you. We just wanted to take a moment to encourage you to review the book. Follow this link: **Blackmist** to be directed to the book's Amazon product page to leave your review.

Every review helps further the author's reach and, ultimately, helps them continue writing fantastic books for us all to enjoy.

———

Want to discuss our books with other readers and even the authors like Shirtaloon, Zogarth, Cale Plamann, Noret Flood (Puddles4263) and so many more?

Join our Discord server today and be a part of the Aethon community.

Facebook | Instagram | Twitter | Website

You can also join our non-spam mailing list by visiting www.subscribepage.com/AethonReadersGroup and never miss out on future releases. You'll also receive three full books completely Free as our thanks to you.

Also in Series
Blackmist
Greenblood
Duskbringer

Want to own your very own Eldritch Horror?

BUY HENRY NOW!

Looking for more great books from Aethon Books?

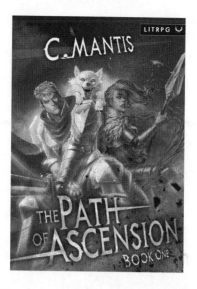

Orphaned by Monsters. Matt must power up to save others from the same fate.

Matt plans to delve the rifts responsible for the monsters that destroyed his city and murdered his parents. But his dreams are crushed when his Tier 1 Talent is rated as detrimental and no guild or group will take him.

Working at a nearby inn, he meets a mysterious and powerful couple. They give him a chance to join the Path of Ascension, an empire-wide race to ascend the Tiers and become living legends.

With their recommendation and a stolen Skill, Matt begins his journey to the peak of power. Maybe then, he can get vengeance he seeks...

Experience the start of an action-packed fantasy adventure that blends everything you love about LitRPG

with Xianxia. With 5 million views on Royal Road, this hit web serial is new-and-improved and now available on Kindle & Audible.

Get Path of Ascension Now!

———

The blood of dragons pumps through his veins. Greatness awaits!

Kobolds cower at the bottom of the foodchain, forced to eke out a meager existence in the most wretched of caves.

Most have made peace with their lot in life; one of eating scraps and carrion. They hide and run from predators, delaying the inevitable day when they aren't fast or sneaky enough to make their escape.

But not Samazzar. Sam is different from other Kobold pups.

Traps and caves might keep him and his people alive, but sometimes, just living isn't enough. Dragon blood runs through him, and Sam isn't willing to settle for mere survival. Whether by claw, magic, or cunning, one day he will soar above the plains, predator rather than prey.

And nothing—be it the mockery of his tribe, the hazards of the deep caves, or even the almost insurmountable difficulty of successfully evolving his bloodline—nothing is going to stop him.

GET A DREAM OF WINGS AND FLAME NOW!

———

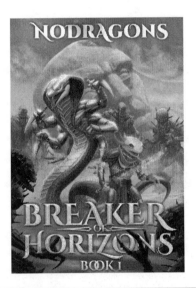

Nic has been Selected.

Chosen to leave his own body behind and become a monster.

Chosen to live or die on his own wits. His own strengths.

He'll adventure out into a new realm as a footsoldier for the System's relentless integration of new worlds. Fighting to break the natives into submission.

But Nic has never loved the System, or cared for his home planet, a depleted husk of a world that the System forgot long ago. With blue skies overhead and green forest to the horizons, he might just fall in love with this strange planet named Earth...

That would leave him with few friends and a thousand enemies. That would leave him clawing, biting, scratching to survive.

GET BREAKER OF HORIZONS NOW!

For all our LitRPG books, visit our website.

ACTUS

Made in the USA
Columbia, SC
26 July 2023

20739104R00248